Praise for *Wolfsong* and the Green Creek series

"An exciting start to the [Green Creek] series." —*Library Journal*

"*Wolfsong* is so well-written that I'm in awe of TJ Klune's talent. The primary character, Ox, has huge feelings he can't articulate. But we know all of them, and we love him. The complex and startling world of Green Creek is the perfect setting." —Charlaine Harris

"One of my new all-time favorite books!" —Giana Darling

"It's a flawless book and shows that you can take the fantastic and make it so very human. I thought the supernatural would be what grabbed me, but instead it's Ox's humanity and humility and loyalty. I hope there will be more. Wildly recommended."
—Mary Calmes

"The prose reads like a simple, placid little pond, and then you jump in and realize it's MILES DEEP. So to conclude this terrible non-review, FIVE BAJILLION STARS." —Emma Scott

"The best part of this book is the pack mentality and how strong of a bond everyone has with each other. Beautiful and I highly recommend!" —K. Webster

"Beautiful, poetic, unbelievably compelling. ALL the stars."
—Juliette Cross

Praise for *The House in the Cerulean Sea*

A *New York Times, USA Today,* and *Washington Post* bestseller!
An Indie Next Pick!
An Alex Award winner!

"It's a witty, wholesome fantasy that's likely to cause heart-swelling."
—*The Washington Post*

"I loved it. It is like being wrapped up in a big gay blanket. Simply perfect." —V. E. Schwab

"Sweet, comforting, and kind, this book is very close to perfect. *The House in the Cerulean Sea* is a work of classic children's literature written for adults and children alike, with the perspective and delicacy of the modern day. I cannot recommend it highly enough."
—Seanan McGuire

"It will renew your faith in humanity." —Terry Brooks

"*1984* meets *The Umbrella Academy* with a pinch of Douglas Adams thrown in. Touching, tender, and truly delightful, *The House in the Cerulean Sea* is an utterly absorbing story of tolerance, found family, and defeating bureaucracy." —Gail Carriger

"*The House in the Cerulean Sea* is a modern fairy tale about learning your true nature and what you love and will protect. It's a beautiful book." —Charlaine Harris

Praise for *Under the Whispering Door*

A *New York Times, USA Today,* and indie bestseller!
An Indie Next Pick!

"*Under the Whispering Door* is a kind book. It broke my heart with its unflinching understanding that grief never goes away. And then it healed me in the next breath." —Cassandra Khaw

"There is so much to enjoy in *Under the Whispering Door*, but what I cherish the most is its compassion for the little things—a touch, a glance, a precious piece of dialogue—healing me, telling me that for all the strangenesses I hold, I am valued, valid—and maybe even worthy of love."
—Ryka Aoki

Praise for *In the Lives of Puppets*

A *New York Times*, *Sunday Times*, and indie bestseller!
A #1 Indie Next Pick!

"*In the Lives of Puppets* is glorious, a thoroughly entertaining and deeply stirring journey through a world of extraordinary robots. The characters here are so vibrant, and the story proves that love stretches well beyond the world of humans." —Chuck Tingle

"*In the Lives of Puppets* is a powerful story of humanity and what survives after we're gone. TJ Klune has created an enchanting tale of Pinocchio in the end times, offering up hard truths alongside humor, kindness, love, and, most important, hope."
—P. Djèlí Clark

"Literature at its very best opens up the potential of a better world than the one we're currently in. Klune's vision of a more considerate and compassionate society is immensely powerful. One can't help but fall in love with this book." —T. L. Huchu

ALSO BY TJ KLUNE
FROM TOR PUBLISHING GROUP

BOOKS FOR ADULTS

The Green Creek Series
Wolfsong
Ravensong
Brothersong

The Cerulean Chronicles
The House in the Cerulean Sea
Somewhere Beyond the Sea

Standalones
The Bones Beneath My Skin
Under the Whispering Door
In the Lives of Puppets

BOOKS FOR YOUNG ADULTS

The Extraordinaries Series
The Extraordinaries
Flash Fire
Heat Wave

TJ KLUNE

HEARTSONG

GREEN CREEK BOOK THREE

TOR PUBLISHING GROUP
NEW YORK

This is a work of fiction. All of the characters, organizations, and events portrayed in this novel are either products of the author's imagination or are used fictitiously.

HEARTSONG

Copyright © 2019 by Travis Klune
Heartsong short story copyright © 2023 by Travis Klune

All rights reserved.

A Tor Book
Published by Tom Doherty Associates / Tor Publishing Group
120 Broadway
New York, NY 10271

www.torpublishinggroup.com

Tor® is a registered trademark of Macmillan Publishing Group, LLC.

The Library of Congress Cataloging-in-Publication Data is available upon request.

ISBN 978-1-250-89042-9 (trade paperback)
ISBN 978-1-250-89041-2 (ebook)

Our books may be purchased in bulk for promotional, educational, or business use. Please contact your local bookseller or the Macmillan Corporate and Premium Sales Department at 1-800-221-7945, extension 5442, or by email at MacmillanSpecialMarkets@macmillan.com.

First Tor Paperback Edition: 2024

Printed in the United States of America

0 9 8 7 6 5 4 3 2 1

For those who are trying to find their way home.

Yes, I have tricks in my pocket, I have things up my sleeve. But I am the opposite of a stage magician. He gives you illusion that has the appearance of truth. I give you truth in the pleasant disguise of illusion.

—Tennessee Williams,
The Glass Menagerie

MOTES OF DUST / SOMETHING MORE

When I dreamed, these pinpricks of light filtered through the trees of an old forest. It was safe there. I didn't know how I knew that. I just did.

I wanted to run as fast as I could. The maddening itch to shift crawled underneath my skin, and I needed to give in.

I didn't.

Leaves crunched underneath my feet.

I ran my hand along the bark of an old elm. It was rough. And then it was wet from a trickle of sap. I rubbed it between my fingers, sticky and warm.

The trees whispered.

They said, *here here here.*

They said, *here is where you belong.*

They said, *here is where you are meant to be.*

They said, *this is PACK and LIFE and SONGS in the air SONGS that are sung because this is home home home.*

I closed my eyes and breathed.

The light seemed brighter in the darkness.

Little motes of dust swirled.

I brought the pitch on my fingers to my tongue.

It tasted old.

And strong.

And—

A low growl off to my right.

I opened my eyes.

A white wolf stood a ways off in the trees. It had a smattering of black on the chest, legs, and back.

I didn't know it

(*him*)

but I thought it

(*him*)

familiar somehow, like it was *right there* on the tip of my tongue, mixed in with elm sap and—

Its eyes began to burn with red fire.

An Alpha.

I wasn't scared.

It—*he*—wasn't there to hurt me.

I didn't know how I knew that. Maybe it was the trees. Maybe it was this place. Maybe it was the sap coating my throat.

I said, "Hello."

The Alpha snorted, shaking his head.

I said, "I don't know where I am. I think I'm lost."

He pawed at the ground, carving jagged lines in the dirt and grass.

I said, "Do you know where I am?"

And he said, *you are far away.*

He sounded like the voice of the trees.

He *was* the voice of the trees.

The Alpha said, *you don't belong to me you aren't mine you aren't MINE but you could be you could be because of who you are.*

"I don't know who I am," I admitted, and it was a terrible thing to say aloud, but after the words were out, I felt . . . lighter.

Almost free.

The Alpha took a step toward me. *i know i know child but you will i promise you will you are important you are special you are—*

Lightning flashed, and I saw I was surrounded. Dozens of wolves were prowling among the trees. Their eyes were red and orange and *violet—*

The trees snapped from side to side in the harsh wind.

I thought I was going to get blown away, carried into the black sky above and lost in the storm.

The wolves stopped.

They tilted their heads back in unison.

And howled.

It tore through me, and it was *breaking* me, it was *crushing* my bones into powder. I couldn't move, couldn't breathe, couldn't find a way to stop it, and I didn't *want* to. That was what hit me hardest, that I didn't *want* it to stop. I wanted to be consumed, to feel my flesh tear and bleed onto the earth beneath my feet, to sacrifice myself so that I would know I mattered, would know that I meant something to someone.

The Alpha said, *no you can't that's not what this is this is DIFFERENT this is MORE because you are MORE and—*

Hands settled on my shoulders.

A voice whispered in my ear.

It said, "Robbie. Robbie, can you hear me? Hear my voice. Listen. You're safe. I've got you. Would you hear me, dear? Please."

The hands tightened against my shoulders, fingers digging into my skin, and I was jerked *backward*, flying through the trees. The wolves were screaming, screaming, screaming their songs of fury and horror, and as the world began to crack around me, as it shattered into pieces like so much glass, one wolf stepped out of the shadows.

It was dark gray with flecks of black and white on its face and between its ears.

And in its mouth, it carried—

. . .

I gasped as I sat up, chest heaving. For a moment I didn't know where I was. There were wolves and trees, and they were breaking, and I had to put them back together. I had to find all the ways to make the pieces fit, to make them whole again so I could—

"You're all right," a kind voice said. "Robbie. You're okay. It was just a dream. You're safe."

I blinked rapidly, trying to catch my breath.

The man next to my bed looked worried, the deep lines on his craggy face pronounced. He was wearing his nightclothes. His feet were bare, thin and bony. His hair was long gone, liver spots on his scalp and the backs of his hands. He was hunched over, more so with advanced age than concern. But his eyes were clear and kind, and he was *real*.

Ezra.

I immediately calmed.

I knew where I was.

I was in my room.

I was in the house I shared with him.

I was *home*.

"Jesus Christ," I muttered, looking down at the tangle of blankets around my waist and legs. I was sweating, and my heart thundered in my chest. I rubbed a hand over my face, trying to get rid of the afterimages dancing behind my eyes.

Ezra shook his head. "The dreams again?"

I flopped back in the bed, putting my arm over my eyes. "Yeah. Again. I thought I was getting past this."

The bed dipped as he sat down next to me. Even though I was overwarm, the air in my bedroom was cool. Spring was late this year, and there were still patches of snow on the ground at the beginning of May, though it was mostly dirty slush. The moon was nearly new, still tugging like a hook in the back of my mind.

Ezra gently pushed my arm away from my face before pressing the back of his hand against my forehead. I could hear the frown in his voice when he said, "You can't force it, Robbie. The more you try, the worse off you'll be." He hesitated. Then, "Did something happen today? You were quiet at dinner. I would hear you, dear, if you'd like to speak on it."

I sighed as he pulled his hand back. I opened my eyes, staring up at the ceiling. My heartbeat was slowing and the dream was fading. I felt . . . calmer, somehow. Able to think. I thought it was because of the man beside me. He grounded me. He was the closest thing I'd ever had to a father, and just having him near was enough to bring me back to reality.

I turned my head to look at him. He was troubled. I reached out and took his hand in mine, feeling the old bones under paper-thin skin. "It's nothing."

He snorted. "I find that hard to believe. You may be able to fool all the others, but I'm not like them. And you know it. Try again."

Yeah. I did know that. I searched for the right words. "It's . . ." I shook my head. "Do you ever think that there's something else out there? Something more?"

"Than what?"

"Than this." I couldn't find another way to put my muddled thoughts into coherent words.

He nodded slowly. "You're young yet. It's not uncommon to think such things." He looked down at our joined hands. "In fact, I expect it's quite normal. I was the same when I was your age."

I felt a little better. "All those centuries ago?"

He chuckled, rusty and dry. It was a sound I didn't hear as often as I'd like. "Cheeky," he said. "I'm not *that* old. At least not yet." His laughter faded. "I worry about you. And I know you're going to tell me not to, but that won't stop me. I'm not going to be around forever, Robbie, and I—"

I groaned. "Not this again. You're not going anywhere anytime soon. I won't let you."

"I don't know if you'll have much say in the matter."

"Yeah? Try me." I was uncomfortable with the idea. He was so fragile. So breakable. Humans generally were, and I couldn't stand the idea of something happening to him. He was a witch, sure, but magic could only do so much. I'd asked him once what would happen if he took the bite. I told him we could run together when the moon was full, and he'd hugged me close, rubbing my back while he told me that witches could never be wolves. Their magic would never allow it. If he was ever bitten by an Alpha, he said, the wolf magic and witch magic would tear him apart. I never asked him about it again.

He squeezed my hand. "I know you would do much for me—"

"Anything," I corrected. "I would do anything."

"—but you need to prepare. You can't become stagnant, Robbie. And that means you need to start thinking about what lies ahead. It's that something more you just spoke of. And as much as I wish I could be with you forever, it won't always be this way."

"But not anytime soon, right?" I asked quickly.

He rolled his eyes, and I loved him for it. "I'm *fine*. I've still got a few tricks up my sleeve. It's nothing you need to worry about."

"That's funny, coming from you."

He frowned. "Don't think I don't see how you've turned this conversation around on me."

"I have no idea what you're talking about."

"I really hope you don't expect me to believe that. What was the dream about this time?"

I turned my head away from him. I couldn't look at him when we talked about this. It felt strangely like betrayal. "It was the same one."

"Ah. The wolves in the trees."

"Yeah." I swallowed thickly. "Them."

"The white Alpha?"

"Yeah."

"What do you think it means?"

I shrugged. "I don't know." It could mean anything. Or nothing at all.

"Did you recognize it?"

I shook my head.

"And there were others."

"A lot of them."

"And they were howling."

Singing, I almost said, but caught it at the last second. "It's like they were calling me."

"I see. Was there anything else? Anything different?"

Yes. The gray wolf with black stripes on its face, carrying a stone in its jaws. I'd never seen it before. I pulled my hand away from him and rubbed the juncture between my neck and shoulders. "No," I said. "Nothing else."

I thought he believed me. And why wouldn't he? I was always honest with him. He would have no reason to think otherwise. He said, "You've always struggled with finding your place. It could be just as simple as a manifestation of wanting somewhere to belong."

"I belong here. With you." The words tasted like they burned. Smoke and ash.

"I know. But you're a wolf, Robbie. You need more than what I can provide. These bonds you've made with the pack . . . they're temporary. To keep you from turning Omega. It's a strain on you. I can see that, even if you can't."

I smiled tightly as I turned back toward him. "It's enough for now."

He patted my knee through the blankets. "If you're sure." He didn't sound convinced.

"I am. I didn't mean to wake you."

He laughed again. "Sleep is an elusive thing for me these days. It happens when you get older. You'll learn that one day. It's late. Or depending on how you look at it, early. Try to get some rest, dear. You need it."

He stood with a grunt, his knees popping. The sleeves of his nightclothes pulled back on his arms, revealing old tattoos that seemed dull and faded.

He was at the door when he stopped and glanced back over his shoulder. "You know you can talk to me about anything, right? Whatever you tell me, it would stay between us."

"I know."

He nodded. I thought he was going to say something more, but he didn't. He closed the door behind him, and the floor creaked as he walked down the hallway of our small home toward his bedroom.

I listened for his heartbeat.

It was slow and loud.

I turned over on my side, arms underneath my pillow, my chin resting against my wrist. My bedroom's only window opened on a lonely stretch of woods.

The dream was already fading. Where once it felt vibrant and alive, it was now mostly translucent. I could barely remember the taste of sap on my tongue.

I listened to Ezra's heartbeat as I closed my eyes.

I didn't dream again that night.

IT WAS ENOUGH / QUIET AS A MOUSE

Near the Canadian border and at the edge of the Aroostook National Wildlife Refuge—a mixture of an old- and new-growth forest that never seemed to dry out—was a town forgotten by the human world.

And it was better that way.

From the outside, Caswell, Maine, was nothing. There was no major highway for miles. The only way one would know Caswell had a name at all was an old sign along a two-lane road. The sign was faded red, held up by two posts with chipped black paint. Gold letters said WELCOME TO, and white against black said CASWELL. Below these words was EST. 1879. At the bottom was a small painting of a tree with a farmhouse and silo set in the distance behind it.

Anyone who found their way to Caswell (usually by accident) would see old farmhouses and streets without a single traffic signal. There was a small grocery store, a diner with a blinking neon sign that said WELCOME, a gas station, and an ancient movie theater that showed films from days gone by, mainly grainy black-and-white monster movies.

That was it.

Except it was a lie.

No one lived in the old farmhouses.

People worked in the store and the diner and the gas station. Even the movie theater.

But none of them stayed *in* Caswell.

Because just outside of the nothing town was Butterfield Lake.

Large walls surrounded it on all sides, the stone at least four feet thick and reinforced with rebar.

Inside those walls was a compound.

And it was here that the most powerful pack in North America—and possibly the world—resided.

I didn't live in the compound. It made my skin feel electrified. I didn't like it.

Off Butterfield Lake was Woodman Road, made of dirt and

gravel. If you followed Woodman Road all the way to the end, you'd come to a metal gate. And through the gate, deeper into the woods, was a small house.

It wasn't much. It'd once been for loggers who had harvested the trees through the middle of the twentieth century. There were two bedrooms. A small bathroom. It had a porch with two chairs on it. The kitchen was efficient enough for two men, and that was it. That's all it was.

It was enough.

Most of the time.

There were days when I needed the quiet. To be away from everyone else.

Days when I'd shift and run through the wildlife refuge, feeling the wet earth beneath my paws and the leaves slapping against my face. I'd keep going until I could go no farther, my lungs burning in my chest, tongue lolling from my mouth.

I'd be deep in the refuge, away from the sights and sounds of the compound. From the other wolves. From the witches. Even Ezra. He understood.

I'd collapse under an ancient tree, lying on my side, chest heaving. It was instinct that led me here, and I'd roll in the grass, turning over on my back and letting the sun warm my belly. Birds sang. Squirrels ran, and though I could chase them and eat them, I usually let them be.

I had a strange relationship with trees.

My mother placed me in one moments before my father murdered her.

I was six years old.

Memories are funny things.

If asked what I was doing exactly one year before on any given day, chances are I wouldn't remember unless someone reminded me.

But I remember being six with a startling clarity.

Some of those days, at least.

They were bright flashes, moments that prickled against my skin.

I remember a pack. There were six of us. One was an Alpha, strong and kind. She pressed her nose against my hair and breathed me in.

One was her mate, an older woman who, when she laughed, would tilt her head back and grab her sides.

One was a woman named Denise. She was quiet and beautiful. When she moved, it was like she barely touched the ground. I asked her once if she was an angel. She picked me up and tickled my sides.

Her mate was a Black woman with bright white teeth and a wicked smile. She had a garden. She gave me tomatoes and we ate them like they were apples, juice and seeds dripping on our chins.

The other was my mother. Her name was Beatrice. And she was the most wonderful person in my entire world. We slept in the same room. She would whisper to me at night and tell me that we were safe here, that we didn't need to run anymore. That we could have a home. That she would never let anything happen to me. I believed her. She was my mother.

I didn't understand why we were running or for how long we'd done so. There were nights when we'd slept in an old car that she prayed over before she tried to start, saying, "Come on, please, God, just give me this." She'd turn the key and the engine would sputter and sputter, and then it would catch, and she'd crow, slapping her hands against the steering wheel, grinning brightly at me as she said, "See? We're okay. We're okay!"

Denise found us sleeping in the car off a dirt road, hidden behind a copse of trees.

My mother woke me up, clutching me against her chest. I looked outside the windshield to see a strange woman sitting on the ground in front of the car.

She waved at us.

"Wolf," my mother whispered.

The car wouldn't start.

It didn't even click.

The strange woman cocked her head at us. She spoke in a quiet voice, but my ears were sharp, and I could hear her. She said, "It's okay. I'm not going to hurt you."

We'd found ourselves in another wolf's territory.

She took us to the Alpha at an old cabin that had two chimneys.

My mother held me close.

The Alpha's eyes flared red.

My mother trembled.

I said, "Do you have any food? We're hungry."

The Alpha smiled. "Yes. I believe we do. Do you like meatloaf?"

I didn't know what meatloaf was. I told her as much.

The smile faded. "Why don't we see if you like it? If you don't, we can make something else."

I loved meatloaf very much. I didn't think I'd ever eaten anything so good before. I ate until my belly ached.

The Alpha was pleased.

We stayed.

The first night, my mother curled around me. She kissed the top of my head and whispered, "What do you think, cub?"

I yawned. I was tired, and sleeping in a bed for the first time in a long time felt good.

"Yeah," she said. "I think so too."

Days passed. Weeks.

The Alpha said, "His father?"

I was drawing at the kitchen table. They had given me all the crayons I could ever want. There were markers too, but they were mostly dry because their caps were missing.

"Hunter," my mother whispered in a choked voice. "I thought he was . . . I thought that he was my—"

I looked up to see she was crying. I could taste it at the back of my tongue. There was a sour scent in the air, like something had spoiled.

I didn't recognize it then for what it was.

Later, I would know.

It was shame.

Before I could go to her, the Alpha rose and wrapped her arms around my mother. She held on tightly and told her that she understood.

The sour smell faded after a little while.

We had months. Months where we were stationary and it seemed like we had found a place to belong. We were like a tree, and our roots were growing into the dirt, getting stronger as the days went by. Our bed began to smell like us. It was nice.

It didn't last.

Everything burned.

I woke to the smell, and it wasn't like shame.

It was fire.

Wolves were howling.

My mother lifted me from the bed.

Her eyes were wide and panicked.

There was a loud crash from somewhere in the cabin, and I heard the shouts of men. It was the first time I'd heard a male voice in a long while, because the Alpha didn't allow men in her pack. She said she had no use for them and winked at me, telling me that I was going to be the exception. It made me the happiest I'd been in a long time, because I'd be a good man. The best there ever was. My mother told me as much.

We went out the window. It was dark when she dropped me to the ground. One of my bare feet landed on a rock, and it cut me.

I cried even as it slowly began to heal.

My mother covered my mouth with her hand as she lifted me up.

She ran. No one could run as fast as my mother. I'd always believed that.

But on this night, she couldn't run fast enough.

The tree she took me to was old. Ancient. Denise had told me that it was special, that it was the queen of the forest and protected all that it towered over.

In the spring, foxes came and had their kits in the hollow at its base. It was empty when my mother shoved me inside it. There were dead leaves and grass inside, and it was soft.

My mother crouched low, her black hair hanging around her face. She had soot on her cheeks, her hands. She wore glasses even though she didn't need them. She said they made her feel better about herself. Smarter, somehow. She thought it was silly, but I'd never seen anyone more beautiful.

She said, "Stay here. Whatever you do, whatever you hear, you don't leave until I come back for you. Even if you hear someone calling your name, you don't move. It's a game, little wolf. You're hiding, and you can't let anyone find you."

I nodded because I'd played this game before. "Quiet as a mouse."

"Yes. Quiet as a mouse. Here, hold these for me." She took the glasses off her face and set them on my own. They were too big and sagged onto my nose. She reached out and touched my cheek. "I love you. Forever."

And then she shifted.

Her wolf was gray like storm clouds. She had black lines on her snout and between her big ears.

She looked back at me once, and her eyes flared orange.

And then she was gone.

I stayed in the tree. It was a game, and I didn't want to lose.

Even when I heard wolves crying out in pain, I stayed.

Even when I heard men yelling, I stayed.

Even when I heard the crack of gunfire, I stayed, though I covered my ears.

I stayed even when I heard a voice calling my name as the sky began to lighten.

A male voice.

And it was *familiar*, like I'd heard it before.

It said, "Robbie, where are you, son? Come out, come out, come out."

It said, "Don't you recognize me?"

It said, "Robbie, please. I'm your daddy."

Quiet as a mouse, I stayed.

Eventually the voices faded.

But still I stayed.

Later I would be told I was in that hollow for three days. I didn't remember most of it, only brief moments when I found an acorn and ate it because I was hungry. Or when I had to pee, so I went in the corner, the scent making me gag even hours later.

Wolves found me eventually.

They covered my eyes as they pulled me out. They asked me who I was. What had happened. Who had done all of this.

"I'm quiet as a mouse," I told them as they took me away. "I'm thirsty. Do you have water? My mom will be thirsty too. She runs really fast. I'll find her. I'm good at tracking. She won't run from me."

I saw the remains of the cabin, charred and still smoking.

I never saw Denise or her mate again.

I never saw the Alpha or her mate again.

But I did see my mother once more.

There was blood in her fur, and I screamed at the flies around her head, but the wolves carried me away.

Memories are funny things.

I carried them like scars.

From the outside, the compound inside the walls around Butterfield Lake looked like a postcard. The houses were big and well-kept. Docks led from most of the houses down to the lake. Children ran on the dirt paths, laughing and yelling at the giant wolf that chased them. They were on their way to the house at the east end of the lake, which had been converted into a school. I'd gone to one like it far away from here, and I'd learned how to write and how to divide and how to track and parse through all the delicious smells and howl at the moon.

Some of the little ones crashed into me, grabbing my legs, demanding I protect them from the big bad wolf chasing them.

One little cub—a boy named Tony—crawled up my legs and chest, wrapping himself around me. He knocked my glasses askew as he shrieked that he didn't want to be *eaten*, save me, Robbie, save me!

I laughed as I spun him around, the other children surrounding me and demanding that they have a turn. I growled playfully at them, baring my teeth. They did the same.

"I don't know if I can save you," I told Tony. "You might need to save *me*."

Tony gasped. "I can do it! I've been learning! Watch!" He squinted at me, clenching his jaw until his face started to turn an alarming shade of red. And then, brief though it was, his eyes flashed orange.

"Wow," I said. "Look at you. You're doing so good. You're going to make an amazing wolf one day."

He squealed in delight, wriggling in my arms so much that I almost dropped him. The other children wanted to show me *their* eyes too, and most of them were able to flash the bright orange. The ones who couldn't looked disappointed, but I told them it would happen when they were ready, and they grinned.

The wolf who had been chasing them—their teacher—growled lowly, and I set Tony down. The children took off toward the school.

"Handful, huh?" I asked the wolf.

She snorted, pressing up against me, and the bonds between us lit up. It was like a tight string plucked in the dark, reverberating in my head. I closed my eyes at the weight of it, and I—

(*i see you*)

I took a step back at the strange voice in my head.

I didn't know what it was. I didn't recognize it. It hadn't come from anyone I knew. No one in the compound, at least. It echoed in the dark, and then it was gone.

The wolf cocked her head at me, and I felt the question she was asking without speaking.

I forced a smile. "I'm fine. Didn't sleep very well last night. Big day. You know how I get."

The wolf chuffed, scratching at the ground. She pressed against me once more, and her scent on my skin was sweet and warm. She lifted her head and pushed my glasses back up my face with her nose. The lenses fogged briefly, and she chuffed again as I scowled.

"Yeah, yeah. You've got a class to teach, Sonari. Get a move on."

That thread between us was plucked again, and she trotted off, following the children.

I stared after her. I felt the beginnings of a headache coming on. I rubbed at my neck, fighting the urge to shift and run into the trees. It was an itch I couldn't scratch. At least not yet. I had a job to do.

People—wolves and witches alike—waved at me as I walked through the compound. I called out greetings in response but didn't stop to talk. I had places to be, people to see. They didn't like it when I was late.

A few wolves didn't acknowledge me, but I was used to it. I was in a position they thought I hadn't earned, given how short of a time I'd been here. I didn't give two shits what they thought. I had the trust of the Alpha of all and her witch, and that was all that mattered.

But most were friendly. They said my name like they were happy to see me, like I mattered. I breathed in the air of the compound and the forest, listening to the wolves moving around me, the day just beginning. It was like it had always been since I'd arrived in Caswell. It was busy, so many moving parts working together.

There was a house set away from all the others, back in the trees. The children didn't go near it. Most of the adults didn't either. It was a normal house with dark green shutters and white paint on the siding. But standing next to it felt like moving through water, and it made me sneeze.

A wolf stood in front of the house, arms crossed over his considerable chest as he leaned against the door. He nodded at me as I approached. "Robbie."

"Hey, Santos. Guard duty again?"

He squinted at me. "Luck of the draw."

"Seems like you're always lucky, then."

He shrugged. "Someone's gotta do it." He jerked his head toward the door behind him. "It's not like it's tough. Guy can barely move. Just as long as I don't have to clean him after he shits himself, I'm fine with it. There are worse jobs."

The wards around the house made my skin crawl and my nose itch. I didn't know how Santos could stand being so close to the barrier magic. A code, like a metaphysical keypad that only certain people had the combination to, would part the wards. Most didn't go in unless Ezra was with them, and even then, it was quick in and quick out. You didn't dwell with the prisoner. Monsters needed to be locked away for the good of all of us. Even so, I was curious about him, about what he'd done. Only a few people knew. I wasn't one of them. "He talk at all?"

Santos slowly shook his head. "You know he doesn't. Completely blank. Doesn't even know who he is, much less where he's at." He got a strange look on his face. It wasn't mean, but it was unpleasant. "Why do you care?"

I frowned. "I . . . don't know. I don't."

"Of course not," he repeated, and there was a nasty curl to his lips. Santos didn't like me. "Don't you have someplace to be? Ezra went by a while ago, which means you're already late."

I cursed. "I don't know why he didn't wait for me."

"He knows how you get in the morning."

"Yeah, yeah. Keep it up, Santos. See how far it gets you."

He laughed, mocking. "Sure, Robbie."

I waved and left him to it. I glanced back over my shoulder at the house once more. I thought I saw movement in one of the windows, but I told myself it was just a trick of light and shadow.

The biggest house in the compound was a two-story cabin with a large covered porch that looked out onto the lake. The windows were open, letting in the cool air. I climbed the porch stairs, the wood creaking underneath my boots. I hesitated for a moment before opening the door.

The interior of the cabin was spacious. A fire roared in the fireplace, and wolves were hurrying around the ground floor. A few spared me a glance, but most of them ignored me. They were busy, and the Alpha of all liked to keep it that way.

I climbed the stairs to the second floor, stepping close to the banister as a woman I vaguely knew flew down the stairs. She grinned at me as she passed, but otherwise didn't stop. The house was loud and always moving, people coming and going.

I reached the top of the stairs. To my left, five doors led to bedrooms and bathrooms. To my right were a closet and a pair of doors that led to the office. I felt something strong pulse within me. It tugged me toward the double doors.

She knew I was here, even though the room was soundproof.

It was part of being the Alpha of all. I belonged to her, and she could find me always.

I knocked before opening the door.

Ezra sat in a chair in front of a heavy desk. There was an empty chair next to him. He didn't turn to look at me, but I felt his magic curl over me. I relished the feel of it more than I ever did with her. I thought she knew that, but we never spoke of it.

And there, sitting behind the desk, was the Alpha of all.

Michelle Hughes folded her hands in front of her and said, "You're late, Robbie."

OUTRIGHT DEFIANCE / LITTLE WOLF

When we'd been on the run, hunters chasing after us with a frightening persistence, my mother did everything she could to keep things normal for me.

Sometimes we could afford a cheap motel. They were always dingy and smelled awful, but she said we needed to be thankful for the little things.

Some nights she stayed with me, curled around me, whispering quietly in my ear.

She would tell me about a place where we could be free. Where we could shift and feel the earth beneath our feet without worrying someone would hurt us. She told me there was a rumor of a place, far, far to the west, where wolves and humans lived together in harmony. They loved each other, she whispered, because that's what pack was supposed to do.

And she told me other stories, little things that made me ache.

About how her grandfather had been sweet and loving. He would always give her fruit candies when no one was watching.

About the first time she shifted and saw the world in shades of wolf.

About how she had made mistakes, but she couldn't be too angry because those mistakes had brought me to her.

She said that in a perfect world, my father would love us. He wouldn't care what we were. That he wouldn't have used her. That when I was born, things would have changed for him.

"No one can know the minds of men," she said, her voice so bitter that I could taste it. "They tell you things, and you believe them because you don't know any better."

I would reach up and tell her not to cry.

Sometimes she even listened to me.

"Sorry," I muttered as I closed the door behind me. "Got tackled by a bunch of cubs."

Ezra chuckled. "They do seem fond of you."

I patted him on the shoulder as I stood next to his chair. "Thanks for waiting for me."

He arched an eyebrow at me. "I told you to get up. It's not my fault you're lazy."

"And it's not *my* fault your idea of morning consists of getting up before the sun rises. There's something seriously wrong with you."

"Cute," Ezra said. "Ageism at its finest." He looked at Michelle. "You see what I have to put up with?" He smiled at her.

She didn't smile back.

Ezra had been her witch for years. When she'd taken over as Alpha of all, he'd come along with her. He was the one who'd come to fetch me last year per her request and brought me back to Caswell. Their relationship confused me. All the witches to wolves I'd met before had an almost symbiotic relationship with their Alpha. Ezra and Michelle seemed to be on good terms, but they had a history I wasn't privy to. I'd thought about asking after it, but I never did. Part of it was not wanting to ruin what I had by dredging up memories they obviously didn't want to talk about.

"Come here," Michelle said. She added "Please" almost as an afterthought.

I walked around the desk and stood next to an old bookcase filled with texts and tomes that held the history of the wolves. I didn't want to seem too eager. We were still learning about each other, but we had time. When I first met her, I'd thought her cold and calculating. It took me a long time to see through it. It wasn't a front exactly, but more the byproduct of being in her position. Once you got through the façade, she was a good Alpha.

And she trusted me.

Gave me a home.

I owed her.

She stood, and I tilted my head in deference, exposing my neck. Her eyes flashed red, and she trailed a finger along my throat. Her scent was spicy and sharp.

"Ezra tells me you were dreaming again," she said quietly.

I glanced at him before looking back down at her. She was a short woman, slight and pale. But I wasn't fooled, nor had I been when I'd first met her. She was stronger than any Alpha I'd ever come across. Part of it was being the Alpha of all. Part of it was from her lineage.

If it came down to it, it wouldn't be a fair fight. She could take me down with ease.

"It wasn't . . ." I shook my head. "It wasn't anything. Just a dream."

"The same one, though." She tapped her fingernails on the desk.

"I guess," I said begrudgingly.

"And what do you make of it?"

"It's nothing. Just . . . probably something from before."

Her expression softened. "He can't hurt you anymore. He's been dead a long time, Robbie. The wolves that found you saw to that. Those hunters are gone."

"I know," I said honestly. "It's why you shouldn't worry about it. I'm fine." I smiled to reassure her.

She looked dubious. "You'll tell me if it happens again."

"Of course."

"Good. Thank you, Robbie. You're a good wolf. You may have a seat."

I felt warm at the praise from my Alpha. I went back around the desk, shooting a glare at Ezra for opening his mouth when he shouldn't have. He'd hear from me later. I couldn't have Michelle doubting me.

Ezra ignored me, as was his way.

I sat down next to him, slumping in my chair. Ezra kicked my foot, and I sighed as I straightened my back, hands folded in my lap.

Michelle sat back down across from us. She lifted her tablet from the desk and started typing on the screen. "I have an assignment for you. Out of town." She glanced at me before looking back down at the tablet. "Out of state, actually."

That caught my attention. Normally if she sent me anywhere, it was within a few hours' drive of Caswell. There were extensions of her pack throughout Maine, wolves who worked around the state, mostly in the bigger cities like Bangor and Portland. They lived in small groups, working with the humans who were unaware of what they were, especially those in positions of power in local government. When I first arrived I'd made the mistake of calling it her *agenda*, and she'd corrected me immediately. She didn't have an agenda, she said. She merely wanted to expand the reach of the wolves. I didn't understand why she needed to do this, given that no one was trying to fight against her. And why would they? She was the Alpha of all for a reason. And while her word was final, it wasn't absolute. She listened to her pack, heard their worries and concerns. If she could help them, she did.

I thought at first the wolves were scared of her.

I thought at first *I* was scared of her.

But there's a thin line between fear and awe.

I tried to tamp down my eagerness. "You're serious?"

She nodded toward Ezra. "He thinks you're ready."

Maybe I wouldn't have to yell at him after all. "I am."

"Then consider this a test," she said. "To see if he's right."

"I think you'll find I usually am," he said mildly.

The skin around her eyes tightened briefly. I wondered what they'd been talking about before I showed up. "We'll see, then, won't we? There's a pack in Virginia. It's small—an Alpha and three Betas. We haven't heard from them in a few months."

I frowned. "Hunters?"

She shook her head slowly. "Not that I'm aware of. More of a . . . disagreement in the way things should be run. I need you to impress upon them that open lines of communication are paramount to the survival of our species. It's imperative, especially in these troubling times, that we have each other's backs as much as possible. I've sent you the file."

I pulled my phone from my pocket and clicked on the Dropbox app to download the attachment. The first page was a picture. The Alpha stood in the center. She was smiling. She was younger than I expected her to be. She could have been in high school. She was holding a sign that said SOLD! in bright lettering. There was a run-down house behind her that looked barely livable.

Standing with her were three men. Two were young. One was old enough to be her father, though they looked nothing alike. He was Black. She was white. They were all smiling.

The rest of the file contained information on the pack. I was right. The Alpha *was* young, having just turned twenty. I couldn't imagine having that kind of power at that age. I read that she'd gotten it from her mother when she'd passed on a year prior.

"No witch?" I asked, reading through the notes.

"No," Michelle said. "They were never big enough to need one. Her mother was a friend of mine. Kind. Patient. Willing to work for the good of the pack. Her daughter is headstrong. I know that she'll fall in line with proper motivation."

I looked up at her. "How did her mother die?"

"A car accident, of all things. Her daughter was in the car with her but wasn't seriously hurt. The power of the Alpha passed along to her. She's been... difficult ever since. But when one is as young as she, one tends to get ideas about the way things should be run. She hasn't been in touch, and it appears she has cut off communication with us."

"She wants independence," I said, going back to the picture. They looked happy. "You can't fault her for that."

"I don't," Michelle said sharply, and I felt the pull in her voice, the undercurrent of the Alpha. "But there is a difference between independence and outright defiance. This is the way things are done, Robbie. You know that. She has her own pack, yes, but all wolves are under my jurisdiction."

I did know. There were outliers, sure, wolves who tried to remain hidden from the reach of the Alpha of all. And if they didn't have an Alpha of their own, they ran the risk of turning Omega, losing their minds to the wolf, forgetting they had ever been human.

And if it got that far, there was only one thing that could be done.

It was always quick. Or so I was told. I'd never seen an Omega put down.

I never wanted to.

"Maybe they just forgot to check in," I said. "You know how things get. They're busy living their own lives. It happens." I didn't know why I was pushing this. Maybe it was because I understood the desire to be free, to not have anything hanging over your head.

"We'll see," Ezra said.

"We?"

He looked at me. "Of course, dear. You don't think I'd let you go by yourself, do you?"

I'd hoped. And even though part of me was relieved at the idea of having him there, the other part of me wanted a little independence as well. "Alpha Hughes won't need you here?" I asked innocently.

He grinned. "Oh, I'm sure she can do without me for a couple of days. Can't you, Michelle?"

"Yes," she said. "I suppose I can."

"And it's not like we'll be gone long," Ezra continued. "It's a day's drive to Fredericksburg, if we keep at it. We'll be back before there's any time to miss us at all."

I groaned. I loved him, but the idea of being cooped up in a car with him for hours on end was going to drive me up the wall. He had terrible taste in music.

He laughed like he knew what I was thinking. "It won't be so bad. Give us a chance to take a break. Meet some other wolves." His eyes were sparkling. "Maybe even find yourself someone special."

Fuck this. And him. "You are *not* going to pimp me out to another wolf. Not again."

"Please. There was no pimping. It's not my fault the last one was . . . well. Exuberant."

"Exuberant?" I exclaimed incredulously. "She killed a goddamn bear and left it in front of the house!"

"It was a small bear," Ezra told Michelle. "Probably only a couple of years old. Still, impressive, if you think about it. She certainly proved her worth. Anyone would be happy to have Sonari as a mate."

"She snuck into the house and licked me while I was sleeping!"

"She wanted you to smell like her. Nothing wrong with that."

I crossed my arms and sank low in my chair. "You've got a seriously skewed view of right and wrong. You don't *lick* people when they haven't asked for it. And she's a teacher. Who knows what she's telling all those kids about courting?"

"I'll keep that in mind for next time. Let an old man have his fun, Robbie. Is it so much to ask to want to see you happy?"

I sighed, knowing I'd lost. I couldn't deal whenever he got sentimental, and he knew it. "Just . . . if it happens, it happens, okay? I'll know when it's right. I don't want to force it."

"I know you don't. Now, if that's all, I'll take my leave. I have things to attend to before we depart."

Michelle nodded. "That's fine. I want you to keep in touch for as long as you're there, if you should find the need to stay longer than a couple of days. Keep me informed."

"Of course, Alpha. Robbie, would you please—"

"Robbie stays."

That caught him off guard. He looked between us. "Come again?"

Michelle looked stern. "I need to have a discussion with my second."

I blinked in surprise. She'd never called me that before. I hadn't even known that was on the table. Granted, she didn't seem to have any other wolf who *could* have been her second—none that I knew of, anyway—but hearing it spoken aloud made me want to howl with joy.

"Of course," Ezra said, bowing low. He stood upright again and squeezed my shoulder. "I have much to prepare for. There is a young witch named Gregory I need to speak with. He's bright and eager, though a little foolhardy, even as he asks question after question. Reminds me of someone I know. I'll see you at home, all right? We'll leave bright and early, so don't stay out too late."

I nodded, barely hearing his words. I was still stuck on *second*.

He closed the door behind him, leaving us alone.

I tried to find the words to show my appreciation, practically vibrating in my chair, but Michelle spoke first. "Are you happy here, Robbie?"

"Yes," I said immediately, and it was mostly the truth.

She watched me for a moment before nodding. "These dreams you're having."

I shifted in my chair. "Everyone dreams."

"I know that. But is this different?"

"I'm a wolf. I dream of wolves. I don't know how else to dream. It's always been this way." It was close to a lie, but not so close that she'd be able to tell.

"You're important to me." She said it stiffly, like she wasn't used to expressing her emotions. Oh, Michelle cared about her pack, but sometimes her concern felt . . . mechanical. Almost perfunctory.

"Thank you, Alpha Hughes. I won't let you down."

"I know you won't." She glanced over my shoulder before looking back at me. "I need you to be on your guard."

I was confused. "For what?"

"The wolves in Virginia. They . . . we don't know what they'll do. What they'll say."

I wasn't worried. "It's probably just a simple miscommunication. Easy fix."

"Maybe," she said. She began to tap her fingernails on the desk again, a habit I thought came from nerves. "But if it's not, do what you need to in order to protect yourself. I expect you to return whole. Stick close to Ezra. Don't be out of his sight."

"Is there something else I should know?"

She shook her head. "Just keep an eye out, okay? That will be all."

I stood as she did. I was surprised when she came around the desk again and took my hand in hers. Her eyes filled with red, and calm washed over me. It was soothing, being here with her. Part of me balked at how easy it was, but I knew my place. I was a Beta wolf. I needed an Alpha.

I needed her.

"You don't need to worry about me. I can take care of myself."

She smiled, though it didn't reach her eyes. "I know you can. But you're mine. And I don't take that responsibility lightly."

I left her standing there in the middle of her office.

* * *

When I exited the house, the day was bright. I hoped winter was finally on its way out. The air still had a crisp bite to it, but the sun was warm.

I thought about going home, but I wasn't ready to face Ezra. I was still a little pissed off he'd been talking to Michelle about me behind my back. I knew he did it out of concern, but it still irritated me.

And the thought of being cooped up with him for a long car ride didn't help.

Instead of turning toward home, I left the compound and headed for the refuge.

The thick trees blocked out most of the sunlight. There were still patches of snow on the ground. I stopped as I entered the tree line, cocking my head and listening to the sounds of the forest. It was teeming with life. In the distance, deer were grazing. Birds were calling, calling, calling.

I crossed an old, rarely used dirt road.

I was alone.

I stretched my hands over my head, popping my back.

I needed to run.

I left my clothes and glasses in some bushes near the road. I dug my toes into the earth, slowly breathing in and out.

It started in my chest.

The wolf and I were one.

The first time I shifted hurt more than anything else I'd felt. I'd been on the cusp of puberty, and my skin felt like it was on fire. I screamed for days on end, my voice breaking and going hoarse, but still I screamed.

The wolves I'd been with weren't pack, but they were close enough. They cared for me even though I wasn't theirs. The Alpha held me against his chest, brushing my sweat-slick hair off my forehead. "Find it," he said, his voice a growl. "Find your tether, Robbie. Find your tether and clutch it tightly. Let it wrap around you. Let it pull you to your wolf."

"I can't," I cried at him. "Please, it hurts, make it stop, make it *stop*."

His hands tightened around me, his claws dimpling my skin. He said, "I know it hurts. I know it does. But you are a wolf. And you will shift. But before you can, you have to find a way back."

My back arched against his chest as I seized, my hands digging into his thighs. He grunted when my claws burst from the tips of my fingers, slicing into him, drawing blood. My mouth filled with saliva at the smell of it, coppery and sharp. The animal in me wanted to rend and tear until he let me go, but he was stronger than I was.

And just when I thought I could take no more, that I would rather die than let it go on, I heard her voice.

She sang, "Little wolf, little wolf, can't you see? You are the master of the forest, the guardian of the trees." She laughed. "Always quiet as a mouse. Let them hear you now."

Memories can be funny things.

They can come when you least expect them to.

And when you need them most.

That was all she was. A memory.

But I latched on to it.

That first shift was a haze of instinct under the biggest moon. I barely remembered any of it, just the need to chase, chase, chase. The other wolves followed, howling so loudly that the very earth trembled with it.

Later, when I could run no more, they curled around me, my belly full of meat, and I slept.

The first shift was always the hardest.

Now?

Now it was easy.

The tether was there, as it always was.

My muscles began to quiver.

My bones began to shift.

There was pain, yes, but it was a *good* pain, and it hurt in such a terribly wonderful way.

I fell to my knees and I was

I am

wolf

i am wolf and strong and proud and this forest is mine this forest is home this

is where i am
this is where i am
this is
squirrel fuckin squirrel
i am going to chase you
i am gonna eat you
run run run
howl and sing and let them hear
there is
(robbie)
(robbie)
(ROBBIE)
????
is that
what is that
another wolf
is that another wolf
who are you
you aren't here
where are you
i can't find you
BUT I CAN SMELL YOU
I CAN SMELL YOU
(robbie robbie robbie)
why are you here
why are you with me
(i see you)
(i see you)
what is

who is
who am
who am i
i am
wolf
i am
i am
i

gasped as I broke out of my shift, falling to the ground, skidding on leaves and pine needles. I landed on my back, chest heaving as I stared through the canopy above. There were flashes of blue sky beyond green leaves.

But all I felt was the blue.

"What the fuck?" I whispered.

I pushed myself up off the ground. I grimaced as a cut on my shoulder began to stitch itself back together. I shook my head, trying to clear my mind.

I stood slowly, head cocked.

Listening.

I would have sworn there had been another wolf in the refuge.

One I didn't know.

I stood still.

Waiting for something. *Anything.*

Nothing happened.

I looked around.

Only trees.

I was alone.

My skin was chilled.

"Great," I muttered. "Now you're hearing things. Fan-fucking-tastic."

I decided to head for home.

. . .

I didn't tell Ezra what I thought I'd heard.

We had other things to worry about.

PROTECT ME / TRUST YOU

"Jesus Christ," I moaned. "How can you call this *music*?"

Ezra grinned. "Feel free to stick your head out the window like a good wolf if you think it'll help."

"That's speciesist. You should feel really bad and apologize." But I rolled down the window anyway. It was warmer than it'd been in Maine. I was stiff and sore, ready to get the hell out of this car, especially since we'd been listening to a woman wail in Italian for the past hour. Ezra thought opera would teach me to be *cultured*, but it was mostly torture. It didn't help that we were stuck in traffic as we neared Fredericksburg, a small city outside of Washington, DC. The air was thick with exhaust, and I was pretty sure we were going to be poisoned and die.

"I feel really bad and apologize," Ezra recited dutifully.

"I don't believe you."

"Ah. Well. At least I tried." But since he wasn't a *complete* asshole, he turned down the woman screeching about her lost love or spaghetti or whatever. "We're almost there."

"That's what you've been saying for the past two hours."

He glanced over at me. "How did I not know that you were like this?"

I hung my hand out the window, tapping it against the side of the car. "Because we've never had to go this far before."

"We could have flown."

I rolled my eyes. "Yes. Because a werewolf in a small enclosed metal tube with a bunch of strangers and screaming children is always a good idea."

"You've never flown before."

I shrugged. "Never had the need to. And I don't like the idea of being so . . . high. I like having my feet on the ground."

The car inched forward. "It's not as bad as you think."

"I think it's really bad, so." A sign up ahead said our exit was only a few miles away. I was relieved. We'd reach the pack before nightfall. "Do they know we're coming?"

"They've been notified, yes. They didn't respond, but we've done our due diligence."

"And what do we do if they're not there?"

I felt him looking over at me. "Where would they be?"

"I don't know. But if they cut off contact with Michelle, what makes you think they're going to want to see us?"

"Because they're not stupid," Ezra said patiently. "They know there are rules in place for a reason. If they're not there, we'll wait for them. They have to return sometime. It's their home. They wouldn't leave it behind. Territory is important to a wolf, especially to an Alpha."

"And if they attack?"

He sounded surprised. "Why would they?"

"Maybe they don't want to see us. Maybe there's a reason they stopped responding."

"Be that as it may, whatever their reason is, our job is to make sure they understand the rules and are following them."

We hadn't yet come across a pack that was truly defiant once we reminded them of their place. Sure, there were always going to be disagreements, but Michelle wasn't so stuck in her ways that she wouldn't listen to the problems of the wolves.

We were her emissaries, an extension of her, and a few of the packs disliked me on sight because of it. I always explained to them that I understood what they were doing and that I was an intermediary. A peacemaker. I carried their concerns back to the Alpha of all, and if she thought the concerns had merit and needed her intervention, she would meet with them face-to-face. Everyone left feeling like they'd been heard. Sometimes changes were made.

Sometimes they weren't.

But still.

This felt a little different.

"If anything goes weird, you stay behind me," I told Ezra.

He laughed. "Protect me, will you?"

"Yes."

"I believe that."

"Good."

"Even though you know I don't need it."

"Whatever. Just let me have this, okay? It'll make me feel better."

"All right, Robbie. Whatever you need."
We drove on.

They were waiting for us.

They lived outside of Fredericksburg, the town dropping away into rolling farmlands the farther we drove. I was disconcerted by the sprawling fields that replaced the trees, but to each their own. I'm sure they found a place to run when they needed it.

The GPS led us to a gravel driveway at the end of a one-lane road. The sun was beginning to set, and the sky was the color of a bone-deep bruise. Thunder rumbled in the distance behind heavy clouds.

The car hit a deep pothole, and I bounced in my seat. I turned to snarl at Ezra to slow the hell down, but he came to a stop, his gnarled hands tightening on the steering wheel as he stared straight ahead.

The gravel driveway opened up to a large circle in front of an old house. It was different than the picture Michelle had sent to me. That house had been run-down, looking like it'd be easier to level it than to repair. But it looked as if they'd fixed it up nicely. The paint on the porch was new, and so were the shutters. The roof had been replaced, as had the siding. The bones of the house were the same, but they'd managed to make it look almost new.

And they were standing in front of it.

My skin prickled with unease at being in the territory of an unknown Alpha without permission.

An older Black man stood in front of the others. His arms were crossed over his chest as he watched us through the windshield. His expression was blank, but his eyes were bright orange. Even over the rumble of the engine, I could hear the low growl in his throat.

Two younger men stood behind him. Fraternal twins, a rarity in born wolves. Both were pale, their hair black and curly. One was thinner than the other, and he looked nervous, eyes darting to his brother before going back to us.

His brother had a scowl on his face. His arms and chest were thick with muscle. I had years on both of them. If the file was correct, they were barely seventeen.

The older man turned his head slightly. He looked like he was about to speak, but instead he stepped to the side, revealing the Alpha.

She looked tired and as pale as the twins. Dark circles blotched the skin under her eyes, and she was thinner than she'd been in the photograph, though it had only been taken a few months before. Her hair was pulled back in a loose ponytail, and her eyes were dull until they filled with red. It rolled over me, foreign and immediate.

She was pissed.

Resigned, but pissed.

They were expecting us.

Ezra was frowning, his knuckles white on the steering wheel.

"Turn off the car," I said quietly. "And stay inside. Be prepared to move if I say."

"But—"

"Please."

He sighed. "Would you hear me for a moment before going out there half-cocked?"

"Yes. Always." My fangs were itching in my gums. "But they're listening to us right now."

His smile was faint. "I know. They're scared, though they shouldn't be. We aren't here to hurt them. Keep a level head. We are all part of the greater good. Sometimes we have to be reminded of that. You're a good boy, Robbie. I have faith in you. They don't yet. But they will."

I took a deep breath and let it out slow.

I reached for the door handle. I was about to pull it when Ezra gunned the engine. It was loud in the quiet, drowning out all other sound. The wolves in front of us winced. He leaned over quickly, his breath hot against my ear. He whispered, "Say little, but listen well."

He took his foot off the gas, and the engine idled.

I stared at him before shaking my head.

He turned off the car as I opened the door, pushing my glasses back up on my face.

The Beta wolves growled in unison, but they fell silent when the Alpha held up her hand.

The gravel crunched under my feet as I moved in front of the car, maintaining a distance between us. I wasn't stupid enough to believe I could get any closer without invitation. We were already encroaching.

My palms were sweating as I curled my hands into fists. My claws hadn't popped through, but it was close. I hadn't lost control of my shift since I was a cub. I didn't know why it felt so close now. I opened my mouth, popping my jaw, keeping my fangs at bay by sheer force of will. A show of aggression would be the worst thing right now.

So I did what I was taught.

I tilted my head to the side, exposing my neck. I flashed my eyes at the Alpha.

"We mean you no harm," I said in a low voice. "I come on behalf of the Alpha of all, who sends her regards. Alpha Hughes is worried about you. She hasn't heard from you in a while."

"We're fine," the bigger brother growled. "We don't need you. Go away."

"John," the Alpha snapped. She turned her head to the side, though she never took her gaze away from me. "Not another word."

John looked like he was going to argue, but he snapped his mouth closed instead, glaring at me.

The Alpha said, "If I asked you to leave and tell Alpha Hughes that we appreciate her concern, would you?"

"Probably not," I said honestly. "And even if we did, we would have to come back, and possibly in greater numbers."

The brothers didn't like that. Their fangs dropped.

"But I don't want that to happen," I added quickly. "I'd rather it stay just between us."

The Alpha laughed, though there was no humor in it. "Just between us. And whoever else you tell upon your return."

She was smart. I would do well to remember that. "Only those who need to know. I'm not one to spread the business of packs to those it doesn't concern."

She was quiet, always watching. Then, "Who are you?" She glanced over at the car and then back at me. "And who's the witch?"

"He's Ezra. The witch to the Alpha of all."

She looked confused. "I thought— What happened to her previous witch?"

I didn't know what she was talking about. Ezra had been Michelle's witch for a long time. "I think you might be mistaken. I've only ever known Ezra. But I haven't been there long. Perhaps there was someone else, but it's him now."

She nodded slowly. "And you are?"

"Robbie. Robbie Fontaine."

The brothers continued to scowl at me.

The Alpha's expression never changed.

But the older man... It was fleeting, the barest of expressions. There and gone.

As if he knew my name.

My reputation must have preceded me. I didn't know if that was good or not.

"Robbie," the Alpha said. "Robbie Fontaine."

"Yes."

And she asked, "Who are you?" like it was *more* than just a question, *more* than what the words seemed to indicate.

Little wolf, little wolf, can't you see?

It tugged.

It pulled.

"I am the second to Alpha Hughes," I said, and the urge to shift was harsh and grating.

She shook her head. "I know that. I can see *that*. That's not what I'm asking."

I opened my mouth—to say what, I didn't know—when the car creaked behind me.

The wolves looked away from me toward Ezra as he climbed out of the car. I cursed silently as he grunted. He shuffled over to my side, wincing at the pains of his old body. He muttered about the idiots standing before him.

"I told you to stay in the car," I said under my breath, though everyone could hear me.

"You looked as if you could use some backup," he said, sounding far more cheerful than the tense situation called for. He bumped his shoulder into mine before bowing as low as he could. He barely grimaced at the pain in his back. "Alpha. Thank you for hearing us out. As my young friend said, we mean you no harm. All that we ask is for an exchange of information. Nothing else."

"An exchange?" the Alpha asked dangerously. "An exchange implies you have something I want."

"Oh, I imagine we can come up with something," Ezra said. "All we ask is that you listen to us, and we promise to listen to you. You have my word."

The Alpha appeared to relax slightly. She nodded at both of us before glancing back at her pack. I don't know what they saw on her face, but they didn't seem pleased. She turned toward us again and said, "One night. You can sleep in the barn. In the morning, you leave, no matter what's been discussed."

"Agreed," Ezra said as if it were the easiest thing in the world.

"My name is Shannon Wells," she said, her voice quieter. "And I am the Alpha. This is John and his brother, James."

John's scowl deepened.

James gave a nervous little wave.

"And this is my second," Shannon said, jerking her head toward the other man, "Malik."

Malik didn't say a word.

"You are welcome in my territory," Shannon said. "But if I suspect there is anything untoward happening, I will kill you both, consequences be damned. Do you believe me?"

"Yes," Ezra said. "I do."

"Good. Pull your car up next to the barn. It's almost time for dinner. You can join us if you wish. I'm sure you have much to say, whether I want to hear it or not."

* * *

The interior of the farmhouse was more modern than I expected, though it still seemed to be a work in progress. It smelled faintly of wet paint, so it had to have been a month or two since they'd done it. Mostly it smelled like the four of them, like a pack home should.

Off to the left of the entryway was a large living room, a sectional couch surrounding a TV mounted above a fireplace. I was amused to see a stack of old black-and-white monster movies on a bookshelf. They all seemed to be about werewolves.

"I like them," a voice said.

I glanced over to see James standing beside me, nervously wringing his hands. "Yeah? I've seen a lot of them. Pretty good. Funny. Got a bunch of stuff wrong, but some of it isn't so far off. Makes you wonder if any wolves actually worked on them, you know?"

He nodded, looking relieved. "It's—"

"Jimmy," John said, voice rough. "Come here."

Jimmy's eyes widened, and he took a step back toward his brother. John wrapped an arm around his shoulders, glaring at me as if he thought I was about to attack Jimmy. His expression softened as he glanced over at Jimmy. He leaned over and kissed the side of his head. "Stay by me, okay?"

Jimmy looked annoyed but didn't argue.

Malik disappeared up the stairs in front of us without a look back as Ezra crossed the threshold. Shannon came in behind him and closed the door.

"No wards," Ezra said as if he were commenting on the weather.

"No witch," Shannon said. "Though I think you already knew that."

"I could help you with that, if you'd like."

"I wouldn't like that at all."

Ezra's only reply was to nod. He stood with his hands clasped behind him, waiting for Shannon to take the lead.

"Upstairs is off-limits," she said, and I couldn't get over how young she was. "I don't want you in our rooms. Malik has an office downstairs where he works, and we can use that after we eat."

"Of course," Ezra said. "Whatever you think is best, Alpha." He looked over at me and smiled.

Dinner was, in a word, awkward.

Malik stayed silent, always watching.

Jimmy tried to keep the conversation going, but anytime I tried to answer him, John would tell his brother to be quiet.

Shannon didn't look apologetic in the slightest. I didn't blame her.

It wasn't until Ezra spoke, halfway through the meal, that it took a turn.

He wiped his mouth almost daintily before spreading his napkin back on his lap. "John, was it?"

John tightened his grip on his fork. "Yeah? What about it?"

"Are you all right?"

"Fine."

"You're happy?"

"Yes." He didn't sound happy.

Ezra nodded, glancing at Jimmy. "And you take care of your brother, I see."

John looked at Shannon, who jerked her chin in response. He

said, "I do. But he takes care of me too. It's what we do for each other. We're pack."

"He's bigger," Jimmy said, sounding proud.

"And he's smarter," John said, sounding pissed off, but not at his brother. All the venom in his voice was meant for us. I wondered what he'd been told. Why his animosity was so blatant.

"Good," Ezra said. "Keeps things even. You depend on one another."

"But we can take care of ourselves," John retorted. "Jimmy may be small, but he can kick your asses if he needs to."

"I'm hard-core," Jimmy agreed.

Shannon sighed.

Malik didn't say a word.

"I bet you are," I said. "People make assumptions about things they shouldn't. I bet you prove them wrong all the time."

Jimmy grinned at me.

John did not.

"And you're in school?" Ezra asked as if we were among friends.

They looked to Shannon again. She nodded.

"We're almost done with our junior year," John said begrudgingly. "We have a few weeks left until summer break."

"And are there any other wolves at your school?"

Jimmy shook his head. "No. We're the only ones. And we don't tell anyone about us." He fidgeted in his seat. "Promise."

"I'm glad to hear that," Ezra said. "Most people wouldn't understand."

Malik cleared his throat and spoke for the first time. His accent was thicker than I expected, sounding sweet and almost musical. "And you should be studying for finals since you've finished, correct?"

Jimmy groaned.

John rolled his eyes.

"Yes," Malik said. "Such a terrible life you lead. Up, up. I'll take care of the chores tonight. Jimmy, I want to see that math book open. John, I've looked over your essay and made some suggestions. Read through it and make any changes you deem necessary."

Jimmy looked like he was going to argue, glancing at me, but John grabbed him by the arm and pulled him toward the stairs.

Shannon looked up at the ceiling as the boys made enough noise for a dozen people. "They'll hear every word you say, even if they're not supposed to listen in."

"We're not *listening*!" Jimmy shouted from somewhere above us.

"I'm sure they will," Ezra said with a chuckle. "It's not every day they get to hear from another pack."

Malik and Shannon exchanged a look. "We're fine on our own. We don't need anyone else."

"Wolves are pack creatures," Ezra said.

"And we have a pack."

Ezra sipped his tea. "I can see that. Your mother took them in, correct? After they had no one else?"

"Yes. They've been with us since they were little. They don't know anyone else." Her eyes narrowed. "And they won't have to. They're not going anywhere." It was a challenge.

I was alarmed. "Oh, hey, no. Of course nothing's going to happen. That's not why we're here." And, because it felt right, I added, "And I'm sorry to hear about your mother. Alpha Hughes spoke highly of her."

Shannon stared at me without acknowledgment.

"Why are you here?" Malik asked.

"Because Alpha Hughes was worried," I said. "She cares about all the wolves. She's not trying to take anything from you. Not your pack. Not your territory. All she wants are open lines of communication. We're better off together than we'll ever be apart. There is strength in numbers."

"Protection," Shannon said, flipping the spoon next to her plate over and over.

"Exactly," I said, relieved.

"From what?" Malik asked.

I blinked. "From the outside world."

Shannon snorted. "And what would you know about that? Alpha Hughes sits on her throne in her little walled kingdom. She doesn't know shit about us. What it means to be in the outside world."

I glanced at Ezra. He didn't look at me. "That's not true. She . . . she would be here herself if she could."

Shannon picked up on the traitorous skip in my heartbeat. "I doubt that."

"Be that as it may," Ezra said, "it wouldn't hurt to check in every now and then. It prevents . . . complications. Shannon, if we could—"

"Alpha Wells."

Ezra wasn't ruffled. "Alpha Wells, if we could speak privately. Just the two of us. I'm sure I can impress upon you what my young friend here means when he says strength in numbers."

There was a long moment of silence. I tried to catch Ezra's gaze to tell him that was a bad idea, that Michelle wanted us to stick together, but he only had eyes for the Alpha.

Then, "Fine." Shannon stood from her chair. "Malik, we'll use your office."

He nodded. "If you're sure."

"I am. The sooner we hear what they've come to say, the quicker they'll leave."

"That's all I ask for," Ezra said. He grunted as he stood slowly. He looked stiff, more so than usual. That car ride hadn't done his body any good. I'd have to keep an eye on him. "Robbie, perhaps you'd help Malik with clearing the table. It's the least we could do for our hosts."

No, I did *not* want to help Malik clear the table. But Ezra shot me a look that told me to keep my mouth shut. I knew he could take care of himself, but wolves hunted by dividing and conquering. I just hoped they didn't think Ezra was the weakest part of us. They'd be mistaken.

Shannon led Ezra out of the dining room and down the hall. I heard a door shut, and their words and heartbeats disappeared.

"It's soundproof," Malik said. "You understand."

I flexed my hands on my thighs. "Of course. She . . . she seems like a good Alpha."

"She is."

"And John and Jimmy are good."

"They are."

I licked my lips. "That's all that matters."

Malik looked amused. "Is it? How kind of you to say." He stood and began to gather the dishes on the table. Not wanting to seem rude, I rose and did the same.

He led the way back into the kitchen. The window above the sink was open, and crickets were humming, frogs croaking. I set the dishes in the sink. I was about to go back for more when he said, "Robbie Fontaine."

"Yeah?" A burst of laughter came from just overhead. The house settled around us, its bones shifting.

"Where are you from?" He wasn't looking at me. Instead, he stared out the window.

"Caswell."

"Always?"

"No. I . . . moved around a lot."

"Did you."

I rubbed my neck. Ezra wasn't the only one suffering from the long car ride. "Long story."

"We all have those, I think."

"Yeah, I guess we do. It's not . . . important. I was orphaned when I was a kid. A few packs fostered me. One helped me with my first shift, and I stayed with them for a while."

"But?"

I shrugged. "I don't know. I liked being on the move. I know it's not ideal for a wolf. Pack ties and all. But it seemed like the right thing for me to do. I wanted to see as much as I could."

Malik turned around, leaning against the sink. "And what did you see?"

"The good in us," I said honestly. "The wolves . . . we may not have the numbers we used to, and we may not always agree with the way things are, but pack is pack. It's important. I was accepted most everywhere I went. And even though the bonds between us were always temporary, it was enough."

"To keep the Omega at bay."

"Yeah. Exactly. I was never in any danger of that. I knew myself well enough to never have that happen to me. And then I was summoned to Caswell, and I've stayed there ever since."

"Summoned? Where were you before?"

I frowned at him. "Before?"

"Before you were summoned."

I shook my head. It was starting to ache. "It's not important. All that matters is Ezra came for me, telling me I was needed."

"By Alpha Hughes."

I didn't like the censure in his voice, though I couldn't exactly fault him for that. "I know she has a . . . reputation. But I don't know that it's deserved. I can't imagine what it must be like to be an Alpha, you know? All that power. But then to be the Alpha of all? It has to take a toll on a wolf. She handles it well," I added quickly. "Just give her a chance, okay? I don't know what Shannon has heard. I don't know what's happened to her. I know it sucks that she had to lose her mother like she did and become something before she ever thought she would. And I'm in awe of what she's made here. But I wasn't lying when I said we're stronger together."

"Temporary."

I frowned. "What?"

"The Alpha of all. Michelle Hughes. She's temporary. She's not meant to be—"

I stumbled. I didn't know what happened. One moment I was listening to Malik, hearing his words, and the next, the pain in my head detonated with a dull *whumpf*. My fangs dropped, cutting into my lip. Blood trickled down my chin. I was astonished to see my claws were out as I brought them to my head, pressing my hands against my skull.

It was

(*little wolf little wolf*)

like I'd lost control, like I couldn't

(*can't you see*)

breathe, I couldn't breathe and I was going to fucking *shift* in this house and

(*i see you i see you i'll*)

I had to get out, I had to get out so I didn't hurt anyone, so I didn't hurt those boys

(*never let you go*)

because I could *never* hurt anyone, I could *never*—

Malik said, "Robbie."

And just like that it was over.

I looked up as I slowly lowered my hands. My fangs had pulled back, my claws retracted.

Malik was watching me warily. His own claws were out, and his eyes were orange.

"I'm sorry," I choked out as I wiped the blood from my lip. "I didn't—I didn't mean—I don't know what the hell just happened."

"You lost control of your shift." He didn't move toward me.

"I know. I don't know what set it off." I shook my head, trying to clear the fog. "I promise this hasn't happened in years. If it had, I never would have come here. Michelle wouldn't have sent me. I wouldn't put those kids in danger."

His own claws pulled back slowly. "I believe you." He hesitated. He looked toward the hallway. The only sounds were the house settling and the boys above us. "Can I trust you?"

That caught me off guard. "Uh . . . yes? I mean, yes. Of course you can."

He moved quicker than I expected. He wrapped his hands around my biceps, his cheek grazing mine. My eyes fluttered involuntarily at the touch of another wolf. It wasn't sexual, it was instinctual. He was a stranger, but it felt warm. There was a scent to him, something I couldn't quite catch. It was faded, like a dream. "Tonight," he whispered fiercely. "After your witch sleeps. Meet me behind the house. Say nothing to anyone."

And then I was alone in the kitchen.

"It isn't much," Shannon said as she opened the barn door, "but it'll do for one night."

"It's not the worst place I've slept," I told her, and she looked at me weird. I shrugged. "Swamp. Long story. Lots of bugs. I got a tick on my—you know what? Probably don't need to tell you that. You don't need to hear about bugs on my junk."

"Right," she said slowly. "John and Jimmy brought out blankets and pillows. They've made you a pallet. Everything is new, so the pack smell shouldn't be too overwhelming."

"You get a lot of guests?" I asked, looking up at the hayloft above us. Two bare bulbs hung from the ceiling, their light low. It smelled like pack, but there was something more to it. Something different. Like there'd been another wolf at some point.

"Better to be safe than sorry," she said. Fucking Alphas. Always cryptic.

"It'll do just fine," Ezra said. "You're very kind, Alpha Wells. I'm glad we made this trip. I believe Alpha Hughes will be pleased to hear of this place and all that you've made for yourself."

"I suppose she will," Shannon said. "We'd offer you breakfast, but the boys have school, and I have work. It's a madhouse here in the mornings. No time for anything."

"Not necessary," Ezra said. "We'll be on the road at first light. It's a long trip back, and I know we'd like to be home as soon as we're able."

"I bet you would," Shannon said coolly. "I'll keep up my end of the bargain so long as you keep yours." She glanced at me once more before she turned and left the barn, closing the door behind her.

We waited until her footsteps reached the house. I opened my mouth to speak, but Ezra shook his head. He slid the sleeve of his shirt up slightly, pressing his fingers against a faded tattoo. It flared weakly, and the sounds from outside the barn became muffled. His magic washed over me in a comforting wave.

He sighed. "There. They shouldn't be able to hear us, but it's not so intrusive that they'd notice unless they come back. I don't want to make an Alpha angry." He looked ragged.

I took him by the arm and led him toward the pile of blankets at the rear of the barn. "What happened with her?"

Ezra smiled tightly. "She's young. Hardheaded. Not unlike a certain wolf I know."

"Yeah, yeah."

He laughed, though it sounded tired. "She has a chip on her shoulder, and I don't know if I can fault her for that. The loss of her mother was painful. She didn't have time to prepare."

I helped him down onto the pallet, making sure he had the majority of the blankets. Now that it was dark, the air was cool, and I didn't want him to get sick. I could deal with being a little cold. "It must have been a shock."

"It was," Ezra said. He patted the blanket next to him, and I collapsed at his side. I stretched, groaning as my back popped. "And that much power without warning would be a lot for anyone to handle. But couple that with the loss of her Alpha *and* her mother . . . well. She felt the need to close her ranks."

I turned my head toward him, pressing my forehead against his hip. His hand went to my hair. "She told you all this?"

"She did indeed. I think she just needed someone to listen to her. Someone who could understand."

This was uncharted territory. Ezra had known loss, just like the rest of us, but from what I could gather, his was catastrophic. His entire family had been brutally taken from him. From the bits and pieces I'd collected, rogue wolves were to blame. I didn't understand how he could know forgiveness after that. I hated the hunters, and not just for what they represented. Everything had been taken from both of us. I could never forgive that. It didn't matter who they were. I wanted to kill every single one. I would never forget.

"I'm glad she had you to talk to," I said quietly.

He hummed under his breath as he scratched my scalp. I refused to make a sound of pleasure, though I was already practically showing him my belly. "And I'm glad I have you, dear. I don't know what I'd do— What's this?"

His hand left my hair and went to the corner of my lip. He pressed a finger against my skin before pulling it away.

On the tip of his finger was a rusty flake of blood I'd missed.

"Bit my lip," I said quickly. "Accident."

He brought his finger up to the front of his face, staring at the flake. "Is that all it was?"

Can I trust you?

"Yeah. That's all it was. We need to get some sleep. We've got a long drive tomorrow. I'll even let you play your shitty music."

He chuckled as he lay back against the pillow. "How kind of you. You know, if you actually had some culture, perhaps you could—"

"That's never going to happen."

I grinned as he swatted me upside the head.

A moment later, the magic around us dissipated and the crickets began to sing.

VIOLET

I dreamed of the forest.

Of bright sunlight and the songs of wolves.

In the trees, great black birds croaked.

The white Alpha wolf prowled in front of me.

He said, *little wolf little wolf.*

I whispered, "Can't you see?"

The black birds said, *you are the master of the forest.*

I whispered, "The guardians of the trees."

The trees began to move.

The earth shifted and broke apart underneath them, their roots roiling like so many snakes. They left divots in the ground as they pulled back, forming a giant circle around us.

We stood in a clearing.

"What is this?" I asked.

But the white Alpha wolf was gone.

In his place stood a black wolf.

I fell to my knees in front of him.

He leaned forward, breathing hotly against my face through his nose.

He pressed his snout against my forehead, and I said, "*Oh.*"

(*robbie*)

A rush of images. A cacophony of sound.

(*robbie*)

"What is this?" I asked the black wolf, my voice breaking into pieces.

(*ROBBIE*)

I turned my head and—

Ezra was snoring beside me.

The trees were gone.

I was in the barn, skin slick with sweat.

"What the fuck?" I muttered, scrubbing a hand over my face.

"*Robbie.*"

I jerked upright. *That* voice was real.

"Come outside," it whispered.

It took me a moment to recognize it.

Malik.

I glanced down at Ezra. His face was slack as he snored loudly, lips flapping slightly with each exhalation. I moved carefully to avoid waking him. I stepped over him before bending over to lace up my boots. I glanced back at him once more before heading toward the door.

The stars were bright in the sky above the farmhouse. The moon was hidden behind a fat cloud, casting everything in shadow. Malik stood near the porch of the house. He put a finger to his lips as I approached, jerking his head toward the house.

I nodded in response. I was curious about this. About what he wanted. Why it had to be such a secret.

He began to walk away from the house toward an empty field.

I followed him.

I kept a few feet between us. I'd heard three separate, slow heartbeats from the house, so I knew his pack was sleeping and not lying in wait. I didn't know this man, but I didn't think he was stupid enough to try to start something. Not if he wanted to avoid bringing down the might of the Alpha of all on his pack.

In the distance, far from the house, a large structure rose at the opposite end of the field. It was an old silo, and he led me toward it.

He moved quickly and quietly, not quite jogging, but his legs were longer than mine, and I had to hurry to keep up.

The cloud moved away from the half moon. My skin thrummed. I jerked my head to the right, sure there was another wolf running beside me.

There wasn't.

We were alone.

He stopped about three hundred yards from the silo in the middle of the field.

A breeze blew through the tall grass. It sounded as if the earth was whispering.

He asked, "Can I trust you?" again without looking at me.

What the fuck was going on? "Yes."

"What I am about to show you will stay between us. Do I have your word, wolf?"

I hesitated, but it was brief. "Yes."

"Your first instinct will be to shift. Don't. Your second instinct will be to speak. Don't. You'll stay still. You'll stay quiet until I say otherwise. Do you understand?"

"Yes." Quiet as a mouse.

I thought I heard my mother laugh.

"As we get closer, you'll feel magic. You'll..." His shoulders slumped. "It's there for a reason. No one can know. Not any of your wolves. Not your Alpha. Not even your witch."

Magic? How the fuck was there magic? "I don't know if I can—"

He whirled on me, eyes blazing. His hand was around my throat before I could take a step back. "You *must*," he growled at me. "Many things depend on it. If you speak even a *word* of what you see, then all the death that follows will be stained upon your fangs and claws as if you were the one who dealt the killing blow."

I didn't struggle. I brought my hands up and circled his wrist. "Okay, I get it. Christ. Let me go."

For a moment he didn't. Instead his hand tightened around my neck. I flashed my eyes at him, a bright beacon in this dark field.

His own eyes faded back into darkness.

He let go and stepped back.

"Why is there magic? You don't have a witch."

"No," he said. "We don't."

He turned and began to walk toward the silo.

I stared after him for a long moment. And then I did the only thing I could.

I followed.

We were close to the silo when I felt it.

The magic.

It bowled over me, and I staggered at the strength of it, taking in a great gasping breath. It rocked through me, and my head snapped up toward the sky, back arching as if I was electrified. There was something *familiar* about it, something just out of reach. It was bright and all-consuming and *green*, there was so much green, green like a forest alive and ancient.

But there was blue in it too, shot right through the middle, cutting the green cleanly in half. It was mourning and sorrow, deep and wild. A tear slid down my cheek as I gritted my teeth.

"Ah," Malik said. "I see. So it is."

The magic loosened its hold on me, and I took a lurching step forward, struggling to breathe as I hunched over. "What did you do to me?" I panted.

"Nothing you weren't ready for. Not another word until I tell you. Stay there. I'll let you know when you may enter."

I wiped my face with the back of my arm, unsure why there was a goddamn lump in my throat, why I felt filled with so much grief that I could fucking taste it.

Malik was at a door at the base of the silo. He didn't look back at me. He knocked once. Twice. Then three more in rapid succession.

He said, "Hello, little one. It is I. Malik. I am here. You are safe. I promise."

It was only then that I heard it.

Another heartbeat.

It was quick, like the flutter of the wings of a bird. It felt *small* somehow, and as Malik opened the door, I was hit with the scent of another wolf.

A child.

But something was wrong. It didn't feel like any other wolf I'd felt before. I didn't know what it was, but it felt like something close to *sickness*, like a fog that reminded me of how humans smelled when they were slowly dying. It wasn't *quite* there yet, but it was close.

Too close.

Malik disappeared into the silo, leaving the door open behind him. I heard him speaking in soft tones, saying "Hi" and "Hello" and "Were you sleeping? I'm so sorry to wake you, little one. But I promised I'd return. It's just for tonight. Just to be safe."

"I know," a small voice said in response, and my chest hitched.

"I've brought a friend," Malik said. "He is good. Not like the bad wolves. He's important."

"He won't hurt me?"

"No. No one will ever hurt you again. I won't let it happen."

I waited.

Then, "Okay."

I was startled out of a daze when Malik said, "Robbie. Come. Now."

I didn't want to.

I wanted to run in the opposite direction.

Find Ezra.

Get in the car and leave this place behind.

Forget we ever came here.

I took a step toward the open door as a dull light switched on somewhere inside.

It wasn't too late.

Just turn around.

Turn around.

I reached the door.

Looked inside.

The silo was mostly empty. A battery-powered lantern sat on an old crate off to one side, barely casting enough light to illuminate the floor.

Malik stood in the middle of the silo. A dusty old tarp lay off to one side.

At his feet was a wooden hatch.

And from between the slats came thin fingers reaching up with tiny claws at the tips.

The silo creaked around us.

"What have you done?" I asked quietly.

"The only thing we could," Malik said. "To keep him safe. There are things at play that you can't possibly begin to understand. This is your first lesson about the great wide world outside the walls of your compound."

He bent over and lifted the wooden hatch. The hinges were rusty, and they screeched as it opened.

At first there was nothing.

I didn't move.

"I can smell him," the child said from the hole in the floor. "I can *smell* him."

"Good. What do you smell?"

There was a hissing growl in response. "It's dirty. Unclean."

"Look underneath. Find it."

"I can't. I can't *I can't I can't I can't—*"

I took a step back.

A boy burst from the darkness. He moved almost quicker than I could follow. He was thin but clean, and half-shifted, hair sprouting along his brow as his face elongated in a furious snarl. He landed against the side of the silo, the claws from his hands and feet piercing the metal, holding him in place. He turned his head toward me and roared.

And then came the unimaginable.

Light filled his eyes.

It was violet.

An Omega.

Before I could even begin to process what I was seeing, he launched himself at me. My training kicked in and I fell to my knees, leaning back against the floor. His claws swiped at my neck, missing my throat but nicking my chin.

He crashed down on the other side of me, limbs flailing as he rolled into the other side of the silo near the door. He was already up and moving even as I rose. He hit my back, claws digging into my shoulder. I grunted and reached behind me, grabbed him by the armpits and flipped him up and over me until his back was against my front. He struggled, but I wrapped an arm around his chest, and my other hand went to his throat.

He immediately stopped moving, going limp as he sucked in air. He turned his head toward me, staring at me out of the corner of his violet eye. "It's there," he whispered. "Underneath it all. It's still there." He began to chant. "It's still there. It's still there. *It's still there.*"

I pushed him off me as I staggered back. Malik caught the boy, holding him close as he muttered into Malik's neck.

"Now you see," Malik said quietly as he stroked the boy's back. "This is your first lesson. Does it burn, wolf? Does it burn?"

The boy—once he determined I wasn't an immediate threat—calmed, and his eyes faded to an emerald green that sparkled in the low light. He was pale-skinned with light-colored hair that hung almost to his shoulders. The sweats and loose T-shirt he wore looked mostly clean, though there were smudges of dust and bits of hay from when he'd attacked me.

He crawled back toward the hatch on all fours, his black claws the only sign of his shift. I thought he was gone for good as he disappeared into the hole, but he reappeared a moment later, dragging a heavy blanket behind him. I watched as he made a small nest on the floor. He growled at me before looking up at Malik. The older wolf sat down next to him as the boy pulled the blanket up and over him, hiding away underneath, his head in Malik's lap.

I didn't move.

"There," Malik said, running a hand over the top of the blanket. "There we are. So much excitement for one day."

"And it smells in here," the boy muttered, voice slightly muffled. "Like shit. Like animals. I miss the barn."

"I know. But it's just for tonight." Malik looked up at me. "Soon all will be well again."

I had questions. Too many questions. They swirled in my head, *who* and *how* and *why why why*. The boy looked like he was eight or nine. But he was already shifting, which was impossible. He shouldn't have been able to even *half* shift until closer to puberty.

And then there were his eyes.

Those violet eyes.

The question I asked wasn't one I planned. "What's his name?"

Malik was surprised. I could see that clear on his face. "Brodie."

I nodded. "Brodie." Then, "Is he yours?"

"Blood? No. Pack? Yes."

The boy moved underneath the blanket, but he didn't speak.

I felt helpless. The stench I'd smelled earlier, that *sickness*, was heavy in the air. It came from the boy. But other than being an Omega, there didn't seem to be anything wrong with him. Still. It was enough. "This is why you cut off contact."

"Not intentionally," Malik said. "We . . . lost track of time. An oversight."

It wasn't a lie, but it felt like it was close to one. There was more, but he wasn't offering it.

"How did it happen? How is this possible?"

The boy growled.

Malik hushed him gently, his hand moving up and down the boy's back. "You need to open your eyes, Robbie. There is much to this world that has been hidden from you by design. Things you haven't been told."

Fuck him for being so vague in the face of all of this. "Maybe if you would just *tell* me, I could—"

Malik shook his head. "It's not my place. The damage it could do would . . . I fear it would be permanent."

I scowled at him. "You aren't making any sense."

"There is a prisoner. In your compound."

"What?"

He didn't flinch at the anger in my voice. The boy growled again but otherwise didn't move. "A prisoner. Someone with a great and terrible power. You must go to him. You must end his life. Only then will everything become clear."

"Are you out of your fucking *mind*?" I demanded. "Do you know what—"

"Step. *Back*."

I hadn't even realized I was moving.

A hand appeared from underneath the blanket. The claws were sharp as they scraped along the floor. Black hair burst up along the back of the hand before it receded and the hand pulled back under the blanket.

A clear warning if there ever was one.

I did as asked, standing near the door.

"I know you're confused," Malik said, voice barely above a whisper. "And I know you're scared."

"I'm not—"

"I can *smell* it on you," the boy growled.

Goddamn kids. "Fine. Whatever. I'm scared. But how the fuck else should I—"

"Focus, Robbie."

I shouldn't have come out here. "How do you know there's a prisoner?"

Malik's mouth twitched. "I wasn't sure until now. Thank you for confirming it for me."

"Oh, fuck you." I wasn't impressed. I *wasn't*.

"He is the cause of this." He nodded down toward the boy. "Somehow. It's an infection, and you must stop him while there's still time to keep it from spreading."

I shook my head. "That's impossible. There are wards in place. Ezra put them up himself. There's no way the prisoner can ever—"

"This boy is part of my pack. *Our* pack."

"He can't be," I said, and a wave of dizziness washed over me. "He wouldn't be an Omega if he was. His eyes would be orange and—"

"And yet they aren't," Malik said simply. "He is Omega, even though his Alpha is Shannon. His brothers are Jimmy and John in all but blood. And he belongs to me just as much as I belong to him. He is ours. There are bonds between us all, threads that tie us together, rotted and fetid though they are. They're tenuous, but they gain strength every day because he *wants* them to. This isn't because he doesn't have anyone, Robbie. I assure you he does. It's because of what has been done *to* him. He is a wolf diseased, and there is only one cure: the death of the person who has infected him and all those like him."

His words struck me cold. "All those like him."

"Yes."

"Meaning there are others."

"Yes."

"How?" I asked helplessly. "We would *know* if there were. If Omegas were rising, if something was happening to cause them to be this way. We would *know*."

And then he said, "They do," like it was the easiest thing in the world, like he wasn't upending everything. "They do, Robbie."

I didn't believe him. I couldn't. It would mean . . . Christ, I didn't even want to think about it. "Why should I believe anything you're saying?"

Malik looked disappointed, as if it should be obvious. "I have taken great risk to bring you here. All it would take would be for you to turn around and report everything you've seen. To wake your witch and bring him here."

"What makes you think I won't do just that?"

He shrugged. "Because part of you knows I'm telling the truth. You can feel it, can't you? It's hidden in shadow, buried deep inside. Something . . . off. Do you dream?"

The walls were closing in. I rubbed at the skin between my neck and shoulders. I closed my eyes and tried to breathe. "We all dream."

"We do," Malik said, and his voice was deeper, almost a growl, like his wolf was just underneath his skin. "Some of us dream in shades of blue. Or green. Or of a field filled with violets that embed themselves in our skin. What is it you dream of?"

There was
an alpha
a strong alpha
black like night

*he stands in a clearing
he sees me
he says little wolf little wolf
he says robbie
he says robbie
he says*

"Nothing," I said hoarsely as I opened my eyes. "I dream of nothing."

"I don't believe you."

I shook my head as I took a step back. "I don't care. You're harboring an Omega. He could hurt people, Malik. Innocent people."

"He's just a child."

"I know that. But he won't be able to control it. Do you want to be responsible for that? If he escaped and made his way into town? And if Alpha Hughes finds out you have him here, she's going to dismantle your pack. They're going to take him away and—"

Brodie said, "They're in pain." His voice was quiet.

"Who is?" Malik asked, though he never looked away from me.

"All of them," Brodie said, and the blanket shifted as his head appeared, eyes glowing in the dark. "They howl. It hurts. A limb severed. It's pack and pack and pack. They hunt. They kill. They *fight* because it's what they're supposed to do. The Alpha said they would tear the world apart. It's the only way they know how." His eyes seemed to get brighter. "There is a song to be sung. And there is one who sings it above all others. His scream. I hear it. A wolfsong." He squeezed his eyes shut tightly. "I hear it all the time because I hear *them*." His chest began to heave. "I hear them, I hear them, I *hear them*—"

"Hush, child," Malik said, pressing a hand against Brodie's forehead. "No need for that now. You're safe here."

The boy began to cry bitterly, tears spilling down his cheeks before he turned and pressed his face against Malik's chest. "Please don't let them take me, Malik. Please don't let them take me away again. I won't hurt anyone. I promise. I promise."

"I know you won't," Malik said. "And no one will take you from your pack." Malik looked back up at me. "Ever."

It was said in defiance.

And I believed him.

Ezra was still snoring when I returned to the barn.

He looked as if he hadn't moved at all.

I slumped against the door, sliding down to the ground.

I tilted my head back toward the ceiling.

Through broken slats overhead, I could see the bright outline of the moon.

※ ※ ※

"I'm pleased with our visit," Ezra said as we stood next the car. The sun was barely cresting over the horizon, and the air was warm. "I know Alpha Hughes will be too, so long as communications reopen."

Shannon nodded. The house behind her was quiet, though I didn't think it would be for long. John and Jimmy would wake soon, and we would be gone. "Extend my apologies to the Alpha. Let her know that we've been busy. It was an oversight. Nothing more."

"Of course," Ezra said. "It happens to the best of us. Let us know if there is anything you need. The Alpha of all is here for you, as she is for all wolves, no matter who they are." He glanced at me, a quiet smile on his face. "Or where they came from. Who knows? One day John or Jimmy might hear her call and feel the need to rise in rank. They seem capable." He chuckled.

Shannon didn't laugh. "We'll see." She took a step back toward the house. "I gotta get back inside. We have a busy day ahead of us. I don't want them to be late for school."

"I'm sure," Ezra said, even though it was barely past six. "We'll take our leave. Robbie? Would you mind driving? These old bones are a little stiff this morning. I'll even let you pick the music."

"Yeah. That's fine." I took him by the arm and led him around to the passenger side. I opened the door and helped him in. He sighed gratefully as he sat down. He told me not to fuss as I tried to buckle his seat belt. I told him to shut up and let me do it. He rolled his eyes, but his lips were quirking. I stood upright and closed the door.

Shannon said, "Robbie."

I glanced at her.

She didn't speak again.

She didn't flash her eyes.

Instead she pleaded without words or a show of power.

Malik came out onto the porch behind her.

He leaned against the rail, arms over his chest.

It would be so easy.

So easy.

To do the right thing.

To tell everyone what I'd seen.

There were rules in place to protect us all.

And this pack was breaking them.

I could almost see it.

The aftermath.

They would descend on this place.

Shannon and Malik would fight.

They would lose.

John and Jimmy would be torn from their pack.

And the Omega would be destroyed.

It'd happened before.

It would happen again.

I nodded at them and rounded the back of the car.

Right as I was about to walk by Shannon, she grabbed my hand and squeezed.

Something pressed against my palm.

I looked down at a piece of paper.

She didn't say a word, only shook her head.

I shoved it in my pocket.

We were almost to the main road when I looked in the rearview mirror.

Shannon and Malik were gone.

"Are you all right?" Ezra asked.

"Yeah," I muttered as I rolled down the window. I was getting tired of people asking me that question. "I'm fine. I didn't sleep very well is all. Sleeping in a barn isn't all it's cracked up to be, apparently."

Ezra patted my knee. "We'll be home soon enough. You did well, dear. I know it's not easy going into another Alpha's territory without knowing what awaits you. I'm proud of you."

We headed north.

· · ·

Ezra went inside to pay for gas the first time we stopped.

I pulled out the crumpled piece of paper.

It was a valentine.

Across the top was a cartoon wolf, head tilted back, a tiny heart over his head.

Above it were the words I HOWL FOR YOU!!!

And below it was a phone number with four more words in a shaky scribble.

FOR WHEN YOU'RE READY.

DREAMED IN SUCH SHARPNESS / KILL US ALL

"And that's it," Michelle said, sounding dubious. "That's all it was. They were *busy*."

"It happens," Ezra said as we sat in her office. "Life often gets in the way when we least expect it to. I don't know that they can be faulted for that so long as it doesn't continue. Especially after all they've been through."

She sat back in her chair, the light from the screen of her computer reflecting in her eyes. "Neither of you suspect anything different?"

"I certainly don't," Ezra said. "Though I'm not a wolf. I'm not as . . . adept at picking up deception. And since they don't have a witch, I feel we need to look to Robbie in this regard."

They both turned to me.

I swallowed thickly.

"Robbie?" Michelle asked.

What makes you think I won't do just that?

Because part of you knows I'm telling the truth. You can feel it, can't you? It's hidden in shadow, buried deep inside. Something . . . off. Do you dream?

I did. I dreamed in such sharpness that it felt like reality.

I said, "They're busy." Truth. "They have two young wolves." Truth. "The Alpha herself is young, as you know." Truth. "It would be a lot for anyone." Truth. "But Alpha Wells is capable of many things." Truth. "And I have no reason to believe she's not doing what she thinks is right for her pack." Oh, how easy it was to lie without actually lying.

Michelle nodded slowly. She was listening for any skip of my heart. There was none. "And they know they need to remain in contact from this point on?"

"They do," Ezra said. "I impressed upon Alpha Wells when I met with her the importance of open lines of communication. She . . ." He stared off into nothing, mouth open.

I reached over and touched his arm.

He blinked as he looked at me. "I'm sorry. I just . . ." He shook his head. "Getting older. I recommend you avoid it if at all possible. The mind has a tendency to wander with age." He smiled ruefully. "The Wells pack is in good hands, I think. They have much to learn, but I don't know if we need to worry about this just yet. There are bigger things to focus on."

Like an Omega hidden in the floor of a silo surrounded by unknown magic.

"Robbie, would you excuse us for a moment?" Michelle asked. "I need to have a word with my witch." She glanced at me. "You did well. Thank you. And I'll need you again in the next couple of days. My computer keeps making weird noises at me. I want you to take a look at it again. You know I'm terrible when it comes to such things."

She was. She didn't know a damn thing about technology. I'd always found it slightly endearing, how frustrated she could get.

I hesitated. If I didn't say anything now, I never could. They wouldn't trust me again if they ever found out I'd kept this from them.

And yet.

"Go," Ezra said. "I'll catch up with you later. Take a shower. You stink."

I nodded at both of them and left the office, closing the door behind me.

The compound was busy, but I barely saw any of it.

I was lost in my head.

I had just lied to my Alpha.

Lied to Ezra, her witch.

And for what? A pack I didn't know that was harboring an Omega? What the fuck was wrong with me?

I accidentally bumped into another wolf. I apologized.

She frowned. "It's okay." But she hurried away, glancing back at me over her shoulder.

I stared after her as she disappeared into the crowd of people.

Something was . . . off.

People were milling about as always.

No one stopped to talk to me as they always had.

No one waved.

They glanced at me, but when they saw me watching them, they'd smile and look away. The barest of acknowledgments.

Not like they were scared of me, but . . . I didn't know.

I shook my head.

I was tired. That was it. I was tired and seeing things. Transference or some such bullshit. I felt guilty and I was projecting it onto others. It was nothing.

It was fine.

It was *fine*.

I needed to go home. Take a shower. Get some sleep. That's all.

With a plan in place, I moved on.

And yet . . .

All I could think about was the look on Malik's face as he cradled the Omega child in his arms, an Omega child caught partially in his shift, though he was too young to be able to turn wolf.

Can I trust you?

I'd said yes. I didn't know why.

Why I'd said yes. Why he'd asked. *Why* he'd shown me what he had.

He didn't know me. He didn't know anything about me.

And yet . . .

There is a prisoner.

In your compound.

The ground swayed beneath my feet.

My head was starting to hurt.

I was going home.

I was going *home*.

Except I stopped in front of the house that held the prisoner. The one no one talked about. We all knew, sure, and we stayed away, but who they were and what they'd done was need-to-know only.

Santos was there again. Luck of the draw.

Funny how that worked.

He said, "I heard you left."

"Assignment. That was all." And, "It was only a couple of days." And, "It was easy." And, and, and, "Who's in there?"

His eyes narrowed. "Who's in *where*?"

I felt feverish. Overwarm and overbright. The sun pounded against

my skull. There was magic here, oh yes, but it was *familiar*. I knew it because I knew Ezra. I knew the scent and taste of it. Magic was
(*a fingerprint*)
unique to . . . the . . . user.
The ground rolled.
I took a stumbling step forward.
"What the fuck is wrong with you?" Santos growled, catching me before I fell.
"I don't know," I gasped, trying to ignore that voice in my head, that voice that said *a fingerprint* because it came from *somewhere* inside, and I didn't know it. I didn't recognize it. I didn't fucking *recognize it*—
That had to be it.
That had to be what this was.
Whoever was in the house was leaking magic, and it was warping everything around me. Whatever wards were around it had cracked, and this witch was using it to their advantage. Never mind that they were supposed to be stripped of their powers. No matter that whatever they'd done had been so egregious that they had to be locked away. It wasn't working.
"Who is it?" I said through gritted teeth. "Who's in there? Can you hear me, you bastard? Who the fuck are you?"
Santos shoved me back.
I fell to the ground, skidding in the dirt.
His eyes were orange as he glared down at me. "I don't know what the hell you think you're doing, but you need to stop. You need to—"
I opened my mouth to tell him to fuck off, but no sound came out.
I looked up at the sky.
It was blue, blue, blue.
And then I screamed, my claws digging into the earth.
The sky was on fire.
It burned.
It burned and I—

what are you doing
 robbie
 robbie
 please don't

please don't do this
oh my god what's wrong with you
you're not
please please please i don't want to die
please you're hurting me robbie you're hurting me
oh god no
no
let me go let me go LET ME GO LETMEGOLETME
robbie
robbie
ROBBIE

Blood filled my mouth when I opened my eyes.

It tasted good. Like fear. Like whatever I'd hunted down had been scared of me.

I craved it.

I rolled it over my tongue, coating it.

I swallowed it down, but there was always more.

So much more and I—

"There you are."

I turned my head.

Ezra sat next to my bed in my room.

My mouth was not filled with blood. In fact, it was dry. I was thirsty.

"What happened?" I asked, voice breaking roughly. I cleared my throat. "Did I hurt someone?" I almost didn't want to know the answer.

Ezra shook his head, expression pinched. "No. Of course not. You passed out. Santos found you. Said you were... It doesn't matter what he said. How are you feeling?"

"Like it's the morning after a full moon. Foggy. Dull."

"Hmm. Have you overexerted yourself, perhaps? It happens."

"I don't know. I just..." I shook my head. "What if something's wrong with me?"

He scoffed. "There's nothing wrong with you. I would know if there was. Would you hear me, dear?"

That made me feel better. If anyone knew how to fix this, it would be Ezra. He knew me better than anyone. "Yeah. Of course."

"You're special," he said, pressing his hand against my brow.

"More than you could ever know. And I will do anything for you. Would you do the same for me?"

"Yes. Yes." My headache was fading. The blood in my mouth was nothing but a dream.

He nodded slowly. "Good. That's good, Robbie. I can't imagine what it's been like for you all these years. But there is nothing to worry about. You're tired. Stressed. The dreams you're having aren't helping. I don't know what they mean, and maybe they mean nothing at all. But maybe they do. I could ease you from them if you'd only ask. Take them away like they were never there at all." His hand pressed harder against my brow. "Leave you to sleep and—"

He didn't make a sound when I grabbed his wrist and snarled, "*Don't.*"

He smiled sadly, even though I could feel the bones of his wrist grinding together. "Because they're yours?"

I nodded as I let him go. He pulled his arm back, and I wondered if he would be bruised. I felt bad, but not enough to apologize. I trusted him, but I didn't want him digging around in my head.

"Okay, Robbie. If that's what you think. I'm here if you ever change your mind." He frowned. "Or just need to talk. Can I give you some advice?"

"Yes."

He sighed as he sat back in his chair. He looked pale, skin tight from worry. "You have questions, I know. Questions about who is in that house. Santos said as much, and I should have prepared for this better."

I sat up quickly. "I wasn't trying to—"

He held up a hand, cutting me off. "I thought it was for your benefit. I did. Given your history, it seemed like the wise thing to do." He shook his head. "I should have known better. Secrets never help anyone, especially ones so monumental. The man inside that house did terrible things to many people. There was death because of him. And the only thing we could do was to keep him locked away from the rest of the world and strip him of all his power."

"But how were you able to keep the witch from—"

"Witch?" Ezra asked. "What witch?"

"The witch inside the house. The prisoner."

Ezra laughed. "Oh. *Oh.* Dear, there is no witch inside the house.

It's a wolf. A great and terrible wolf who wanted something that did not belong to him. But he can no longer hurt anyone. He's . . . empty. A husk, hollowed out and dim."

A wolf? But I'd felt . . . I could have sworn there was *magic*, and it was *leaking* from inside, *leaking* until it— "A wolf," I said weakly.

"Yes, dear. One whose name we do not speak because he lost the right." He looked grim.

"What did he do?" I asked, sure I wasn't going to get an answer.

Ezra sighed and looked down at his hands. "He took a boy once. A little boy. A princeling, or as close to one as we have these days. This wolf hurt the boy terribly, and it was only by the grace of the moon that he was saved. But not before the wolf forced upon him unbelievable torture that no child should ever have to know." He looked terribly sad. "I wouldn't expect you to understand such things. You would never hurt someone who didn't deserve it. And while the boy wasn't exactly . . . innocent, what was done to him was madness."

"What the hell?" I asked incredulously. "What do you mean he wasn't innocent? He was a *child*."

"I know, I know," Ezra said, holding up his hands as if to placate me. "But even children are capable of things we wouldn't expect. And when you come from a family like his, one needs to exercise an abundance of caution. His family . . . they're . . . well. Let's just say they want something they can never have. Something that doesn't belong to them." He stared at me hard. "Something that will go against the very nature of the wolves."

Alarm bells were going off in my head. I thought the walls were closing down around me. "What? What do they want?"

He reached out and pressed a hand against my arm, fingers circling my wrist. I could see the bruise already starting to form from when I'd grabbed him earlier, the dull ink on his arm red and inflamed.

"To see your Alpha gone," he said. "To see the Alpha of all come tumbling down and to send our world into chaos. To integrate humans into the wolf pack. You of all people should know the danger of humans and what they're capable of. This family does not care. They would take all that we've worked so hard for and enforce their will upon the wolves. And I cannot stand for that."

"Why did you never tell me about this?" I demanded. "How the fuck am I supposed to protect her if I don't know about any of this?"

He looked frail and weak. His hand shook against my wrist. "Forgive an old man," he said quietly. "All I wanted to do was to keep you from all the darkness. To give you a life where you would only know peace after all you've been through. I made a mistake. I underestimated you, dear. I shouldn't have. You deserve better from me." He took a deep breath. "I don't know what's coming. I don't know what the future holds for all of us. But if we are to survive, it's important that you know who our enemies are. The man in the house. The prisoner. He is an enemy, but he's been declawed." He looked thoughtful. "But even then, he seems to be capable of some kind of hold. I wonder why that is? Tell me, dear. Why now? Why did this come about now? Did someone say something to you?"

Dangerous ground. "It's all secret," I said. "And I don't like secrets." It was a deflection, careless and rough.

But it worked.

He nodded. "I know you don't. But it's for your own protection. And for the protection of us all. He won't be the last. I feel we are in for perilous times ahead." He looked older than I'd ever seen him before when he said, "It's time you know who the *real* enemy is. The ones who would take everything from us."

"Tell me. Tell me. *Tell me.*"

Ezra said, "They are the Bennetts. And they will destroy everything if given the chance."

He left me after securing a promise that I'd rest. He took my glasses from his coat pocket and set them on the nightstand next to the bed. Silly wolf, he said. You don't need these. I love you, I love you, I love you.

I didn't reply.

He was at the door when I said, "Omegas."

He stopped. He didn't turn around. "What about Omegas?"

"Have you ever seen one?"

He didn't hesitate. "Oh yes. Poor creatures. Feral and dark. I can only imagine what it would feel like to have everything ripped from you, to have your tether shredded until it hangs in tatters. I think I would lose my mind too." He glanced back at me over his shoulder. "Why do you ask?"

"Just wondering what else I haven't been told."

He winced. "I deserve that. And no, dear, I promise that you know everything I do. I won't keep these things from you any further. You aren't a child."

"No. I'm not."

He nodded. "Sleep, Robbie. We'll talk more in the morning." He closed the door behind him, leaving me alone.

I collapsed back down on the bed, trying to focus.

Bennett.

That name.

I *knew* that name.

Didn't I?

Of course I did.

It was lost somewhere in the fog, out in the fringes, but I *knew* it.

Barely spoken aloud anymore.

They had betrayed the wolves.

They were the enemy.

And if they thought I was going to stand by and let them take my Alpha from me, then they were mistaken.

I would do anything to protect her.

Anything.

I didn't dream of wolves.

Instead, there was a shadow above my bed.

I couldn't move.

I couldn't scream.

It leaned over me and whispered in my ear.

It said—

I opened my eyes.

The sky was gray through the window.

I blinked as I yawned, jaw cracking.

I heard Ezra moving downstairs in the kitchen. I could smell the terrible coffee he always made. I grinned to myself.

I pushed myself up out of bed, scratching my bare stomach as I popped my back.

I felt . . . good.

My head was clear.

I looked around for the jeans I'd been wearing the day before. They were folded on top of my dresser.

I frowned. For the life of me, I couldn't remember taking them off and putting them there.

I shook my head. It was nothing. Yesterday was... well. It was what it was. And even if I only had a vague recollection, it was *fine*. Michelle was happy. Ezra was happy. I'd done a good job. They cared about me, and I couldn't ask for anything more.

I grabbed the jeans and sniffed them. They smelled all right. There was the scent of a foreign wolf on them, and... hay? When the fuck had I been around hay?

Whatever.

I pulled them on, letting them rest low on my hips. My wallet was in the back pocket. The front left pocket was bunched up, and I reached in to push it down.

Something was inside.

I pulled it out.

A small piece of paper. A sticky note. Bright orange.

There were two letters written on it in my own handwriting. Dashes too.

I _ _ _ _E

I didn't remember writing it.

I knew what it meant. It was a game from my mother, like Hangman. She used it to teach me how to spell.

INSIDE

I stared down at it. When had I put it there? When had I *written* it?

I went to my closet and opened the door, shoved aside the hanging clothes. There, at the back of the closet, was a small wooden panel. Even if someone was looking for it, they'd miss it. Ezra didn't even know about it. I'd waited until he was out of the house the second week I'd been in the compound before I made it, cutting the wood at the back of the closet.

A hint of claw grew from my right index finger, and I pushed it into the hairline crack at the top. I pulled.

The panel fell away.

Inside (INSIDE) was a box that carried all my secrets.

I pulled it out and sat on the floor, the box in my lap.

It was plain and made of pine. It'd once been a jewelry box, but my mother had sold all its contents to fund our escape.

Now it was filled with little details.

Her driver's license. She wasn't smiling. I touched the small photo before setting it aside.

Sitting in the box in a corner was a stone wolf.

A gift for the one who would complete me. It'd been carved by the Alpha who taught me how to shift. He said I needed to keep it safe. Keep it whole. It was small and made of black stone, the ears perked, the tail curled around the wolf's legs. I lifted it out and—

Underneath was a folded . . . card? I didn't recognize it.

I set the stone wolf aside.

The card fell over in the box, opening slightly. A cartoon wolf at the top. I HOWL FOR YOU!!!

I picked it up and opened it.

A phone number and four more words.

FOR WHEN YOU'RE READY.

I frowned down at it. I didn't know where it had come from. I thought back over the past few days. I'd . . . what? I'd gone to see Michelle a couple of times. She'd summoned me. Told me I was a good wolf. That she was proud of me. Ezra had been there. He was smiling. It was fine. It was great. It was wonderful. It was

(*can i trust you*)

just on the tip of my tongue, but I couldn't remember, I couldn't

(*wolfsong*)

focus on, I couldn't fucking *focus*.

Why did it matter?

Maybe one of the younger wolves had snuck it into my pocket and I'd forgotten I'd put it in the box. Rumor had it that a bunch of the girls (and some of the boys) had a crush on me. It was sweet. I sure as hell wasn't going to do anything about it, but still. I had to give whoever it was props for being so forward.

I put the other items back in the box and closed it. I set it in the small opening and put the panel back in place. Maybe Ezra would know what this was about.

I opened the bedroom door. "Hey, Ezra," I called out as I walked out of my room. "You're never going to believe what I found. It's—"

A pure white wolf stood at the end of the hall. Its head almost touched the ceiling. Its ears twitched.

I froze.

The hallway began to twist and bend, the siding cracking as pictures fell from the wall, glass shattering on the floor. The wolf took a step toward me as the ceiling split. The walls were *bending*, and I couldn't move, I couldn't even take a step back, and the wolf, the *wolf* took another heavy step toward me, its paws almost as big as my head. Its claws scraped against the wood floor, leaving long scratches.

The house disintegrated around me, the walls exploding outward, the ceiling rising and cracking.

And then it stopped.

The wolf grinned.

It had many teeth.

I said, "Who are—"

The wolf ran at me.

I braced for impact.

The moment before it struck me, its eyes filled with a bright and terrible red, and the Alpha—

Passed right through me.

I bent over, clutching my head, the paper digging into my ear as wolves howled in my head, pulling, pulling, pulling.

They sang:

I HOWL FOR YOU!!!
I HOWL FOR YOU!!!
I HOWL FOR—

"Robbie?"

I opened my eyes.

Ezra stood at the end of the hall, head cocked, wiping his hands on a dish towel.

The house was as it always was.

The pictures hung on the walls.

The ceiling was intact.

There were no grooves in the floor.

"You said you found something?" Ezra asked. "What is it?"

I stared at him.

He smiled.

"Nothing," I said slowly. "It was . . . nothing. Just . . . a book I thought I lost."

He nodded. "Funny how that works, isn't it? We don't even realize what we've lost until it's right in front of us once again. It's good to see you up and about. Come. Let's get you fed."

"Be right there," I said.

He turned and went back to the kitchen.

I looked down at the crumpled note in my hand.

FOR WHEN YOU'RE READY.

GUNMETAL SKY / NEVER FORGET

My mother and I didn't have many things. She said it was easier that way when you were always on the move. But she let me have books. A few of them, at least.

She said it was important. That I needed to learn.

She taught me how to read herself. There were nights when we'd be sleeping in the car, and she'd make sure to park near a streetlight so I could see.

She would make a nest in the back seat using old blankets and a flat pillow. I loved them because they smelled like her. She would always lie down first and pull me against her chest. Sometimes she would sing. Other times she would cry.

I didn't like those other times.

But then she'd hand me a book and ask me to read to her. "It makes me feel happy," she said. "You have a pretty voice."

And so I'd read to her, stumbling over the words I didn't know.

"Sound it out," she'd say.

I would.

If I couldn't figure it out, she never got angry.

"No, Robbie. It looks like a *g* and an *h*, but sometimes it makes a *ffff* sound."

"A-and the wolf looked through the w-window. He saw the pig inside. 'I'll huff and I'll puff, and I'll b . . . *blow* your house down.'"

She kissed the side of my head. "Yes. That. Yes."

Sometimes I could smell her tears, even if I couldn't hear them.

. . . . .

I walked into the compound under a gunmetal sky.

The wolves waved at me.

I waved back.

Children ran squealing around me. I thought it was weird that they were out and about, given it was a weekday. They should have been in school.

"Play with us," they begged. "Chase us. Shift and *chase* us!"

They all laughed when I bared my teeth at them.

They waited for me as I walked around the back of a house.
I took off my clothes.
Folded them.
Stored them near a back porch.
A piece of paper stuck out of one of the pockets.
I shoved it back in.
The bones and muscles under my skin began to shift, and I
am wolf
i am wolf and there
there are cubs
cubs to play with
cubs to chase
cubs to love
cubs to protect
i will
catch them and play with them and nothing will ever hurt them

A boy followed me as I shifted back hours later. He was bright-eyed with a devilish smile.

He turned away as I dressed myself. He was bouncing on his toes like he was excited.

"Had enough yet, Tony?" I asked him as I put my glasses on. "You can turn around now."

He grinned at me as he did. "Your wolf is so big! Am I going to be big like you?"

"Bigger," I said as he took my hand in his, tugging on my arm. "I bet you'll be the biggest wolf there ever was."

His eyes were wide. "Really?" he breathed. "Whoa. Even bigger than an Alpha? Mom says I'll be a Beta, but maybe if I get big enough, I could be an Alpha too!"

"I don't know," I said seriously. "Being an Alpha is a lot of hard work."

"I can do it," he said. "I'd be the best Alpha in the world. And when I'm the Alpha, you won't have to be sad all the time."

I blinked. "What? I'm not sad all the time. I'm not sad at all."

He frowned as he looked at my fingers. "Mom says blue is sad. And you smell like blue. Like the ocean."

I knelt down before him. "What do we say about smelling other people without their permission?"

He scowled. "Not to do it."

"Right. Because it's impolite."

He shook his head. "It's not—I'm *not* being impolite. It's . . ." He scrunched up his face. "You're my favorite. After my mom. And dad. And brother. And Ms. Dunstrom, but she's my teacher, so she doesn't count. So you're like, my *fifth* favorite." He looked proud.

I was touched. "You're one of my favorites too."

"I *knew* it," he crowed. "I tried telling all the other kids, but they didn't believe me."

I laughed. "Maybe keep that to yourself. It'll be our little secret."

Something crossed his face then, something dark that looked tragic on a child so young. I could almost *taste* it, and it was like ash on my tongue.

"What's wrong?"

He looked away but didn't let go of my hand.

"Hey, it's okay. You can tell me. Did something happen?"

He shrugged, though he looked uncomfortable. "It's . . . a secret too. Like how you like me better than everyone else."

"Okay. Is it a secret that will get someone hurt?"

He hesitated before shaking his head.

"Are you in any danger?"

He shook his head again.

"Is it something only for your mom and dad? Like a parental secret?"

"I don't know," he said, brow furrowing. "I mean, I heard my mom and dad *talking* about it, but it wasn't *their* secret."

"Did they know you were listening?"

The ash was replaced with the sourness of shame. So, no. They didn't know. I suspected as much. "I didn't mean to," he said, kicking at the dirt. "It was just . . . they were talking, and they said your name, and I wanted to hear what they were saying because I like you a lot."

"Ah," I said. "I like you too, Tony. But I don't know if what they were saying was meant for either of us to hear. You should probably just forget you heard anything, okay?"

"But you're *blue*," he said fiercely. "I know it. And they said you weren't always blue, that when you were here before, you were green and happy and it was awesome." He looked up at me. "What was it like when you were here before? Why were you blue when you came back?"

Gooseflesh prickled along the back of my neck. "From where? One of my trips? Sometimes I have to go see other wolves, and it can be tough because not everyone wants the same thing. It's just . . . how it is."

He shook his head. "Not *that*. I know about *that*. I'm talking about *before*. When you left for a long time. I don't remember 'cause I'm too little, but when you used to live here with the pack."

"I think there's been a mistake, cub," I said. "I never lived here before Alpha Hughes summoned me. Ezra found me and brought me back with him. It wasn't . . . I've only been here for a year. You know that."

He scrunched up his face. "Where did you live before?"

"All over," I told him. "With many different wolves."

He didn't look like he believed me. "But Mom said they already knew you. And that you were different. And she doesn't lie about anything because lying is bad."

His parents. Griff and Maureen. We could have crossed paths before. I didn't remember it, but it was possible. But I didn't remember them before I'd come to the compound, and I'd never been to Caswell before that. After my own mother, I'd bounced around to different packs. I tried to remember all of them, all their names, but there were so many. It was all bleeding together. I stayed with some longer than others, but I'd never—

"Blue," Tony whispered. "It's all blue."

I forced a smile on my face. "Hey. Nothing for you to worry about. Listen. Let's just keep this between us, okay? I won't tell your parents if you don't say anything to anyone else. Is that okay?"

"Another secret?"

I nodded.

He didn't look as happy about this one. "Okay."

I hugged him close, and he giggled as he pressed his nose against my neck and inhaled. "And I promise to work on the blue thing. Thanks for telling me. I'm glad I have someone like you watching my back."

"I'm glad you're feeling better," he whispered. "Alpha said you were sick and in bed and that's why we haven't seen you in a few days, even when it was the full moon. I thought wolves didn't get sick."

My hands shook. A few days. A *few days*. But that would mean—

"Why aren't you in school?"

He laughed. "It's Saturday, silly. I don't have to go to school on Saturdays."

"Of course not," I said, and my skin was buzzing. "No one goes to school on Saturdays."

He broke away from me as a group of boys on the other side of the house called his name. "Bye, Robbie!" he called over his shoulder as he ran off to his friends.

I stayed behind the house for a long time.

"I don't know what's wrong with it," Michelle said, sounding irritable. She pressed a button on her keyboard, and the computer chimed. "It never does what I want it to do, and it needs to update every five seconds."

"Maybe not *that* much."

"It seems like it."

"It doesn't help that you're banging on it."

She sighed. "Sometimes hitting things makes me feel better."

"Be that as it may, I don't know if electronics respond to physical violence. You can't Alpha your way through a Windows update."

She shoved back from the desk, her chair bumping against the bookcase. It rattled quietly as she stood. "Just... can you fix it, please? I don't have time to deal with it, and you understand these things better than I ever will. There's a pack coming in next week, and I don't want to have to spend my time worrying about this."

"Anything big?" I asked. Normally I'd keep my mouth shut, but I was her second by her own words, and I felt a little braver than normal.

She eyed me for a moment before shaking her head. "No. Passing through and want to pay their respects." She stood from her chair, motioning for me to take it. "I have to go to a meeting in town. Can you take care of this by the time I get back?"

"Do I need to be involved?"

"I don't believe so. I want Ezra to check the wards around Caswell.

Make sure they're intact. Can't be too careful these days. All manner of things can try and sneak through."

I thought they were being paranoid, but so long as I didn't have to walk with Ezra as he fucked around with the wards, it was fine with me. It was long and boring, and listening to Ezra mutter at invisible walls did not make for an enjoyable afternoon. "I'll take care of it. It'll be done by the time you get back. You work too hard. Especially since it's Saturday."

She didn't flinch. Instead she looked relieved. "Thank you. You're a lifesaver." She headed for the door as I sat down in her chair. She looked back at me as she put her hand on the doorknob. "Let yourself out after you've finished. And Robbie?"

I looked up at her over the monitor. "Yeah?"

She looked like she was going to say something, but instead she shook her head. "Nothing. Thank you. I don't know what I'd do without you."

She was gone before I could respond.

I felt warm from my Alpha's praise. It was a little thing, but it felt like a fire burning in my chest. It almost made me want to tell her I seemed to have misplaced a few days here and there, and had she possibly seen where I'd put them?

I shook my head.

I sounded like such a cub.

"All right," I muttered as I cracked my knuckles. "Let's see what we've got."

She had spyware.

And adware.

And it was a fucking *mess*.

"Jesus Christ," I muttered. "No wonder everything is going so slow." I ran the security software. While the system check was running, I sat back in the chair, the back of my head hanging off the back. I looked up at the towering bookcase behind me, seeing old books with golden script on their spines with such titles as *The History of Lycanthropy* and *The Moon and You: Fact and Myth*.

I stood up to browse the shelves while the computer did what it needed to. Michelle had never said I *couldn't*, and while she wasn't necessarily here to say otherwise, it still felt like I was skirting a line.

"It's just history," I whispered to myself. "I'm allowed to learn."

I was alone in the office of the Alpha of all.

What could it hurt?

With Tony's voice whispering in my ear and the vision of a white wolf in a crumbling house, I brushed my fingers over the covers. Some, especially near the top of the shelf just out of reach, were covered in a thin layer of dust, as if they hadn't been taken from the shelf in years. I could see *which* books had been taken down, given there was no dust in front of them, but they were all rules and regulations, ancient laws that governed the wolf world.

In other words, all crap.

Except.

There were two volumes near the top right corner, shoved between larger books. One looked very old, the words on the spine once gold but now faded. The other, the thinner of the two, had no title on its spine.

"What's this?" I asked no one in particular.

I glanced back down at the computer.

Only halfway done.

The house was empty.

Outside, I could hear wolves talking to each other.

Rain was coming. It'd be here within the hour. I could smell it.

Against my better judgment, I pushed the chair against the bookshelf. I climbed on top of it. It wobbled but held.

The thick layer of dust on the top shelf caused my nose to itch. Whatever these books were, they hadn't been moved in a long time. I pulled them both out, the older book on the top. My skin started buzzing at the faded gold pawprint embossed on the cover.

The pages were stiff, almost like cardboard. The words on the first few were illegible, the handwritten notes having faded with time. I made out a couple of dates in the top right-hand corners. If it was real, the book I held was over four hundred years old.

I stopped when I came to a page that held a drawing.

A beast.

A monster.

A wolf, but one unlike any I'd ever seen before. It stood upright on two legs, the muscles thick in its calves and thighs. Its arms were long and ended in misshapen paws almost like hands, with hooks for claws.

Words were written underneath, some more legible than others: *lost* and *broken* and *tether* and *mate* and *pack*.

"An Omega?" I mumbled, brow furrowing.

I could make out one more word, and it chilled me to the bone. *Sacrifice*.

I looked away from the beast to the margins of the page. Written in much newer ink, in different handwriting, were more words.

Is this what he could become? Should we have killed him when we had the chance? I don't know. They assure me he's trapped forever.

And what of the other? He's more than what I thought. He's an Alpha. I don't know how. I don't know why. But if this is true, if the beast can rise, then an equal and opposite must also rise.

Ox.

Ox.

Ox.

I closed the book. I reached up, meaning to set it on top of the bookcase. A sharp burst of laughter from just outside the house startled me. I almost fell from the chair. I caught myself at the last moment, but the old book slipped from my fingers. I winced as it slid *behind* the bookcase, clattering down to the floor.

"Shit," I muttered. I'd have to move the whole bookcase to get it out. I looked down at the smaller book. The cover was blank. The book itself was wrapped with a leather strap. Initials were carved into the leather.

TB

I couldn't think of anyone with those initials.

I stepped down from the chair, clutching the book to my chest.

It wasn't from a witch. It didn't smell like magic.

I undid the leather strap and let it dangle.

Inside, the pages were lined and yellow, filled with barely legible chicken scratch. I made out words like *power* and *creek* and *father* and *sons*. It was the same handwriting that had been in the margins of the other book.

I turned to the first page.

There was an inscription, written with a delicate hand, so much different than all the pages that followed.

To my beloved—
Never forget.
—E

Two things happened at once.
The computer chimed,
and
my phone rang in my pocket.
I startled, dropping the book onto the floor. I cursed as I pulled my phone from my pocket, glancing down at the screen as I pushed the chair back under the desk.
UNKNOWN
I frowned at the phone. I thought about ignoring it.
I answered it instead.
"Hello?"
A crackle of static filled my ear.
I pulled the phone away to look at the screen again. The call was connected. I put it back against my ear. "Who is this?"
The phone beeped as the call dropped.
I looked at it again and—
I was standing next to the bookcase, the leather tome in my hands. The chair was pressing against my thigh.
My phone was in my pocket.
The computer was still updating.
I blinked slowly.
I felt like I was underwater. Like I had when I'd gotten close to the house under guard.
I looked down at the book. The inscription on the first page was the same.
I flipped to the second.
There was a date from years before across the top right corner.
It took me a moment to read the first few lines.
They said, *I have made mistakes. So many mistakes. That's the terrible gift of hindsight; it allows you to see everything in such startling clarity. My father always said if wishes were horses, beggars would ride. I didn't understand what he meant. Not then. Not before it was too late.*
I do now.

Elizabeth thinks I should call him. I doubt he'd even pick up the phone. He's always been hardheaded, and it's undoubtedly gotten worse because of what we did. What I did. I don't know how to make him understand. That we couldn't take the chance that his father had done something to him, put something in the marks carved into his skin when he was a child. A fail-safe in case his plans didn't go through. Gordo wouldn't—

The computer chimed.

The scanning software had finished.

I grimaced as my head began to throb.

The book fell to the floor.

I stumbled toward the desk, hands flat against it.

My phone began to ring.

My claws dug into the wood.

The computer chimed again. And again. And again.

My phone wouldn't stop ringing. The combined sounds rattled around my skull.

I said, "What is this? What is this? *What is—*"

"—this?" I asked as we walked through the woods.

He laughed, taking my hand in his. I couldn't see him, not really. It was static and snow, a vague outline of a person, but it was right. Oh god, it was *right*. "It's nothing. Just . . . why do you ask so many questions all the time?"

I bumped my shoulder against his. "I need you to come with me. That's what you said. You have to know how that sounds. All mysterious."

"It's . . . goddammit. I'm not trying to be *mysterious*."

No, I didn't think he was. I—

—fell back into the bookcase, hands covering my face, muttering, "No, no, no, this isn't real, this *isn't real*, this isn't—"

"—anything bad," he said. "It's . . . I hope it's good."

"You hope," I teased him, feeling lighter than I had in a long time. The trees were *green*, the sky was *blue*, and the forest was *alive*. There was a hum beneath my feet, deep in the earth, and I knew its power, I knew what it was capable of.

He squeezed my hand in his, and if I listened, if I focused hard enough, I could hear and *feel* the blood moving through his veins, the quick, birdlike beat of his heart. He was nervous, the tang of sweat sharp and sour, but there was so much more to it. It was—

—books falling around me as I crashed into the bookcase and—
—grass and—
—I tilted my head back, my fangs dropping and—
—lake water and—
—I fell to my knees and—
—sunshine. It was sunshine, the feel of warmth on my skin, soft and melodic, a song whispered under one's breath. It was a caress, and he was laughing, and the sun was shining on his blurry face and he said, "I hope. I hope more than anything. I see you, you know? I see you. And I'll—"

"Never let you go," I whispered, my face pressed against the floor.

The computer was silent.

My phone was silent.

I lifted my head.

The little leather book lay off to my left.

I stood slowly.

Something fluttered to the floor.

I looked down.

There, by my foot, was a note.

I could see four words.

FOR WHEN YOU'RE READY.

I nudged it with my boot.

It fell open.

The phone number was the same. One I didn't know.

Without thinking, I pulled my phone from my pocket.

I dialed the number.

It rang once. Twice. Three times.

Then, "Hello?"

I didn't speak.

"Hello?" the woman said again, sounding annoyed. "Listen, buddy, if you think panting in my ear is gonna get you anywhere, maybe we should meet face-to-face and I'll show you just how wrong you are."

"Who is this?" I asked, voice barely above a croak.

"Who the fuck is this?" she demanded.

I cleared my throat. "This is . . . Robbie. Robbie Fontaine. I found your number in my pocket."

"Robbie? What the hell—hold on a second." There were muffled voices in the background, and I thought about throwing my phone.

Throwing it and tearing off my clothes to shift and run toward the refuge. It was safe there. It was safe, and I would find the ancient tree, and all would be well. All would be—

"Robbie. What's going on? I didn't think we'd hear from you so quick, or even at all. What—"

"Who are you?" I demanded.

"Who am I?" She paused, and the silence tore at my head. "Robbie . . . it's Shannon. Alpha Wells."

Oh fuck, an Alpha. "Alpha. I'm sorry. I didn't mean to yell at you. I just . . . I didn't know where I'd gotten this number. How *did* I get this number?" I thought back over the past few days. No Alpha had come to Caswell. I would remember. I'd met with Ezra and Michelle, and she'd said . . . she'd said . . .

I frowned. What had she said?

I couldn't remember.

"Robbie," the woman said. She sounded strangely flat. "I gave my number to you. Before you left Fredericksburg. A week ago."

I was startled into a laugh. "Fredericksburg? Where's that?" My palms were slick with sweat.

"Shit," she muttered. "Fuck, how the hell did they— Malik. Do you remember Malik? What he showed you? What he—"

"I don't know any Malik," I bit out. "I don't know what you think he showed me, and with all due respect, Alpha Wells, if this is some kind of joke, it's not funny. At all. I can't—"

"The prisoner. In your compound."

That knocked my breath from my chest. "How the hell did you—"

"It doesn't *matter!*" she cried into the phone. "If they took this from you, then they know. I gotta get home. We have to run. The others are already on their way. They need to know what they're walking into—"

"I don't know what the fuck you're talking about," I snarled. My vision was tunneling, and I thought my phone was going to shatter with how hard I was squeezing it.

"I know," she snapped. "And it's because it was *taken* from you. I don't know how, but I know why. Robbie, get to the prisoner. I don't care how you do it, but get to him. You'll see. Delete this phone call. Don't let them know you called this number. I have burner backups and I'll call you when we're safe. It's almost time. Find the prisoner. Do you hear me? *Find him.* You find him and you kill him."

The phone beeped in my ear as the call dropped.
I lowered it slowly.
On the blue computer screen was a message in a gray box.
UPDATE COMPLETE! RESTART?
In the corner was the date and time.
12:47 PM
May 9, 2020

IT WAS HUMAN / YOU ARE WOLF

I burst out of the house. Rain slashed against my skin.

I tilted my head back as lightning crossed the sky in a bright flash.

I shoved the journal in the top of my jeans, pulling my shirt over it to keep it dry.

The compound was mostly empty, everyone having hurried inside to escape the storm. The surface of the lake was black.

I turned toward the house set back from all the others. I could barely see it through the rain.

Find the prisoner. Do you hear me? Find him.

I was moving even before I realized.

Santos wasn't on guard duty. It was a younger wolf I vaguely recognized. He looked miserable standing out of the rain on the old porch. He brightened as I approached. "Robbie. Hey! What brings you out in this weather?"

I climbed up the porch, that old familiar magic washing over me. It vibrated against my skin, and it felt like home. It took me a moment to remember the wolf's name. "Daniel. I just . . . was out," I finished lamely.

He didn't notice. "Oh man, why? I hate the rain if I'm not shifted. But I can't shift here when I'm working. Sucks, right?"

"Tell you what," I said, thinking quickly. "Why don't you get out of here? I'll take over for you. What time were you supposed to be relieved?"

He looked wary. "Not until three. But why would you want to do that? You're the second. You shouldn't have to be here."

I shook my head. "Nah, it's all right. Ezra and Alpha Hughes are out checking the wards. I need something to do. Besides, me being a second doesn't mean I shouldn't share in the responsibilities. I'll cover for you. I promise. If anyone asks, I'll make sure they know it was my idea."

"Wow," he said. "Dude, that's awesome. Thank you." His gaze

darted away. "There's this girl, and I'm courting her, but she's being... well. You know."

"Nikki, right?"

His smile was wide. "Yeah. Nikki. Oh man, she is the *best*. When she acknowledges my existence, at least. Do you think she'd like to run in the refuge with me? In the rain? That's romantic, right?"

"Very," I assured him. "Why don't you go ask her and find out?"

"Yeah, you know what? I think I will. Thanks, Robbie. This is fucking awesome." He gripped my shoulder and squeezed as he grinned at me. He stepped off the porch.

"Hey, Daniel?"

He glanced back at me. "Yeah?"

"Just to be safe, what's the code to get inside?"

His smile faded. "I don't think that's a good idea."

"I know," I said. "But it's okay. It's best that I know. Since Alpha Hughes and Ezra are out, I need to make sure that if I need to get in, I can."

He bit his bottom lip. "Well, I guess that makes sense. I mean, if they're gone, you're pretty much in charge, right? Being the second."

I grinned at him, although I'd never felt less like smiling. "Exactly. You got it. And I *really* don't want to go inside. Trust me on that. But you gotta be prepared, you know? Just in case."

"Just in case," he echoed. He turned, but not before looking over his shoulder through the rain toward the other houses. There was no one else there.

He went to the door of the house. His nose wrinkled as the scent of magic intensified. A red circle appeared on the door, glowing dully. The circle was filled with lines, sectioning off the interior. And inside each of the boxes the lines created was a symbol. It was simple, a combination of shapes: squares, smaller circles, and triangles. He didn't touch them, just pointed at a combination. "Circle. Rectangle. Octagon. Heptagon. Circle again. Easy, right?" He took a step back and the bigger circle faded. He looked uneasy. "Just don't go in, okay? Not without the Alpha here. Or Ezra. The prisoner was already fed before they left. No one is scheduled to go back inside until tonight."

"Got it," I said easily. "Hey, say hi to Nikki for me, all right? And I heard she gets impressed the bigger the deer you bring her."

Daniel laughed, shaking his head. "Women, right? Always wanting a bigger deer." He stepped off the porch into rain. "Thanks again, Robbie. I don't care what anybody says. You're a good guy."

"Yeah," I said quietly as he walked toward the lake.

I forced myself to wait until he disappeared around the front of another house, passing out of sight. I strained my ears, listening as hard as I could. Through the sounds of the rain, I could make out the faint voices of other wolves, but they were all coming from indoors. If Michelle and Ezra were actually checking the wards, I had time, but I had to move fast, just in case.

I turned back toward the door. I felt the familiar pull of Ezra's magic as the circle flared to life.

What had the inscription inside the book said?

Never forget.

Easier said than done, apparently.

Because I *had* forgotten. And if everything the Alpha had told me over the phone was true, I'd been *made* to forget.

Why?

An even darker thought followed.

What else had I forgotten?

I told myself that Ezra and Michelle Hughes were trying to *protect* me. They loved me. They'd told me as much. And their heartbeats didn't betray any lie. And maybe, just maybe, they had nothing to do with this.

I took a step back from the door. The circle faded.

What the fuck was I doing? I couldn't go inside. If they found out, everything would be ruined. Oh, I could probably spin it away, telling them that I thought I heard something from inside, thought something dangerous was happening, but would they believe me?

"Fuck," I whispered.

I turned away from the door.

For a moment I thought I saw a wolf standing on the dirt pathway leading toward the house.

I see you.

Oh god, I wanted to be seen. I wanted to be seen so badly.

I blinked and the wolf was gone, if it'd been there at all.

The circle burst onto the doorway as I stepped toward it again. This time I didn't hesitate.

Circle.
Rectangle.
Octagon.
Heptagon.
Circle again.
The magic pulsed once. Twice. Three times.
The red faded.
And then the lock in the door clicked.
Last chance. Last chance to forget all this idiocy, last chance to walk away and tell Michelle and Ezra that something was wrong.
I opened the door.

* * *

The interior was like any other house in the compound.

I didn't know why I was so surprised. It was sparsely furnished, and it smelled unlived-in and musty, as if the windows hadn't been opened in a long time. There were no lights on, and as the door closed behind me, the entryway fell into a dull gray light that filtered in through the heavy drapes on the windows.

Off to my left was a sitting room with an unlit fireplace and a high-backed chair in front of it. The bookshelves were bare.

The sitting room opened to a kitchen that looked empty. There was no table. No stove. No microwave. No fridge. The floor was ancient linoleum, cracked and faded.

The floor creaked under my boots as I took a step away from the door.

I inhaled deeply.

There was no wolf in the house.

There *had* been. I picked up faded notes of Daniel and Santos and a few select others who had access. Michelle had been here too, though it didn't seem recent.

Ezra permeated everywhere because his magic was in the walls, in the ceiling, in the floor beneath my feet, and he'd *told* me it was a wolf, he'd *told me it was a wolf*—

A heartbeat.

From down the hallway in front of me.

There were three doors. All of them were closed.

It wasn't the heartbeat of a wolf.

It was human.

The heartbeat was slow and steady, a repetitious beat on a hollow drum.

I followed it.

It didn't come from behind the first closed door.

Or the second.

It was the last door at the end of the hall.

Nothing hung on the walls. No paintings. No pictures. The house felt blank. Unused. Hollow.

I hesitated in front of the last door before knocking.

The heartbeat inside didn't speed up.

"Hello?" I said. "My name is Robbie. I'm here to . . . check on you."

No response.

"I'm going to come inside. I would really appreciate if you didn't attack me or anything. Because honestly? I've had a very weird day."

Nothing.

I took a deep breath as I put my hand on the doorknob.

I expected the door to be locked. It wasn't.

The knob twisted easily. I pushed the door open.

The hinges made no sound.

The room was filled with shadows. There was an empty bed, the blankets pulled tight in the corners. A rug lay on the floor at the foot of the bed.

The windows were covered in the same thick drapes, barely letting in any light. I could hear the rain through the walls. It was getting louder. In the distance came a peal of thunder.

A chair sat in the middle of the room.

And in this chair sat a man, facing away from me. He didn't move.

"Hello?" I said. My voice cracked. I cleared my throat and tried again. "Hello. Can you hear me? My name is—"

"Ahhhhhh," the man said.

A chill ran down my spine. I left the door open as I stuck to the wall, inching my way around the man.

He didn't move, staying perfectly still.

It made everything worse.

I didn't know why I expected a great flash of *something* when I saw his face. I was too worked up, my senses heightened.

He was a thin man, almost gaunt. His cheekbones were sharp. His hair was cut short. He wore jeans and a chambray button-down shirt. His feet were bare. His hands were in his lap. He sat statue-still, the only movement the shallow rise and fall of his chest as he breathed. His skin looked bleached white, as if he hadn't stepped out into sunlight in a long time.

His eyes, though.

His eyes were like the house.

They were blank. Unseeing. He barely blinked.

I pushed myself off the wall, taking a step toward him, making sure to keep my distance as I circled him. My claws prickled against the palms of my hands.

"What's your name?" I asked him in a low voice.

Nothing. Like no one was home.

"What are you doing here?"

Silence.

"Why did the woman say I needed to come here?"

He stared straight ahead.

I was sweating. And I was scared. "What have you done?"

He didn't flinch at the harshness in my voice.

I stopped in front of him. A few feet separated us. I hunkered down on my heels so we would be eye level.

He looked right through me. I wasn't sure if he knew I was there at all.

He was younger than I expected him to be, though whatever had been done to him seemed to have aged him prematurely. The hair at his temples had turned white, and there were heavy black circles under his eyes.

He breathed in. He breathed out.

His heart rate never changed.

I asked, "Do you know me?"

Nothing.

"Do you know Ezra?"

Nothing.

"Do you know Alpha Hughes?"

Nothing.

A memory filtered in through the storm in my head.

It's time you know who the real *enemy is.*

The ones who would take everything from us.

They are the Bennetts.

And they will destroy everything if given the chance.
Was that real? Or was it just a dream?

I asked, "Are you a Bennett? Are you part of their pack—"

He moved quicker than I expected. I cried out in alarm as he leapt from his chair. I fell back onto my ass as he stalked toward me. I growled at him as he stood above, head cocked, eyes still horribly blank. His arms hung at his sides like they were boneless.

He said, "Ah. Ah. Ahhhh."

I pushed myself away from him, my boots slipping on the floor.

He took an answering step toward me. And then another. And then another.

He only stopped when I did, my back against the wall. I had nowhere else to go.

I looked up at him, claws digging into the floor.

His mouth opened and closed soundlessly, his brow furrowed in deep lines like he was thinking as hard as he could. He blinked slowly.

And then he sat down on the floor in front of me. One of his bare feet pressed against my calf, causing my skin to crawl.

He opened his mouth again.

He said, "Ahhhhh. Ahhh. Ah." The skin around his mouth tightened. "Ahhh am. Ah am. I am. I am."

"You are," I whispered.

"I am. I am. I *am*." He was getting frustrated, practically spitting the words. "I *am. I am. I am.*"

I never should have come here. I needed to get out while I still could.

I started to get up but stopped when he lashed his hand out, wrapping his fingers around my ankle, squeezing tightly. I thought I felt a flash of heat, but it was faint.

"Bennett," he said through gritted teeth.

I could barely breathe. "Bennett. You're a Bennett?"

He shook his head jerkily, like it was being controlled by strings. "No. *No* Bennett. I am. I *am*." He bared his teeth at me. They were yellowed, though they still looked strong. "I am. I am. Witch. I am *witch*. I am *witch*."

He couldn't be. I would have smelled the magic on him as soon as I walked into the house. Ezra had said this was a wolf. That was a lie. The man said he was a witch. That was a lie.

Unless...

Reality felt thin, like a translucent membrane.

I wanted to tear it apart.

"Witch," I repeated. "You're a witch."

He nodded, head snapping up and down. He still held on to my ankle. If it came down to it, I'd break his wrist. Hell, I'd break his entire fucking body. I wasn't going to die here. Not in this house.

"But you don't have magic."

"Ta," he said. "Tay. Tay. Ken. Tay ken."

"Taken."

He nodded again. *Yes.*

"Taken. Your magic was taken from you."

Yes. Yes.

"Ripped from you before they put you in here."

Yes. Yes. Yes.

"Because of what you did."

And *that* got a reaction out of him. He narrowed his eyes, and his grip on my ankle tightened to the point where it'd probably leave a bruise if I were human. He snapped his mouth at me, teeth clicking together again and again.

"Because of what someone else did," I said.

Yes. Yes. Yes.

"Do you . . . do you know who I am?"

"Rob. Bee."

I swallowed thickly. "How do you know me?"

He said, "You. Are. Wolf."

He said, "You. Are. Pack."

He said, "You. Are. Bennett."

No. No, no, no—

I kicked him. He grunted as my boot caught him in the chest, knocking him back. His fingernails scraped against my ankle before he let go. He fell back onto the floor, head bouncing against the wood. I pushed myself up, ready to tear him to pieces.

He was staring up at the ceiling, barely blinking, his head near one of the legs of the chair he'd been sitting in.

"You don't know what the fuck you're talking about," I snarled down at him. "You don't know me. You don't know the first thing about me. I'm *not* a Bennett. The Bennetts are traitors. Ezra said—"

He laughed. It sounded wet and harsh.

It went on and on before dissolving into heaving gasps, tears streaming down his face as he smiled.

"Fuck this," I muttered.

I headed for the door.

Before I could walk through it, he spoke again.

"Dale," he gasped through his tears. "I am Dale. I am Dale. *I am Dale I am Dale I am Dale I AM DALE I AM—*"

I closed the door against his screams.

I called the number from the note again as I stood on the porch, running a hand over my face.

It rang and rang.

No one answered.

Ezra and Michelle returned to the compound as the rain began to let up later that afternoon. I watched them as they approached the house. Ezra was soaking wet, though he didn't look as if he minded. Michelle held an umbrella.

"Robbie?" she asked. "What are you doing here?"

I shrugged. "Daniel needed a favor. Figured I'd help him out. Courting is a lot of work."

"It is," Ezra said slowly. "Not that you would know anything about that yet."

I rolled my eyes. "I'm twenty-nine years old. I have plenty of time."

Ezra and Michelle exchanged a look. Michelle said, "You don't need to worry about this place. It isn't your job. We have plenty of people who—"

"It's fine," I said, and Michelle narrowed her eyes at the interruption. I added, "It was a good deed, you know? I hope those crazy kids make it. And I'm sure Santos or someone else will be back soon to take over for me."

"Santos is off-compound," Ezra said. He stood at the bottom of the steps, looking up at me. "On assignment."

I kept my expression neutral. "Is he? Where did he go?"

"It's not your concern," Michelle said sharply.

I arched an eyebrow at her. "I'm your second. You said so yourself. Shouldn't I know these things?"

Her eyes flashed red. "I don't appreciate your tone."

I nodded as I felt her pull like a hook in my brain. "My apologies, Alpha. I don't mean anything by it. I just thought . . . well. I thought I'd be kept in the loop should anything happen."

"And you will be," she snapped. "If I feel it needs to be brought to your attention. This didn't."

"Okay."

She blinked. "Okay?"

"I believe you. If you say I don't need to know about it, then I don't need to know."

Ezra stared at me thoughtfully. "Did you go inside the house?"

"I did. Thought I heard something." I shook my head. "It was nothing. Guy inside was sitting in a chair in his room."

"Did he say anything to you?"

I laughed. I felt cold. "Didn't seem like he was aware of anything at all. He didn't act like any wolf I've ever seen before."

"No," Ezra said, "I don't suppose he did. Why are you here?"

"I told you. I was doing Daniel—"

"A favor, yes. I heard that part. But why?"

"Because he's a good guy. Deserves every happiness. Don't you think so?"

"Of course I do," Ezra said. "I just . . . Would you hear me, dear? I worry about you."

The stress drained from my body, shoulders slumping. I was very tired, and it wasn't helping that I didn't know what the fuck I'd seen in the house. What it meant. "I know. But you worry too much. I can handle myself. I'm not a cub."

"I know you're not," he said gently. "But there are things at play here. Things that go beyond your understanding." He raised a hand before I could speak. "And it's not because we—*I*—don't trust you. You know that's not the case. But there's a need for sensitivity, for . . . discretion. And with these dreams you're having, it's probably not helping matters. You've been out of it for a few days, you know."

I smiled grimly at him. "It's Saturday."

"Yes, dear. It is."

"I was out of it for a little while."

"Yes. You were. You've been overworked. That, coupled with these dreams you seem to be having—"

"Why?" I asked him. "What was wrong with me? And why didn't you say anything to me? Seems like I should have been told that I was missing three days."

"Because it's nothing to be concerned with," Michelle said. "Ezra assures me that you're well, all things considered. With everything going on, I don't like having to worry about you too. I need you to be strong, Robbie. For me. For your pack."

I didn't know why I said what I said next. It wasn't planned. It wasn't something I considered. But it came out all the same.

"Ezra told me about the Bennetts."

She didn't react. "Did he?"

"Yes. He said they were the enemy."

She glanced at Ezra. He wiped the rainwater from his face. "He needed a history lesson. So he could understand."

"And do you?" Michelle asked me. "Do you understand?"

You. Are. Wolf.

You. Are. Pack.

You. Are. Bennett.

I said, "Oh yes. I do. More than you know, I think."

She didn't like that. "What's that supposed to mean?"

It felt like we were dancing, and both of us were trying to lead. It went against everything I knew, every instinct I had. She was my Alpha, and I was pushing her—toward *what*, exactly, I didn't know. But still we danced. "All I ask is that I be kept informed. I can't do my job if you don't tell me what's going on. Even if you don't think it concerns me. What will I do if something happens to you? To both of you?"

Ezra's expression softened. "Nothing will happen to us, dear. I promise."

"No one can promise that. Things happen every day. It could be something mundane." *Like a car accident*, a tiny little voice whispered, and it felt like there should have been more to it, but it was lost in the fog. "Or it could be a boy in a tree, trying to be as quiet as a mouse."

I saw the moment it clicked for her. She was feeling *something*, and it was making her uncomfortable. "It's not . . . that won't happen. Not here. Not to us. And never to you. You're safe, Robbie. I swear to it as your Alpha. Nothing will happen to you."

It already had. And I thought she knew that. Both of them did.

"Why don't you head on home?" Ezra suggested. "Get some rest. You're obviously still a little under the weather."

"I've had enough rest," I told him. "I don't need any more. I think I'll go for a run, if I'm not needed here anymore."

"That sounds fine, Robbie," Michelle said. "Stretch your legs. I need you at your best. Do what you have to."

Oh, I would.

I nodded at both of them as I stepped off the porch into the rain.

I stopped only when Ezra said my name.

I didn't turn around.

"How did you get inside?" he asked.

"The code. I put in the code on the door. Why?"

"Interesting," he said. "And there weren't any . . . complications?"

I looked back at him over my shoulder. "No. Should there have been?"

He smiled. "Of course not. Go run, dear. Feel the grass under your paws. The lake water in your mouth, and

(*sunlight all the sunlight it's warm it's home it's*)

the rain on your face. I wish I could run with you, but we both know you'd leave me far, far behind."

"As if I could ever do that."

He chuckled. "As if you could ever. I'm glad you know that, dear." He waved a hand at me. "Off with you."

"Alpha," I said with a nod, before leaving them both standing in front of the house.

A VOID / MY INSANITY

I called the phone number twice more.
No one answered the first time.
I waited a day before calling again.
There was a mechanical message.
"The number you are trying to reach has been disconnected or is no longer in service. If you feel this is an error, please hang up and try your call again."

* * *

I barely slept.
I heard Ezra outside my door numerous times.
Sometimes he would knock and ask if I couldn't sleep.
Other times he would do nothing.
Every morning I'd wake up and check the date on my phone to make sure I wasn't missing days.
I wasn't.
I waited.

* * *

Santos returned on Tuesday, along with three other wolves.
They didn't speak to anyone as they went to the Alpha's house.
I thought about following them, but I didn't.
I watched as they entered the house, closing the door behind them.
They stayed there for a long time.

* * *

"She likes me," Daniel whispered excitedly on Wednesday morning. "She *likes* me. We're going to run together on the full moon, and then we'll be happy forever. She's my mate, you know? I think she's my mate, and I'm going to give her my wolf. Do you think she'll take it?"

* * *

On Wednesday afternoon, Santos was once again guarding the little house.
I didn't approach him.
I didn't need to.

I am Dale, the man inside had said. The prisoner. *I am Dale. I am Dale.*

Wednesday night I had dinner with Ezra.

He said, "I'm sorry. I never meant to cause you any frustration. I only want what's best for you. I only want to keep you safe. These dreams... I could see they were pulling at you. They were hurting you. I thought... I thought I could help. I thought I could stop them. But I went too far. I never should have done so without your permission. Would you hear me, dear? Would you believe an old fool and forgive his mistakes?"

I said, "Yes. Of course. Of course I forgive you."

And what was absolutely fucking wild was that I *could* forgive him. I *did*. Here, in this house, just the two of us, I thought it was the easiest thing in the world.

I slept a little better that night.

I looked down at the note hidden away in the box in the back of my closet.

I HOWL FOR YOU!!!
FOR WHEN YOU'RE READY.

On Thursday she said, "The Bennetts."

I looked up at my Alpha as she stood above me. I was showing her how to work around an accounting program she was having trouble with, and she hadn't said a word in close to ten minutes, just listening and watching as I rambled.

Until she said those two words. Apropos of nothing.

Nothing could be done about the way my heart sped up. She heard it. We both knew she did. "What about them?"

"Do you know them? Have you ever met one in all those years before you came to me?"

You. Are. Bennett.

I shook my head. "No. Look, here. There's a tutorial that'll show you better than I could how to—"

"They want something that doesn't belong to them."

I lifted my hand from the computer mouse so I didn't break it. "Why?"

She placed a hand on my shoulder. I didn't look at her. "They're stuck in the old ways. And it has twisted them into something unrecognizable. They would do me harm, Robbie, if only they could get to me. To any of us. Do you believe that?"

I said, "Yes," and it wasn't a lie.

She squeezed my shoulder. "I should have told you this a long time ago."

"Why didn't you?"

"Because I needed you to heal. You came to Caswell a shell of a man. I needed to give you time for the bonds to form between us. So that you could trust me, and so that I could trust you."

"Do you? Trust me?"

"Yes." Her heart didn't skip a single beat. But I also knew Alphas were much more in control than any Beta wolf.

"You trust me to protect you?"

"Yes."

"To keep you safe?"

I nodded, still staring straight ahead at the computer screen. "I won't let them get to you."

She sighed. "I know."

I didn't dare look up at the empty space where the leather journal had once been.

It ended on Friday morning.

The storm that had lingered over Caswell was gone.

The sky was blue, blue, blue.

I stood in the refuge, and all those trees rose up around me, and if I thought hard enough, if I *believed* in what I dreamed, a man stood next to me, a man who said he had something to show me.

I know he did.

I *know* he did.

But he wasn't real.

He wasn't there.

I was alone.

I saw a white wolf in the trees. It had black on its chest and back.

I saw a black wolf in the distance. It—

My phone rang.

A few birds took flight from the canopy above me.

They looked like ravens.
The screen said UNKNOWN.
I thought about ignoring it.
Going back to the compound.
Being surrounded by my pack.
Living the life I had the way it was supposed to be.
My name was Robbie Fontaine.
I was the second to the Alpha of all.
I lived with (and loved) Ezra. He had saved me.
Given me a place.
Given me a home.
Yes, things didn't make sense. Missing time. These dreams.
But I could explain them away if I really wanted to. I could just . . . be.
Would you hear me, dear?
Yes. Yes I would.
The phone stopped ringing.
I breathed in. I breathed out.
And then the phone started ringing again.
I stared down at the screen.
UNKNOWN.
But was it? Was it *really*?
"Little wolf, little wolf," I said. "Can't you see?"
The skin between my neck and shoulder felt like it was on fire.
The phone beeped as I connected the call. I brought it to my ear. "Who is this?"

"Robbie? I need you to listen to me. We don't have much time. You need to—"

"Shannon? Alpha Wells?"

"*Yes*," she snapped. "Did you find him? Did you find the prisoner?"

The day grew brighter around me. I pressed a hand against the tree to ground me in reality. The membrane was thinner still. "Yes."

"Did you kill him?"

"*Kill* him? What the fuck? No, I didn't kill him. I don't know who the hell you are, but you need to—"

"His name is Robert Livingstone," Shannon said, and I fell silent. "A witch. And he's the reason all of this is happening. To us. To you. You need to—"

The ground rolled beneath my feet. "He's not—that's not his name. I don't know who that is, but he's not who's in the house." Unless he was lying, but with the amount of effort it took and with the way his mind seemed destroyed, I didn't think that was possible.

Silence. Then, "What?"

"The man. He's a witch. But his name isn't Robert Livingstone."

"He *talked* to you?" Shannon demanded. "He told you his name? Jesus Christ, Robbie, he could be fucking with your head. They told us he was—Goddammit. Who did he say he was?"

I am.

I am

I am—

"Dale."

"No," she whispered, sounding terrified. "No, no, no. Oh fuck, that's ... That means ... Robbie. I need you to listen to me, okay? I know you don't remember me. I know you don't have any reason to trust me. But I *need* you to hear me."

Would you hear me, dear?

My claws dug into the bark of the tree. Sap spilled over my fingers.

"We've met before. Days ago. You came to my house. You met my *pack*. Malik. John. Jimmy. He showed you his monster movies. You slept in my barn. You ate at my table."

The colors of the world around me began to bleed together. My stomach clenched and my knees felt week. "I've never met you before in my life."

"You *have*," she snarled. "And they know it. Your Alpha. Your witch. He took it from you, and then they came for us. They sent wolves after us, Robbie. They sent them to find us. I recognized one of them. We were already gone, but I stayed behind to watch. Santos. His name was Santos."

"No," I muttered. "No, that's not ... it's not—"

"Lignite."

"What?"

"Get to Lignite, Virginia. In Botetourt County. It's a ghost town, but there's a truss bridge there. Meet us at the bridge as soon as you can."

"Why the hell should I do anything you're asking?"

There was a voice in the background. It was quiet, and I couldn't make out the words. "But—" Shannon said. "How could he—"

The voice spoke again.

"Fine, but if this fucks him up— Robbie. Are you listening?"

"Yes."

"I need you to think. I need you to think *hard*. Can you do that for me?"

I closed my eyes. "Yes."

"Before the witch came for you, before you were brought to Caswell, where were you? What do you remember?"

"He found me. Ezra."

"I know that. But *where*?"

"I don't... It's..." I pulled my hand away from the tree and pressed my fist against my face. The entire world smelled like smoky sap, and I was *drowning* in it. And where *had* I been when Ezra came for me? What had I been doing? I remembered him standing in front of me, telling me he needed me, telling me that I was special, that he would take me to a place I could belong, where I would never have to be alone again, and his words were *everything* I had ever wanted. *Everything* I ever needed. He told me I would do great things, that I was important, that I was exactly what he was looking for, that I I I I I I—

I was nothing.

Because there was *nothing*.

It was an empty space.

A void.

"Who am I?" I whispered.

"I will tell you," she said. "I'll tell you *everything*. That whole place, all you know, everything you *think* you know, it's a *lie*. Robbie, I promise you, I will show you the truth. I'll show you the way home. Don't you want to know what's real? I can *give* that to you. And they'll be here to—"

"Who?"

"I—can't. Robbie, just get here. Do you hear me? It's not safe for you anymore. Get to Lignite. Get to the bridge. Do it now before it's too late. Everything depends on it."

"But—"

The phone beeped in my ear as the call dropped.
I looked at the tree.
Sap poured down the trunk.
It looked like it was bleeding.

I read once that insanity is doing the same thing over and over again and expecting a different result.

Here was my insanity:

I walked back into the compound.

Some of the wolves waved at me. Some did not.

I smiled at those who did. I smiled at those who did not.

Little cubs ran around me, shouting my name, demanding that I lift them up and spin them around.

I did.

God help me, I did.

Tony screamed in delight, just like all the others.

What was it like when you were here before?

Why were you blue when you came back?

I almost dropped him.

He looked up at me with wide eyes, nostrils flaring. "Blue," he whispered. "It's all blue."

Sonari said, "Hey, Robbie." She smiled as the cubs took a step away from me. They weren't frightened of me, but they knew something was wrong.

"Hi," I said. "Sorry, I've—I've got to run."

Her smile faded slightly. "Oh. Hey, that's okay. Maybe we can talk later?"

"Sure. Yeah."

"Are you all right?" She looked concerned. "You look like you've seen a ghost."

I left them standing there. I could feel their eyes on me as I walked away.

Santos was on guard duty.

He stood in front of the house.

He said, "What are you doing here? Alpha Hughes said you're not allowed back at the house. It's for your own good."

"Where did you go?"

He glared at me. "Fuck off, Fontaine."

I didn't know how it happened. One moment there was distance between us. The next I had him pressed up against the porch railing, the wood cracking under our combined weight, my claws in his throat. A small drop of blood trickled down his neck.

"Get the fuck off me!" he cried.

"What did you do?" I whispered hotly in his ear. "What the fuck did you do?"

"Jesus *Christ*, have you lost your damn mind? What the hell is wrong with you?"

He tried to shove me away.

I let him.

His blood was on my hand, deeply dark.

I wanted to taste it.

More of it.

I wanted to tear him apart.

I whirled around and headed for the woods.

He shouted after me.

I ignored him.

The trees swayed as I walked through the forest.

Black birds (ravens? Why were there so many ravens?) swirled overhead. My mother told me once that a group of ravens was called an unkindness. "I don't know why," she said as we lay in the back of the car, waiting for daylight. "It's odd, isn't it? There's another name for a massing of ravens too, though it's strange. When they come together, they're also called—"

"I know what they're called," I said to the trees, to the birds, to the earth beneath my feet.

The ravens laughed at me. They screamed, *Little wolf, little wolf, what do you see? We take to wing above you, flying in a conspiracy.*

An unkindness of ravens.

A *conspiracy* of ravens.

I turned my face toward the sky.

The birds were gone.

I looked ahead.

The path through the trees was empty.

I looked to the right.

A white wolf, black on its chest and back.

I looked to the left.

A pure white wolf stood side by side with a black wolf.

Their eyes burned red, and I swore the black one had violet mixed in.

It wasn't possible.

I ran.

Tree limbs slashed against my face, cutting into my skin. Blood began to fall even as the scrapes healed almost immediately. My glasses were knocked askew, and someone snarled in my ear, "Take those fucking things off. You don't need them."

I gasped as I stumbled, sure that a man, a gruff man, an *angry* man was standing next to me.

He wasn't.

I was alone.

I sucked in a breath, trying to clear my head from a maelstrom of voices that spun furiously like a tornado. They were shouting at me, dozens of them, telling me to *listen*, that I needed to *listen* and it would all make sense, it would all become clear.

My chest burned as I took off again.

Someone was running next to me. A large blond man, a wicked grin on his face.

He said, "You think you're faster than I am?"

I laughed. "I know I am."

"Oh, you're in for it now. You think you got this, Fontaine? I'm not going to go easy because you've got my brother wrapped around your finger. I'll—"

I screamed in horror when he burst into a cloud of dust. It sprayed my face, and I—

I ran into the house I shared with Ezra.

It was empty.

No one was home.

I shut the door behind me, slumping against it.

Outside, something prowled back and forth on the porch.

Its claws clicked against the wood.

It snorted air out its nose.

And then it howled.

The house shook around me, the door vibrating against my back.

The song

(*wolfsong*)

was long and loud, and my bones quaked at the sound of it. I said, "No, please, please don't do this, please don't do this. Who are you? *Who are you!*"

The howl faded into nothing.

The house creaked and settled around me.

"I'm Robbie Fontaine," I said to no one. "I'm the second to the Alpha of all. I am home. I am loved. I have many responsibilities. I live with my friend. He is—"

And they knew it. Your Alpha. Your witch. He took it from you.

I could only scream. "Get out of my head!"

I pushed myself off the door, storming down the hallway to my room. I looked around wildly, sure someone would be waiting for me, waiting to take all of this away, to make me sound, to make me *whole*, to put some sense back into the world around me.

There was no one there.

"Don't you want to know what's real?" I said with a grating laugh. "I can give that to you."

Backpack hanging on the closet door.

I grabbed it and opened the closet.

I stuffed it with a pair of jeans. With socks. A couple of shirts. I pulled out the panel from the back of the closet. It broke in my hands. It didn't matter. I grabbed the secret box and upended it into my backpack, spilling its contents inside.

My mother looked up at me from her driver's license photo lying near a wolf of stone.

"Quiet as a mouse," I told her.

She didn't reply.

I zipped the bag closed. I lifted it up and over my shoulder. It was heavy against my back, grounding me. It felt like the only real thing in all this unreality.

I turned toward the door.

Ezra said, "Going somewhere?"

He stood hunched in the doorway. He looked tired. And sad.

"I need a break," I said evenly. "I need to get away for a couple of days."

"If you give me a few minutes, I can throw some things in a bag. We can go together."

I shook my head. "No. It's not— I need to do this. On my own. It's important."

"Why?"

"I need to clear my mind."

"There's nothing wrong with your mind, dear. There never has been. You're just tired. Maybe you should get some rest."

I laughed. "I don't *need* any more rest. Look, I just want a couple of days, okay? I never ask for anything."

"No. You don't." He looked like he was going to reach for me but thought better of it. His liver-spotted hand curled into a fist instead. He was shaking. I thought he was scared of me, but I couldn't smell fear on him. "It's the worst thing about you."

"Then give me this. Just . . . let me go. For a little bit."

"Where will you go?"

"Away."

He sighed. "Would you hear me, dear?"

And it was *so easy* to say yes. *So easy* to say of course, of course I will hear you. Every part of me *screamed* to do just that. It rolled over me in a calming wave, and for a moment I thought how ridiculous I was being. I was in the middle of a breakdown, that much was clear, and here was this man, my *friend*, who wanted nothing more than to keep me safe. He loved me, and I loved him. I loved him.

I loved him.

And even as a sharp lance of pain pierced my skull, I said, "No."

Silence fell between us, stretching until it was almost unbearable. Then, "What?"

"No. Not this time. Not now. Just let me go. Please. That's all I'm asking. Just let me go."

"You're scaring me, Robbie."

I laughed. "You have no idea."

"We need to fix this. We need to fix this *together*. I don't know what's going on in that head of yours, but I promise that I can help—"

"I don't want you in my head," I snapped at him. "I don't want *anyone* in my head."

I was surprised when he took a step back out of the doorway. "Fine. If that's the way it is, then go. I don't know what's going on, but I won't stop you. If this is something you need to do, then do it. I'll make sure Michelle knows."

I gripped the strap of my backpack tightly. "Thank you."

He grabbed my bicep as I left the room.

I didn't look at him.

He said, "Your home is here. It's always here. Remember that. No matter what happens, I want you to remember what we have."

I pulled my arm out of his hand. "I know. And it's the best home that I've ever had. I'll come back."

"Oh, I know you will."

I left him standing in the doorway.

I expected him to follow me.

He didn't.

* * *

I stayed out of the compound, circling around it as I headed into town. I could hear the wolves laughing and shouting. I could hear the cubs screaming in happiness.

I pushed it all away.

The main road through Caswell was mostly empty on this Friday. The few businesses that we had were open. The marquee of the movie theater was lit up, lights flashing. Anyone passing through wouldn't think twice about it.

There was a large garage next to the theater. Inside was a small fleet of vehicles.

I grabbed the keys for a compact car off the corkboard.

I shoved my bag into the back seat before climbing in the front.

I gripped the steering wheel, breathing in and out.

In and out.

"Okay," I whispered. "Okay."

I hit the clicker on the visor above my head.

The garage door opened.

Weak light spilled in, the rain lessening.

I turned the key in the ignition.

The car rumbled to life.

I gave myself one last chance.

One last chance to stop this.

One last chance to go back to the compound.
I gunned the engine.
It whined laughably.
I put the car into Drive and pulled out of the garage.
I headed south.

PACK

Once, when I was just a cub, my father sat me in his lap.
He said, "There are things you don't understand."
He said, "Things that you're too young to hear."
He said, "But I need you to hear them anyway."

I looked up at him with stars in my eyes. I loved him. He wasn't like us, but he was my father, and it was all that mattered.

He said, "You have something in you. Something that will grow and grow and grow. It's a bad thing. You have to fight it. You can't let it consume you. It's a monster, Robbie. And it will eat you if you let it. And then *you'll* be the monster."

I trembled in his arms. "I don't wanna be a monster."

He brushed my hair off my forehead. "I know. And I will do everything I can to make sure it never happens. But if it does . . . well." He smiled. "We'll worry about it then, won't we? Can you keep a secret?"

I nodded. "Yeah. Tell me."

He leaned over, his lips near my ear. He whispered, "There's a monster inside all of us. But some of us learn to control it."

The farther away I got from Caswell, the more it pulled in my head.

I was in Connecticut when I pulled over to the side of the road and vomited. I retched until I was dry-heaving, a thin line of noxious spittle hanging from my bottom lip. I spit as my stomach rolled.

The air was hot, rising from the black roadway in wavy lines.

I sat back in my seat, wiping my mouth.

"Fuck," I muttered as I closed my eyes.

I allowed myself another minute before I closed the door and pulled back onto the road.

I slept that night near a field in a tiny village in Pennsylvania with the odd name of Bird-in-Hand.

I lay in the back seat, overwarm and aching, the moon and stars as bright as I'd ever seen them.

My sleep was thin and restless.

My mother was in the back seat with me, running her hands through my hair as I sounded out words from the book she'd given me. The pages in the book were filled with wild things, great and horrible beasts that raised their claws. I struggled with some of the words, but she helped me through them.

"Good," she said into my hair. "You're doing so good."

She was crying.

When I looked up to ask her what was wrong, why she was sad, why she was *blue,* she wasn't there.

I didn't know if I was awake.

It was early evening when I found it.

As I saw the red wooden sign with LIGNITE in white, I knew.

Lignite was dead. It'd been dead for a very long time.

A few buildings remained, their bones nothing but piles of stone, a vague outline of what had once been.

The forest had overtaken it.

The trees were thick.

The road into Lignite was small and covered in potholes. I hadn't seen another car in a long time.

I didn't know where to go.

A bridge. Shannon had said there was a truss bridge, but I didn't know what the fuck a truss bridge *was.* My phone was no help. I had no service. The GPS had cut out ten miles back, and I didn't want to turn around. If I did, I thought I would keep driving.

I stopped the car on the side of the road near an old collapsed building. It was cooler than I expected it to be when I opened the door and got out of the car. An electric hum ran through my skin, and I fought the urge to shift. It felt safer.

"Hello?" I said.

My voice echoed around me, and it was as if the trees were greeting me.

Hello . . . ello . . . lo . . . lo . . . lo.

I was alone.

I closed the car door. The sound was startling in the great quiet.

I looked around, unsure of where to go.

Through the trees to my right, I thought I saw the flash of *something* in the failing sunlight. I walked toward it.

The trees felt different here, unclaimed.

This wasn't wolf territory, or at least it wasn't currently.

I growled at a rodent that skittered off through the forest.

The flash came again, brighter than it'd been before.

It looked metal.

I began to run.

I ran alone. No wolves.

It didn't take long.

The bridge was as old and dead as the buildings. The struts below had turned brown with rust. The metal railings along the top were in better shape, though not by much. The trees around the bridge swayed in the cold breeze.

Before I stepped onto it, I hesitated. My shadow stretched out long in front of me, looking monstrous.

The pavement was cracked, the yellow dividing line faded into almost nothing.

The bridge groaned.

I didn't look back.

I stepped onto the bridge.

Nothing happened.

I took another step. And then another. And then another.

In the middle of the bridge, the moon caressed my neck, prickling my skin.

"I'm here," I said.

Nothing.

"I'm here."

Nothing.

I raised my voice. "I'm here! Goddammit, you told me to come here, you told me to find you, and I'm *here*!" I spread out my arms as I spun in a slow circle. Above, the first stars were coming out, and the moon, the fucking *moon* was calling for me, saying *i see you here you are you are here you are you are you are*.

"What do you want from me? What more do I possibly have to give! Do you know what it took for me to get here? *Do* you? You're all fucking with my head, and I won't—"

"Robbie."

I whirled around.

A young woman stood on the bridge. She looked wary, and she

stepped no closer, but she was an *Alpha,* and I fought against the instinct to bare my neck to her.

"Who are you?" I asked harshly.

"Alpha Wells. Shannon. We spoke on the phone. Do you remember?"

I glared at her. "Of course I remember. You told me to get here. You sounded fucking nuts, but here I am. You said you had answers."

She nodded. "I do. Though not all of them."

"Malik," I said suddenly, and she narrowed her eyes. "John. Jimmy. Those are the names you told me. Your pack."

"Yes."

"Where are they?"

Something complicated crossed her face, there and gone. "Why?"

"Is this a trap?"

"No, Robbie. It's not a trap. Not for you, anyway." She looked over my shoulder in the failing light. "Are you alone? Did you tell anyone you were coming here?"

"No."

She cocked her head as she listened to my heartbeat. I bristled but said nothing. "Do you want to hurt me?"

That shocked me into laughter that echoed around us before I cut it off. "What? Why the hell would I want to hurt you?"

"I had to ask. To make sure you're you."

That discordant feeling returned, the divide in my head where things were real and unreal at the same time, separated by a thin veil made of glass. "Who else would I be?"

"A weapon," she said quietly. "A monster capable of great harm. Savage. Fang and claw hell-bent on spilling as much blood as possible. Feral."

I took a step back. "I've . . . never done that. I've never hurt *anyone.*"

(what are you doing
robbie
robbie
please don't
please don't do this
oh my god what's wrong with you
you're not

please please please i don't want to die
please you're hurting me robbie you're hurting me
oh god no
no
let me go let me go LET ME GO LETMEGOLETME)

The bridge creaked beneath my feet as more stars appeared. I tilted my head back, stretching my neck, barely holding the shift at bay.

"I'm not a monster," I told the waning moon.

"We were wrong," Shannon said as my eyes flooded with orange fire. "We thought . . . we thought we knew what had happened. In the compound. We were wrong. All of us. We made mistakes. And we suffered because of it. But it wasn't as bad for us. Because we had each other. We're pack. Even after all we'd lost, we're pack. We're together. But I understand loss. That void. Where something is taken. Torn away. I can only imagine what it must have been like for them."

"Who?" I demanded, my voice a low growl, more wolf than man. "Who are you talking about? Why am I here? What have you done? I'm not a monster. I'm not a weapon. For fuck's sakes, you're describing an Omega. Can you see me? Can you see what I am? I'm a goddamn Beta!"

She said, "I thought I knew. What it meant to be Omega. What they were. I was wrong. Brodie showed me that. And I will never let him go."

"I don't know who you're talking about."

She smiled sadly. "I know. But you will. One day all will be well and we will live free and without fear." Her eyes flooded with red. "I'll fight for that with everything I have. Can you say the same?"

"Alpha, I mean no disrespect, but can you get to the fucking point? Because I'm getting real tired of your shit."

She nodded. "You're right, of course. Here. Let me show you."

She tilted her head back toward the moon, her shift starting to overcome her. Her face elongated as thin white hair grew around her nose and mouth. The white faded into rust red, almost like a fox. And she *was* foxlike, her snout shorter than most other wolves I'd seen. It took me a moment to recognize her for what she was.

A maned wolf.

I'd never seen one before.

I didn't even know there *were* maned wolf shifters.

She didn't howl. Instead, a deep guttural bark crawled from her throat and out of her mouth, reverberating along the bridge and slamming into me. She did it again. And again. And again.

The sounds faded away into nothing.

"What is this?" I asked her. "What is—"

An answering howl.

I fell to my knees.

An Alpha.

A second howl rose up from the trees, singing in chorus with the first.

A *third* Alpha.

I pressed my hands against the ground, claws scraping into the pavement.

The howls came again, and I could *hear* the voices in them, saying *we're coming we're coming WE'RE COMING*.

I stood quickly, my half-shift overcoming me. I growled at the Alpha across from me. She was going to kick my ass, but I'd go down swinging.

I rushed toward her.

And slammed into an invisible wall as a burst of magic sprang up around me.

I fell back, nose bloodied and broken. It began to knit itself back together, and I wiped the blood away, flicking it onto the ground. I pressed my hand against the barrier. It felt familiar, just off enough to be unknown, but still recognizable.

It felt like Ezra.

I tried to push through it, but it was unyielding. I slashed at it, my claws sending out bright sparks. It didn't change no matter how hard I struck.

"Yeah," a voice drawled from behind me, "that's not gonna do anything. Jesus Christ, kid. You can't still be *that* stupid."

I whirled around.

An older man stood at the other end of the bridge. The tattoos on his arms were bright in the low light, lines and symbols that meant old magic. A raven on a bed of roses on one of his arms fluttered its wings, beak opening soundlessly. The man had one hand raised toward me. The other was—

His arm ended in a stump at the wrist.

"Witch," I hissed at him. I ran toward him only to smash into *another* barrier. It knocked me back, but I stayed on my feet. I snarled in anger.

He rolled his eyes. "Or maybe you can still be that stupid. Good to know some things don't change, no matter—"

A low growl came from the shadows behind him.

The witch sighed. "Yeah, yeah. I hear you, you overgrown mutt."

I recoiled as a large brown wolf stepped onto the bridge. Its eyes were violet.

An Omega.

It pressed up against the witch, bumping its snout against the stump of his arm.

"I know," the witch said. "Hand, sanity, blah, blah, blah. Look. It's him. It's really him." All the bravado seemed to fall away from the witch as he looked at me. His eyes were wet as he shook his head. "Christ, kid. Aren't you just a sight. All that hair, man. You used to keep it short. Still have the glasses, though. Figures."

"Let me out," I snarled at him, banging my hands against the barrier. "You can't keep me in here forever!"

The witch laughed, though it sounded hollow. "I know," he said as the brown wolf tilted its head. "But better to be safe than sorry. Especially after . . ." He shook his head. "It doesn't matter. Not now." He was plaintive when he said, "Kid. Robbie. Look at me."

I bared my fangs.

"You know me."

I slammed my hands against the barrier again. "I *don't*."

He said, "You do. You know me very well. Somewhere deep inside, you do. It's there, I think. Still. Locked away behind a door. My name is Gordo. And I'm the witch of a wolf pack. *Your* wolf pack." He took a step toward me even as the brown wolf growled in warning. "We've waited for this moment for a long time. We . . . tried, kid. We tried so hard to find you. To get to you. You know me. *You know me.*"

He dropped his hand.

The barrier fell away as the magic dissipated.

I charged at him.

He didn't stop me as I wrapped my hand around his throat and lifted him off the ground. The brown wolf snarled in fury, but they *smelled* like each other, their scents mixed in, all dirt and leaves and rain and *ozone*. They were mated. I squeezed the witch's neck tightly as I glared at the wolf. "You back the fuck off or I'll tear out his throat." It was stupid to threaten the mate of a witch, but I was out of options and in a full-blown panic.

"I think," the witch gasped, "he's kind of got a point. I'd rather keep my throat as is, if it's all the same to both of you."

The brown wolf wasn't having it. Before I could sink my claws into the witch's neck, the brown wolf slammed into me with its head, knocking me off my feet. The witch fell to the ground as I rolled into the side of the bridge. I was up on my feet immediately, ready to lash out at the Omega.

But he didn't come for me.

He stood protectively over the witch, eyes bright in the looming darkness.

"Well," the witch said, flat on his back in the road. "This is going better than I expected. I'm still alive, so that's a plus. Mark, would you please get your fucking dog junk out of my face?"

The brown wolf *sat* on him, looking rather pleased with himself before he caught me watching. He snapped his jaws at me but didn't move.

The witch wheezed. "You . . . fucking . . . *dick.*"

A sound from behind me.

I looked back over my shoulder.

Alpha Wells—Shannon—was gone. But in her place stood two wolves.

One pure white.

One pure black.

The white wolf had red eyes.

The black wolf did too. But there was *violet* swirling within them, like he was . . . like he could be—

My shift melted away beyond my control.

They took a step toward me in unison, shoulders brushing. The white wolf was smaller than the black but emanated such power that I could barely breathe. It felt almost *regal*, like this wolf was royalty.

But it was the black wolf that held my attention the most. Its eyes never left mine as it walked toward me, claws clicking on the pavement.

This wolf was different.

This wolf was *more*.

My eyes stung, and I didn't know why. My hands shook.

I heard a whisper in my head, faint but undeniable.

It said *packpackpack*.

"Who are you?" I said in a broken voice. "What do you want with me?"

The Alphas stopped a good twenty feet away. As I watched, they began to shift. The white wolf became a blond man, younger than I expected. He was strong and slender, the red fading from his eyes until they were blue, blue, blue.

But the other wolf.

Oh god, the *other* wolf...

His skin was tan. His eyes and hair were dark. He was big, so big that I thought he would fill up the entire world. He popped his neck side to side as the black hair receded, as the fangs slid back up into his gums.

A single tear slid down his cheek. He didn't wipe it away. It hung on the curve of his jaw for a moment before it splashed onto the road.

"Hello, Robbie," the man said. His voice was deep, the words slow and filled with so much *blue* that I could barely breathe. But there was green in them too, green relief that was like the forest around us was in full bloom. "I know you're scared. I know you have questions. And I will do my best to answer all of them. But we have to go while there's still time. I need you to trust me."

I was in a daze. The wolves from my dreams were here in front of me. I didn't know if I was awake. "Who the hell are you people?"

The man nodded. The other Alpha at his side gripped his hand, mouth a thin line. The big man was an all-encompassing presence, but the other one...

The other one was dangerous.

And he said, "My name is Joe. Joe Bennett."

My shift returned, sudden and savage.

My fangs dropped as I roared at them. At *him*.

The witch shouted at the brown wolf, telling him to get the fuck *off* him even as the wolf growled. The Alphas stood there, barely affected.

Bennett. They were coming for Ezra. They were coming for the

Alpha of all. I knew this because Michelle had told me. They were traitors, they were monsters, they were the *enemy*, and I would do what I had to in order to protect what was mine.

They stood their ground as I ran toward them.

The muscles in the bigger man's legs flexed as he began to crouch, eyes flashing impossibly in shades of red and violet.

The other one, the *dangerous* one, popped his claws and—

"*Robbie!*"

Everything stopped.

My breath hitched as a fourth man stepped out from behind the Alphas.

A wolf.

He looked like the dangerous Alpha, all blond and blue-eyed. They had to be brothers.

He took measured steps, barely looking as if he touched the ground with his bare feet. His jeans were rolled up above his ankles, and he wore what looked like a work shirt, gray with thin red stripes, the hem hanging around his waist.

There was a name embroidered in a patch on his chest.

ROBBIE.

The world tilted.

He took another step toward me. The darker Alpha reached out to stop him, but the other Alpha shook his head once.

I barely noticed.

I couldn't look away from the man in front of me.

His smile was a trembling thing. I thought for a moment he was *scared,* but the scent that assaulted me wasn't *fear.*

It was sorrow.

Oh god, there was an ocean of blue pouring from him. There was hope, yes, green along the surface, but it was overwhelmed by the sea that engulfed him.

He said, "Hey."

He said, "Hi."

He said, "Hello."

He said, "I see you, you know?" and "I see you" and "I'm sorry, I'm so sorry we let you go, I'm so sorry *I* let you go, but I swear to you, I *swear* it'll never happen again. You're safe. You're safe now. Finally, after all this time."

I was surrounded.

I could do nothing about it.

I was trapped.

He took another step toward me, hands coming up because he *knew* what a cornered animal would do. He *knew* that I was on the edge, and the moon was so bright, so strong, so fucking *close*.

He said, "Listen."

He said, "I need you to listen, okay?"

I jerked my head as the wolf and witch behind me began to move.

"Robbie," the wolf in front of me snapped. "Look at me."

I did. I was helpless *not* to.

He nodded. "Good. That's good. It's me, Robbie." He took a deep breath. "It's me. It's Kelly."

And I said, "Who?"

His face crumpled immediately, and I was *submerged* in the blue, drowning in an ocean that rose around me. He hurt. He hurt so fucking bad that I didn't know how he could stand it.

"Kelly," he whispered. "I'm Kelly."

The witch said, "Can we do this later? We need to leave. *Now*."

The Alphas took a step toward us.

The man in front of me—Kelly—shook his head furiously. "Wait. Just—"

Gordo said, "We don't have *time* to wait," as the brown wolf growled low in its throat. "They'll be right behind him. And if it's really my father, then we need to—"

They shouted after me as I ran toward the side of the bridge. Kelly screamed my name as I vaulted over the edge. My clothing tore as I fell, wind whipping around me. Muscle and bone groaned and broke as I listened to the moon.

I landed on the ground as a wolf, dust billowing around me.

I

need to

run

run

escape

find a tree

hide

quiet as a mouse

i am wolf

i

barely made it from under the shadow of the bridge before my shift was ripped from me in a terrible burst of magic, causing me to fall to my knees, and I was surrounded by wolves.

One was large and gray with flecks of black and white on its hind legs. It had violet eyes.

The second and third wolves were smaller. They were white and brown with black hair across their backs. Their eyes were orange, but they stood side by side with the Omega like it didn't matter, like they weren't *scared*.

I punched the ground in fury, my muscles rippling under my skin as I fought against the magic that held the wolf at bay.

The wolves stepped closer.

From above, the witch appeared, looking down at us. "Chris," he snapped, "Tanner. Carter. Pulling him out of his shift won't last. Don't hurt him. You hear me, whatever you do, don't—"

They were distracted.

I lunged for the Omega wolf, as it was closest. The other two wolves yelped and stumbled back, tripping over each other and falling to the ground in a tangle of limbs.

I feinted left as they started to recover. The gray wolf fell for it, and I went right.

I took off, running as fast as I could, crossing under the bridge.

I didn't make it far before the Alphas crashed down in front of me, muscles coiling.

I skidded on the ground, rocks tearing at the soles of my feet.

They took a step toward me.

I took an answering step back, only to hear a low growl behind me. I looked over my shoulder. The other wolves had recovered and were coming toward me, slowly and deliberately, like they were hunting.

"Fucking werewolves," the witch said as he and the brown wolf slid down the hill next to the bridge. "And we just *had* to do this so near a full moon. Because of course we did. Hey, let's just make things as difficult as poss— Mark, if you don't stop pushing me, I will *end* you."

The brown wolf huffed in annoyance as they came to stand next to the Alphas.

"Robbie."

I whirled around.

The man from the bridge pushed his way between the wolves.

Kelly.

The gray Omega tried to stop him, but he pushed its head away, gaze never leaving me, as if he thought I would disappear right in front of him.

I was surrounded.

"We're not going to hurt you," Kelly said. "I swear it."

"You're Bennetts," I bit out, trying to force my shift. My skin rippled, but I couldn't burst through. "You're the enemy. You want to kill my Alpha."

He looked stricken. "No. That's not—"

But *oh*. He *lied*. His heart tripped the *smallest* amount, the barest of stutters.

His eyes widened. "Not like— Robbie. It's not *like* that. You have to believe me. You've been lied to. They did something to you. Something to your memory. You know me. *You know me.*" And he stretched the collar of his shirt away from his neck. The shirt with my name on it.

There, at the juncture of his neck and shoulder, was a scar.

The perfect formation of a bite.

And he said, "You're my mate."

It was like a punch to the stomach. I couldn't breathe. I couldn't focus. "No. No. No. You're not. You're *not*." I bit through my lip, blood filling my mouth. "I don't *have* a mate. I would know if I—"

"Would you hear me, dear?"

The ocean parted.

Calm washed over me.

All would be well.

Ezra stood on the bridge above us, looking down.

He smiled. "Bennetts, Robbie. All of the creatures before you are Bennetts. And they want to take you away from me. All they do is *take*." He shook his head. "I can't let that happen, I'm afraid. It's time for this to end, one way or another."

The wolves around me howled a ferocious song.

It sounded like war.

Ezra nodded. "Ah. I suppose it was inevitable. Some things never change. All this fighting. All this bloodshed. Aren't you tired? You have suffered. *I* have suffered. And yet you persist."

The struts above us began to shake and groan.

Rust sprinkled down on us.

Ezra gripped the railing, his tattoos beginning to shine.

"*Move!*" Gordo shouted.

The bridge broke apart. The wolves around me darted out of the way when large sections of stone and metal crashed down around us. Kelly grabbed me by the arm and *yanked,* almost pulling me off my feet. I swiped at him, going for his face, but he ducked before my claws could tear into his skin.

"What are you *doing!*" he shouted at me. "I'm trying to *help*—look out!"

He shoved me out of the way as a beam hurtled toward us, slamming into the ground where I'd once been standing. From above came the grating screech of metal as what remained of the bridge folded in on itself, slumping down toward the ground.

It looked like . . .

Stairs.

Ezra had made a staircase.

The metal reformed with every step he took toward us.

I watched as he stood upright, his hunch gone.

The liver spots on his hands and head faded.

White hair sprouted along the top of his head, thin and wispy.

His tattoos were as bright as I'd ever seen them, brighter than I thought possible, like they were new, like they'd just been carved into his skin.

The deep lines on his face filled, though not completely.

He looked years younger. *Decades.*

"There," he said, sounding breathless. "Do you know how hard it is to maintain that level of magic at all times? Such a waste."

He grunted as the brown wolf charged him. Gordo shouted furiously as the wolf was knocked away with a wave of Ezra's hand, slamming into one of the steel beams with a devastating crunch. The wolf cried out in pain, a long and mournful sound.

"You," Ezra said to the witch. "How you look like your mother."

He barely blinked as Gordo raised his arms, magic building.

The black wolf stood at his side, eyes red and violet.

"What do you think you could do to me?" Ezra asked. "Don't you see how easy this was for me? No matter where you go, no matter what you do, I will *find* you, Gordo. And I will take everything until you return what belongs to me."

"We never took *anything* from you," Gordo snapped. "And even if we had, do you really think we'd just let this go? After everything you've done?"

Ezra looked saddened, shaking his head slowly. "A demonstration, perhaps. Would you hear me, dear? Robbie, would you hear me?"

"Yes," I whispered. Always.

Gordo's eyes widened. "Trigger. It's a goddamn *trigger*—"

"Kill them," Ezra said. "Kill them all."

I would do what he asked.

They were the enemy. The witch would be the first to die.

Except I didn't reach him.

I leapt for the witch, claws extended.

A gray-and-black wolf came between us.

It whimpered as my claws sank into its hair. Into its skin.

Blood spilled over my hands.

"No!" Gordo cried.

The gray-and-black wolf fell to the ground, my claws still inside it.

It looked up at me with orange eyes.

I stared down at it.

A tatter of clothing hung on its chest.

I watched as wolf blood spilled over the patch with my name on it.

I slowly pulled my claws out.

The wolf whimpered.

I stood as blood dripped from my fingers.

The black Alpha tilted his head back and howled. It rolled through the destruction around us, echoing into the forest.

For a moment nothing happened.

"Yes," Ezra said mockingly, "because your wolfsong will do you any good so far from home—"

There came an answering howl.

And then another.

And another.

And *another*, until the forest was *alive* with wolves. Flashes of violet lights began to fill the forest. Wolves stood on the remains of the bridge overhead, peering down at us, their eyes glowing.

Violet.

We were surrounded by Omegas.

"Curious," Ezra said, sounding unafraid as he turned his gaze upward. "I've often wondered how you did it, Alpha Matheson. Taking what I created and making it something else entirely. Is it just you? Your pack? The territory? No matter. It's—"

The gray-and-black wolf was moving, even as it bled.

It jumped for Ezra.

Ezra caught it by the throat. His tattoos grew brighter until I could barely look at him. "A lesson, I think. You will learn what happens when you try to take from me." He shook the wolf like it weighed nothing. The wolf tried to snap at his arm, his face, but it couldn't reach. "Yes, you will learn very well. Let's see what happens when your wolf is stripped from you."

The wolf lost its shift. One moment it was scrabbling, jerking side to side, and the next he was fully human, nude, with blood coating his side. Kelly.

It was Kelly.

What happened next was over in a matter of seconds.

He cried out as the tattoos on Ezra's arm crawled over his wrist and hand. Ancient symbols appeared on Kelly's face. Kelly's head rocked back, teeth grinding together.

The symbols twisted as if alive, rising up and attaching themselves to his lips, little tentacles that pulled on his mouth, forcing it open.

And then they poured down his throat.

Kelly made no sound as his body shook. His hands flexed and closed. Flexed and closed.

His skin lit up, pulsing once, then twice.

His eyes flickered orange.

And then the orange disappeared.

Ezra tossed him to the ground.

He lay on his back, blinking up at the dark sky. The wolves surrounded him, hackles raised, growling loudly.

Ezra sighed. "It didn't have to be this way. All I want is what belongs to me. Surely you have to see that. All this fighting. All this death. What has it brought you in the end? I may have underestimated the bond between you all, and that's my mistake. But it's one I won't make again. Robbie, if you please. Come with me. I have much to tell you. Would you hear me, dear?"

Yes.

Yes.

Yes.

"He's lying," Gordo snarled, cradling the brown wolf's head in his hands. "My father is *lying* to you—"

"Father," I whispered.

Ezra said, "I am Robert Livingstone. It's lovely to meet you again, Robbie. Now come. We have work to—"

A small figure landed on his back, half-shifted, claws sinking in.

It was a boy.

And his eyes were violet too.

"Brodie, *no!*" a woman screamed from above us.

Ezra grunted as he was knocked forward toward the wolves. The Omega was fierce behind him, hands moving up and down quickly as he scraped into the witch's back.

Ezra reached up behind him and grabbed the boy by the arms, lifted him up and *over* his head, and threw him at the Alphas.

And for the first time since I had known him, I saw fear on his face.

And I *smelled* it.

He looked around wildly, taking us all in.

He held his hand out for me.

I stepped forward to take it.

A hand wrapped around my ankle.

I looked down.

Kelly panted up at me. "Don't. Please don't go. Please. Stay with me."

The moon and the stars shone down on the scar on his neck.

"Robbie?"

I turned to look at Ezra again.

He held his hand out for me, his fingers trembling.

I hesitated.

He nodded slowly as he dropped his hand. "I see," he whispered. "You too. Just like everyone else. How you betray me."

The Alphas snarled as they took a step toward him.

"You think you've won?" Ezra said as Omegas filled the coming night with their fury. "This is just the beginning. And I won't stop until I have what belongs to me. I will tear the world apart." His tattoos flared to life once again.

"Get *down*!" Gordo screamed.

And without thinking, I collapsed on top of Kelly, covering his body with mine.

He whispered, "I found you."

And then the world filled with a bright flash of light, and everything exploded.

LIKE AN ECHO / A DOOR

I was lost in the dark.

Voices rose around me.

"He's not breathing, oh my god, he's not *breathing*—"

"Carter, would you stand the fuck *back*? You need to let me help him!"

"What did he do? What the hell did your dad *do* to him? He doesn't smell like wolf, he doesn't smell like—"

"I don't know, okay? You've got to let me at him, you've Got to let me— Ox! Get your ass over here *now*."

"Kelly? Kelly! Come on, man, open your eyes. Please, God, open your eyes, please, please, please— Let me go, Joe, you fucking let me go right now or I'll kick your ass. Let me— Ox! Ox, you have to help him. You have to—"

I felt my heartbeat in my eyes as I drifted away.

My head was pounding as I burst through the veil that had fallen over me.

I blinked slowly up at a bare ceiling.

My mouth was sour.

A human had told me once what it felt like to have a hangover. Alcohol didn't affect wolves like it did humans. Our metabolism burned through it too fast. But Jesus Christ, did it feel like I'd nearly drunk myself to death.

I groaned, putting a hand over my eyes. The light around me wasn't bright, but it still hurt.

"Hello."

I dropped my hand and turned my head.

A woman sat on the floor of a large room. For a moment my vision blurred and I *swore* it was Alpha Hughes, and I wondered what had happened. What I'd done. If I'd hurt anyone.

But it wasn't the Alpha of all.

She was older, for one, and so beautiful that it took my breath away. She was dressed simply, wearing loose-fitting pants and a shirt with an oversize neckline that hung off one bare shoulder. Her long, light hair was up in a messy bun, strands hanging around her face.

No, this wasn't Michelle.

For one, she was smiling quietly, and it looked like she meant it. She was tired, but her back was ramrod straight, her head tilted toward me. Her hands were folded in her lap.

A wolf.

A powerful one at that, though she wasn't an Alpha.

"Hello," I said. My voice came out rough and weak. I cleared my throat. I was thirsty.

Her smile widened briefly. "How are you?"

"I don't know."

She nodded. "That's okay. It's to be expected, I think. Many things have happened. Not knowing is perfectly understandable. Can I tell you something?"

I nodded. If it weren't for how shitty I felt, I would have thought this a dream.

"Your hair is long."

"That's what you want to tell me?"

She chuckled. "No. It's just . . . an observation. Different, but not in a bad way. What I want to tell you is that you're not a prisoner, no matter how it looks at the moment. Do you understand?"

"No."

"We have to be careful. Precautions. We don't know how much of a hold has been put over you, and while I don't think this will be permanent, we need to hedge our bets."

"I don't know what you're talking about."

She pointed toward the floor in front of her.

A line of gray powder went from one side of the room to the other, separating us.

I inhaled.

It burned.

I said, "Silver."

"Yes. So if you feel like attacking me, don't. It would only end badly for you. And no one wants that. Especially no one here."

I sat up. I was on a small cot, a scratchy blanket covering me. I pushed it off and put my legs on the floor. My feet were bare. The floor was cool. I only had on a pair of sleep shorts. My stomach grumbled.

"Hungry?" she asked.

"A little," I admitted begrudgingly.

"I'll take care of that in a bit. I'd like to have a chat, you and I. Your glasses are on the floor under your bed with your backpack."

I narrowed my eyes at her. "I don't need the glasses."

She bit her bottom lip like she was trying to keep from laughing at me. "Oh, I know. Funny to hear that coming from you, though. I always thought they made you look handsome."

"You act like you know me."

"It's not an act, Robbie." Her smile faded. "No, it's not an act at all. And though I may not know exactly the man before me, there are still bits of you I recognize. Like looking through a fractured mirror."

I pulled the blanket into my lap. "Please don't stare at my bits."

The smile returned in full force. It took my breath away. "There you are. I wonder . . . is it like an echo? Somewhere deep inside, locked away. What makes a man when so much has been taken from him?"

"Where am I?"

She said, "In a moment. Firsts things first. My name is Elizabeth. I am a wolf, as you've no doubt figured out already."

"Not an Alpha."

"No, though I've known a few in my time. Most of them are good. Some . . . some were not."

"I know you."

She looked startled and strangely hopeful. "You do? Tell me."

"You look like him."

"Who?"

I swallowed thickly. "That . . . man. On the bridge. The Alpha." I frowned. "And the other man. The one who . . ."

I found you.

I bent forward, sure I was going to vomit. I gagged, my nose bumping against my knee.

The woman watched me.

The dizziness passed. I coughed and grimaced. "Shit."

"Shit," Elizabeth agreed. "The Alpha is my son. Joe. And the other man you refer to is also my son."

"Kelly."

"Yes. In fact, my eldest was there too, though I don't think you got to meet him properly. There will be time for that later. Why did you help him?"

I snapped my head up. "What?"

"Kelly," Elizabeth said. She looked down at her hands. Her nails were short and neat. "You helped him."

"I didn't mean to."

She laughed but didn't say anything else.

"You're a Bennett."

"I don't know that I appreciate the derision in your voice. It's a nice name. One I'm proud of despite everything."

"Joe is your son. Which makes him a Bennett."

"Yes. That's usually how it works."

"Which means Kelly is a Bennett."

"It's good to know your talent for stating the obvious remains remarkably intact," she said dryly.

I stood quickly, the blanket falling to the floor.

She didn't flinch as she looked back up at me. She wasn't scared. If anything, she was curious.

"What do you want with me?"

"Ah. I want many things with you, Robbie. But we'll get to that in time. You're under a sort of thrall. Or so I'm told. You do stink of magic. It's almost unbearable."

I took a step toward her.

She remained still.

"You want to kill my Alpha."

She said, "Michelle Hughes."

I nodded.

"Then yes. I do."

I snarled at her.

She shrugged. "I'm not sorry about that. Alpha Hughes has taken something that doesn't belong to her. Many somethings, in fact."

I rushed toward her.

The silver line burned. "Ow, *ow*, mother*fucker*!" I hopped back, looking down at my toes as they blackened before beginning to heal. "That hurt!"

"I should think so," she said. "You're a wolf. It's silver. It's supposed to hurt."

I glared at her. "You said I wasn't going to be harmed!"

"Yes. I did. But I can do nothing when you do it to yourself. You always were a little eager."

"Lady, I don't know who the fuck you are, and I don't know who the *fuck* you think I am—"

"You're Robbie Fontaine," she said. "Born January 21, 1991. You're twenty-nine years old. Your father was a hunter. Your mother was a lovely woman. She died protecting you. In fact, her last act was to ensure your survival."

"Oh, so you can read a file. I'm sure you've got all that shit on me—"

"You hate Brussels sprouts," she said, and I gaped at her. "You think they stink. Same with pickles, though you do like cucumbers because of the way they crunch in your teeth, especially when you've shifted. You like to read. Weirdly, and endearingly, you have an affinity for romance novels from the eighties. You're computer smart and a little real-world stupid, though it comes from your desire to see the good in everything and everyone. You like trees. You can spend hours lying underneath one, just staring up at the sky through the leaves." She blinked rapidly against the sheen in her eyes, but she never looked away from me. "You're a good man. A lovely man. And I've missed you so."

"What is happening?" I asked hoarsely.

"Something that should have happened a long time ago. And I'm sorry that it didn't. We were . . . we were confused. Angry. At what, I don't think we knew. Not exactly. But . . ." She sighed. "I can't promise you it's going to be easy. I fear the days ahead will provide us with more questions than answers. And with all that we have to face, I don't know if we have the time."

"Where am I? Why are you keeping me here? What the hell do you want from—"

A door opened.

Another woman walked through and closed it behind her. She was muscular and tan, and her head was shaved on one side. On the other, her brown hair was parted over the top of her head, hanging in sharp spikes on the shaved side. Her green eyes were bright and wide as she glanced at me before looking at Elizabeth on the floor.

Human. She was a human.

But she smelled like wolves. Overwhelmingly so.

She crouched next to Elizabeth, their shoulders bumping together. "How's it going?"

"It's going," Elizabeth said.

"That good, huh?"

"He thought about attacking me but burned his toes."

The woman shook her head. "Men. They never learn."

"No, I don't suppose they do."

"I'm standing right here," I snapped.

"Observant," the woman said. She eyed me up and down. "He's bigger. Wider, I think. Looks like he's finally gotten some muscle. Still short, though."

For reasons I didn't care to think about, I covered my bare chest with my arms. "Would you stop ogling me!"

They ignored me. "Needs a haircut," the woman said.

"Eh. I kind of like it long." Elizabeth frowned. "Huh. That's not the first time I've said that. Interesting."

The woman slowly turned to look at Elizabeth. "Did you just make a *sex* joke? Oh my god, I'm going to tell *everyone*."

"Robbie," Elizabeth said, "this is Jessie Alexander. You met her brother, Chris, during your little bridge adventure. One of the wolves."

I scowled at them.

"Yeah, that sounds about right," Jessie said. "Good to know that dipshit look on his face hasn't changed. Kelly's asking about him."

That caught my attention. "He's awake?" I demanded. "Where is he? What happened to him? What did Ezra do to him?" The silver was once again singeing my toes, but I didn't care. There was a pulse in my head, and it was Kelly, Kelly, Kelly.

Elizabeth cocked her head. "Interesting. Yes, Robbie. Kelly's awake. He has been for a while now. We were waiting on you. It's been six days since the bridge."

My knees weakened, and I took a stumbling step back. "No. That's not . . . that's impossible."

"I think you'll find many things you thought impossible are now reality," Elizabeth said, not unkindly. "I don't know what will happen, Robbie. I don't know if anything can ever go back to the way it once was. This . . . world. This life. Sometimes I think we're cursed. After everything we've been through, everything we've done, there's always more. Mistakes were made, and I—"

And then I said, "To my beloved. Never forget."

The wolf mother moved quicker than I could follow. Her eyes blazed as she stood before me, just on the other side of the line of silver. Her claws were long black hooks that gleamed in the low light. "Where did you hear that?"

My shoulders slumped. "There was a book. In Michelle's office. I found it."

"What is it?" Jessie asked. "What's he talking about?"

"A gift," Elizabeth said. "To my late husband. It would seem Alpha Hughes has kept something else that doesn't belong to her. Good to know."

She turned and stalked from the room.

"Well, shit," Jessie said, staring after her. "Way to go."

"I don't know why I said it."

"Yeah. You usually don't. It's part of your charm." She shook her head. "Look, Robbie, I know you have questions. Probably a lot of them. And we're going to answer them. I swear. It's just . . ." Her expression hardened as she looked at me. "It's just a lot to take in right now. We never thought we'd see you again."

"You're lying," I whispered, even though her heartbeat was even.

"I'm not. And you know it. This is your home. We're your pack." She took a deep breath. "Thirteen months ago, you were taken from us. Stolen away by the man you call Ezra. His real name is Robert Livingstone, and he took your memories. Of this place. Of all of us. Of the man you love. The man you're mated to."

"No," I told her as the room grew brighter. "No. No. No. That's not real. None of this is real. You're lying. You're all fucking lying. You're Bennetts. You are the *enemy*. You are—"

"If I'm lying, then why do you have a mate mark on your shoulder? Mystical moon magic bullshit."

My hand went to my neck. "Are you out of your goddamned mind? I don't have a—"

My fingers traced over bumpy scar tissue, ridged and hard.

I turned my head.

There, between my neck and my shoulder, was the imprint of fangs in my skin.

"It was a glamour," Jessie said quietly. "Gordo was able to destroy it, though he can't do much more right now, given all the energy he expended in the last week. It's like it is with the Omegas. He thinks there's a door. It's locked, and we don't have the key."

My fingers shook as I pressed down into the scar tissue.

"Welcome home, Robbie," she said as she turned toward the door.

But she stopped with her hand on the doorknob.

Her shoulders were stiff.

She didn't turn to look at me when she said, "And I know you won't understand, but I've waited a long time to tell you this. If you ever lay your hand on my brother again, it'll be the last thing you do."

And then she was gone.

I paced back and forth around the room, looking for weaknesses. There were none.

The line of silver was absolute. The walls were made of thick concrete.

I listened for the sounds of anyone above me, but I heard nothing—not because no one was there, but because there was an *absence* of sound. The room was soundproof.

It didn't stop me from yelling until my voice was hoarse.

I sliced the walls with my claws, causing sparks to shoot out around me.

I threw my weight against the line of silver.

I prowled the edges of the room.

"It's a trick," I muttered to myself, refusing to look at the mark on my shoulder. "That's all this is. A trick. They're trying to trick me. Trying to get in my head."

And fuck, did it make me angry.

It was while I was making yet another path around the room that I saw it—a blinking light up in the far corner near the ceiling.

A camera.

I was being watched.

I glared up at it. "Is this what you want?" I shouted. "I don't know who the fuck you think I am, but you're *wrong*. Let me out!"

Of course, there was no response.

Which made me *angrier.*

I overturned the cot, throwing the thin frame against the wall, where it snapped and fell to the ground in pieces.

It wasn't enough. I needed to break it more. Except I tripped over my backpack, which had been underneath it.

I landed on the ground, hard. I groaned as I rolled onto my back.

I hoped whoever was watching me got a good laugh out of that, and that they choked on it.

I sat up, pulling my backpack toward me. My glasses sat on top of it, thick frames with nonprescription lenses. I put them on, brushing my hair back off my face. I unzipped the main pocket of the bag, sure that most of my hastily packed belongings would be gone.

They weren't.

Everything still seemed to be there.

In the bottom left corner was my mother's driver's license.

Next to it was a stone wolf.

The journal I'd found in Michelle's office sat underneath them both.

I grimaced as the mark on my neck pulled.

I pulled the backpack into my lap, hugging it close.

And then I did the only thing I could.

I waited.

* * *

Time became elastic. I didn't know if it was day or night. I was disoriented. The room around me was large, but it felt like the walls were inching closer and closer.

It might have been only minutes or it could have been hours and hours before the door opened again.

The Alphas walked in, followed by the witch.

I hugged my backpack closer in case they were here to take it from me. If they were, they were in for a fight.

The witch shook his head at the sight of me. "I should have broken those damn glasses while I had the chance."

I snapped my teeth at him. "I'd like to see you try."

Gordo rolled his eyes. "Sure, kid. I'll get right on that."

The Alphas didn't speak. The bigger one stood with his hands folded behind him, a grave look on his face. The other one—Joe—was next to him, their arms brushing. It struck me then that they moved in sync with each other. Even their breathing was in unison. I didn't know how there could be two Alphas in a pack, but here it was, right in front of me. They were a pair. Mated. It should have been impossible.

And yet here they were.

Another man came in behind them, closed the door, and leaned against it. His head was shaved to the scalp, and he had a thick beard, but it didn't completely cover the tattoo on his neck. A raven, the wings spreading out over his throat, tail feathers disappearing into the collar of his shirt.

The same raven that was on the witch's arm.

So that's how it was. Witch and wolf. Alpha and Alpha.

I'd have to remember that if I got out of here. Michelle and Ezra would want to—

Grief.

A wave of blue, a riptide pulling me under.

Ezra. The way he'd smiled at me. The way he'd held my hand. Touched my hair. Cared for me. Protected me. Loved me.

But he wasn't Ezra at all.

They'd called him Robert Livingstone.

He'd called *himself* that. And if Michelle didn't know, then she was in danger.

Unless.

Unless she *did* know.

I'd never felt more lost.

"Where am I?" I asked miserably, not expecting an answer.

"Green Creek," Gordo said, crouching down to inspect the line of silver.

"I don't know where that—"

"Oregon."

My eyes bulged. "*What?*"

The Alphas didn't speak. The man against the door frowned.

The witch stood again. He glanced down at the stump of his arm, scowled at it, and then glanced back at the Alphas. "You sure about this? We don't even know if it's going to work. It probably won't. Aileen and Patrice think it's gone too far."

That didn't sound good. "Then maybe you shouldn't even try."

Gordo laughed. "Yeah, sure, kid. We'll keep that in mind." He shook his head. "I'll be damned if it isn't good to hear your voice, though."

"He's different," the man against the door said. "Holds himself differently. Moves differently."

"That's what happens when your mind is wiped," Gordo told him. "There's a difference between destroying a specific memory and taking years' worth. My father went too far. It's like a blank slate. Or close to one. You notice the little flashes, though? The glimpses peeking through?"

The man nodded.

"He couldn't take everything," the witch said. "Though I'm sure he tried. I bet he even tried to put in *new* memories, but that's probably beyond even him. And I don't think it would've worked on Robbie."

"Why?"

"You heard what he said at the bridge. He underestimated the bonds in the pack." Gordo glanced at me. "He didn't know just how strong Robbie was. He had to have fought like hell against my father. He wouldn't have made it easy to do what he did." His voice held a note of pride, and it took me a moment to realize it was directed toward me.

"I don't believe you," I told them helplessly. "Ezra wouldn't . . . he's not *like* that."

Gordo snorted. "You keep telling yourself that. The stories I could tell you would make your toes curl. Let's just say I'm not sending him a card for Father's Day this year. And the name Ezra is fake, kid. He's Robert Livingstone. Try to keep up, all right?"

The man against the door covered a smile like it was a secret.

The Alphas still didn't speak.

"Okay," Gordo said. "Let's get this shit show on the road. Mark, the others ready?"

The man stepped away from the door, pulling it open behind him. A burst of sounds and smells and *color* filled the room. He raised his voice and said, "You guys good?"

"Yeah," a male voice called from somewhere above us. "But I'd hurry up if I were you, bird neck. We're getting antsy up here. Carter's shadow is trying to hump his leg—"

"He is *not*!" another voice cried. "Rico, for fuck's sake, would you keep your goddamn mouth shut?"

Mark's lips twitched. "They're ready." He closed the door again and stepped forward until he was behind Gordo, putting a hand on his shoulder.

Gordo took a deep breath and closed his eyes. The tattoos on his arms burst brightly, and the room filled with the ozone smell of magic. I hissed at it, and him, but he ignored me.

Mark's eyes began to glow.

Violet.

And I was distracted by it, distracted by what it meant, what was happening to me here, in this place. The raven on his throat fluttered its wings, and then—

Gordo kicked his leg out, foot scraping through the line of silver, breaking the barrier. "Ox, *now*."

The big Alpha was moving even as the silver parted.

He was on me before I could react.

He wrapped his hand around my throat, pushing me back. I fell to the ground as he landed on top of me. I tried to knock him off me, but he was too heavy. His face was inches from mine. I whimpered as his eyes filled with a swirling mixture of red and violet. They were endless pools of Alpha and Omega, and I couldn't look away.

And then he roared as loud as I'd ever heard.

The call of an Alpha.

I seized underneath him, an electrical shock rolling through me. My head snapped to the right and I was

(*in a clearing the moon bright and full and and and*)

screaming at the force of it, screaming though no sound came out, and I couldn't fight it, couldn't fight the

(*stars all those stars like ice like bright ice*)

strength of the Alpha above me, and he was tearing me apart, shredding me into tiny pieces and there was

(*a door there was a door a door a door a*)

I stood in the clearing under a brilliant night sky.

I wasn't alone.

Behind me was a door, an old metal thing that didn't cast a shadow.

In front of me was a group of people. The Alpha called Ox. The Alpha called Joe. Gordo. Mark. Elizabeth. Jessie. Four men I didn't recognize, though one looked like a bigger version of Joe and and and—

Kelly.

Kelly.

Kelly.

I screamed for him as my back arched off the ground, but the Alpha on top of me held me down, his hand tightening around my throat, and he roared at me again, and in my head, I heard thunderous voices, and they said *BrotherSonLoveFriend hear us hear us because we are pack and pack and PACK—*

The door behind me groaned in the clearing as I turned toward it.

A hand folded into mine.

I looked over. He was faint, a thin outline, faded.

He said, "I see you. I'll never—"

He was torn away as the door behind us screamed in metal. It pulsed, the surface becoming liquid glass, and a hand shot out of the door, covering my face and *pulling* me toward it. I cried out as I slammed into the door and began to sink into it.

I reached for the pack, begging them to save me.

They didn't.

None of them.

I

(*would you hear me dear*)

(*would you hear me*)

(*even in this place i can find you*)

(*because i love you i need you i can't live without you*)

(*they are trying to keep you from me*)

(*but they don't know do they*)

(*just how strong you are*)

(*and you're mine you're mine you're*)

I gasped as the clearing disappeared. The weight holding me down shifted as the Alpha slid off me, collapsing to the floor. I blinked against the light overhead.

"Shit," I heard Gordo mutter. "Goddammit. God*dammit!*"

"Hey, hey," Mark said, and I turned my head to see him cupping Gordo's face. "It's okay. We thought this would happen. At least now we know. You did what you could."

Joe knelt beside the Alpha, the one they'd called Ox. "All right?"

"More than I expected," he mumbled. "I can't—" He shook his head. "It was different. The door. It wasn't like it was before with the Omegas. I couldn't break it. Hell, I couldn't even touch it."

"That's because dear old dad learned a few tricks," Gordo said tiredly as Mark dropped his hands. "But fortunately for us, so have I."

Now.

Now.

Now.

I rolled back, bringing my legs up and over me, my hands flat on either side of my head. I pushed forward as I kicked my legs out, flipping up and landing on my feet.

They barely had time to react before I was through the silver line. I crashed into Gordo, shoving him into Mark before heading for the door.

I threw it open just as Joe shouted, "He's coming up!"

A set of stairs rose before me. I climbed them as quickly as I could, muscles stiff but holding. Another door at the top was partway open. Before I reached it, a face appeared—a man with dark skin and bushy eyebrows. "*Mierda*," he breathed, eyes wide. "This is gonna suck."

He slammed the door shut.

It didn't matter.

I threw myself against it, and it cracked in its frame before the wood splintered, exploding outward as I stumbled through it, managing to stay upright. The man at the top of the stairs was knocked off his feet, but I paid him no attention.

I was in a house.

A goddamn *house*. Sunlight streamed through the windows.

People were shouting all around me, but I ignored them. I charged toward one of the windows and crashed through it, the glass slicing into my skin.

I landed on the ground, curling into myself and rolling to absorb the impact. I was on my feet even as the glass continued to fall.

There was another house in front of me, a blue house next to a dirt road surrounded by an old forest. It all felt surreal, like I was caught in a dream. It smelled different, more potent, the scent in the air filled with wolves and magic, causing my chest to burn with each breath I took. I was so far from home. I looked around wildly before deciding on the road.

I made it three steps before my legs were kicked out from under me. I barely had time to make a sound before I hit the ground again, this time flat on my back.

A woman stood above me, pointing a crowbar at my face.

Jessie grinned. "Hey. This is fun."

I snarled at her as I knocked the crowbar away, gasping as my skin began to burn. There was fucking *silver* in the goddamn metal. Before I could even begin to think who the fuck would do something like that, she attacked.

I jerked my head to the right and the crowbar hit the dirt. She grunted when I kicked her in the hip, but she was already moving again by the time I sat up. She raised her thigh to her chest before kicking out toward my face.

I caught her foot.

She barely looked surprised.

I twisted it, intending on breaking her fucking ankle, but she moved with it, throwing herself to the side. She landed roughly, the crowbar bouncing from her hand.

"You *dick*," she groaned. "I'm going to kick your fucking—"

I was already up and moving, heading for the road.

I made it three steps before I was stopped again, a hand on my shoulder. I bared my fangs as I whirled around. The man didn't seem scared. "Hey, Robbie. I'm Chris. Good to see you again, dude."

I shoved him hard, sinking my claws into his chest, but he grabbed my hands as he grunted, pulling me down with him. He kept the momentum going as we fell back, his legs folding between us, feet pressed against my chest. He kicked me up and over him, and once again I landed flat on my back.

I really fucking hated this pack.

I was up on my feet again when a strangled yell came from behind me and some douchebag landed on my back, causing me to take a stuttering step forward. Legs wrapped around my waist and arms went around my neck, cutting off my airway.

"Hey," he panted in my ear. "It's me, Tanner. And honestly? I really didn't think this through. So if you could not hurt me, that'd be—"

I grabbed him by the arms and *yanked* as I bent forward, throwing him over my back. He landed with a jarring crash on the ground in front of me. He was older but strong. Another fucking wolf.

I went for his throat.

Jessie was there again, silent and deadly, crowbar forgotten on the ground. She cocked her fist back, broadcasting her next move a mile away. So imagine my dismay when, instead of punching me in the face, she wrapped her *other* hand around the back of my neck and pulled me forward, her knee going into my stomach.

She laughed as I bent over, my breath knocked from my chest. "I'm enjoying this far more than I expected. No offense."

I flashed my eyes at her, but she wasn't intimidated. I didn't know who the hell this human was, but I was pissed.

The man who called himself Tanner picked himself up off the ground, wincing as he did so. "Jesus. I thought being a werewolf meant I would be all badass at everything I did. This is frankly embarrassing."

From behind me came the telltale click of a gun.

I turned.

Standing on the porch was the man who'd been at the door near the top of the stairs. His eyes were cold, mouth set in a thin line.

Another human.

And he was pointing the gun at me.

"Yeah," he said. "*Lobito,* you don't want to fuck with me right now. I swear to God I'll shoot you in the fucking *balls* if you—"

My hand burned as I stooped down and picked up the crowbar, then hurled it at him. He barely ducked in time as the crowbar flew over his head and embedded itself in the side of the house.

He stared at me. "Oh, I am going to shoot you *so fucking much*—"

Ox burst through the doorway, pushing the man's arm down as he started to raise the gun.

"Oh, come on," the man said. "Just a little. Just a little gunshot. I won't aim for anything important."

"Your bullets are silver, Rico," Ox said.

The man frowned. "I know that. Oh. Right. It'll kill him." He squinted at me. "Are we sure that's not a good idea? I mean, if I hit him in the leg, we could always amputate it before—"

I snarled at him, keenly aware of the others moving slowly around me, circling.

Hunting.

Joe appeared behind him, followed by Gordo and Mark.

The odds were absolutely against me.

Good.

Fuck them.

Fuck them all.

They wanted to see what I could do?

Fine.

I grabbed Tanner, as he seemed to be the weakest of the wolves. He squawked angrily as I hurled him at the man named Chris. They fell back in a tangle of limbs.

I turned toward Jessie.

She was still smiling.

"What the fuck is wrong with you?" I demanded.

She shrugged. "I missed having someone scrappy to spar with. The others tend to be all brute strength. It's pretty insufferable when you think about it. Men."

"Chris," Rico said, "your sister is being mean again."

"She's got a point," Ox said mildly, as if they hadn't just kidnapped me and weren't trying to kill me.

"Tanner, would you get *off* of me?"

"I'm trying, but your foot is in my asshole!"

Joe sighed. "This isn't going like I thought it would."

"Come on," Jessie said, beckoning toward me as she bounced lightly on her feet. "Let's see what you got."

She wanted it?

Fine.

I went left.

She fell for it. *Again.*

I jerked right, grabbing her by the arm, spinning her around until her back was against my chest. And still she laughed like she was having the time of her life. I wrapped my arms around her and began to squeeze as hard as I could, intent on breaking her ribs.

"Not a victim," I heard her whisper before she kicked her legs up off the ground, throwing her entire body back against me. I couldn't stay upright, and for what felt like the millionth time in the past five minutes, I found myself on my back, staring up at the blue sky.

She was up before I could even consider moving. She stood above me, head cocked. "Huh," she said. "That was easy. I expected more from—"

She grunted as I returned the favor, sweeping my legs against her, sending her to the ground.

"Oh," Rico breathed from the porch. "You shouldn't have done that."

Jessie wasn't smiling anymore.

I turned, planning on running from these idiots, but I came face-to-face with another woman, this one smiling serenely. I hadn't even heard her approach. She was barefoot.

"Hello, Robbie," Elizabeth Bennett said. "You're looking less pale today. All this exertion is doing wonders, I think."

I punched her in the face.

Well, I *tried* to punch her in the face.

Except she caught my fist with one hand before I could connect.

"You *really* shouldn't have done that," Rico said from the porch. "I'm going to enjoy this. Destroy him, *mamacita*."

She squinted at me. "I don't know if all this violence is necessary."

I threw another punch.

She caught that one too.

She shrugged. "Okay, maybe a little necessary."

A bright flash exploded in my skull as she fucking *head-butted* me, her forehead crashing into mine. I gasped as stars shot across my vision. I staggered back, blood trickling down my face. Before I could recover, I bumped into something big. Something *hairy*.

I turned slowly as I wiped the blood away.

A gigantic timber wolf stood there, jaws open, fangs bright in the sunlight. Its eyes were violet, and before I could get a handle on the fact that there was yet *another* Omega, the large blond man standing next to the timber wolf said, "Hey. My mom just fucked your shit up. That's hysterical." He tried to take a step toward me, but the timber wolf moved between us, crowding against him. The man turned his blue eyes toward the sky as he sighed. "Dude, we've *talked* about this. Boundaries, okay? Just because you've got this stupid idea in your wolf brain that you need to be my shadow doesn't mean you can stop me from punching Robbie. Everyone else has gotten a chance. I want a turn."

The timber wolf growled.

The man scowled. "Don't you take that fucking tone with me. I don't need you to—"

"Robbie."

Grass.

Lake water.

Sunshine. So much sunshine. As if the world was on fire.

Kelly stood on the porch. His skin was pale, eyes sunken in his head. He stood between Ox and Joe. But he wasn't leaning on them. He was standing on his own, and even though he looked exhausted, he wasn't letting that stop him.

I'm your mate.

He wasn't like he'd been at the bridge.

Because he no longer smelled like wolf. Oh, the thick scent of *packpackpack* still poured off him, and he was theirs just as much as they were his, but it wasn't the same.

He was human.

Ezra had taken his wolf away.

The others disappeared.

I only had eyes for him.

He nodded slowly.

He said, "I know."

He said, "I know you're scared. Confused."

He said, "But we're not going to hurt you. You're safe, Robbie."

He said, "You're home."

I took another step toward him.

"That's it," he said, stepping away from the Alphas. Joe looked like he wanted to stop him, but he kept his hands at his side. "Hey. It's okay, Robbie. It's okay now. You're here." He smiled, though it was broken. "You're with me now."

It would be so easy.

To go to him.

To let him fix all of this.

To have him take me away.

And part of me wanted to. Part of me *believed* him. A quiet part, whispering in the dark, but there nonetheless.

But it was a trick.

It had to be.

They were Bennetts. And they were the enemy.

He knew then. The moment before I made my decision. I didn't know how. But he did.

Even as my muscles coiled, the skin around his eyes tightened.

There was an opening to my right. Chris and Tanner were spread too far apart.

The secret part of me whispered for me to stop. To stay. To *listen*.

I ran.

"Gordo!" Ox shouted.

The ground cracked under my feet. I zigzagged just as a column of rock rose from the split earth. Dirt hit my face. There was a loud *whoosh* as the rock grew, but I spun around it, heading for the forest.

As I hit the tree line, howls rose up behind me. And I swore there were Omegas running through the woods around me, eyes violet and hungry.

The chase was on.

GREEN CREEK / ON SUNDAYS

I thought about shifting, about putting my paws into the earth.
I didn't.
I was in a strange pack's territory, so far from home. I didn't know what would happen if I shifted. Even though I wanted nothing more than to feel the pull of the wolf, I couldn't take the chance of running into someone who didn't know about wolves.

Tree limbs slashed against me, the wind whipping through my hair. I could hear voices of humans and wolves from behind me as they chased me, and I made a split-second decision to move toward the sound of cars ahead. It sounded like there was a town somewhere in front of me, and if I could make it to it, they'd have to stop. The wolves wouldn't take the chance of exposing themselves to a group of unsuspecting humans.

It didn't take long to reach pavement. An old truck almost struck me as I stepped out onto the road. The tires screeched, and I raised my hands in front of me, the sharp smell of oil and exhaust assaulting my senses. The grill of the truck was less than a foot away as it came to a stop.

A woman leaned her head out the window. Her eyes were wide.

"*Robbie?*" she gasped. "What the hell are you—"

She cursed as I ran past the truck. The engine squealed as she threw it in reverse. I glanced over my shoulder to see her spinning the steering wheel expertly, the old truck wheezing and groaning as it whipped around, the smell of burning rubber filling the air.

Ahead, I could see the outline of buildings.

A town, just as I'd thought.

I saw an old sign set back in the trees, almost overgrown by bushes.

GREEN CREEK

The words were faded.

But underneath seemed to be a more recent addition, carved into the wood.

A wolf, head tilted back in a silent song.

It struck me as I crossed the town line that I was wearing shorts and nothing else.

I didn't have time to worry about it. If anything, I hoped people would see it and believe I was being chased. That I'd been kidnapped and attacked. There was still blood on my head, though the wound had closed. I'd find a cop, tell him about the weird people in the house at the end of the dirt road, and then I'd figure out what to do next.

The *problem* with that is the first human I came across said, "Robbie? Holy shit, when did you get back? When did they find you?"

I had no idea who he was. He was standing in front of a hardware store, a broom in his hands. His eyes were wide.

"You have to help me," I told him. "I've—there are people after me. I don't know who they are. They took me—"

He nodded, taking a step toward me. He looked around as if to make sure we weren't being overheard. He lowered his voice and said, "Is it a . . . wolf thing? Like, bad wolves or hunters again?"

I gaped at him. He wasn't a wolf. He wasn't in a *pack*. How the fuck did he know about any of this?

"Let me call Ox," he said, reaching into his pocket. "He's your Alpha. He'll know what to—"

I took off down the road, leaving him staring after me.

There was a diner ahead, warm and inviting. I could see an inflatable palm tree near the door. OASIS, the sign in the window said.

A few people sat at the counter, cups of coffee in front of them. They all turned as I pushed through the door, a bell ringing overhead.

"I need help," I said, even before the door closed behind me. "I need—"

An older white man sitting at the counter said, "Robbie? Hey! Holy shit, you're back! Where have you been?"

Jesus fucking *Christ*.

Everyone smiled at me as the man stood with a grunt. Their smiles faded as I took a step away from him. "Are you bleeding?" the man asked as he squinted at me. "Did it heal already?" He shook his head. "Shape-shifters. I'll never get over it. Well, that isn't exactly true. I did get over it when the pack paid for the motel room to get fixed after that whole mess with the Omegas. And that crazy hunter woman who loved God a little too much. And the bar exploding." He paused, considering. "A lot of shit happens with shape-shifters, huh? Crazy."

Before I could even begin to process *that,* an alarm began to blare.

I covered my ears as I winced. It sounded like an old tornado warning system, and it was *everywhere.* The people in the diner stood quickly, and I was shocked when the older man in front of me pulled out a gun. "Saddle up, boys," he said. "I haven't had a drink since I found out about werewolves, and I ain't gonna start now. I'm ready to kick some ass and take some names." He cocked the gun.

Who the fuck *were* these people?

"We need to wait for the Alpha, Will," a woman said. She was wearing a waitress uniform. She was Black and plump, her hair hanging in thick locs on her shoulders, and I was shocked into a stupor when she flashed violet eyes at me. "He'll know what to do. Ox knows everything."

The man with the gun—Will, apparently—snorted. "I hear you, Dominique. But who knows what's going on now? Best to shoot first and ask questions later." He laughed, as if he wasn't standing near an Omega. "Besides. The Alphas said we have to be on guard. And Ox knows what he's talking about. His momma taught him that, God rest her soul. Men! Follow me!"

I barely had time to step out of the way before the diner emptied, the others following Will outside. They all clapped me on the shoulder as they rushed by. One flashed his eyes at me. It was another fucking Omega.

I was left alone with the waitress.

She eyed me warily. "You came back."

"Omega," I growled at her.

She took a step back, wringing her hands. "Okay. I get it. Jessie said that you were—"

I started to walk toward her when the alarm grew louder. It pounded in my head. I bent over, trying to block it out, but it was no use. By the time I stood back upright, the Omega was gone, the door that led back to the kitchen swinging on its hinges.

I ran out of the diner, hitting the sidewalk.

People rushed around me as the alarm continued to blare.

I watched as windows were shuttered in the businesses up and down the street. People inside pulled down metal grates, and even from a distance, I could feel the burn of silver as it reflected in the sunlight. The grates had *silver* built into them, as if the entire fucking town *knew* about wolves and their weaknesses.

Aside from the diner behind me, only one other place wasn't being closed up.

A shop across the street. It looked like a mechanic's. One of the garage doors was wide open. Maybe there'd be a phone inside I could use. I didn't know *who* I was going to call, but it felt like the only option.

I wouldn't realize my mistake until later.

I ignored the sign above the garage and the single name on it.

I ducked into an alley as that old truck reappeared down the main thoroughfare. The woman from before was hanging out of it, driving at a crawl, shouting my name. She had a phone to her ear. "No," she was saying, "I don't know where he— Rico, I swear to God, if you yell at me one more time, I'm going to break up with you, and you will *never* find someone as good as me as long as you live, you hear me? Send the wolves. They can sniff him out—"

She drove right by me, still yelling into the phone.

I stepped out from the shadows of the alley. The street was almost empty now, the businesses all closed up. I looked up and down the road. No pack. No wolves.

I took off across the street, waiting for someone to shout my name, tell me to stop.

No one did.

The garage was empty and smelled of oil and metal and wolves. A car sat up on one of the lifts. An SUV had its hood up, sunlight filtering in through the skylights overhead. There were three doors inside the garage. One looked like it led out to the back. Another led to the front of the garage and what seemed to be a waiting room.

The third door led to a small office with an ancient desk and a newer computer. The keys on the keyboard had smudges of oil on them. The screen of the monitor was dark.

Next to it was a phone, the cord spilling off the side of the desk.

I picked it up and breathed a sigh of relief when I heard the dial tone above the siren ringing through the streets of Green Creek.

That relief, so green in all this blue, disappeared a second later.

I didn't know who to call.

Ezra wasn't...

He wasn't who he said he was.

I'd *seen* the way his body changed, the years fading off him as he descended from the ruins of the bridge. He hadn't been slumped over like age had ravaged his body.

And he'd said his name was Robert Livingstone.

Gordo had called him *father*.

Which meant—

Fuck. I didn't know what it meant. It was lost in the storm in my head.

Alpha Hughes, but then...

I had no one.

I had no one I could call.

I was alone.

It wasn't grief that hit me then, but it was close. It was something alive and dark, clawing at my chest.

I put the phone back in its cradle.

I had nowhere to go.

No friends.

No family.

No pack.

Nothing.

My chest hitched. I let out a shuddering breath, eyes stinging.

And then I saw it—the photograph next to the computer.

The glass covering the photo was dusty, covered in smudged fingerprints, as if it were picked up often.

I recognized the house I'd just escaped from in the background, a dusting of snow on the ground around it.

And standing in front of it was a wolf pack.

Ox was there, arms across his chest, a quiet smile on his face.

Joe stood next to him, head tilted back in laughter.

To Ox's right was the witch, Gordo. He was scowling, but there was a vibrant spark in his eyes.

Mark held on to Gordo's elbow, as if he were about to turn the witch toward him. The raven on his neck looked so real, I expected it to fly away.

On Joe's other side were Tanner and Chris and Rico. They appeared to be wrestling, with Chris standing in the middle, holding Tanner and Rico in headlocks on either side of him. He was grinning, a big goofy thing that made me ache.

Next to Rico was Carter, glaring at the timber wolf, who had its tongue lolling out of its mouth. But his hand was on its back, fingers curled into the hair.

And then . . .

I saw me.

I looked different. My dark hair was shorter, the sides shaved with length left on top. My green eyes were bright, my glasses sitting crooked on my face. I looked loose and happy. I wore a leather jacket that looked a little big on me, with a patch on the front that looked like a raven. I thought it was Gordo's.

I wasn't looking at the camera or at any of the others.

I only had eyes for one person.

And oh, was he *smiling* at me as if I were the only thing in his entire world. Our hands were joined between us, and Kelly Bennett had stars in his eyes. He was taller than me, his head tilted downward as he watched me. I looked as if I were in the middle of telling a story he'd heard a million times. And even though it looked cold, he was wearing a thin shirt. No jacket. Peeking out from the collar was a dimple in the skin.

The top of a scar.

Without thinking, I reached up and touched my own neck. Rigid bumps extended down to the top of my shoulder.

It was a glamour, Jessie whispered in the storm.

All those times I'd thought I felt something there.

All those times I'd rubbed my neck, sure something was off.

I picked up the photo, bringing it close to my face, sure I'd be able to see whatever trick this was. Photoshop. It had to be Photoshop. It was the only thing that made sense. They'd lifted my image and put it in this picture.

But for the life of me, I couldn't ever remember a time I'd been so happy.

The glass above my face was smudged the most, as if whoever sat at this desk had brushed a finger over it more than the others.

I was startled when the frame splintered in my hands, the glass suddenly filled with a spiderweb of cracks.

I felt weak.

Tired.

The photo slipped from my hands and landed back on the desk. The glass broke, and the back of the frame popped off as it bent. The photo landed facedown, and I could see words written on the back of it, though I couldn't make them out.

I pulled the back of the ruined frame off, letting it fall on the desk.

I could see the words clearly now.

SUNDAY TRADITION
FEB 3 2019

I couldn't breathe.

The walls were closing in.

I had to get out of here.

I had to leave.

I stumbled from the office and headed toward the front. I pushed through the other door just as the siren cut off midscream, and I was *assaulted* by images hung on the walls.

There I was, standing between Chris and Rico, my arms around their shoulders.

There I was, bent over the open hood of a car, Rico scowling above me as I held a hammer.

There I was with Tanner, wearing a work shirt similar to his, ROBBIE stitched into the patch on the chest.

There I was alone, sitting at the counter that stood right behind me now, my head tilted to the side as I held a phone against my cheek with my shoulder, typing on the computer.

There I was, my head pressed against Ox's forehead, his hand wrapped around the back of my neck, fingernails a little dirty.

There I was standing in front of the shop, surrounded by all of them, the name GORDO's on a sign above us. All of our arms were crossed, and somehow I just *knew* we were supposed to be unsmiling, but my lips were quirked, and Tanner and Rico looked like they were struggling not to laugh. Chris was winking at the camera. Gordo was scowling. Ox was intimidating.

But we were together.

All of us.

I fit with them. Somehow, in these photos, in these frozen memories I couldn't remember, I fit.

I belonged with them.

To them.

This Robbie, whoever he was, had a home.

There was a corkboard next to the photos on the wall. Above it was a framed certification of some kind. And on the board were notices for a school play, a garage sale from six months ago, a request for a specific part someone was looking for, and—

And me.

A flyer with my picture on it.

Stark black words across the top.

HAVE YOU SEEN ME?
ROBBIE FONTAINE
MISSING SINCE 2/17/19

"It was a Sunday," a voice said from behind me.

I looked over my shoulder. Everything felt like it was in slow motion.

Kelly stood in the open door at the front of the shop, smiling tightly. He was breathing heavily, as if he'd just run and wasn't used to the exertion. A sheen of sweat was on his forehead, and he reached up to wipe it away.

Whatever he saw on my face caused his heartbeat to trip all over itself, and the blue came back, sharp and all-consuming. He wasn't smiling anymore.

I didn't know what to say.

He let the door close behind him.

Whatever else he was feeling through all that grief, he wasn't scared. There was no fear in his movements, though he kept his distance, staying near the door.

Outside and across the street near the diner, I could see Carter watching us, talking into a phone. I couldn't focus on what he was saying. Everything felt too loud. It didn't matter. I no longer had the strength to run.

Add in the fact that the timber wolf was sitting on its hindquarters next to him right out in the open, and I didn't know what was real.

"It was a Sunday," Kelly said again, voice quiet. "We have this . . . thing. On Sundays. No matter what's going on, no matter what we're doing, we come together as pack. We make a lot of food, but it's not really about that. It's about being together. As a family." He shrugged awkwardly. "We've always done it. Goes back a long time. Before me and Carter and Joe."

I found my voice, rough though it was. "Tradition."

The look of hope on his face was like the sun coming out from behind the clouds. "Do you remember—"

"No. It was on the back of the photo in the office."

The hope shattered, but he covered it up quickly. "Yeah. I . . . That's Gordo's. He used to act like he didn't give a shit about all of this, but after he and Mark . . ." He shook his head. "It doesn't matter. It was hard on him. I didn't expect that. I knew the two of you were close, but his anger almost matched my own, and I thought—I don't know what I thought."

I didn't either. Here was this man, this stranger, who claimed we were connected. That we were *mates*. And I didn't know him. "Why?"

"Why what?"

"You say I was taken. Me. Why?"

He looked over his shoulder at the window. Across the street, Carter started to take a step toward us, but Kelly shook his head. Carter didn't look happy, but he stayed where he was. The timber wolf bumped his head against Carter's chest.

Kelly turned back to me, squaring his shoulders. "We think it's because of your connection with Alpha Hughes. You were part of her pack. Before you came to ours. Years ago. We weren't here when you arrived. My brothers. Gordo. The others, they thought you were going to spy on them."

I was shocked. Nothing made sense. "*Years?*" I asked incredulously. "Are you really trying to tell me I've been in this pack for *years?*"

"Yes," he said simply.

I put my hand against the wall to hold me up. I breathed through my nose. "Ezra wouldn't—"

And though he was no longer a wolf, I swore his eyes flashed.

"Ezra doesn't exist. Not like you know him. Not like he led you to believe. His name is Robert Livingstone. I don't know what you've been through or what he's done to you, but he's not who you think he is. He's warped you somehow. Messed with your head. He took all of us away from you." The last words came out in a thin choke. "He took *me* away from you. And he took you away from me."

I shook my head. "I can't—it doesn't—it's not *possible*."

"It is," he said sadly. "And I'm sorry, Robbie." He took a step toward me. "I'm sorry this is happening to you. I don't know what it's like to be in your head right now. All of this, these last few days, I know it sounds crazy. But I have no reason to lie to you. Listen, okay? Listen to my heart."

I was helpless to do anything but.

"You were gone," he said, taking another step. "On assignment. Helping Omegas. We've got this system. It's complicated, but think of it as a sort of underground railroad. Long story, but you were helping an Omega get to a pack that would take them in. You went alone because it was just up into Washington. A quick trip."

He might as well have been talking about someone else. I had no memory of any of it. But his heartbeat never wavered. It was light and quick, like he was nervous, but steady.

"And something happened there," he continued. "He changed you, whether it be to act as a mole or a weapon, we don't know."

He was so close.

I took a step away from him, but my back hit the wall, the photos rattling. I shook my head. "No, that's not—he wouldn't *do* that to me. His name is Ezra. He found me. I was lost and he found me. He gave me a home. He gave me a purpose. He gave me *focus*—"

"He lied to you," Kelly said. He sounded like he was pleading. "You have to see that. He's not who he said he was. He's not—"

I laughed. It sounded crazed. Everything was spinning out of control. "I'm not who you think I am. Look, I don't know what they've told you, I don't know what you think—"

"I don't *think*," he snapped at me, and oh, *there* was anger, fierce and burning. "I *know*. I know you, Robbie. I see you."

"Don't. Don't you fucking do this. Get out of my head. Get out of my *head*!"

I didn't mean to do what happened next. It just happened.

One moment his eyes were wide and he was reaching for me, hand trembling, and the next he was gasping as I lashed at him, claws out. It was a shallow cut, two grooves on his forearm that immediately filled with blood.

He pulled away quickly, eyes wide and shocked.

A coppery tang filled the air.

A loud roar come from across the street, but I didn't care. I reached for Kelly again.

And he *flinched*.

He was *scared* of me. The wound wasn't closing.

Because he was human. Breakable and soft.

A red sheen fell over my vision.

I whirled toward the wall of memories that meant nothing to me.

There I was. Smiling and happy. Like I belonged.

And it was all a lie.

I howled in rage and began to tear the photographs off the wall. The frames and glass broke apart as I threw them on the floor. I barely noticed, only wanting to get rid of this goddamn imposter grinning at me mockingly.

I gouged the wall with my claws, chunks of plaster landing on my bare feet. Glass cut into my soles, but I ignored it. I felt the squelch of blood with every step I took, the scent mingling in with Kelly's wound, and it drove me fucking crazy.

I saved the flyer for last.

HAVE YOU SEEN ME?

I tore it down.

It wasn't enough.

I grabbed the corkboard, ripped it off the wall. I hurled it toward the front window, which shattered as the heavy board struck it, spilling glass onto the sidewalk.

Kelly said, "Don't, Carter, *don't!*"

Thick arms wrapped around me, pinning me. I struggled, screaming and kicking, but it was no use. Carter held firm. I lifted my legs and pressed my feet against the ruined wall, leaving bloody prints as I kicked off it as hard as I could.

Carter stumbled back, but he didn't let go.

"Stop," he growled in my ear. "Robbie, Jesus Christ, *stop*!"

I laid my head against his shoulder and howled my fury, a frenzied song filled with horror.

And then it all left me, just as quickly as it came.

I sagged against Carter.

I breathed heavily. I thought I was hyperventilating.

The timber wolf stalked in front of me, eyes bright and violet. Its lips pulled back in a sneer, nose twitching.

"Let me go," I gasped. "Please. Just let me go."

"Can't do that," Carter said, sounding winded. "Who knows what you'd try and do?"

As much as I hated to admit, he had a point.

Before I could say anything else, a wolf pack gathered in front of the garage.

"Well, shit," Tanner said. "How many times do we gotta fix the goddamn windows here?"

"Eh," Chris said, crouching down and squinting at the damage. "Could be worse. At least no one's guts or bones are hanging out this time." He frowned. "That seems to happen to us a lot. I wish I'd known that before the whole, 'hey guys, werewolves are real, do you want to be in a pack?'"

"Too soon," Rico muttered. He was glaring at me, and I thought I saw real hatred in his eyes. "I still have nightmares about it."

Elizabeth was trying to get a look at the cuts on Kelly's arm, but he wasn't having any of it. He pushed her away, trying to come toward me, but stopped when Ox flashed his eyes and stepped into the shop. Beyond him, Joe was out in the streets, talking to a gathering crowd of people. He glanced back at me and then turned toward the people, speaking in hushed tones. Jessie was with him, standing close to the Omega woman from the diner. She was whispering in Jessie's ear. Jessie looked stricken.

"You're fixing all of this," Gordo said, looking disgusted as he stared at the wall I'd destroyed. "I don't care if your brain is scrambled. You can patch it and install new windows. And I swear to God, if you give me any shit for it, I will turn you inside out."

"He threatens a lot," Mark said, sounding amused. "You get used to it." He blanched. "Or you will. Again." His brow furrowed.

Gordo snorted. "Real helpful, Mark."

Ox stood before me. He looked like a mountain, solid and sure. He said, "Let him go, Carter."

"I don't know if that's a good idea—"

"Carter."

"Fine. But if he goes for Kelly again, I'll rip him in half. I don't give a shit what anyone says. No one touches my brother. Ever." He squeezed me so hard I thought my ribs would break, and then he let me go.

I sagged forward, legs unable to support me.

But Ox.

Ox caught me.

He cupped my face, and oh my god, he was *Alpha,* he was Alpha, and the wounded noise that punched out of me was low and miserable.

His eyes filled with a swirling mixture of Alpha red and Omega violet.

There was a whisper in my head, crawling along tangled knots that felt like they were rotting. It said *i know i know i know you're frightened i know you're confused but listen listen listen.*

I could do nothing else.

He said, "You're mine, Robbie. My wolf. My pack. My Beta. My love. My brother. And I won't let anything happen to you. No one will take you from us ever again."

He bent his face toward mine and pressed a soft kiss against my forehead.

And I said, "*Oh,*" before all I knew was darkness.

WEREWOLF JESUS / MY FATHER

I wasn't a prisoner. They tried to make that much clear.

That didn't stop them from keeping me locked behind a line of silver in the basement of the house at the end of the lane. Oh, they fed me and made sure I had anything I asked for, but it didn't matter, as I didn't ask for much. I barely talked.

Kelly didn't come down. At least not for the first couple of days.

When I was alone, I prowled along the edges of the room, trying to find any weaknesses. Even though I knew I was being watched, I still tried.

There was nothing.

Even the free-standing toilet next to a partition was bolted down. I could rip it up, but then I'd have to shit in a corner.

"You're not the first person to be held down here."

I grunted but didn't turn around, running my hands along the wall. I was surprised he was the first. I thought it would be someone else—Elizabeth or the Alphas.

"Sucks, right? I was down here a few times. Kinda pissed me off, but what can you do?"

That caught my attention. "Why?"

"Why what?" Carter asked.

"Why were you down here?"

"Oh. Well . . . it's a long story."

"I'm not going anywhere."

Carter snorted. "Funny. I don't know why I forgot how funny you could be. It's annoying."

I didn't say anything.

He sighed. "Listen, you can—would you look at me?"

I thought about ignoring him. I turned around instead.

He looked exasperated as he pushed himself off the wall. "There. Was that so hard?"

"Where's your shadow?"

"Fuck if I know." He shook his head. "I ditched him in the woods. Figured it'd give me a few moments alone with you. He's not going to be happy when he finds me, but fuck that guy. You know how hard it is to jerk off when a wolf is watching you?"

I gaped at him.

He rolled his eyes. "Don't look so offended. We don't have boundaries here. The quicker you learn—*re*learn—that, the better off we'll be. It's probably not healthy, but it works for us." He paused. "Well, most of the time." He shuddered. "I could have gone through the rest of my life without knowing Joe is a screamer."

I laughed. I didn't mean to. It caught me off guard. He looked just as surprised as I did. He stared at me in wonder with that dopey look I was coming to expect from him. I knew what he was going to say next even before he opened his mouth. "I missed that. You. Laughing. It's a good sound, man."

I looked away.

He sobered. "Anyway. My dad . . ." He swallowed thickly. "My dad used to bring us down here when we were little. Told us that it wasn't a place for us to play. But you know how it is. You tell a kid not to do something and they just have to do it. He yelled at us a few times. Especially when they had this rogue wolf down here who—uh, doesn't matter. I stood where you are now. A couple of years ago."

I lifted my head. "Why?"

He rubbed the back of his neck. "I don't know how much I'm allowed to tell you."

"Then why are you here?"

He shrugged. "To see you. Probably threaten you a little, if I'm being honest."

"How's that working out for you?"

"Okay. So far. I mean, you're the one behind the silver and I can go outside whenever I want."

I scowled at him. "I don't like you."

He nodded. "Oh, sure. Most don't. I tend to grow on people, though. Like a fungus. Give it time. You'll love me soon enough. You did once. I can wait for it to happen again. I'm irresistible that way." He waggled his eyebrows at me. He looked ridiculous.

"Go away."

"Nah," he said easily. "I'm not—"

A snarl came from somewhere up inside the house.

Carter rolled his eyes. "Dammit. He found me quicker this time. Motherfucker."

The timber wolf appeared through the open door. It—*he*—didn't look pleased. He growled under his breath as he circled Carter. He narrowed his eyes as he glanced at me, and it was all the warning I needed. Fucking with Carter meant the wrath of the wolf. "Dude, stop it," Carter said, shoving the wolf's head away. "Go upstairs. I'm trying to talk to Robbie 2.0."

The wolf did not go upstairs. Instead, he sat down next to Carter, his massive head cocked.

"Good job," I said. "He really listens to you."

"Oh, fuck you, man. Seriously."

"Why doesn't he shift?"

"He can't," Carter said. "Or won't. We don't really know. He just stays as a wolf. It's kind of his thing."

"Like watching you masturbate."

"I hate everything. Including you."

"I'm heartbroken. Really. Why don't you let me out and I'll do my best to make amends."

Carter squinted at me. "Are you hitting on me?"

Jesus Christ. "No, Carter. I'm not hitting on you."

"Really? Because it sounds like you are."

The wolf bared his fangs. Ah. So that's how it was. Before I could comment on it, his eyes flooded with violet.

"An Omega," I said quietly. Because of course he was. I'd never seen so many of them in my life.

"Yeah," Carter said, looking at the wolf. "We don't know where he came from or how he came to be stuck like this. The Omega thing we've pretty much got figured out, but beyond that? I don't know."

I blinked. "What do you mean you've got it figured out? How the hell is there an Omega here? Why isn't he hurting anyone?" The woman in the diner. The Omegas in the woods. The fucking *kid* at the bridge. Brodie.

And with that, another memory.

Chris. Tanner. Carter. Don't hurt him. You hear me, whatever you do, don't—

"You're an Omega too."

"Yeah," he said, and he let his eyes fill. The violet was shocking, even though I knew it was coming. "And that's why I was down here where you are now. In fact, there was a time when our roles were switched. You stood where I am, and I was in there behind the silver."

I slumped against the wall, sliding down to the floor. "I don't understand. How are you able to control it?"

"Long story," he said again. "But the gist of it is Ox is like Werewolf Jesus, and there was this beast who murdered my dad and Ox's mom and then stuck his hand inside Ox and ripped out his guts—taking Ox's Alpha power away from him, even though he was still human—and then *he* turned into the Alpha for like six seconds. Then Joe ripped the bad guy's head off because of love and stuff, and since said bad guy was, like, leader of the Omegas, the Alpha power went *back* to Ox, and when he was turned into a wolf, there was a door that we closed, but then we shattered it because Mark and I got bit by a carrier of a magical Omega virus—Pappas, poor guy, got shot by someone who took the Bible a little too literally—and Ox became the Alpha of the Omegas, and now here we are." He shrugged. "Might have left out a few details here and there, but that's the nuts and bolts of it." He grinned at me. "You get all that?"

I stared at him.

His smile faded a little.

I said, "What."

"Yeah, right? It sounds crazy, but that's how it went. Some explosions too."

"And I was here for all of it."

"Most of it, yeah." His grin returned, taking on a wicked curve. "You wanted to fuck Ox for a long time. Or so I'm told. Tried to get all up on that Alpha junk."

I choked. "*What.*"

"Ah," he said. "I feel better now that that's all out in the open. So, I was reading up on amnesia, and Wikipedia told me that if I show you pictures, you'll remember. That didn't work so well at the garage, but that was probably a little overwhelming, right? At least now you know we aren't bullshitting you."

"I don't know that at *all*—"

He ignored me. "So, here. Take a look. Let's see if we can get the brain juices flowing. I mean, if we can control the Omega shit, who's to say we can't do something like that for you?" He pulled his phone out of his pocket. He took a step toward the line of silver, but the wolf was up in a flash, standing in front of him.

Carter thumped him upside the head. "Would you stop it? He can't hurt me. He's trapped." He looked at me earnestly. "We love you."

I was convinced the Omega in him was eating away at his brain. "Fuck you."

"No, thanks. I'm good." He tapped on the screen of his phone before holding it up against the barrier. "Take a look."

"Go away."

"Come on, man. Just look. What harm could it do? I mean, you could go crazy again and try to break things, but since you only have your backpack and your bed that we've already had to replace, that's all on you." He wiggled the phone at me.

I sighed as I pushed myself up off the floor.

"There we go," he said cheerfully. "That's it."

"You're an asshole," I muttered as I walked toward him.

The timber wolf growled at me. I flashed my eyes at him in warning.

I looked at the phone. "Instagram. You want me to look at your Instagram."

"Wow," Carter said. "I don't think I've ever heard so much disdain in such few words. Yeah, man. Look at my Instagram."

I did.

There were photos of the pack—all of them in some, just a few of them in others. One had Carter scowling in the mirror of a bathroom, the glowing violet eyes of the timber wolf in the background.

I was there too. Or rather, the version of Robbie they claimed to know. It was discordant, this feeling, recognizing my face but not remembering anything about who that person was supposed to be. I was laughing, I was smiling, I was staring up at the moon with a look of wonder.

The most recent one, in the top left corner, was of Kelly and me. We were sitting under a tree. Kelly lay with his head in my lap. My hands were in his hair. The caption said one word. Gross.

"Elizabeth said I was taken over a year ago."

"That's right."

"Why is that the last photo you posted, then? Why haven't you done more since?"

He took the phone away, looking down at the screen. A complicated expression crossed his face, and the room filled with the scent of blue, bright and cold. "Things just sort of... stopped. After you were gone. It didn't seem right, I guess." He cleared his throat. "I know you don't remember, but I do. And man, I gotta tell you, it sucked. For all of us. It hit harder for Ox and Gordo and especially Kelly, but yeah. We all felt it. Pack. It's all about pack."

"Oh."

"Yeah," Carter said. "Oh. It's like... part of us was missing." He looked up at me, mouth set in a thin line. "I don't expect you to understand, because you can't, obviously. You don't know. I think you might be better off because of it. It hurt, man. The hole in all of us was ragged and never seemed to heal. Even when we figured out where you were, like, eight months after you left, it still hurt. And I know you—"

The ground tilted beneath my feet. "You knew where I was?"

His eyes widened. "Oh shit. Totally forget I said that. I wasn't—dude, that's not what I meant at *all*."

The wolf tried to pull him away as I stepped right up to the line of silver. My skin tingled. My nose itched.

The timber wolf tried to pull Carter away, but he didn't budge.

"You care about me," I said in a dangerous voice. I felt like hunting. Carter was the perfect prey. "You love me. It's all about pack. That's what you said. All those wonderful words painting such a pretty picture. And if everything you've all told me is to be believed, I was part of this. This house. This town. Your pack. I was *taken* from you. I *left*. I was *stolen*. Which is it? And now you tell me you knew where I was this whole time? And you left me there?" I cocked my head at him. If not for the silver between us, my teeth would be in his throat. "Sounds like I didn't belong here as much as you're all claiming. Maybe I left because I wanted to. Because I didn't want to put up with all your bullshit."

I thought he'd cower and mutter and disappear up the stairs and try again another day. No. He looked pissed. He squared his shoulders, his lips curling. His blue eyes gave way to violet, and I could feel his animal lurking underneath. "After what you did? You're fucking lucky we even kept tabs on you at all when we found you. Even Rico said to just leave you where you were."

"What did I do?" I asked. It was a challenge, and I wanted to scream at him to fucking break the line of silver, to let me out and decide this like wolves. Oh, the timber wolf would be on me before I could get a hand on him, but I didn't care. Fuck them both. "Come on, *man*. Tell me what I did. You're angry. I can see it. You have been ever since you saw me at the bridge."

He faltered. He broke. He recovered. He said, "If you lay a hand on Kelly again, I'll tear off your fucking arm."

I smiled at him, a nasty thing that felt foreign on my face. "Try it, Bennett. See how far you get."

He left then. He didn't look back.

The timber wolf trailed after him. He stopped in the doorway, looking at me over his shoulder.

I turned my back to him.

Eventually he left too.

I dreamed, that second night, and it was blood and fire.

I screamed for someone to find me.

No one did.

I woke on the third day in the basement to something different. My mouth was dry and my eyes were gummy and stuck. I groaned as I sat up on the cot.

"Good morning," a quiet voice said.

I looked up.

Kelly sat against the far wall near the door. He had a blanket covering his lap. His arm was bandaged. He looked frail and weak, dark circles under his eyes, like he hadn't been sleeping. I wondered if he had nightmares.

I closed my eyes, hoping I was still dreaming.

I opened them. He was still there.

He pushed his hair off his forehead. He needed to get it cut. It was—

I stopped myself from thinking anymore. It didn't matter.

I grunted at him. If I didn't talk, maybe he'd go away.

"Are you hungry?"

Or maybe he'd just sit there. Goddammit. "No."

"You should still eat."

"I'm not hungry."

He shrugged. "It's there when you're ready." He nodded toward a tray on the floor. There was cereal in a chipped bowl and a small cup of milk. A spoon. A banana. A napkin. When I was fed, one of the humans would come with Ox or Joe and set the tray over the silver. I didn't smell the Alphas this time, though. Kelly must have done it himself.

It meant nothing.

He shivered, and before I could stop myself, I asked, "Are you cold?"

He nodded slowly. "Yeah. It's weird. I don't know how humans can stand it. I'm always freezing now, even when I'm outside." He chuckled, though it sounded forced. "Dumb, right? All the little things I never really thought about. Shifting. Being warm. Being able to smell my pack. Hearing where they were at all times. It's frustrating. I feel so . . ."

"Human."

He nodded. "Yeah. Jessie and Rico are . . . well. They're trying to help, but they don't get it, you know? It's like I'm locked in a windowless room and I can't find my way out."

"Yeah," I said, pointedly looking around the basement. "I wouldn't know anything about that."

He startled. "Huh. I never thought about it that way."

"Why don't you just have your Alphas bite you? Change you back?"

"We don't know what Livingstone did to me," Kelly admitted. "Not really. It's not so much that he trapped my wolf as much as he just . . . took it away."

I couldn't look at him.

"See?" he said after a moment. "Even a week ago, I'd have some idea of what you were thinking. Or feeling. Emotions have a scent to them. You don't really think about it much until it's gone."

"Scent memory."

"Yeah. Like that. Little reminders that open up something you haven't thought about in years. Smoke does that for me. I don't like the smell of smoke. It hurts."

Before I could stop myself, I asked, "Why?"

He picked at the blanket in his lap. "My father."

"What was his name?"

"Thomas."

"Thomas Bennett." TB.

"Yeah. He . . . died."

"I'm sorry."

He arched an eyebrow. "Are you?"

I shrugged. "I don't know. Did I know him?" Those last four words caused my head to spin.

"No. It was before you. Years ago." He paused like he was thinking hard. Then, "Seven years, to be exact. Seven years in a couple of weeks. Wow. I don't . . . That's a long time. Longer than I thought."

"How old were you?" And, "How old *are* you?"

His lips quirked. "Almost twenty-one then. And I'm twenty-seven now."

Only a couple of years between us. He looked younger than that. "What does your father have to do with smoke?"

He didn't look away when he said, "He burned. After he was killed. On a pyre in the woods. Wolves came from all over. We cried and howled. And I never forgot how the smoke smelled."

I didn't know what to say to that. Consoling him felt fake. I made a mistake instead. "Did Michelle come here too?"

His expression hardened. "No. She wasn't invited."

"Why? She's the Alpha of all. And if your family is as important as you're all telling me, then—"

"You really don't know, do you?"

I scoffed at him. "Just figuring that out, are you? Good for you."

He didn't take the bait. "My father was the Alpha of all. Like his father before him. He left Michelle in charge after Joe was hurt. When he was a kid. He brought us back here so that Joe could heal. So we all could heal."

He . . . took a boy, once. A little boy. A princeling, or as close to one as we have these days. This wolf hurt the boy terribly, and it was only by the grace of the moon that he was saved.

Reality shifted yet again. I searched my memory for *anything* about this, anything about the history being laid out before me, but once again came up empty. "How do I not know about any of this? Why didn't I know anything about your father?"

"We think he took everything away," he said, meaning Ezra. Or whoever the fuck he was supposed to be. "Like my wolf. He just wiped it out. Everything having to do with us. Your time here. Everything we went through." He gnawed on his bottom lip. "And there might even be a chance he took things from before you came. But if we don't know about it, and you don't, then it's kind of pointless to even think about."

I reached up almost unconsciously to touch the mark on my shoulder.

His gaze tracked my movement, but he didn't say anything about it.

"How long was I here?"

He hesitated. "You showed up about a month after we left. We were gone for almost three years, and you were part of Ox's pack by the time we got back. We think you were sent to spy on the pack while it was fractured. But something changed. You stayed."

"But that's—that would mean I was here for *years*." I stood up from the cot, letting the blanket fall to the floor. I began to pace, my head full, thoughts racing.

He never looked away from me. It was as if he thought I was going to disappear if he did. "You were. Middle of 2013 to when you were taken, in the beginning of 2019. So almost six years."

Six years. If he—and all of them—were to be believed, then Ezra took the better part of a decade away from me. "Why would he do this?"

Again he hesitated. I wondered if the others were listening in. I could hear their hearts and breaths above me. Not all of them. Joe and Ox. Elizabeth. Mark. The others didn't seem to be in the house.

He said, "Michelle . . . you always had a soft spot for her. You were with her for a year before she sent you west to Green Creek. And even with everything that happened after, even after all she did, you still believed there was something good in her."

I shook my head. "I know her. She wouldn't—"

He stood, grimacing. His eyes burned with something fiery that had nothing to do with being a wolf. It was all human anger. "She would," he snapped. "And I'm sorry to have to be the one to tell you this, because it hurts me, okay? To have to see that goddamn look on your face. But she did this. To you. To me. All of us. What happened to you may not have been by her own hand, but she *knew* about it. She is *complicit*. The stories I could tell you about her, about what she's done, Jesus Christ, Robbie."

"I don't believe—"

"She sent hunters here to kill us," he said hotly. "All of us. Including you. You pleaded with her. You *begged* her. And she didn't listen. After Carter and Mark were infected by whatever magic Livingstone put on them to turn them and all the others into Omegas—"

"*What?*"

"—she told us we had to kill them both. Put Carter and Mark down. Her words." He was breathing heavily. His hands clenched into fists. "We said no, so she sent hunters to Green Creek to kill every single one of us. We survived. The hunters didn't. But other people died too. Good people. And *still* she refused to listen to us."

"That's not like her," I growled. "She wouldn't—"

He scrubbed a hand over his face. "Do you hear yourself? I know it's a lot, okay? But you have to meet me halfway. You have to listen to what I'm trying to tell you."

"I don't even know you," I said coldly. "If this is all real, then that person you knew, that guy in the photos, on the missing poster, that guy you all seemed to be desperate to find, he's gone. This is what I am. This is *who* I am."

He was angry. It smelled like a forest fire. I wanted it to consume me, to burn the flesh from my bones just so I could find relief from the storm in my head. But it was good. Anger I could deal with. Anger I could handle. The begging, the pleading, the look of cautious hope and affection in his eyes—I didn't want that.

He spoke as if each word was getting punched out of him. "Memories are all well and good, but they aren't everything. You're still you. You're still the man I lo—"

Words. Like grenades about to explode at my feet. Instead I picked them up and hurled them back. "I don't love you."

He paled. He opened his mouth, but no sound came out.

I was sweating. Aching. Everything hurt. "I don't know you. How the fuck could I love you? You have to see that. You said we were mates."

"We *are*—"

"Then why don't I feel you? Mate bonds connect two people. Two halves of the same whole. It's a gift. A treasure. Something wonderful. And that's not us. There's nothing between us. For all I know, this mark I have was put there by your witch. That woman Jessie, she said Ezra put a glamour on me. Covered it up. What if there was nothing there to begin with? What if it was something Gordo did to me? To fuck with my head. To cause as much pain as possible."

He was shocked. And devastated. The forest fire had turned to ice. It was all blue. "We wouldn't do that. *He* wouldn't do that."

I shrugged. Aloof. Cold. Dismissive. "How the hell am I supposed to know that? I don't know any of you. Say what you're telling me is true. It means nothing now. I don't remember—"

The blue receded. It still pulled at me, but something else replaced it. Something that felt like resolve. He said, "You're lying."

I narrowed my eyes at him. "Really? Listen to my heart, Kelly. Oh. Wait. You can't do that, can you?"

He didn't flinch. And I *admired* him for it. It came out of nowhere, and it slapped me across the face because I was *impressed*.

Before I could recover, he said three words that sucked the air from the room.

"Do you dream?"

Ah. Ah, god.

He nodded slowly. "You do, don't you? Dreams of wolves. Of forests. Do you know why?"

I took a step away. He scared me. I didn't want to hear any more. I put my hands over my ears. I hunched over, trying to block it all.

It didn't help.

He said, "That was us. We didn't know if it would work. Even with the combined power of the pack and all those witches who came to help us, we didn't know if you'd hear us. But you did, didn't you?"

"No," I muttered. "No, no, no."

"It started a few months ago. You dreamed of Alphas. Of wolves in the trees. You saw them. You saw *me*."

No.

No.

No.

"A pure white wolf," he said. "My brother Joe. A black wolf. My brother Ox. You saw us. You *saw* us."

And I said, "The wolf wasn't always pure white."

Silence.

Then a whisper. "What?"

I gritted my teeth. My head was

(*you don't belong to me you aren't mine you aren't MINE but you could be you could be because of who you are*)

breaking apart, *I* was breaking apart, little pieces of me falling away

(*i know i know child but you will i promise you will you are important you are special you are*)

and I could do nothing to stop it. I didn't even know if I *wanted* to stop it.

I heard myself speak.

I said, "There was a white wolf. But he had black. On his chest. And back. And—"

Somewhere above, a woman choked on a sob. It sounded like Elizabeth. Quick and light, a sharp inhalation of breath followed by a stuttering exhale.

I looked up at Kelly as I dropped my hands.

A tear slipped from his right eye onto his cheek.

And he said, "That . . . that was my father."

He left a short time later, never having said another word.

HIGH SCHOOL GIRLS / SEE YOU AGAIN

He came back the next morning.
I ignored him.
He was fine with it. He had his blanket. And a book. He sat against the wall near the door, opened it, and began to read.

I lay on the bed, staring up at the ceiling.

It was a game.

I would win.

I lasted an hour.

"What day is it?"

He marked his place in his book before closing it and looking up at me. "Wednesday."

"The date."

"May twentieth."

The bridge incident was after the full moon. It'd been over a week. Everyone in Caswell had to know I was gone. I wondered if they were looking for me. They had to know where I was.

I said, "Don't you have a job or something?"

"I do." That was it. That was all he said. He was waiting to see if I would ask more.

I wasn't going to fall for it.

It took two minutes before I couldn't stand it any longer. "What?"

He arched an eyebrow at me.

I hated him. "What do you do?" Then, as if I couldn't help myself, "What did *I* do?"

"You worked at the garage with Gordo and Ox. Chris and Tanner and Rico."

I was dubious. It made sense, seeing as how much I'd been on the wall, but I couldn't believe it. "Me."

"Yeah."

"But I don't know anything about cars."

He smiled. It was quiet and soft, and I forced myself to look away. "Yeah, no. You absolutely don't. You once caused an engine to catch on fire."

I scowled at him. "There's a lot of parts inside—"

"You were supposed to be rotating the tires."

Well, fuck. "Oh."

"It was impressive. Rico and Chris put it out before it caused too much damage, but Gordo decided then and there you could never touch a car again. He put you at the front desk answering phones and handling customers. It worked for you. People . . . they liked you." I looked up when his voice took an odd tone. "Some of them *really* liked you. High school girls especially. This one guy kept bringing in his daughter's car. She swore there was a rattling sound every time she drove it."

"There was nothing wrong with the car."

"No. She just liked to put her underage boobs on the counter for you to look at."

I was scandalized. "I would *never*—"

He laughed. "I know, but she didn't. She tried, though. Got to give her some credit."

"I . . . liked it? Working there," I added quickly. "Not the underage . . . whatever." I looked down at my hands.

"You did. You made it your own. You updated all the computers, added new programs. Gordo bitched and moaned, but he always does. You could tell . . ." He cleared his throat. "You could tell he liked having you there. The others did too. One of the guys, I guess."

"They haven't been down here," I said, keeping my voice even.

He said nothing.

I looked back up at him.

He was picking and choosing his words carefully. "They're giving you space. They don't want you to be overwhelmed any more than you already are."

I nodded. That wasn't all of it. There was something else, something bigger. I was too scared to ask what it was. Knowing meant facing something I wasn't ready for.

I don't know what he saw on my face, but he said, "Maybe we can ask them. You know. To stop by. When they have a moment."

I shrugged. "It doesn't matter."

"Okay."

"But that didn't answer my question."

"Which one?"

My hands tightened in my lap. "What you do. How you can be here in the middle of the day."

"I work for the town. So does Carter."

That wasn't surprising. "Doing . . . ?"

"He's the mayor of Green Creek."

My head shot up so hard, my neck cracked. "He's *what*?"

He was struggling not to laugh. "Yeah, that was pretty much my reaction too. You saw how the humans in town didn't seem too fazed by werewolves?"

My head spun. "That's another thing that doesn't make sense. How the hell did they find out?"

He sobered a little. "When Michelle sent the hunters to Green Creek, they went after the whole town. Cut us all off in the middle of a snowstorm. It was unavoidable that the people would find out about us. About the pack. You can't go to war in the streets without repercussions. The storm was bad and a lot of people had already evacuated, but many stayed. And they were caught right in the middle. Rico's girlfriend—the woman in the truck who saw you when you were running crazed through town—"

"I wasn't *crazed*, what the hell—"

"Sure you weren't," he said. "She owns a bar in town. Called the Lighthouse. Bambi gathered everyone who remained—"

"Bambi," I repeated.

He nodded. "Bambi."

"The fuck."

He was solemn when he said, "You don't want to underestimate her. She will kick your ass. She almost shot Mark in the head after he backhanded Mom accidentally on purpose."

I swallowed my tongue.

He waved it away. "The Omega in him was eating him whole. He's better now."

"That's good," I said faintly.

"Anyway, Carter was in the bar and shifted in front of all of them because the timber wolf was trying to kill Mark and Gordo—"

"What is *wrong* with this town?" I whispered fervently.

"—and all the humans saw everything. And then a few days later, the main hunter—a woman named Elijah—tried to blow up the bar with everyone inside. But she failed and only ended up killing herself.

And everyone pretty much saw all of it. So that's how they found out about werewolves."

He said it like it was nothing, like he wasn't upending the entire world. "And they just *accepted* it."

He sounded amused when he said, "Mostly. There were a few outliers. People who couldn't handle it. People who were afraid."

I hesitated. Then, "Did you kill them?"

"Uh, no?" He was baffled. "Why would you think that?"

"I don't know," I admitted. "How else would you stop them from telling everyone?"

He snorted. "So you automatically went with murder. Good job."

"Hey!"

"The few who couldn't deal, they . . ." His brow furrowed. "Well. Gordo altered their memories. Took it all away."

"Like father, like son." I meant it as a halfhearted joke, but the words were bitter, and it fell flat.

His gaze sharpened. His voice was hard. "No. Not like that at all. Gordo isn't his father. He did what he did to protect us. *And* to protect the humans. He did it so no one would get hurt. As for the ones who remember, they're not pack. Think of them as pack-adjacent. We don't have bonds with them, but we do have an understanding. We protect them. This place. Green Creek is . . ."

"Different."

He nodded. "It is. Our family has been here for a long time. Generations. The land here, it isn't like it is anywhere else. There's a power to it. It sings. I think it was always meant for wolves."

"And all of this somehow led to Carter becoming the mayor."

"Weird, right? I don't even really know how it started. I think someone said something to him, and the next thing I knew, elections were being held and he was running unopposed. The previous mayor decided it was better if there was someone younger running the town. And since we already own most of Green Creek, it was easier if it was one of us. Keeps things simple."

Jesus Christ. Michelle had to have known about all of this. And she kept it from me. "And you work for him?"

He blushed a little like he was embarrassed. "I'm a deputy."

"What."

He rolled his eyes. "We had a couple of deputies here, but one of them died because of the hunters. We didn't want something like that to happen again, so it just made sense that we had someone who knew what they were doing."

"What," I said again.

"Yeah, yeah," he said. "Get it all out. I've heard it all. Rico kept asking me if I was going to pitch my own TV show. Called it *Werewolf Cop*. Said we'd make a fortune in merchandising and syndication." He rubbed his jaw thoughtfully. "Not a bad idea if you think about it."

"This is stupid," I said. "All of this is stupid."

He sighed. "And yet, it's the way things are. You . . ." He trailed off, looking distant.

I didn't want to know. "I what?"

He ran his fingers over the pages of his book. I could just make out the cover, a snarling dog underneath the word *Cujo*. "You were excited about it," he finally said. "When I told you. I wasn't sure it was for me, but you said I would do a good job. That people would rest easier knowing I was out there." He took a deep breath. "Because you felt the same way. Knowing I was there."

I couldn't find a single word to say. It was all too much. This life. We were talking about me, but it might as well have been someone else entirely.

He shrugged awkwardly. "Hey, it's okay. I'm not trying to make you feel bad or anything. It's just the way it is. Or was."

I nodded as I swallowed, throat clicking.

He smiled, though it didn't reach his eyes. "Maybe we should—"

I stood. "They're coming down."

"Who?" He fumbled with the book, dropping it to the floor as he stood.

"Alphas," I growled.

Ox came through the door first. He wore a uniform I recognized. His name was embroidered on a patch on his considerable chest. His fingers were stained with oil, and he had a rag hanging out of his back pocket.

Joe followed behind him.

Without thinking, I stepped forward quickly, wanting to get to Kelly, to drag him behind me, to shield him away.

Clarity came when I smashed into the line of silver. I hissed as my skin singed, backing away.

Joe looked curious, glancing between Kelly and me.

Ox's expression was blank.

"Kelly," Joe said. "You okay?"

"I'm fine," Kelly said, sounding exasperated. "I'm getting really sick and tired of that question."

"As your Alpha, I—"

"I'm older than you," Kelly retorted. "I changed your diaper when you shit yourself. You may be my Alpha, but I've wiped your ass, Joe."

Joe grinned at him. He reached over, wrapped his arm around Kelly, pulled him close, kissed the side of his head.

Someone snarled angrily.

It took me a moment to realize it was me.

I stopped, mortified.

"Huh," Joe said, a glint in his eyes I didn't like. "I wonder what that's about."

Kelly shoved him off. "Not now."

"As your Alpha—"

"Asshole."

Ox said, "Hello, Robbie."

Two words. That's all it was. Two simple words said in greeting.

And it made me tremble. There was such power emanating from him, and it was overwhelming, but it was so serene and calm. I'd never met another Alpha like him. I wanted to bare my throat to him, even as I warred with myself, the baser part of me gnashing its teeth because I already *had* an Alpha.

Or maybe I didn't.

I was so far from home.

He nodded as if he understood. As if he could read all my thoughts and everything I felt. For all I knew, he could. I'd seen the red and violet mixing in his eyes. He was different. He was *more*.

I was in awe of him.

I was terrified of him.

My fear extended to all of them, this pack, but him especially. Him and Kelly. For entirely different reasons.

My throat closed.

He said, "Would you like a shower?" His nose wrinkled slightly. "I think you could use one."

That sounded wonderful. But there had to be a catch. "Yes." Then, "Please."

He hummed under his breath. "In a moment, Kelly is going to break the line of silver. Will you attack him?"

I shook my head.

"Will you attack us?"

"No."

"Do you believe I can stop you if you try?"

"Yeah. Yes."

And then he said, "I'm trusting you, Robbie," and I wanted to howl at the moon.

"Yes. Yes. Yes." I was panting.

He nodded again. "Good. You won't be alone. Consider it a safety measure. It's nothing we haven't seen before, so I don't think you'll need to be worried about it."

Nudity to wolves was natural. Still, it felt like showing part of myself I wasn't ready for. "You?"

He tilted his head. "Would you prefer someone else?"

I glanced at Kelly but didn't reply.

"Okay," he said slowly. "That's fair."

"Ox," Joe said, a warning in his voice.

"I won't hurt him," I snapped. "He's . . ." I didn't know what he was.

Joe threw up his hands. "Fine. But we'll be right outside the door."

"Carter said you don't have boundaries here."

Joe gaped at me before recovering. "Uh. Yeah. I guess. I've seen Carter's dick more times than I care to think about." He frowned. "I really regret saying that out loud."

"And yet there it is," Ox said dryly. "Thanks, Joe."

Joe grinned at him adoringly. It took my breath away. They were close. It wasn't like it was in Caswell. At least it wasn't for me. Sure, I'd had Ezra, and he'd—

I hung my head.

"Kelly," Ox said.

Kelly stepped forward, a determined look on his face. He hesitated as if he thought the silver was still going to hurt him.

It didn't.

He pushed a foot through the powdered silver, and the line broke. The sounds became louder, the smells stronger.

I sucked in a deep breath as my ears twitched.

I could run. I'd done it once.

Maybe I wouldn't make it very far. Probably not even out of the house. But I could try.

I was tired of running.

Kelly stepped back, squaring his shoulders like he expected me to burst forward.

Instead, I walked slowly across the line.

He looked relieved. I thought he was about to reach out, like he was going to take my hand, but he didn't.

Ox did. Ox touched me.

He put a hand around the back of my neck.

He pressed his forehead against mine.

His eyes seemed endless.

I could do nothing but watch him.

I breathed him in.

My hands shook.

My knees were weak.

He whispered, "Hello, Robbie. I'm so very pleased to see you again."

* * *

I was in a daze as they led me up the stairs. Ox was in front, then Kelly. I was behind him, with Joe bringing up the rear.

The window at the top of the stairs had been replaced. You couldn't tell I'd broken it only a couple of days before.

Aside from us, the house was mostly empty. Music was playing in the kitchen. Dinah Shore. Elizabeth Bennett was sashaying away, her dress flaring out around her legs as she sang that she didn't mind being lonely because she knew in her heart I was lonely too. She smiled at me, the sun like a spotlight through an open window over the sink.

"I like this song," she said. "Don't you?"

I could only nod.

Joe shook his head and went to her. She laughed in delight as he bowed before her, one hand behind his back. She took his other hand in hers, pulling him close. We left them dancing in the kitchen as if all was right in the world.

Ox headed for another set of stairs.

There was a beautiful painting hung halfway up, a violent slash of color on a white canvas. I didn't understand it. I wanted to touch it.

"She painted it," Kelly said from behind me. "Mom. She's good. I don't always understand it, but I don't think that's as important as how it makes me feel."

I nodded but didn't speak.

We reached the second floor. All the doors were open save one. I sucked in air greedily, taking in the scents of *packpackpack*. Ox and Kelly didn't mention it. The only closed door reeked of Kelly, and I didn't want to ask. I couldn't. I wasn't ready.

The bathroom in the hall was bright and airy. Fresh flowers sat on the windowsill. The white claw-foot tub was spotless. There was a towel folded on a small bench next to it.

"I'll be outside," Ox said, nodding toward the bathroom, "when you're finished. You and I are going to talk."

Ah. The catch.

"Okay," I said meekly.

He stepped out of the doorway and leaned against the wall.

I stepped inside.

Kelly followed, closing the door behind us. It latched firmly. There was no lock. It would have been pointless.

I didn't look at him when I asked, "Is one of those rooms mine?"

Or ours.

"It was," he said from behind me, voice even. "But after... everything, we moved."

"To where?"

He chuckled. "Not very far. The blue house. It used to be Ox's. He lived there with his mother."

"Oh."

"We shared it with some Omegas who stayed here."

My eyebrows felt like they were trying to crawl up into my hair. "We *what*?"

He pushed by me, rubbing his bandaged arm. He nudged the towel to the side before sitting on the bench next to the tub, hands flexing on his knees. He looked up at me. "For a while they had nowhere else to go. Many stayed with us until we could place them in packs throughout North America. A couple even went to packs in Mexico. We ate a lot of food that trip."

"We."

He shrugged. "You and me and Carter. We drove. It was nice. Rico taught me enough Spanish to get by."

"He doesn't like me very much."

Kelly hesitated. "You . . . Give him time. He'll come around. It's been a lot. For all of us."

I stayed near the door, suddenly uncomfortable. "Brodie."

"Yeah. He was one of them. Alpha Wells is a good wolf. They'll take care of him."

"Who brought him?"

He looked away. "Gordo. And Mark."

"When?"

His hands tightened on his knees. "A few months ago."

We were both thinking it. Ox probably was too.

Gordo and Mark had crossed the country to bring an Omega child to be placed in a wolf pack that was less than a day's drive away from where I'd been. And they'd known it. They'd known I was in Maine. Carter had said as much.

They hadn't come for me.

They hadn't even tried.

My hands went to the plain white shirt I was wearing. Elizabeth had given it to me, along with a few others. They were new, she'd said. They kept them for anyone passing through who needed them. They smelled faintly of pack, but not like it would have been had they shared their own clothes with me.

I started to pull it up.

I stopped.

He arched an eyebrow at me, like a challenge. "It's nothing I haven't seen before."

My face grew hot. "Right," I muttered. "Just . . . no ideas, okay?"

He laughed, but I didn't think it was *at* me. "I don't think you'll have to worry about that. Not really."

I was almost insulted. I was proud of my body. I was strong. I was young. I was capable of providing for my—

Fuck.

He wiped his eyes. "No, oh god, get that wounded look off your face. Christ." He took a deep breath. "I'm ace."

I frowned. "What's that?"

"Asexual."

"Oh. *Oh.*" I scrunched up my face. "Like . . . really?"

Now he was laughing at me. "Like, really."

"How did that work?" I blanched. "Holy shit, ignore me. Seriously, don't think you need to explain—"

"If that's what you want," he said, and that was it.

I scowled at him.

He smiled at me.

I lasted a few more seconds. "Are you *sure*?"

"I am," he said simply.

"But." I waved my hand in the direction of my neck and the scar on it that extended near my shoulder. "And. Like. You know."

He laughed again. I thought I even heard Ox snorting outside the door. "We made it work. It's not that I'm repulsed by sex or anything. It's just not everything to me. There's more to us than physical intimacy. Or there was."

"Oh." I bit the inside of my cheek, but the words came out in a rush. "And I was okay with that?"

"You were," he said, and his voice took on a wistful tone that made me feel like I was intruding. "We made it work because we . . . well."

Blue.

The room filled with blue.

It was smothering.

I wanted to go to him. It was like a pull. Toward what, I didn't know.

Instead I pulled off my shirt and let it fall to the floor.

"You can stop flexing," he said, the blue fading slightly.

"I'm not."

"Really," he said. "So your pecs usually bounce up and down like that normally? That's something you should probably get checked out." He looked me up and down, but there was no stink of arousal coming from him. Instead, it was warm, like a heavy blanket on a winter day. "You're bigger than you were. Harder."

"I'm . . . sorry?" I wasn't sorry at all.

He shook his head. "It looks good on you." He reached over, pulled the shower curtain back. He turned the faucet. Water began to pour into the tub. "Best get to it. You need it. Even I can smell you, and my nose is weak as hell."

I took a deep breath and reached down, slid my sleep shorts to the floor, and stepped out of them. And I absolutely did *not* strut toward the tub, even if he had to cover up his laughter with the back of his hand.

I stepped into the tub and pulled the curtain closed. I twisted the lever near the tap, and the showerhead poured water down on me.

I groaned in relief.

"None of that," Ox muttered through the door. "You'll have time later."

I almost fell down.

Kelly stuck his head through the curtain. "All right?"

Of course he couldn't hear what Ox said—he was human. "I'm *fine*," I snapped at him, pushing his head out and closing the curtain again. "Your Alpha is making insinuations."

"Knock it off, Ox!"

"No!" Ox called back.

"Fucking werewolves," Kelly muttered before sitting back on the bench. It creaked under his weight, and I just stood under the water. I didn't remember anything ever feeling so good.

"Ace, huh?"

"Ace," he agreed.

"That's . . . okay."

"Glad you think so."

And something settled in my chest that I didn't even know was askew.

It felt dangerous.

FIX YOU / ENIGMATIC DICKS

We walked for a long time.

Ox never left my side.

The sky was cloudless and the sun was warm.

He'd offered me shoes, but I'd shaken my head. I liked the grass between my toes.

He led me through the trees. I didn't know where we were, but I followed him as if it were the most natural thing in the world. I glanced back over my shoulder. Kelly stayed behind us, trailing his hands along the trunks of trees. He smiled at me when he caught me watching him, but never spoke. I'd insisted that he come with us. Ox agreed.

"Where are we going?" I asked Ox.

"You'll see."

"Is it about me?"

"In a way."

"Oh."

We didn't speak much after that.

We came to a large clearing.

It was familiar, like it was right on the tip of my tongue, but I couldn't place it. It was a maddening itch I couldn't scratch.

Ox was watching me. Kelly too.

I didn't know what they wanted from me.

I said, "What is this place?"

"It's ours," Ox said. "The pack's. Our territory. Many things have happened here. Good and bad." He looked off into the surrounding trees. "I learned the truth here. About wolves."

I crouched down to the ground, pressing my hands flat against the grass.

The earth felt alive, but it was foreign. Unknowable.

I stood back up.

Ox said, "I don't know how to fix you. And for that, I'm sorry. I thought—" He shook his head. "It's not like it was with the Omegas. Whatever Robert did to you, it's more than I am."

Robert. Ezra. Robert. And all at once, it hit me again, a devastating wave of loneliness. I had no one. I had nothing. Everyone was a stranger, even if they thought otherwise. I knew nothing about them. I was a deserted island in a sea of blue.

"Hey," Kelly said.

I looked over at him.

His brow was furrowed. His nostrils flared from muscle memory. It took him a moment to remember that nothing would come from it. His expression stuttered and shook. It was brief. He tried for a smile and nearly got there. He said, "That doesn't mean we're giving up. It's just . . . we have to think about it differently. Try to find another way."

"And what if there's nothing you can do?" I asked.

He shrugged. "Then we work with what we have. You're here, Robbie. That's all that matters."

It wasn't enough, and it made me angry. Which is why I said, "Ezra isn't all bad. Or whatever his name is. I know he's . . . he's *done* things to you. To all of you. But he was kind to me. He loved me. He told me. He didn't lie to me about that."

Kelly and Ox exchanged a look, and I wondered if I'd once been part of it, these secret communications between members of a pack.

"I believe *you* believe that," Ox said slowly. "And maybe even part of him did. Or does. I'm not trying to take that away from you."

"Then what *are* you doing?" I demanded.

"Going for a walk," he said easily, as if it were nothing.

He continued on, crossing the clearing, leaving me to stare after him.

"Yeah," Kelly said as he came to stand next to me. "It's an Alpha thing. Don't try to question it. It'll only make him more insufferable. Joe won't tell me, but I think part of being an Alpha is learning to be an enigmatic dick."

"I heard that," Ox called over his shoulder. He didn't stop when he reached the edge of the clearing. He crossed into the tree line, hands clasped behind his back.

"His eyes," I said.

"The violet?"

I nodded.

Kelly dug one of his shoes into the ground. "Weird, right?"

"Werewolf Jesus."

Kelly snorted. "Carter." He sighed. "Dumb, but he kind of has a point. Ox is different. He was a human Alpha before Joe had to bite him."

"How?"

"We don't know. There's never been anyone quite like Ox. You certainly thought so when you first came here. You kissed him once."

"I did *what*?"

Kelly laughed. "Yeah. I wasn't here for it. It was when we were out in the world."

"But he has Joe!"

"Didn't stop you."

"Oh my god," I said faintly. "I'm going to be straight-up murdered. That's what's going on, right? You are taking me out in the middle of the woods to kill me."

"Nah," Kelly said. "We'd just do that at the house. Easier to clean up that way."

That didn't make me feel any better. "You sound as if you've done that before."

"We have," he said grimly.

I blinked in surprise. "Who?"

"It was bad. Before Ox was the Alpha of the Omegas, he . . . was lied to."

I didn't want to know. I said, "Who?"

Kelly looked at me. His eyes were bright. He wasn't a wolf, but he made a good human. I didn't know how to tell him that or even why I thought I should. It would remind him of all that he'd lost because of me. "Michelle Hughes," Kelly said.

I closed my eyes.

"Before we knew about the infection, before we knew how it spread, Omegas were coming here. Drawn like Green Creek was a beacon. We didn't know why at first. But almost on schedule, one would come every couple of weeks. They were lost. Vacant. Driven by instinct."

"Why did they come here?"

"Part of it was Ox. But a bigger part, we think, was Gordo. Magic has a signature, a fingerprint. But it's born of blood, and Gordo is his father's son. And since it was Livingstone who infected the wolves to turn them Omega, they were drawn to Gordo's magic. They hated it, but they couldn't stop even if they wanted to. Most of them tried to come after him."

I opened my eyes. "Who did they kill?"

"Michelle sent a man named Pappas here—"

"Pappas?"

"You after you."

"What?"

"A man named Osmond was Michelle's second-in-command. He betrayed everyone for the beast. Then you were Michelle's second. After you came here and stayed, Pappas took over."

My head hurt again. "I don't know Pappas."

"He's dead. One of the hunters Michelle sent to Green Creek."

"Michelle wouldn't have her own second killed—"

"He was infected too," Kelly said. "Robbie, she's not . . ."

"She's not what?" I asked, trying to keep the anger from my voice.

"She's not a good person," Kelly said. He looked defiant. "I don't know what you think or what she's told you, but—"

"You don't know her. Not like I do. Not like—"

"She told Ox to kill an innocent woman," Kelly snapped. "An Omega. She said it was the only way. And we believed her because we trusted her. She said there was nothing to be done to help her, nothing that could save her. Ox did what she asked. I don't give a *damn* what you think of her, not when I remember feeling what Ox felt in that moment, when he took the woman's face in his hands and twisted until her neck broke. And she wasn't the only one. We sent many Omegas back east because Michelle said she'd deal with them. And she did. By killing every single one of them. And you were furious about it. Or at least the Robbie I knew was."

I was speechless. Surprised, even, at how much those words hurt.

Kelly was breathing heavily. He grimaced and looked like he was about to say something else. Instead he huffed out an angry breath and followed his Alpha, leaving me to stare after him.

There was a bridge, wood painted red and picture-perfect over a stream.

On one side was a plaque, six words in metal.

May our songs always be heard

Kelly and Ox stood in front of the plaque. Ox reached up and put his arm around Kelly's shoulders. Kelly traced the engraved words with his finger.

I stood away from them. Whatever was going on, it wasn't for me.

I thought about running.

Their backs were turned.

I'd have a head start. I probably wouldn't make it very far, but I wouldn't know unless I tried.

I'm trusting you, Robbie.

I stayed where I was.

They turned to face me. I wanted to ask what the plaque meant, but I didn't. Powerful scents have a way of lingering, and this place was filled with fury and blood and something much, much deeper that pulled at the back of my mind.

Ox left Kelly standing near the bridge. He came to me. He filled up my entire world until all I could see was him.

He said, "One day and one day soon, I'm going to ask you about Caswell, Maine. I'm going to ask you to tell me everything. The layout. The people there. How strong they are, and if they're willing to fight for Alpha Hughes or against her. Because a reckoning is coming. Alpha Hughes has long held a position that was always meant to be temporary. And we're going to take it back. Do you believe me?"

I could only nod.

He said, "But I'm not going to ask you that today. Because today you don't trust me. Today you don't know me. You don't have any reason to believe me when I say I don't want innocent people to get hurt. That I want as little bloodshed as possible. But anyone who doesn't stand with us stands against us. And it's going to be the last thing they do."

He leaned forward and pressed a kiss to my forehead. He spoke again, lips against my skin. "You have this void. This hole in your head and heart where you know something should be but isn't. It's the same for all of us. We were taken from you, yes, but you were also taken from us."

He stepped back.

And then he said something so ridiculous that I couldn't make sense of it. He said, "It's almost my birthday. I'd like for you to join us this coming Sunday. It's tradition."

Then he stepped around me and started back the way we'd come.

I gaped after him.

Kelly sighed. "I told you, man. Enigmatic dicks. All of them."

"Sorry about this," Kelly said as Ox and Joe looked on.

I said nothing.

Kelly closed the line of silver, trapping me in the basement once again.

Ox nodded at me before heading toward the stairs.

Joe said, "Your tether."

Ox stopped, but he didn't turn around.

Joe said, "Who is it?"

I scowled at him. "Fuck you."

"Simple question."

"None of your business."

"Joe," Ox said.

Joe ignored him. "Is it still your mother?"

Little wolf, little wolf, can't you see?

I snarled at him.

And Kelly said, "*Enough.*"

Joe left then, followed by Ox.

Kelly glared after them before slamming the door shut.

I paced back and forth, prowling the edges of the silver line.

Kelly hung his head, hands pressed against the door. He took a deep breath before turning around. He picked up his blanket and pulled it around his shoulders. He sat on the floor again, back against the wall. He picked up his book but didn't open it.

I said, "This is all shit," and "You all act like you know me," and "You're fucking with my head, this could all be a lie, everything could be a lie. Please let me go. Please just let me go home. I want to go home. *I want to go home.*"

He didn't respond, at least not verbally.

His chest hitched.

I could smell the sting of salt.

He blinked rapidly as he looked down at his book. He didn't turn the page for the longest time.

Kelly didn't come back the next day.

"He's not feeling well," Elizabeth told me. "This human thing is taking some getting used to. His body doesn't do what it once did, and it's frustrating."

"I get that," I muttered. "My head isn't doing what it once did."

She laughed quietly. "Is that right? How curious. Tell me about it."

I didn't. For all I knew, she was trying to gather as much information as possible.

She nodded. "Okay. We can just sit here if you'd like. I often find that silence is special if you're with someone who understands."

I turned away from her and stared at the wall.

Kelly didn't come the day after that either.

Chris and Tanner did, though.

I heard the sound of a million people running down the stairs to the basement. I was surprised when only the two of them burst through the door, jostling each other.

They stopped when they saw me watching them.

"Hey," Chris said.

"S'up," Tanner offered.

I nodded at them. My hair fell onto my forehead, and I pushed it back.

"I could cut that for you," Tanner said. He scratched the back of his neck. "If you want."

"Don't let him," Chris warned. "I let him do it to me when we were thirteen because he said he could give me lightning bolts and make me look cool for this girl with really big ... eyes. Instead I looked like I had a bad case of mange and got grounded for a week. The girl moved to Canada." He frowned. "But not because of my haircut. I don't know why I made it sound like those two things were related."

"Don't listen to him," Tanner said. "He never had a chance with that girl to begin with."

I said, "You're scared of me."

They took a step back in unison.

"Why?"

"We're not scared," Tanner said.

"Why would we be scared of you?" Chris asked.

"People lie. Scents don't."

Chris said, "Look, Robbie, it's—"

"Chris? Tanner?"

"Uh-oh," Tanner said.

"He's so high-strung," Chris muttered.

Rico appeared in the doorway. He was frowning, and when he saw Chris and Tanner standing in front of me, he narrowed his eyes. "What the hell are you doing down here?" He glanced at me coolly. "*Lobito*. You're looking . . . alive. How wonderful for you."

Lobito. *Little wolf* in Spanish. Like he knew. Like someone had told him. Joe had known about my tether, and here was Rico saying things like he had a right to. I didn't like it. Or him.

But he had already dismissed me. He was glaring at Chris and Tanner. "Lunch is ready. You know we only have an hour. Get upstairs."

Chris said, "We were just—" as Tanner said, "We only wanted to—"

"I will shoot you both in the goddamn *assholes* if you don't move," Rico said.

They moved. Chris waved at me as Tanner nodded.

They were up the stairs a moment later, leaving Rico and me alone. He turned to me.

It hadn't been a mistake before, what I'd seen. There was real hatred in his eyes.

He said, "I never wanted to find you."

He said, "I never wanted you to come back."

He said, "I don't know what that makes me. But I don't know how to forgive you, and I don't think I ever will. Magic. It was magic, but it was still you." He looked stricken. His hands tightened into fists at his sides. "I have a gun. It's loaded with silver bullets. And I know how to use it very well. The others think they can fix you. That they can get back all that was taken from you. Maybe they can. Or maybe they can't. And you have to ask yourself if that's even something you want. Because of all it would bring back. The truth of it all. Either way, the *second* I think something is off or that you're going to hurt someone I care about, I will put a bullet in your head, consequences be damned."

He spat on the floor between us.

And then he left too, slamming the door behind him.

Kelly came back on Saturday.

He looked tired.

He said "Don't worry about it" when I asked him.

I was desperate for a friendly face. The confrontation with Rico the day before had left me shaken. I didn't know what was happening. My dreams were vivid, bright colors and wolves and trees, but they were all mixed together. It was disorienting.

I said, "Why?"

"Why what?" he asked, blanket in his lap. He set his book on the floor beside him.

"Why are you keeping me here?"

"You belong here."

He sounded so sure of himself. "What's stopping them from coming for me?"

Them. He didn't need me to clarify. "Wards."

"Wards can be manipulated."

"They can," he said slowly. "But not these. At least we don't think so. It isn't just Gordo's magic. There are . . . others involved."

"Others," I repeated.

"Witches."

"Who?"

He shook his head. "I can't answer that. At least not now."

"Because you don't trust me."

"Do you trust me?"

I didn't answer.

I didn't need his scent to know that that hurt him. He covered it up quickly. "My father taught me that generals of old used to meet on the battlefield before the fighting started to parlay. War is . . . expensive. Casualties come at great cost."

"And you all think it's going to come to that."

"It might. Or it might not. We're on one side of the country. They're on the other."

"Am I your prisoner?"

"Yes," he said bluntly. "You are. And it has nothing to do with whether or not we can trust you. It's because we want to keep you safe. Livingstone has a hold over you. He can trigger you."

"Would you hear me, dear?" I whispered.

Kelly nodded. "How did that make you feel? When he said that?"

"Like nothing hurt. Calm. Happy. Like I was floating." I narrowed my eyes at him. "Is this why you come down here? So you can ask me questions and report back to your Alphas? Did they send you down here to dig for information?"

He shrugged. "Yes. But that's not all it is. I want to see you as much as I can. I want to touch you. I want to lay my head in your lap and have your hand in my hair. I want you to smile at me like you know me. Like I'm the only thing you see."

"Don't," I said hoarsely. "Just . . . don't."

He looked down at his hands.

"I don't know you."

"I know."

"I don't want to."

"I know that too."

"Then *why*?" I demanded. "Why are you—"

His head snapped up. "Because I love you. And I never forgot you. Even when everything was fucked up, even when it all turned to shit and blood was spilled, I did everything I could."

"Then why the *fuck* was I still there?" I roared. "Why did it take you so goddamn long to come for me? If I meant as much to you as you say, if I meant *anything* to your fucking pack, then why did you leave me where I was?"

He wiped his eyes as he sniffled. "Because you killed an Omega. A man who had come to us for help. You came back from your assignment and you tore him to pieces. Chris and Tanner tried to stop you, and you wouldn't let them. Instead, you attacked them. Chris died. His heart stopped beating. I found you, your teeth in Tanner's side, breaking his ribs as he begged for you to stop. I screamed at you. You looked at me like you didn't know me. And then you were gone. The only reason Chris and Tanner are here at all is because Ox and Joe and Gordo managed to save them. It was almost too late for Chris, but he pulled through when Ox bit him. He and Tanner were human before you got to them. They're wolves now because it was the only way to keep them alive. We thought you'd betrayed us. Like Osmond. Like Michelle. Like Richard Collins. Like Gordo's father. That's why we didn't look for you at first. That's why we didn't come for you."

I tilted my head back and screamed.

It echoed throughout the bones of the house that creaked around us.

I didn't stop for a long time.

By the time my voice cracked and broke, Kelly was gone.

IT'S TRADITION / CAN'T FORGIVE

I dreamed in blood.
what are you doing
robbie
robbie
please don't
please don't do this
oh my god what's wrong with you
you're not
please please please i don't want to die
please you're hurting me robbie you're hurting me
oh god no
no
let me go let me go **LET ME GO LETMEGOLETM**

I didn't. I didn't stop. My mouth filled with blood, and I swallowed it down.

They feared me.

And I *reveled* in it.

Elizabeth stood in the doorway to the basement in early afternoon. Her hands were on her hips. Her head was tilted.

She said, "I need your help."

I rolled over on the cot, away from her. I pulled the thin blanket up and over my shoulder.

She chuckled. "That never works on me. I'm a mother. I've raised three boys. You'll lose."

"Go away."

"I need your help," she said again. "It's Sunday, so it's tradition. But it's not just a normal Sunday. We have things to prepare for. Get up."

"No."

"Get up, Robbie."

"Fuck off."

"If that's how it's going to be."

I heard her go back up the stairs.

I couldn't believe it was that easy.

It wasn't.

A few minutes later she came back. She was grunting and muttering under her breath, talking about stubborn wolves who didn't know their asses from their elbows. I didn't turn to look at her. Nothing she could say would—

Cold water sprayed my back.

I yelped and fell off the cot.

Elizabeth stood on the other side of the silver, a nozzle attached to a hose in her hand.

"You're all wet," she said amiably. "Shall I do it again, or are you going to get up and come help me?"

"What is *wrong* with you? Why would you—oh my god, *stop!*" Water filled my mouth and nose. I choked and sat up, water dripping off my cheeks and chin.

"This is hurting me as much as it's hurting you."

"Then why the hell are you *smiling*?"

She shrugged. "Because you keep shaking yourself like a wet dog. It's adorable. Are you going to get up?" She pointed the nozzle at me again.

"You can't just *torture* me into—"

She snorted. "Torture. Cute. If I was torturing you, you'd know it."

I glared at her. "Was that supposed to make me feel better? Because it didn't."

"Oh no," she said. "That wasn't meant to make you feel better at all. It was a threat." She squinted at me. "Do you not know when you're being threatened? That's not good. I'll have to make my intentions clearer, then. Robbie. Get up. You're coming to help me. If you don't, I will torture you."

"Like hell you—aah!"

I got another face full of water.

"I could do this all day," she said. "I'd rather not, since I have so much to do and so little time to do it, but I could. And if not me, then I'm sure I can find someone who would be willing to keep this up in my place."

I sighed and looked up toward the ceiling. My hair stuck to my head. "You mean that, don't you?"

"Yes. I often find that saying what you mean is easier than saying what you don't."

"Fine."

"Good," she said cheerfully. "But I think I'll keep the hose at the ready, just to be safe. It's gotten more of a reaction out of you than almost anything other than Kelly. I'll be sure to let everyone know that. We have many hoses for reasons I don't quite understand." She turned toward the door and raised her voice. "Jessie! Robbie has seen fit to grant us his company. Could you come down and let him out?"

Jessie appeared in the doorway a moment later. "Why is there a hose on the—oh my god."

Her eyes widened as I glared at her, arms across my wet chest.

And then she laughed. She laughed so hard that she bent over, clutching at her sides.

Elizabeth grinned at her. "Quite the sight, isn't he? And look. He's pouting."

"I am *not!*" I snarled.

"You kind of are," Jessie said. She pulled out her phone and pointed it at me. I heard a shutter sound as she took my picture. She showed it to Elizabeth, and that set them both off again. Jessie was still laughing when she came over and broke the line of silver.

I stood.

The women didn't act like I was a threat.

They should have been scared of me.

They weren't.

Jessie leaned against Elizabeth, elbow propped on her shoulder as she shoved her phone back into her pocket. "You know I'll just kick your ass again, right? I mean, if you want to go for it, then let's do it. I could use the workout."

I walked across the line, keeping my head down, grinding my teeth.

"Good puppy," Jessie said, patting me on the shoulder. She didn't even flinch when I snapped my teeth at her.

"There," Elizabeth said. "Was that so hard? Next time just do what I ask and we can avoid all of this. Come, now. We have a big day ahead of us."

She pointed me toward a door down the hall. "Get cleaned up. Meet me in the kitchen."

And then she left, humming under her breath.

"Most everyone is outside," Jessie said as I looked toward a window. "Just in case you were thinking about trying to run again."

"I wasn't," I muttered.

"Sure you weren't. But even if you *were*, we'd chase you and drag you back, and then where would we be?"

"You could just let me go," I told her hopefully.

She cocked her head. "Why? You have nowhere else to go."

And *that* hit me harder than I expected, hearing it so bluntly. She was right. Where *would* I go? Caswell? Back to Ezra and Michelle? Even if I chose to disbelieve everything I'd been told since coming to Green Creek, it wouldn't explain away everything that had happened in the compound. What I'd seen. What I'd heard. All the things I couldn't remember. Tony—the little cub—asking me what it'd been like when I'd been in Caswell *before*, and why I always felt blue.

I felt a hand on my shoulder.

I looked up.

Jessie wasn't smiling. She was hurting too. "I didn't mean it that way."

"Yeah, I think you did. And it's not like you're wrong."

She bit her bottom lip. "Maybe. But . . . look, Robbie. We'll figure it out, okay? You just need to give yourself *and* us time to readjust. You're here, but it's like you're *not* here, you know? Not completely. I can see you standing in front of me, but I can't *feel* you. Not like I could before. Not like I can with the other wolves."

I was confused. "But you're human. How can you feel anything with the wolves? It doesn't work like that."

She nodded slowly. "Not many humans in Maine, huh?"

"Only witches. Alpha Hughes says humans are a liability."

"I bet she does." Jessie sighed. "We're not like other packs."

"You don't say."

She punched me in the arm. It hurt more than I expected. "Don't be a bitch, Fontaine. It's different. With us. Maybe it's having two Alphas. Maybe it's because of Ox and who he was before everything went to hell. But we're pack, just as much as any of the wolves. And the bonds that tie us all together are strong." She hesitated. Then, "Can you feel any of us? Any of the wolves? Anything?"

I started to shake my head but stopped. "There's... when I was in Caswell, I kept seeing things. Hearing things. Wolves that weren't there. Voices."

She didn't react. Her face was carefully blank. "And since you've gotten here?"

"Ox. Loud and clear. But not really anyone else. At least not that I can differentiate."

"Not Kelly?"

My throat closed. I didn't say anything.

She let it go. "Rico and I can't read the wolves as well as they can read us, but it's enough. Chris and Tanner were the same before they..."

The skin around her eyes tightened.

Right. Chris and Tanner. Chris, who Kelly said had actually died. Chris, who was her brother.

The words tumbled out of my mouth before I could stop them. "I'm sorry."

She arched an eyebrow. "Are you? Do you even remember what you're apologizing for?"

"No."

"And yet you said it anyway. Why?"

"Because I'm not a monster. If I did what Kelly said—"

"You did."

"Then..."

She stepped away. "Hall bathroom, Fontaine. You've got five minutes. There are some clothes in there for you. They're yours from before. They might not fit as well, seeing as how you've finally gained some muscle. I'm told they smell like pack. Try not to rip them. If I don't see you in five minutes, I'm breaking down the door and shoving my crowbar down your throat."

I believed her.

The clothes were sitting on the counter.

A plaid button-down shirt.

A pair of jeans.

Boxer briefs.

There was pack scent there, heavy and warm, as if they'd all worn my clothes at one point or another.

But it was one scent I chased after more than all the others.

It was grass.

And lake water.

And sunshine.

I lifted the shirt and brought it to my nose, inhaling deeply.

My chest ached. It was there. Faint, but mixed in with all the other scents.

And it fit. It mingled. It complemented.

Somehow, it—and I—fit with all of them.

I thought I was spinning out of control.

* * *

Jessie wasn't outside the door when I came out.

I heard her laughing in the kitchen at something Elizabeth had said. I pulled at my shirt. Jessie was right. I was bigger. The shirt was too tight in my chest and arms. The buttons were straining.

I looked out the window to the front of the house. There were multiple cars parked in the driveway. The blue house sat behind them, the windows open. Rico and Tanner stood near the porch. Tanner said my name, and Rico turned to look at me through the window.

He frowned before shaking his head. Tanner put an arm on his shoulder, but he brushed it off.

I didn't want to give Rico a reason to shoot me, so I turned away from the window and walked toward the kitchen.

I was cautious. Careful. I stood in the doorway. Elizabeth had to know I was there, even though her back was to me. Jessie too, probably. She wasn't like any other human I'd met. She moved like a wolf.

Elizabeth stood at the sink, peeling potatoes.

A radio sat on the windowsill above the sink. It was old-fashioned, the dial lit up in a bright yellow light. Tammy Wynette was crooning about how she was going to stand by her man. Elizabeth was singing along, her voice quiet and melodic.

Jessie stood in front of the large stove. There were four pots on four different burners, and they were all bubbling. It smelled wonderful. I was ravenous.

I didn't know what to do.

I waited.

Tammy sang, aching and sweet.

Elizabeth swayed back and forth, her summer dress billowing around her legs.

It struck me then just how much I wanted this. It was sudden and fierce. I wanted this. Here. With them. In this place so very far from all I thought I knew.

I didn't deserve it.

My heart hurt.

"You know," Elizabeth said suddenly, "my mother told me once that a watched pot never boils. I always found that fascinating, because it does, eventually, whether you're looking at it or not. Robbie, if you please."

I swallowed thickly.

She took a step to the left, motioning me to join her in front of the sink. She didn't look at me.

I thought she was giving me a choice.

There was no hose in sight.

I took a deep breath and stepped into the kitchen.

She said, "There. That's better. Can you help me?"

"I'm not a very good cook," I muttered as I came to stand next to her. "I burn things. Ezra always did the . . ."

Except he wasn't Ezra.

I wondered how long that would go on.

I thought it might be forever.

She said, "Strange."

"What?"

She handed me a peeler and a potato. "How for everything that's different, some things are always the same. You tried to cook Kelly breakfast once."

"Just once?" I started to peel the potato in slow, even strokes.

"Notice how I used the word *tried*. I woke up and thought the house was on fire."

Jessie snorted but didn't speak.

"I came downstairs," Elizabeth continued. "It was barely light out. You were panicking. There was a black mess in a pan on the stove that you said had once been the beginnings of an omelet. There was egg on the ceiling. You had cheese in your hair."

The potato burst in my hand as I squeezed it too tight.

Elizabeth took the remains from me. "Interesting way to go about it. Good thing it was going to be mashed anyway."

She handed me another.

I started again.

"Your eyes were wide," she continued, "and you told me you didn't know what had happened. Everything had been going well, but then you got distracted by the trees outside the window." She smiled. "You always did love trees. I think you got that from your mother. She could spend hours out in the woods, just walking around."

"You knew her."

She nodded. "Not as well as I would have liked. But yes. I knew her."

"Did . . . you tell me this? Before?"

"I did."

"Oh." I nearly nicked my hand. I gripped the peeler tighter.

"So there you were, burning the meal you'd woken up early to make. You said that you'd always wanted to bring someone breakfast in bed. You'd never had someone before to do that with, and you were so mad that it didn't work out."

"What did I do?"

She bumped her shoulder against mine. "You started over. And that's how I knew that there would be no one else for Kelly but you. Because even though it was hard and turned out rather terrible, you didn't give up. You asked for my help, but when I started cracking eggs, you said you wanted to do it. You told me you wanted me as more of a supervisor than to be hands-on."

"If I had help, it wouldn't be from me."

She looked startled before she laughed. "Yes. That's what you said. So I watched over you, and you started from scratch. It wasn't perfect, and I believe Kelly found an eggshell or two, but you did it. You get frustrated easily, but you learned patience. Don't forget that."

I nodded as she wiped her hands on a dish towel and sashayed away, Tammy ending and the Shirelles taking over, asking if you'd still love me tomorrow.

I looked out the window.

In the backyard, a large table had been set up, a dark green tablecloth set on top of it. Chris and Gordo and Mark were putting chairs around the table. In the center, weighted down, was a bunch of balloons.

Carter stood with Kelly next to a grill. They were close together. As I watched, Kelly laid his head on Carter's shoulder. The timber wolf sat on Carter's other side, stretching his nose toward the meat on the grill. Carter tapped the tip of his nose with a pair of tongs. The wolf growled but didn't try again.

"It's Ox's birthday," I said.

"It is," Elizabeth agreed. "A big one. He turns thirty tomorrow. We're celebrating today because it seemed right. Tradition, you know."

"I don't have a present for him."

"I think you'll find that you being here is more precious than any gift he could hope to receive."

"And besides," Jessie said easily, "you can just put your name on what I got for him. Say it's from the both of us."

"What did you get him?"

She grinned. "A shirt I found online. Three wolves howling at the moon. It's awful. I can't wait to see the look on his face."

How easy they made it sound. "Last year."

Elizabeth and Jessie exchanged a look. "What about last year?" Jessie asked.

I put my hands on the edge of the sink. "Did you celebrate then too?"

"Yes."

"Oh." Of course they would have. I'd only been gone a few months, if what they'd told me was correct. And then, they wouldn't have been looking for me. They still would have thought me a traitor.

Elizabeth was behind me. I hadn't even heard her move. Her chin was on my shoulder, her lips near my ear. She said, "It wasn't the same. Nothing was the same. No matter what happened, no matter everything that came before and everything that followed, it wasn't the same. For any of us."

I looked down at the sink. "I don't know if it'll ever be the same again."

"Maybe not. But we start again. Because even if everything is burnt to a crisp, we can always try again and again. Jessie, I think the carrots are done."

"Yes, ma'am," Jessie said.

I closed my eyes.

Joe and Ox came walking down the road, hand in hand. I was standing on the front porch, my nails digging into the railing.

"All right?" Joe asked as they stopped near the stairs.

I shrugged. "Happy birthday, Ox."

"Thanks, Robbie. I—"

"The people in Green Creek don't know what I did, do they."

Ox tilted his head. He didn't act surprised or like he didn't know what I was talking about. "No. Why do you ask?"

"They weren't scared of me. When I went there. They all seemed happy to see me."

Joe nodded slowly. "We thought it was better that way. In case you ever came back."

I laughed bitterly. "Why? You thought I was a monster. A murderer. And I guess that wasn't too far from the truth. Who was he? The Omega I killed."

Joe said, "Maybe we could do this later—"

"His name was Alan," Ox said, and Joe sighed. "He'd been infected by another Omega in Kansas. His pack was small. He left them because he didn't want to hurt them."

I nodded but didn't look at them. "And he came here looking for help. Because of who—*what*—you are."

"He was one of them, yes."

"There's been a lot? Omegas, I mean."

"Yes."

"And you help them."

"Yes."

"And I killed him."

"It wasn't you," Joe said hotly. I looked up, and his eyes were filling with red. He crossed his arms over his chest. "You had no control. You weren't *you*. This is on Livingstone, Robbie. He took away your free will. He *made* you do this."

"It was still my hands," I mumbled. "Still my teeth. And Chris and Tanner—"

Ox was up on the porch and next to me before I could finish. He wrapped his arms around me, holding me close. I didn't hug him back, my arms dangling at my sides. He squeezed me hard like he was trying to force me into his chest.

"I don't want to remember," I said against his neck. "Because if I do, I'll remember what it felt like. I'll know what it's like to kill an innocent person. How can I come back from that, Ox? How can you even stand to look at me?"

"Because you're mine," he said simply. "And that will never change."

"You let me go," I choked out. "You let me go because you all thought I . . ."

"Fuck," Joe muttered.

"We did," Ox said, and it hurt more than I thought it would. "We were scared. Confused. And we were wrong. It took us longer than I like to think to realize just how wrong we were."

"Maybe it'd be easier if I just—"

"Nope," Joe said. "Get that out of your head right now. You're not going anywhere. I don't care if we have to shove a tracker up your ass, you're staying right here where you belong. We got you back, Robbie. Do you really think we'd let you go?"

"What if it happens again?"

Joe had no response to that.

Ox did, though. He said, "They won't touch you again," and his voice was deep and strong. "I won't allow it. Let them come. We'll show them what happens when you fuck with the Bennett pack."

I tried to pull away from them, but they wouldn't let me. Joe stood on one side of me, Ox on the other. They held my hands. We walked through the house toward the kitchen. Jessie had gone to the backyard. Elizabeth looked up at us, first at Joe. Then Ox. Then me. She nodded. "Good."

And that was it.

She said, "Joe, if you please, the cutlery. Ox, don't lift a finger. It's your birthday and you don't get to do a single thing. In fact, why don't you take Robbie out back? I'm sure the others want to see him."

I didn't know about that, but Ox wouldn't let me go.

He pulled me toward the back door. I could hear the others laughing and talking loudly. The timber wolf growled at something Carter was saying, and Kelly was teasing them both.

Rico saw us first. His expression hardened, but he didn't say a word.

Chris and Tanner were next. "Birthday boy!" Chris shouted. He grinned at the both of us. "And look what the wolf dragged in."

Tanner said, "You're so old now, Ox. You realize that, right? It's all downhill from here. Unless you're lucky like me." He flexed, kissing each of his biceps. "Yeah, that's the good stuff."

Chris shoved him. "No one wants to see that, man. Put those away before you hurt yourself."

Tanner flashed orange eyes at him in challenge.

Apparently Chris couldn't resist. He tackled Tanner to the ground, and they started wrestling as they shouted at each other.

Jessie looked down at them, grimacing. "Men are so stupid. I'm so glad I'm into women these days." She smiled wickedly. "No offense, Ox. You were good for a little while."

My eyes bulged.

"As your Alpha," Joe said as he stepped around us, "I am ordering you never to bring up your history with my mate ever again."

"Oh sure," Jessie said. "I'll get right on that." She paused, considering. Then, "Which is something I said to Ox."

She laughed as Joe growled at her.

"Where's Dominique?" Tanner asked, panting on the ground next to Chris. They'd apparently called a truce.

"Coming with Bambi. Should be here in a little bit."

Ox squeezed my hand before letting go. He pushed me toward the table. He pulled out a chair near the end and motioned for me to sit down.

It went like this:

Ox sat at one end of the table, Joe at the other.

To Ox's right was Mark, a position reserved for the second to the Alpha.

To Joe's right was Carter, the timber wolf lying behind his chair.

I was to Ox's left.

Elizabeth was to Joe's left.

It wasn't lost on me what this meant.

The right was for the second.

The left was a position of trust.

Ox was showing he trusted me.

Rico wasn't happy as he sat on the other side of the table. Chris and Tanner sat next to him.

Kelly pulled out the chair next to me. He sat down. I thought he was going to reach out and take my hand, but he didn't. He kept his hands in his own lap.

He said, "Hello, Robbie."

I was suddenly nervous. I wondered what he'd thought of the breakfast I'd made for him. I muttered, "Hey."

Jessie sat down next to him. On her other side, between her and Elizabeth, was an empty chair. Rico also had an empty chair next to him. It wasn't long before they were filled.

The woman from the truck walked in, keys jangling as she flipped them back and forth. Behind her was the Omega from the diner.

I tried not to stare when Rico got a dopey look on his face as Bambi bent over and kissed him sweetly. Then she pushed him away, ruffling his hair. He didn't seem to mind.

The Omega eyed me warily but was distracted when Jessie pulled her down into the last chair, smiling widely.

And then it was quiet.

The only sounds came from the forest.

It was like we were waiting. For what, I didn't know.

Ox put his hands on the table. He closed his eyes and took in a deep breath. His chest expanded, and he held his breath for a beat, then two, then three before letting it out slowly. He opened his eyes.

He said, "My mother. She liked to dance. In the kitchen. Once, we were doing the dishes, and there was a soap bubble in my ear. She popped it. And then we danced. That was a good day, for many reasons."

Joe's smile was blinding.

"Things have changed since then," Ox continued. "We're not who we once were. We've lived and lost. But I like to think that she's still here. Somewhere. Somehow. And I know she's proud of who I am and what I've made for myself. My daddy said I was going to get shit all my life. He didn't know that I would have pack who would do anything for me, as I would do everything for them. And while we may not be who we once were, we're still here." He glanced at me before looking back out at the others. "We're still together." He raised his glass. The others did the same. After a moment, I did too, though

I felt like a fraud. "To Maggie. To Thomas. To all those we've lost and all those we've found again."

"And to Ox on his motherfucking birthday," Tanner said cheerfully, and most everyone laughed as they raised their glasses even higher.

I didn't.

Neither did Rico.

It was slow, this meal. Leisurely.

I never wanted it to end.

I wanted to go back to the basement and hide away.

I stayed quiet for most of it, taking in all the sights and sounds and smells. There was blue still, clinging and cold. Green too. Relief, though it felt fragile.

It didn't help (hurt?) that Carter got it in his head that he needed to get his brother drunk.

"Think about it," Carter said to Kelly from across the table. "Who knows how long you're going to be human? You gotta go for it, Kelly."

Tanner sighed as he glared down at his bottle of beer. "You know, this whole wolf thing lets me jump ten feet in the air from a crouch, but I can't even get a buzz. What kind of messed-up shit is that?"

Chris nodded. "You did like to drink beer more than you liked to jump."

Mark looked amused. "You can shift into a wolf the size of a small horse, and you regret not being able to get drunk?"

"So much," Tanner said. "I mean, don't get me wrong. The fact that I can shift into a killing machine is pretty damn cool, but fuck, what I wouldn't give just to not be sober for, like, five seconds. Weed doesn't even work on me anymore." He blanched as he glanced at Gordo. "Not that I've ever been stoned before, boss. Because hugs, not drugs. Or whatever."

Gordo snorted. "Bullshit. We got high for the first time when we were what, fourteen? Fifteen?"

"You did?" Mark asked, arching an eyebrow.

"You wouldn't know. That was when you were an asshole and I never wanted to see you again."

"You told me that last week," Mark said.

Gordo rolled his eyes. "That's because you left your wet towel on the floor. *Again.* You're lucky I didn't kick you out right then and there. You would have nowhere else to go, and I wouldn't even feel bad about it."

"I wouldn't take you back," Elizabeth agreed. "You don't know the relief I felt when you and Gordo finally stopped being idiots. I turned your old room into a second studio. I don't plan on changing it back. It's probably for the best that you pick up your wet towels."

Mark laughed at Gordo's smug expression. "Duly noted."

"I'm going to bring Kelly into the Lighthouse," Carter told Bambi, "and you're going to keep bringing drinks until Kelly throws up or goes to sleep, whichever comes first."

Kelly pulled a face. "Let's not do that."

"I got you," Bambi said easily. "He won't be able to leave unless he has to be carried out. What's your poison? You seem like the fruity drink kind of guy. Little umbrella. Sorority girl cocktails."

Chris and Tanner and Carter looked delighted.

Kelly, not so much.

"I'm going to live vicariously through you," Chris said, staring at Kelly. "Just so you know. You're going to describe it in great detail. And you have to sing. Because everyone knows when you get super drunk, you have to sing."

Dominique laughed but covered it up when I glanced at her. She seemed uncomfortable, and Jessie reached over and took her hand. I didn't think she was pack, not like the others, but that didn't mean she hadn't heard about what I'd done. She wasn't scared of me, but she wasn't *not* either.

Rico said, "So we're just going to act like everything is fine. Like this is normal."

And it was weird, because I was thinking the same exact thing.

Everyone fell silent.

He glared down at the table. He was stiff with anger.

Bambi put a hand on his shoulder but pulled away when he didn't react.

Ox frowned. "Rico. Look at me."

Rico didn't.

"Rico."

He huffed but did as his Alpha asked.

"Nothing is normal," Ox said quietly. "It hasn't been for a long time."

Rico shook his head. "Understatement, *alfa*. I get that you're all for the greater good, but I can't do that. I'm not like you." He raised his voice. "Or apparently any of you. It's like you all have memory issues, and not just our Robbie here."

"Not cool, man," Tanner said. He looked nervous, glancing between me and Rico. "He wasn't . . . It's okay."

Rico slammed his hand on the table. The plates rattled. An empty bottle fell over. "It's *not* okay. You didn't *see* what I did." He swallowed, his throat clicking. His eyes were bright and glassy. "You didn't hear it."

Chris rubbed his jaw. "I dunno, Rico. I think I did see it. I think I did hear it. And you know what I had that you didn't? I *felt* it." He winced. "All of it. And I get you're pissed, but let's not do this now, okay? We're here for Ox. We're together. I'm not saying let bygones be bygones, but just . . . curb it for a little while."

"I can go," I said quietly. "If it makes things easier. I don't want to—"

Kelly took my hand in his under the table. He pulled it into his lap and held on tightly.

"No," Ox said. "You're staying right where you are. Rico, you want to have this out? Fine. We'll do it now."

He recoiled slightly. "No, hey, I didn't—it's not like I'm trying to—"

"Yes," Ox said flatly, "you are. And if you have a problem with a member of the pack, then we deal with it *as* a pack."

"Pack," Rico said, sounding incredulous. "He doesn't even know who the fuck he is! We can't *feel* him. Not like we used to. How the hell is he still pack? It broke. The bonds between us *broke*. Maybe it was Gordo's dad, but how do you know? How the hell can you be sure that he didn't *invite* it in? You all saw how he was with Michelle before Elijah came. He was *begging* her. And look what's happened since. Tanner and Chris almost died. An Omega is *dead*. And then we find his sorry ass and we go *save* him, and what happens? Kelly's wolf has been ripped from him—"

"Leave me out of this," Kelly said. "I can speak for myself. Don't you dare try to use me against him. It's not fair."

I thought Rico was going to apologize to Kelly. He didn't. He said, "Fine. Let's leave you out of this. But all the rest? I can't forgive and forget. Not like the rest of you. You're all walking on eggshells around him like you think he's fragile. Well guess what: he's not. I was *there*. I saw what he did, and if I'd had my gun, I would have killed him."

"Holy shit," Carter muttered as the timber wolf whined.

"That's enough," Gordo snapped. "I don't want to hear another—"

"Oh, I bet you don't," Rico said. "I get it, papi. You've got your favorite back. You're good to go." He stood, the table shifting as he struck it with his thighs. "I'm sorry that I'm not all rah-rah Team Robbie like everyone else. But I held my friend as he *died* in my arms, and I can't forget that. I won't. And you all forcing this, acting like everything is fine, isn't helping either."

"Sit down," Elizabeth said.

"Are you even hearing me? I'm not—"

"Sit. *Down*."

The power in her voice was undeniable. Rico opened his mouth again like he was going to argue, but instead he did as he was told.

Joe said, "Maybe we should—" but Elizabeth held up her hand without looking at him, and he fell silent.

"I love you," she said to Rico. "You're important to me. To all of us. And you are justified in your anger."

"*Thank* you, *mamacita*," he said. "It's good to know that—"

"I'm not finished. Don't interrupt me again."

He gulped.

"You're justified in your anger," she repeated. "But it's dangerously misplaced. This is what they want. Doubt. To pit us against one another. Because if we let anger consume us, if we let it take control, then we run the risk of losing everything we love."

"Where was this when Joe decided to break apart the pack?" Rico demanded. "When they all left to go after Richard Collins? Did you tell them the same thing?"

"You weren't even there," Gordo said. "You weren't part of this then."

"Only because you kept it from us," Rico retorted. "We had to find out from Oxnard about all of it. You left a note and you were *gone*. Your life, man. We thought we knew you. We didn't. We thought we knew Robbie. *We didn't*. Because—"

"What do you want?" Elizabeth asked. "What do you hope to have happen here?"

Rico fisted his hair. "Argh. I don't know. But I can't just sit here and pretend nothing has changed. *Everything* has changed."

I said, "I don't remember."

Everyone looked at me.

I wanted to run.

To find a hidey-hole in a tree and be as quiet as a mouse.

My mother laughed somewhere in my head. *Little wolf,* she whispered. *Little wolf. Can't you see?*

I couldn't run. I couldn't hide.

I was very tired.

I said, "I don't remember, and I'm sorry because I don't know if I want to. If I did everything you're saying, then I don't want to remember because I don't know that I would survive it."

Kelly hung his head.

I looked at Tanner and Chris. "I didn't mean to hurt you. I don't know how I know that. But if I was here, if I was part of this pack once, then that would have been what was important to me. It's all I've ever wanted. A place to belong. A home." My voice cracked. "And if I had that, then I would never have done anything to have that taken from me."

Tanner smiled tightly.

Chris nodded, though he looked a little pale.

I looked back at Rico. He was furious, though he kept it coiled inside. "I don't expect you to trust me. Or even forgive me."

"Good."

"But I'm lost," I admitted. "And I don't know how to find my way back. Everything I thought my life was, everything I knew, it was a lie. Because my real life was taken from me by someone I loved. Someone I trusted. I thought I knew the way the world worked. I didn't. I don't know any of you. I wish I did even as I hope I never get my memory back."

It was Kelly who moved then.

He stood abruptly, his chair falling back into the grass.

He let go of my hand as he turned and headed for the house.

"Seriously," Carter said, standing to follow his brother, "fuck you guys. Fuck you very much."

The timber wolf trailed after him, tail swishing back and forth.

Rico scrubbed a hand over his face. "Fuck. Ox, I'm sorry, man. I didn't mean—"

"Yes," Ox said, "you did. You're hurting. I get that. You're angry. I get that too. But you aren't the only one who feels that way. And I think it's time you start remembering that. We're pack, and I'll be damned if I'm going to let it be torn apart from the inside."

Rico nodded jerkily. Bambi leaned over and whispered in his ear, but it wasn't meant for me to hear, so I didn't try to listen. Instead I turned toward the house, hearing Carter and Kelly's muffled voices.

I thought about going after them, but before I could, a phone began to vibrate.

Gordo frowned as he pulled his phone out of his pocket. He glanced down at the screen.

He closed his eyes and sighed. "Well, their timing certainly sucks."

"What is it?" Ox asked.

"Aileen," he said as he looked at me. I slumped lower in my seat. It didn't help. "Patrice. They're early."

HOUSE IN ORDER / PACK DIVIDED

We stood on the dirt road in front of the house, watching a plume of dust rise up behind an old sedan as it drove toward us.

Bambi and Dominique had left already, heading back into town. Bambi said it'd be easier if they weren't there, that it needed to be pack.

I didn't like the sound of that, especially when Jessie told me Aileen and Patrice were witches.

Kelly was pale as he stood next to his brother. Carter looked as if he would have punched anyone who spoke to them, so I didn't try. I thought I was being honest, but I'd fucked up. I didn't know how to make things right.

With any of them.

The car stopped in front of the house.

A woman climbed out of the passenger side, a lit cigarette dangling between her teeth. She was older and worn, her skin wrinkled. But through the smoke came the stench of magic unlike anything I'd ever smelled before. It was rough and wild and made me sneeze.

The driver was a man with bone-white skin. He wore a fedora and sunglasses that covered most of his face. Pale red hair stuck out from underneath his hat, and when he took off his sunglasses, I saw his face was covered with rusty freckles. His magic felt cleansing, like it was made of white light.

Aileen coughed around her cigarette, a wet hacking sound. "Well, shit," she said. "This is more fucked up than I expected. You feel it?"

Patrice nodded. "Deep. Dark. Heavy. Dis isn't gonna be easy."

She sighed. "Yeah. We've got our work cut out for us. Let's see what we see."

* * *

"It's best before the full moon," Aileen said, leading us into the woods. "I'm not a fan of how close it is now, but we should try to get it over with. Don't need to have this one turn into some kind of rage monster if we can avoid it, eh, Robbie?"

She smiled at me.

It didn't make me feel any better.

She was plucking leaves from the bushes around her, folding them into her hand and crushing them together. I grimaced when she opened her hand again and spit into the pile.

"It ain't pretty," she said when she saw me watching her. "A little bit of dirty magic. But it'll have to do. No promises, boyo. It might be too far gone."

"What might be too far gone?" I asked, not liking the sound of any of this.

She laughed until she saw I didn't get the joke. She looked slowly over at Gordo. "You didn't tell him?"

Gordo shrugged. "We got busy. Family problems. And it's Ox's birthday. Almost."

She snorted, exhaling a plume of smoke. "That right? Salutations, and all that. But I thought something was up. You're all jumbled. Out of sync. Keeping secrets. That never works out for anyone."

"That's one way to put it," Rico muttered.

Aileen arched an eyebrow at him. "Is it? Because it's coming off of you almost more than anyone. Got a problem, Rico?"

"Several."

"Then get over it. At least for today. We can't have the negativity. It'll mess things up. A pack divided is a pack that cannot stand true. We just drove two days to get here to help you sorry bunch. You're not a little bitch, so stop acting like one."

He looked outraged as Chris and Tanner laughed behind him.

She plucked a couple of small red berries from a bush, crushed them on top of the leaves and her spit. Seeds and juice squirted out between her fingers. They were poisonous, so I recoiled when she held the mess out toward me and said, "Eat this."

"You spit on it."

"I am aware."

"Then I decline," I said. And then, because she was a powerful witch, I added, "Ma'am."

Rico sounded like he was choking and was angry about it.

"Hmm," Aileen said. She looked down at the wet pile in her hand. "I suppose I can get a slice of cheese and wrap it in it. That's what I do for my dogs." She squinted at me. "Would that help?"

Every wolf growled at her.

"That's speciesist," Tanner said. He blinked. "Wow. Now I understand prejudice. That's eye-opening. Damn. I have fucked up a *lot* in my life. I'm going to start making amends first thing tomorrow. After Robbie scarfs down the spit berries like a good boy."

"I'm not going to eat that," I told her. "It's weird, I know, but I have this thing where I don't eat out of people's hands after they've spat on them."

"You ate cat poop once when you were shifted," Elizabeth said mildly.

I gaped at her.

She shrugged. "Don't look at me. I tried to stop you."

"Dis pack," Patrice said, shaking his head. "Just when I tink I have dem all figured out."

I recovered. "I don't know what you're trying to do to me, but I don't—"

Aileen cut me off. "Sorry, boyo. We're not here for you. Or at least not *just* you. There's not much more we can do that Gordo and your pack haven't already tried. I'm afraid that until we can get to Livingstone, you're going to be as you are now. This is about Kelly."

"Oh," I said weakly. "No one told me."

Kelly was stiff beside me.

"I know." She sounded frustrated. "I get things are moving fast, and there are many moving parts, but I wasn't kidding when I said this could be a problem." She turned to Joe and Ox. "Get your house in order, Alphas. You're not helping anyone the way you are now."

"We're trying," Joe said quietly. "It's complicated."

"Is it?" she asked. "Because as far as I can tell, you're all together once again. It may not be like it was, but it's a start." Then, without looking at him, she said, "Rico, stop scowling."

"I'm *not*," Rico said, scowl deepening.

She flicked him in the forehead. "Stop it."

He growled at her, sounding more wolflike than any human I'd ever heard.

"Eat this," she said to me again, holding out her hand.

I gave it one last try. "But if it's about Kelly, maybe he should be the one to eat it."

"Oh, that's *right*!" she exclaimed. "I don't know what I was thinking."

"Really?" I hadn't expected that to work.

"No. Not really. Don't be ridiculous. Do I need to get the others to hold your mouth open? I'll massage your throat to make sure you swallow."

"Bet he's never heard *that* before," Carter muttered. Then he looked at me. "Have you ever heard that before? I mean, I know Kelly is ace and all, but—"

"Enough," Patrice said. He turned to me. "Dis is your mate."

I looked down at my feet. "So I've heard." I winced as Kelly sighed. "That came out wrong. Do you really think this could help him?"

"I don't know," Aileen admitted. "But we're running out of options. What do you think Robert Livingstone is doing right this second? Licking his wounds? Biding his time? He's not, boyo. He's planning. What, we don't know. Hell, we don't even know *where* he is. But you were taken from him. Whatever he had in mind for you, whatever he was grooming you for, he's had to course correct. Out of sight is not out of mind with him. We don't know what he'll do, but he won't stop."

I felt sick. "All those wolves in the compound. Will he hurt them? There are children there. Cubs."

She hesitated.

And that was enough.

I grabbed the mess from her hand and shoved it in my mouth. I bit down, grimacing at the taste. I swallowed, and almost immediately my stomach cramped. Before I could say anything else, Aileen stood in front of me, her palm inches from my face as she muttered under her breath.

The cramps increased as she pulled her hand away and blew a quick breath in my face.

"Shit," I muttered as I bent over, clutching my stomach. "What did you do to me?" The grass at my feet swayed side to side as if in a breeze. But then it started rubbing against my boots, leaving green smears against black leather. I yelped and hopped back, trying to get away from it. I looked up, and all the colors of the forest started to bleed together. "Um. What?"

Aileen was squinting at me, and I squeaked in horror as her eyes began to move around her head. The left went to her forehead. The right settled just above her lips. "I might have dosed him a little too much."

"Ohhh *shiiiit*," I breathed as her lips flew away from her mouth and settled in a tree branch overhead. "Your mouth is a bird."

"We must hurry," Patrice said, grabbing me by the arm and jerking me through the trees. "Get to da clearing. Now, Bennett pack. As if your lives depend on it."

By the time we reached the clearing, I was convinced the ground was lava and that Rico was going to die.

He wasn't amused when I threw him over my shoulder.

"You'll *melt*," I snapped, hopping over the crack in the earth filled with boiling lava. "I know you don't like me, but I won't let you die."

He pounded his fists on my back. "I swear to God, I will *end* you. Chris! Give me my gun!"

"Nah," Chris said, seemingly unaware that his nose had migrated to his chest above his right nipple. "Think that would be a bad idea."

I jumped over another lava hole. The clearing ahead looked safer, so I set him down. "There," I told him, leaning forward until my cheek grazed his. "You're safe."

He shoved me away. "*Pendejo*. Don't touch me, you fucking weirdo."

Aileen pressed down on my shoulders. I sank to the ground as the grass danced around me. I grinned goofily at Kelly as he sat across from me, his knees bumping into mine. "I don't love you," I told him. "And I know that makes you sad. But I like your face. It's a good face. You should keep it."

His lips twitched. "I'll keep that in mind." He touched the back of my hand. "I like your face too."

I puffed out my chest. "I worked hard on it."

"Cute," Aileen muttered. "Ox, behind Robbie. Joe, behind Kelly. Everyone else, spread out, but make sure you're touching a member of your pack. You need the connection."

The others formed around us. Carter and the timber wolf sat near Kelly. Carter put his hand on Kelly's knee, and the timber wolf laid his gigantic head in Carter's lap. Elizabeth sat on the other side of Kelly, laying her head on his shoulder, closing her eyes. Joe knelt behind them, hands in Kelly's hair.

I tilted my head back when heavy hands fell on my shoulders. Ox looked down at me, and he was the biggest man in the entire world. His head was surrounded with a halo of stars. He looked like a god.

I was distracted from this thought when Gordo crouched next to me. His tattoos glowed fiercely, and the raven in the roses jerked its head from side to side. He reached up and delicately wrapped his hand around Mark's throat. The wings of the raven twin fluttered.

"Where'd your other hand go?" I asked sadly, looking down at the stump pressed against my knee. "You lost it."

Gordo grunted. "Long story, kid."

"Do you miss it?"

He sighed. "We'll talk about it later."

"Okay. Oh, hey, Tanner."

Tanner grinned at me as he leaned against me. "Hey, Robbie."

"Sorry I almost murdered you."

"Um. Thank you?"

I nodded. "I don't know you either, but you seem like a nice guy. I wouldn't hurt you unless you were trying to hurt me. You too, Chris."

Chris shook his head from the other side of Tanner. "It was magic, man. We get that."

"Rico doesn't think so. But don't tell him I said that. *He's standing right there.*"

Rico glared at me as he stood behind Tanner. Jessie rolled her eyes and pulled him to the ground. She held her brother's hand, and Rico grumbled under his breath as he hooked his chin over Tanner's shoulder. "At least we're not all naked this time."

That sounded like a good idea, but Ox stopped me before I could take off my clothes. I looked back up again, and I swore he was the center of the entire universe. His face was the moon, and I wanted to howl for him to hear me.

"Alpha," I whispered to him.

He brushed a lock of my hair off my forehead. "Little wolf."

Aileen and Patrice circled around us. Patrice's lips were moving, but no sound came out. He was bathed in a white light that seemed to emanate from within. The rusty freckles on his face swirled on his cheeks.

"This isn't going to be easy," Aileen said. "Not after everything you've been through. I can't promise anything will come of this. You're fractured. There are cracks. Unless you believe in one another, believe in your pack, it will remain that way."

Rico opened his mouth as if to speak but snapped it closed. He shook his head instead.

I startled when Kelly took my hands in his. He was watching me with those blue, blue eyes. Something stirred deep within me, something primal and brutal. I wanted to tear apart everything that would ever hurt him. It was grass and lake water and sunshine.

I said, "I'm sorry."

He said, "For what?"

I said, "I don't know."

He said, "That's okay."

Before I could tell him it *wasn't* okay, that I wished I could be the man he needed me to be, the man he remembered, that I didn't think anyone had ever looked at me the way he was now, Aileen said, "It begins."

And I—

⋅ ⋅ ⋅

—am alone.
(not alone here we're here we're)
i look up at the night sky.
it's bright.
so many stars.
the brightest are red and pulsing.
others surround them like beacons in the dark.
i reach up to touch them.
they don't burn me.
it's the surface of a lake.
the stars ripple.
they laugh.
they howl.
they sing.
they say
(BrotherSonLoveFriend)
and
(packpackpack)
and it hurts.
it hurts.

it hurts because i can't find them.
i can't reach them.
i can't touch them.
these stars are

"Hey," Kelly says, and I say "Hey" back.

He's smiling, and it might be the best smile I've ever seen.

I dreamed of this, I think. Once.

It's familiar, like we've been here before.

"What is this?" I ask as we walk through the woods.

He laughs, taking my hand in his. "It's nothing. Just . . . why do you ask so many questions all the time?"

I bump my shoulder against his. "I need you to come with me. That's what you said. You have to know how that sounds. All mysterious."

"It's . . . goddammit. I'm not trying to be *mysterious*."

I don't believe him, but it doesn't matter because there is nowhere else I'd rather be.

He says, "I know," like he can hear my thoughts. Maybe he can. It wouldn't be such a bad thing. Having someone know me like that.

He

(*here here here*)

stops. Grimaces. His face contorts. He says, "It hurts, Robbie."

"No," I tell him. "It can't hurt. Not like this. You have to say it isn't anything bad. That you hope it's good. That *I'll* think it's good. That's how it's supposed to go. That's how it's supposed to—"

His back snaps viciously as his face turns toward the sky. His mouth is open, but no sound comes out. The cords in his neck stick out sharply. His eyes are wide, and he's gripping my hand so hard, I think the bones will turn to dust.

But I don't try to pull away.

I can't.

I won't.

Not now.

Not ever.

Symbols appear on his throat, dirty things that split his skin and glow with a sick light. His mouth stretches farther than should be humanly possible, and I cry out as the snout of a wolf appears between his teeth, fangs bared.

Something's wrong.
Because the wolf is sick.
The hair on its snout is patchy, the skin underneath dry and cracked. The tongue is coated with a thick film, and more symbols crawl along it. One fang falls out of its mouth and bounces off Kelly's chest before hitting the ground.
The wolf is rotting.
Before Kelly swallows it back down, I catch the brief glimpse of orange eyes, dull and lifeless and I—
am alone.
he's gone.
the stars are gone.
i am alone in the dark.
except.
a white wolf approaches.
there is black on its chest and back.
its eyes are red.
i am afraid.
i am not afraid.
i am both.
it circles me.
it doesn't speak aloud.
it whispers in my head.
it says
(little wolf, little wolf, what do you hear?)
i don't know. i don't know. I DON'T KNOW I DON'T KNOW I DON'T
(you think yourself lost, but your pack is near.)
i scream in the dark.
the white wolf is gone.
all that's left is the void and i—

—opened my eyes.
I was lying flat on my back, my head in someone's lap.
I blinked.
Kelly stared down at me.
"What happened?" I croaked.
He tried to smile, but it crumbled. "Don't worry about it. Just rest."

He traced a finger over my eyebrows, and I leaned into the touch. I was at peace. I felt safe. And warm.

It didn't last long.

"—and we can't help you, Alphas," Aileen said from somewhere off to my left. "Not when you're so broken. Your bonds—this pack—are stronger than any other I've ever encountered. You've got your missing piece back. But it's not the same. There is dissonance. Much of it can be blamed on the magic in Kelly and Robbie. Even in Carter and Mark, though I think Ox has that mostly under control. But there is distrust here. In each other. In yourselves. You cannot hope to stand and fight for us all when you can't even hold your own pack together."

"We only just got him back," Joe retorted, sounding pissed off.

"And it took how long for dat ta happen?" Patrice asked, voice soft.

There was no response.

"Shards," Patrice said. "Pieces of a whole. But dere sharp. Dey cut. You slice yourselves even as you know it's wrong."

Joe tried again. "If Rico would just—"

"It's not just Rico," Aileen snapped. "Or Kelly. Or Robbie. You've been hurt. I get that. I do. Lord knows I do. But it's coming from all of you. You are a pack divided. And divided you will fall. Because he will *exploit* it. Whatever he wants, whatever he's after, he won't stop. This is nothing but a setback to him. He'll come again and again and again until either he wins or you stop him. The fate of all of us rests in your hands, and *you are not ready*."

"Go easy, Aileen," Patrice said quietly. "Even if dey weren't as dey are, we don't know what would have happened. It's old, dis magic. Unlike anyting I've ever seen."

She glared at him. "I know. But they're not helping. They're spinning their wheels. What *exactly* is your plan, Alphas? You let yourselves become distracted by the Omegas, you watched as a member of your pack was taken from you, and what have you done? How much longer will this go on before you decide to act?"

"Aileen," Patrice warned as Ox and Joe looked contrite.

She sighed. "I know. I just . . . I thought the mate bond between Robbie and Kelly would be enough, even if it's stifled. But it's like it was for Gordo and Mark, only on a bigger scale. Richard Collins had his wolf stifled, shoved down and locked into a box. This . . . this is like Kelly has been *stripped* of his wolf. I've never seen anything like it. Done to witches, yes, but never a wolf. Do you even feel him like the others?"

"No," Ox said. "Not . . . it's not the same. With him or Robbie."

I looked up at Kelly.

He was staring off into nothing.

"We may need ta figure something else out," Patrice said. "Just in case."

"But the Bennetts are our best chance. Our *only* chance. If they can't lead, then who will? What hope do we possibly have? We're running out of time, Patrice. All those witches that turned against us, that were taken out by the Omegas . . . our numbers are dwindling. And we're just letting it happen." She glanced at Ox and Joe. "Figure it out. Before it's too late."

"It's okay," Kelly whispered. "We'll figure it out."

I would have given anything to believe him.

They didn't stay long after, saying they had other matters to attend to. It felt forced, and even though their hearts never stuttered, I thought they were lying. I could see the worried expressions on both their faces.

Before they left, Aileen pulled Kelly aside. He wouldn't look at her when she spoke. I thought about listening in to what she was saying, but I didn't. It wasn't right.

I let them be.

NOT THIS AGAIN / YOU LOVED ME

Bright and early the next morning, Gordo appeared in the basement. He didn't have to kick the line of silver away because there wasn't one. Ox had told me I could take my old room the night before, but I'd gone to the basement instead.

And stared at the ceiling for most of the night.

I was groggy and exhausted by the time Gordo came down, a stern look on his face, arms full of clothes.

"Get up," he said.

I didn't know why I thought it would work. Last time I'd gotten the hose. But still, I turned away from him on the cot, pulling the blanket over my head.

"Last chance, Robbie."

"Fuck off, Gordo."

"All right," he said. "If that's how it's going to be."

I thought he was going to leave.

I should have known better.

One moment I was in my blanket cocoon, and the next the cot was tipping over, sending me tumbling to the floor. "Hey!"

"Shut up. I don't want to hear it. Get dressed."

"No."

He bent over me, eyes narrowed. "Tell me no one more time, I dare you."

I steeled my nerves, looked up at him, and said, "No."

· · ·

Five minutes later I was glaring daggers at his back as I followed him up the stairs. The clothes he'd given me were a little tight, but they smelled like oil and metal and wolves. The shirt had a patch on it, my name stitched neatly into it.

"The sun isn't even up," I grumbled.

"It's good to know your powers of observation are still intact." He paused at the top of the stairs. I almost bumped into his back. He turned around, looking me up and down. He sighed and reached into the pocket of his work pants, which matched the ones he'd given me. He pulled out a pair of glasses and handed them over to me. "Put those on."

"I can see without them."

"Good. Then I'll just break them."

I yelped as he started to do just that, snatched them out of his hands, and put them on. Something soft crossed his face before he rolled his eyes. "You look stupid with those on. You're a terrible werewolf."

"You just handed them to me."

"I know. And I hate myself for it. Come on. You're not going to be late on your first day back. You've already missed enough time as it is, and I will not hesitate to fire your ass." He was about to turn around, but he stopped. His brow furrowed and he frowned. Then, gruffly, "I know you think that it didn't work with Kelly because of you. But that's not it. Or at least that's not *all* of it. If he's anything like me, he would rather have you here as you are than not at all. No matter what happens, no matter how long it takes, don't ever think you won't get to where you need to be. And we'll be right there, every step of the way. Okay?"

I nodded dumbly.

"Okay. Now enough of the feelings shit. I already get too much of that with Mark. Move your ass. Don't make me tell you again."

· · · · ·

Gordo's had been fixed back up, the pictures reframed and hung back on the wall. Some still had obvious tears in them, but tape held them together. Someone had patched and repainted the wall.

My missing poster was gone.

The sun was barely over the horizon as Gordo sat me down at the front desk, pushing me onto the chair. Music poured in through the door that led to the garage. Chris and Tanner were laughing.

"This is yours," Gordo said.

The desk was sticky, and the computer looked like it hadn't been cleaned in months. A phone with multiple lines sat next to it, the handset smudged with something black. "Gee. All of this? You really shouldn't have."

He smacked the back of my head. "Less talking, more listening."

I grimaced as I poked the mouse. It was crusty. "Do you guys ever clean here?"

He almost looked embarrassed. "We didn't—shut up. It was easier when you were here. You kept things clean." Then he grinned. "You made a good office wife."

"Oh, fuck you, Gordo."

"You answer the phones. You schedule appointments. You do intake when people bring in their cars."

"I don't even know the programs you use on the computer," I pointed out.

"You wrote most them. You'll figure it out."

"Oh."

"Yeah, *oh*. You get a break for lunch, and you can take a smoke break or two if you need it—"

"I *smoked*?" I asked, incredulous.

He snorted. "You tried once. Then you bitched for a week after that the smell wouldn't go away." He scratched the back of his neck. "None of us smoke, not anymore, though I would probably kill half of you for a cigarette, Mark be damned. But it's the same principle. Smoke break is just a break. Any questions about office stuff, don't ask me. I don't understand half this shit." He paused. "I may need you to look at my computer in the office. It's beeping. At me. And runs really slow."

"How did you guys ever survive without me?" I asked.

He was quiet for a moment as I turned the computer on. "I don't know. Whatever it was, kid, it wasn't survival. It was a holding pattern. Stasis. And it wasn't good."

I turned to look back at him, but he was already pushing his way through the door. He called out over his shoulder, "And there's a damn Keurig machine that you won't even remember asking for. You said it would make the place look more professional. That's the dumbest thing I've ever heard, but it's there anyway."

Everything was a mess.

I spent ten minutes wiping down the desk and keyboard with an ancient bottle of cleaner I found in one of the drawers. The Keurig sat on a card table next to a water cooler. An assortment of K-cups sat in an old wicker basket on the table. I sighed as I stared down at it. It didn't look professional at all.

Before I could do anything about it, the front door opened.

Rico walked in, followed by Ox.

"—and it sucks, *alfa*, and I know that I'm part of it, but I don't know how to let it go," Rico was saying. "I don't know how to fix . . . this."

He stopped when he saw me standing next to the desk.

I waved pathetically.

"That's why you insisted on picking me up," he said to Ox. It was an accusation.

Ox didn't look perturbed. "I wanted to spend time with you."

"You brought me a muffin. You *never* bring me food. Especially muffins. Seeing as how that's what Joe did when he was jailbait and trying to get up all on your junk, I see right through you, *alfa*. I won't fuck you, *and* I'm still going to be pissed off."

"I like one of those things better than the other," Ox said, patting him on the shoulder.

"It better be the pissed-off thing," Rico grumbled. "Because I'm fucking sexy. Bambi says so."

"Sure, Rico," Ox said. "Whatever you say." He pushed by him and came to stand before me. I itched to reach out and touch him but kept my hands at my sides. "All right?"

I nodded. Then shrugged.

He leaned forward and pressed his forehead against mine. "It'll work out," he whispered, and I heard the low, deep thump of *packpackpack* in my head, foreign and quiet. "You'll see." He stepped around me and went back into the garage. Tanner and Chris called out in greeting as the door swung shut, leaving Rico and me alone.

I fidgeted next to the desk, unsure of what to do, what to say. If I should say anything at all.

Rico sighed. "So I guess you're back, huh."

"I guess."

"For good."

"I think so? I'm still trying to—"

"Would you hear me, dear?"

I snapped my head up.

He squinted at me. "Do you feel like going on a murderous rampage?"

"That's not funny."

He pointed two fingers at his eyes, then at me. "I'm watching you,

Fontaine. If you even step one foot over the line, I will pop a cap in your ass."

I snorted. "Do you hold your gun sideways like a badass when you aim?" I hadn't meant to say that. It just came out. I didn't know where it'd come from.

He was surprised. "You've said that to me before."

"I did?"

He bristled. "It doesn't matter. I will straight-up end you."

"Try it, Espinoza." I sneered at him. "We'll see who ends who."

"Huh," he said thoughtfully. He rubbed his jaw. "Weird."

"What?"

He shrugged. "It's still hysterical hearing someone so short trying to make big-boy threats." He bumped me hard as he passed me by. "Keep working on it. Maybe one day I'll be intimidated, but don't hold your breath. Or maybe do and see how long it takes for you to pass out or die."

It felt like a start.

· · ·

It was awful when it happened.

It was like I lost control of everything.

I was surviving the day by the skin of my teeth. The phone rang incessantly, and by the fifth call from someone I didn't know excitedly telling me how happy they were I was back instead of actually needing to make an appointment, I thought about throwing it across the room and hoofing it back to the basement.

I stayed.

I was in the garage, frowning at an invoice that didn't make any sense, as it seemed as if Gordo was charging next to nothing for a considerable amount of repair work. Gordo was telling me that he only charged people what they could afford, especially when they were hurting financially.

Both of the main garage doors were open, and the air was warm. People walked by on the street. A few of them even poked their heads in to wave at me happily. I waved back, but Gordo told them to come back another time when they looked like they were about to walk in and talk. I was grateful for it, as I was already overwhelmed.

"I'm not in this for money, kid," Gordo said. He was tapping on a tablet he said was used as a diagnostic tool. I wondered if I'd made him get it, as it was more high-tech than anything I'd seen so far. "I like cars. I sometimes like people. I don't give a shit about becoming rich."

"Then how the hell is this place even open?" I demanded. "You can't expect to turn a profit if you don't—"

"Pack finances." He looked up at me. "We don't have to worry about money."

I was horrified. "You do pay me, though, right? I don't work for free?"

He laughed, sounding lighter than I'd ever heard him. "Yes, Robbie. I pay you. We'll get you hooked back up into the pack accounts. Don't worry about it, okay?"

I leaned against the SUV he was working on. "So . . ."

"So?" he asked, looking back down at the tablet.

"How rich are we?"

He snorted. "Get back to work."

And I was going to do just that, except that Kelly Bennett decided to appear right at that moment.

Wearing a deputy's uniform. Tight green pants with a tan button-up shirt that pulled against his torso. He had a mic clipped near his shoulder and a black utility belt around his waist. He wasn't carrying a gun, but I barely noticed because at that exact moment, I discovered my legs decided to quit working and I tripped and fell into the side of the SUV.

Everyone stopped what they were doing to look at me.

"Sorry," I said quickly, using the SUV to pull myself back up. And immediately hit the top of my head on the open hood. "Son of a *bitch*."

"What are you doing?" Gordo asked slowly.

I laughed wildly. "Nothing! It's nothing. Just . . . don't even worry about it."

He turned toward the front of the garage.

"Oh no," he said when he saw who was standing there. "Not this again." He pointed the tablet at Kelly. "I swear to god, if I find an animal carcass brought here at *any point*, I will make both your lives a living hell. Do you understand me? I'm getting too old for this shit."

"I can't believe we have to watch this all over again," Chris said to Tanner. "It was bad enough the first time. Remember when Robbie figured out that he wanted to put himself all over Kelly?"

"Yeah," Tanner said. "How could I forget? We had to tell Ms. Martin that her side mirror was broken by accident instead of telling her the truth, that Robbie got a weird wolf boner and forgot his own strength."

"Maybe it'll be like it was with Ox and Joe," Rico said, tapping a socket wrench against his hand. "Mini muffins, you know? I ate, like, ten of them."

Chris looked scandalized. "You did *what*? That was one of their mystical moon magic presents! You don't touch another man's mystical moon magic present, Rico. They could have killed you, or worse, gotten confused and made you their mate." He frowned. "Are there werewolf threesomes? That sounds complicated. Too many limbs. I don't know anything about being a wolf."

Ox said, "Maybe consider stop talking. And get back to work."

"Sure, Ox," Tanner said. "We'll do just that."

They didn't move.

They stood there staring at me.

Even Gordo.

And Ox.

I ignored them as I rubbed the top of my head. "Hey," I said quickly to Kelly, completely forgetting about the invoice lying on the floor. "What's up? What's going on? What's the haps?"

He bit his bottom lip like he was trying to keep from laughing at me. He blushed slightly as he said, "I just . . . thought maybe we could have lunch? Together? If you're not busy."

I shook my head furiously. "I'm not busy at all. I have absolutely nothing to do."

"*That's* not true," Gordo grumbled behind me.

I ignored him. "I like your pants," I told Kelly seriously and immediately wished I had lost my voice as well as my memories. It was a weirdly dark thought to have.

"That sounded creepy," Tanner called. "Try again."

I glared at them over my shoulder. "Would you *fuck off*?"

Chris pretended to wipe a tear from his eye. "Spoken like he works at Gordo's. I'm so proud. Maybe there's hope for him yet."

"I dunno," Tanner said. "He was weirdly prudish when he worked here before. Robbie 2.0 is like the bizarro version of Original Flavor Robbie."

I hated them all so much. I was never going to forgive them. I turned back to Kelly. "Lunch," I said. "I can do that. Like, you have no idea how much."

"Good," Kelly said softly. "Maybe we can go to the diner?"

I nodded. "Just . . . can you give me a minute? I'll meet you out front. Don't go anywhere, okay?"

"I won't." He nodded at the others and turned back toward the sidewalk.

I whirled around, eyes wide. "What do I do?"

"He's literally standing five feet away," Gordo said dryly.

I lowered my voice. "What do I do?"

Gordo sighed and turned his eyes toward the ceiling. "I deserve this. For everything I've ever done, I deserve this."

Tanner and Chris shoved him out of the way, standing before me with their arms across their chests. They looked me up and down. "He looks like a roughneck," Tanner said. "He's dressed for the part."

"Eh," Chris said critically. "Not quite." He rubbed one of his grimy hands over my face, smudging oil against my skin. "There. That's better. No one trusts a person who works at a garage and doesn't get dirty."

"He looks like one of those cover models on the books he used to read," Tanner whispered. "*The Mechanic's Heart* or whatever." He squinted. "Maybe a little too short, though. Sucks you couldn't figure out how to make yourself taller while you were gone after you tried to kill us."

Gordo choked.

"That might be too soon," Chris said.

"Not helping," I growled at them.

Chris shrugged. "I can smell your arousal. I don't know that I want to help."

"I'm not aroused!"

"Uh-huh," Tanner said. "You hit your head on a stationary object at the first sight of Kelly. Ox once walked into that wall over there, and then he banged Jessie."

"That's my *sister*," Chris hissed at him, turning to glare over his shoulder at Ox, who seemed to be resolutely ignoring everything that was happening.

"I know," Tanner said. "But it's true. And then he walked into the side of the house at underage Joe in tiny shorts. And he eventually banged him too."

I looked pleadingly at Gordo.

He shook his head furiously. "Leave me out of this. I don't know the first thing about—"

Rico coughed roughly. It sounded strangely like *bullshit*.

"You made heart eyes at Mark," Tanner accused. "For *years*."

"I was trying to murder him with the power of my mind," Gordo retorted. "I don't *do* heart eyes. I don't even know what that *is*."

"He's right," Chris said. "Don't take advice from Gordo. You'll end up surly all the time until you're transformed by the power of love."

"I'm not *transformed*—"

"Mark has a magic tattoo on his neck that you put there while he fucked you in the butt," Tanner said. "And wow, I never thought I'd have to say something like that out loud. We really do need to work on boundaries in this pack. New rule. We all mind our own business and never talk about any of this stuff ever again."

"Agreed," Chris said.

And with that, they turned around and left me standing there.

"But—"

"Nope," Tanner said without looking back at me.

"But—"

"Sorry, kid," Chris said. "You did it once already with Kelly. Pretty sure you'll figure it out."

"You guys suck," I muttered. "And *don't* make that into an innuendo."

Tanner snapped his mouth closed, looking disappointed.

"Anyone?" I asked. "Hello?"

They all ignored me.

"I *quit*," I announced savagely.

"You get an hour for lunch," Gordo said in a bored voice. "If you're late coming back, I'll dock your pay."

I threw my hands up and stalked out of the garage.

"So," I said for the fourth time as I sat across from Kelly in the booth. I almost felt bad about the pile of shredded napkins in front of me. I didn't know why I was so nervous. Sure, I had no real idea who this man was, aside from superficial things, but Chris was right; we'd done this all before. I could do it again.

"So," Kelly said, hands folded on the table.

I racked my brain for anything to say. "Do you like . . ."

He nodded at me to continue.

"Things?" I finished lamely.

He bit his bottom lip as he looked out the window. "Things."

I groaned, putting my face in my hands. "Ugh. I'm sorry."

"For what?"

"All of this."

"That's vague."

I dropped my hands and immediately started shredding another napkin. "I don't know what to do."

"About what?"

"This. The pack. Everything." I sighed. "You."

He arched an eyebrow. "Who says you have to do anything?"

I was confused. "I have to prove myself."

"Says who?"

"Everyone."

He shook his head. "I don't think that anyone is saying that."

"Maybe not in so many words. But it's—you can't think that everything is going to be easy. It's not."

"I didn't say it would be. Or that it is."

"Rico said—"

His expression hardened. "I have a good idea what Rico said." He sighed. "Look, Robbie. I know it's tough. And you've got all this shit swirling through your head. But Rico is . . ."

"Justified in his absolute hatred of me?"

He traced a finger along the tabletop. "He doesn't hate you."

I snorted. "Yeah, I kind of think he does. I mean, I don't blame him. I can't. I don't remember what happened, but it was bad."

"It was," he said bluntly. "But that wasn't your fault."

"You all thought it was." And that caused my heart to seize in my chest. This void in my head, this blank space where apparently *years* of memories should have been, was vast. I didn't know how I'd never noticed it before. It was like I'd been drugged. I didn't know how to reconcile what my head told me versus what I was hearing from the man across from me and the others.

He winced. "We made mistakes. All of us. It doesn't make it right. It caught us off guard, and given all that we'd been through, it . . . I don't know. We trusted people we shouldn't have before."

"And you thought I was the same as them," I said dully.

He was frustrated. I could see it on his face, could smell it in his scent. His hands curled into fists. "I . . ."

I shook my head and forced a smile. "It's okay. I don't know that I would have thought any different had it been someone else." I frowned. "And I mean that. I really don't know *what* I would have thought."

He sat back against the booth. "It's not okay, Robbie. And we should have known better."

"But . . ."

"But we were hurting," he admitted. "And we put blame on people who didn't deserve it. I know you don't remember, but my father knew Osmond for a long time. He wasn't *great*, but we thought we could trust him. And then Pappas after you. It turned out he knew far more than he was telling us. In the end, before he turned, he tried to make amends. But by then it was already too late. He was the one who bit Mark and spread the infection to him."

"And Carter?"

Kelly's mouth thinned into a white line. "When we were kids, Carter hated the idea of someone being hurt. He's very protective that way. It was worse when he was shifted, because he would always try to lick everyone's wounds to clean them."

"Instinct."

Kelly shrugged. "Maybe. And it's something he never grew out of. He was there when Mark was bitten. He tried to clean the wound. It spread to him."

"How do they fight it?" I asked. "How are they not completely insane by now?"

"Ox," Kelly said.

"Because he's different. That's what you said."

"He is. I think my father knew that. Saw something in him the rest of us didn't. Oh, we loved him right away. He was this shy, awkward kid. Big, but awkward. And Joe . . . Joe didn't talk for a long time before he found Ox."

"Because someone took him," I said without thinking. "Someone hurt him."

Kelly looked at me sharply. "How do you know that?" His eyes widened. "Are you remembering something?"

I shook my head, and I hated the way his face crumpled. "Something Ezra—" I caught myself. I coughed. "Robert Livingstone told me."

The skin around his eyes tightened. "What did he say?"

I was about to tell him when a terrible thought struck me, one I wished I never had to have. And it tumbled out before I could stop it. "Is that what this is all about?"

He was quiet for a moment, like he was steadying himself. "What?"

"You," I said, and I hated myself for it. But I had to get it out there. I had to know. "The others. The pack. All of this. Is this why you finally decided to come find me? So you could figure out what I'd learned in Caswell?"

"Is that what you really think?"

"I don't know *what* to think," I said roughly. "You said it yourself. You thought I'd betrayed you. You thought I was like this Osmond or Pappas. You let me go. Carter said the pack figured out where I was eight months after I was gone. Elizabeth said I was gone for thirteen months total. That means there was *five* months where you just left me there. Like you—"

Abandoned me is how I meant to finish, but I couldn't get the words out through the lump in my throat. It made me sick to my stomach. The wounded look on his face only made it worse.

He closed his eyes, breathing in deeply through his nose. "Like the only reason we decided to rescue you was because we thought you could tell us what we needed to know about Michelle Hughes and Robert Livingstone."

"Right," I whispered. Then, louder, "I mean, it makes sense, doesn't it? Oh, Rico probably didn't like it, which is why he's acting like he is. But if I did hurt Chris and Tanner, then why the hell aren't they terrified of me? Why are they acting like they give two shits about me?"

He slammed his hand on the table as his eyes flashed open. The noise of the diner died around us as people looked over. People who had waved enthusiastically at me when we'd come through the diner door. People who had told me how happy they were I was finally back and asked just where had I been all this time? Their eyes had shifted side to side, and they'd whispered *pack business, right?* like it was some great secret.

Dominique was behind the counter, watching me like she thought I would shift right then and there and attack.

The humans in the diner didn't know what I'd done. But she did. That much was clear.

"They act like they give a shit because they *do*," Kelly said through gritted teeth. "It took them time—hell, it took *all* of us time—but they know what happened wasn't your fault. You had no control over your wolf."

"How do you know that?" I asked angrily. "Maybe I did. Maybe if I get my memories back you'll see I'm just like Osmond. Just like Pappas. Just like Livingstone or Alpha Hughes or anyone else who wants to hurt you. Maybe there was no magic at all and I did what I did because I *wanted* to." I was panting by the time I finished, my throat raw.

"You weren't," Kelly said. "You *aren't*. You're not like them. You never have been. And you never could be."

I laughed bitterly. "Sure, you can say that. But how do *I* know it? I don't even know who I am."

"He didn't take everything."

"He took enough."

Silence fell over the table, awkward and heavy. I wished Kelly had never come to the garage, or even better, that I was still trapped in the basement behind a line of silver. It seemed safer down there.

Kelly said, "I knew. The moment I saw you standing on the porch when we came back from hunting Richard Collins. I knew."

"Knew what?"

"That you were my mate."

I hung my head.

"Mom always told me when it happened, I would know. She couldn't explain how exactly, but she said it would be like this light. In my head and chest. The clouds would part and there would only be sun where there'd once been shadow."

I blinked rapidly against the sting in my eyes.

He shifted in his seat. "And I guess it was like that. But I wasn't in a position to do anything about it. I was different than I was before I left with my brothers and Gordo. Harder. Less trusting. I didn't want it. I didn't want *you*. I was too focused on trying to keep my family alive. I didn't trust you, especially given all we'd been through. I told myself that I was pissed off about it because you were a stranger and you'd carved yourself a home in the hole we created when we left. It took me a long time to realize I was jealous too."

I looked back up at him. "You were?"

He shrugged. "A little. I didn't know what to make of you. You were always... *there*. There was this one day before the hunters came and tried to take over the town. It was just you and me. We were in the kitchen, and you said something that made me laugh. It took me a moment to realize I was the only one laughing, and when I stopped, you were staring at me like it was the first time you were seeing me. After that, you always found some reason to stand near me."

"Wow," I muttered. "So smooth. I don't know how you were able to resist."

His lips twitched. "I don't know either. It was weird. Good weird, but weird all the same. And I didn't know if I wanted to do anything about it. I knew who I was, and I knew who you were, and I didn't know how to make it work or even if I wanted to."

"The whole ace thing?"

He snorted. "Yes, Robbie. That was part of it."

I hesitated. "I didn't... force you?"

He shook his head. "No. Never."

"Oh. That's good."

"It is." He leaned forward, resting his hands on the table again. It wouldn't take much for me to reach over and take his hand. I didn't. "I know you can't remember, and that's not your fault. But you can't blame us *for* remembering. That's not something we can control. We shouldn't have done what we did. Or what we didn't do. We should have believed in you more."

"Why didn't you?" I asked, needing to hear it from him. "If we were together, why didn't you trust me? Why didn't you do everything you could to get me back? I may not remember what we had, but I know I would do everything I could to get to someone I cared about. Nothing would have stopped me."

He was at a loss for words.

I nodded. That was all the answer I needed.

Then, "I did."

"What?"

"I did," he repeated. "Gordo and me. We looked for months. And then Ox found out what we were doing, and he helped too. It took a long time, but we spread the word through the packs we trusted. This network we have, these wolves and witches and humans who believe in the Bennett pack, they kept an eye out, ears open, for any hint. Any rumor. Any sighting. It took eight months, but then we found you. In Caswell. There was a wolf who said he'd seen you in the compound. He was visiting, and he recognized you from your picture. He said he tried to talk to you, tried dropping a couple of hints, but there was nothing."

I couldn't think of who this had been.

"And it hurt," Kelly continued, "because he said you seemed *happy*. And I almost convinced myself that maybe what we'd thought was right, that you *had* betrayed us. But then I remembered something, and I knew it couldn't be true."

"What did you remember?"

"The way you loved me."

It was a punch to the stomach.

"You loved me," Kelly said softly, "without reservation. Without expecting anything in return. You loved me, and I knew that you wouldn't stop, not unless you were forced to. And I knew then that *I* wouldn't stop, no matter what it took."

"I wish you had," I said hoarsely.

"Why?"

"Because you'd still be a wolf. You wouldn't be stuck like you are. And now we can't fix you, and it's my fault."

"It's not your fault."

I scoffed.

"It *isn't*. We're—goddammit. It's not *just* you, okay? Aileen and Patrice are right. We've lost our way. But that's not forever. We'll find out how to fix all of this. We've come too far, been through too much, to have it all end like this."

"But you're still a human."

"And I hate it," he said. I started to get up, but he reached out and gripped my hand tightly. His skin was warm, his fingers thin and bony. "I feel weak and tired all the fucking time. But it brought you back to me. And I would do it again and again and again. You said you would do anything for someone you cared about. Me too. My wolf was taken from me. I can barely breathe at the loss of it. I feel like I'm cut off from everything I've ever known, and there are days when I think I'm losing my mind." He swallowed thickly. "But I got you back, so it was worth it."

He turned his hand over, his fingers grazing against my wrist. His pulse fluttered just underneath his skin.

"Chris and Tanner have had time," he said. "They've come to terms. And once they knew where you were, we had to stop them, physically stop them, from going across the country and storming the compound and killing everyone who stood between you and them. Jessie too. Rico ... It'll take time, but I know he'll come around. You're home, Robbie. At last."

I held on to him with all my might. I thought he would bruise, but he didn't try to pull away. "What do we do now?"

He cocked his head. "Now? We try again. Maybe things won't be the same, but you're still you. Deep inside. You're still the Robbie I know. And even if things don't work out between us, even if we never get back to where we were, it'll be okay because I'll have you here. And that's the most important thing." He shrugged. "Who knows, maybe you'll want to find someone else to—"

I shook my head furiously. "No. I don't—that's not what I want. I don't want *that*. I want . . ."

I wanted a pack who loved me.

Who trusted me.

Who never wanted to let me go.

Who missed me when I was gone.

Who thought about me and smiled.

I wanted a home.

He watched me as I struggled to put into words this overwhelming desire, this thing within me that I had dreamed about for as long as I could remember. I'd had it once. I wanted it again more than anything.

He said, "Then we start again. We take it one day at a time, and we start again."

"How?" I asked helplessly.

He pulled his hand away, and I bit back a protest at the loss.

I was bewildered when he held it out to me. "Kelly Bennett."

I stared at it. And him.

He wiggled his fingers.

I took his hand carefully. He was breakable. He was soft. I didn't remember him, but I wished I did, because I thought maybe he could be everything. He was a summer filled with green, like so much relief.

It was preposterous. This moment. Him. All of it. But he shook my hand up and down.

"I'm Robbie Fontaine," I managed to say, feeling stupid. "It's nice . . ."

"To meet me?" He sounded amused.

I shook my head. "No. Well, yeah. But it's just . . . nice."

"I think so too," he said, and instead of letting me go again, he kept his hand on mine on the top of the table.

"What if this doesn't work?"

"Maybe it won't," he said slowly. "But that won't be because I didn't give it all I had. I will fight for you, Robbie. No matter what."

I was speechless.

Dominique came then, carrying two plates. "Sorry about the wait," she said. "You looked like you weren't ready yet. You good now?"

"I think we are," Kelly said, and he never looked away from me.

She leaned over, set the plates on the table. Before she stood back up, she kissed Kelly on the cheek. He grinned.

It was breathtaking.

Dominique glanced at me as she turned to leave. She stopped. She said, "We haven't had a chance to talk. I've heard about you."

I rubbed the back of my neck. "Is that bad?"

"Nah," she said. "At least not about you. It was bad. For them." She nodded at Kelly. "I came after everything. Just passing through."

"But you stayed."

She nodded. "Green Creek does that to you. It's not like anywhere else I've been."

"And Jessie's here," Kelly teased her.

"She is," Dominique agreed. "Probably more than I deserve once we figure things out, but she's foolish and doesn't see it." She looked at me pointedly. "I'm not one for pack. Always been a bit of a loner. But it's good having one so close. It takes the edge off, especially with

Ox. Got me this job and everything. Said I could make something of myself. I figured why the hell not. I didn't have anything else to lose. It stuck." She patted Kelly on the shoulder before she turned away.

I watched her leave. "Jessie, huh? I thought she and Ox were... whatever, at one point."

Kelly snorted. "Sexual fluidity is a thing that exists. You lost your virginity to a woman."

I blinked in surprise. "How did you— Oh. Right. What about you?" I balked, horrified. "Oh my god, ignore me. What the hell is wrong with me?"

He laughed until I thought he would pass out. I wanted to hear that sound for as long as I could. For a moment it was like this was a first date, like we were relative strangers just getting to know each other. Like we had all the time in the world.

We didn't, but I could pretend. Because there was a man like sunshine sitting across from me, acting like there was no place he'd rather be than here with me.

Everything would come to a head at some point, and I thought it would be soon.

For now, though, Kelly Bennett was looking at me with such a spark in his eyes that I could barely function.

I said, "So, a cop, huh?"

And he said, "Yeah. A cop. It's not bad. I actually like it more than I expected to. And it helps to have one of us patrolling through town in an official capacity. Makes people here feel safe. And we can keep an eye on things."

"The uniform," I said, feeling my face grow hot. "It suits you."

He grinned as he looked out the window. "Thanks, Robbie."

And on and on it went.

FIREFLIES

The guys gave me shit when I turned up at the garage a half hour late.

Gordo told me not to do it again.

Tanner said that was only because Gordo hated answering the phones.

Chris waggled his eyebrows.

Ox wrapped an arm around my shoulders, and I breathed him in.

Rico shook his head but didn't speak.

It felt like enough.

That night I started back down toward the basement when Mark stopped me, his hand on my arm.

"It's not punishment," he said, "being down there."

"I know."

"Do you?"

"You can't trust me. Not yet."

He shook his head. "It's not—come with me."

I followed him down the stairs.

The silver was gone. Granted, no one had closed the line the night before, but still.

He knelt next to the cot and pulled my backpack out from underneath. I barely kept from grabbing it away from him. But he didn't look inside. Instead, he handed it over.

"Let's go."

And then he left the basement.

The stairs creaked under him as he climbed. He paused at the top. "Robbie."

I sighed as I followed him.

He didn't speak as he led me through the house. Kelly and Carter were clearing the table in the kitchen. Elizabeth sat on the back porch, watching the stars come out. Ox and Joe were near, their heartbeats in sync. The others were at their own houses, and I knew

Mark should have been on his way home to Gordo, but here he was, with me.

He led me to the second floor, down the hall. He stopped in front of a closed door near the end.

He said, "It's your old room from before you and Kelly moved to the blue house."

I nodded, suddenly unsure. I didn't know what to expect. The basement felt safer. For me. For them. "Are you sure it's all right?"

"It is. I spent the day cleaning it out. After you and Kelly moved, we used it for any Omegas who came to us, the ones who needed to be close to Ox." He grimaced. "It was a little musty, but I aired it out as best I could."

"Maybe I should just go back down," I said, tugging on the strap to the backpack. "Full moon is coming at the end of the week. We don't know if anything will happen."

"It won't," he said simply.

"How do you know?"

"Because I know you." And he opened the door.

It was plain. Generic. A bed stood against one wall with a small rug at the end. There was a chest of drawers and a painting on the wall. It looked like one of Elizabeth's. It made me ache.

Mark nodded for me to go inside.

I couldn't move.

He said, "First steps, Robbie. It's all about the first steps. It was Ox's idea. Joe agreed. So did the rest of the pack."

"Rico—"

"Even Rico."

"Really?"

"Really."

"I bet he bitched about it first, though, huh?"

He shoved me into the room. He followed me inside as I set my backpack on the edge of the bed. "Not a lot in here. Most of your old stuff is still in the other house. I wasn't sure if you were ready for it, and Kelly thought it was best to wait. At least for now."

They were right. It'd been a long day, and I wasn't sure how much more I could take.

I looked around the room, trying to take it all in to see if something triggered in me—a thought, a memory, a remembrance of my time spent here.

There was nothing.

"You can do what you want with it," Mark said. "Leave it as is or do something more." He glanced at my backpack, and I had to stop from growling at him. He nodded and took a step back. "No one will take anything from you, Robbie. Not in here."

"You already know what's in the backpack, don't you?"

He didn't try to lie. "Yes. When we brought you back, we had to make sure there was nothing that could hurt us. I went through it myself." He hesitated. "I found my brother's journal in there."

"Of course he's your brother," I muttered.

"Where did you find it?"

"Michelle's office."

"And you took it."

I nodded.

"Why?"

"I don't know," I admitted. "It seemed important."

"It is," he said. "The others don't know it's there."

"They don't?"

He shook his head. "I figured you could be the one to tell them. To tell Elizabeth, when you're ready. It should go to her."

"Did you read it?"

He sighed. "I started to. I was greedy for it, for anything from him. But I realized it wasn't meant for me. At least not right away. It should go to her before anyone else. Then she can decide what to do with it."

I sat on the edge of the bed. "I don't know why I took any of what I did when I left here. It's weird, right?"

He rubbed a hand over his shaved head. "You already had it on you."

I looked at him in surprise. "What?"

"You took that wherever you went," he said, nodding toward the backpack, "when you left on assignment. It wasn't because you didn't trust the pack, it was just an extension of you. You had it with you on that first day you showed up on our porch. Said you traveled light, and for a long time, no one knew what you had inside. We did, eventually, when you let us in." And then, "Still got the stone wolf, huh?"

He said it like it was nothing, like it was just a simple conversation between friends.

I nodded, eyes narrowing.

"Take it out."

My claws dug into my palms.

He said, "I'm not going to take it from you. I just want you to see it."

I almost didn't. I almost asked him to leave. To let me be. I was tired, and I didn't know how much more I could take. I didn't know why I had that damn wolf. It should have been Kelly's.

I did as he asked.

I took it out.

It was heavy and cool.

He said, "I know things don't make sense. That we have a history with you that you can't remember. But I know you fought to keep some part of who you were with everything you had."

"How do you know that?"

"Because you still have that," he said, pointing toward the wolf. "You kept it secret. You kept it safe."

"It was important," I muttered. "I had this cubbyhole in the back of my closet in the compound. I hid it away."

"Like a hole in a tree."

I closed my eyes. "Yeah. I guess."

"And no one was able to take it from you."

"No."

"Good," he said. "And I know you're still you, Robbie. I know it with everything I have, because that's not your wolf. It's Kelly's."

I took in a stuttering breath.

He was in front of me then, and he bent over, trailing his nose along my hairline to my ear. "You took it with you wherever you went," he whispered. "Because you loved it so and couldn't bear to leave it behind. With you, it was safe. With you, *he* was safe. After he was taken from your mind, part of you still held on. Even if you can't remember anything else, remember that. I asked you once why you carried it with you all the time. You said it was because you never thought you could have something so special, and you needed to remind yourself that it was real."

He kissed my forehead and let me be, closing the door behind him.

I sat there for a long time, the wolf of stone in my hands.

I couldn't sleep.

I missed the little house outside of Caswell, though the thought made my stomach twist with guilt.

Even worse, part of me wanted to see Ezra. I felt like I was cleaved in two, and there was this guy, this version of myself who could have spent the rest of his life never knowing where he'd come from, the people he'd once loved nothing but smoke reflected in a fractured mirror. That Robbie would have been none the wiser. If the Bennett pack had kept on thinking that I'd betrayed them, I might have never known reality. It was as if Caswell was a dream, and I'd awoken into a nightmare. How far would they have pushed me? What could they have made me do if I'd never known the truth?

It hurt.

And then there was this *other* Robbie, this Robbie smiling in photographs hung on the wall in a garage in a town in the middle of nowhere. *This* Robbie was happy, this Robbie was loved, this Robbie was *whole*, and here I was, stepping into his shoes like I deserved it. Like I belonged.

I felt like a fraud.

I wanted to believe.

I didn't know how.

I tossed and turned for a few hours. The moon was bright through the window. It whispered to me, and I tried to shut it out. Begged it to leave me be.

It didn't.

And then I felt guilt about *that* too, because Kelly probably didn't feel it like the rest of the wolves, didn't feel that electric thrum coursing through his body, a kinetic and enthralling energy that was wonderfully insistent. He would *remember* what it felt like, would remember the comforting weight of the moon as it called out, singing *here i am my loves here i am because i am always with you i am your mother i am your father and all will be well will be well.*

It was my fault.

No matter what anyone said, if Kelly hadn't been on that bridge, if he hadn't tried to protect me, if he hadn't tried to stop Ezra, he would be as he once was.

He was fragile now.

Breakable.
Soft.
I sat up in my bed.
Maybe...
Maybe he needed me.
To help him.
To protect him.
To keep him safe.

I slid out of bed, dragging the comforter off and trailing it behind me. I barely noticed the stone wolf in my hand.

I opened the door to my bedroom.

The hallway was dark.

The only sounds were the deep, slow breaths of a sleeping pack.

Elizabeth.
Ox.
Joe.
Carter.
Even the timber wolf.

I stopped in front of Kelly's room.

He was sleeping too.

I placed my hand flat against the door.

I whispered, "I won't let anything happen to you. No matter what."

I laid the comforter on the floor, making a little nest. It wasn't going to be comfortable; the floors were wood and the comforter was thin. But it would be enough for now.

I lay down in front of Kelly's door.

Just for a few hours, I told myself. Just to make sure.

As the night wore on, I listened to the sound of his heart, memorizing every beat and tick and stutter. At one point it sped up, as if he were dreaming. I told him that it was okay, it was all right now, he could sleep easy because I wouldn't let anything happen to him.

He didn't hear me, of course, but that didn't matter.

Anyone who tried to get to him would have to go through me.

It wasn't until someone softly tapped my shoulder that I realized I'd fallen asleep.

I blinked in the low light spilling in through the window in the hallway.

Elizabeth said, "Hello."

I said, "Hi," feeling foolish. "I was just..."

She crouched down next to me. She ran a hand through my hair. I leaned in to it, and she laughed quietly at the low rumble in my chest. "You were just," she said, and it was warm and kind.

I nodded. She understood.

"I wonder," she said.

"About what?"

"What makes a man?" Her face was covered in shadow. Her hand never left my hair. "If all he knows is stripped away, what is it that remains?"

"I don't know."

"I didn't either until we found you again. I think I know the answer now. Would you like to hear it?"

"Yes." Almost more than anything.

She said, "What remains is a broken heart shattered like so much glass. Pieces are missing, and the ones that are left don't fit like they used to. But still it beats, because no matter what is taken away, no matter what is lost, it needs to continue. To survive. You are a survivor, Robbie. And not even magic can take that away from you."

I closed my eyes, struggling to breathe.

She sang then. Softly, just a song for her and me. She didn't mind being lonely, she told me, because her heart told her I was lonely too.

We stayed that way as the sun rose.

* * *

It was an adjustment—Green Creek and all it entailed.

I tried to memorize the names of everyone that came to see me at Gordo's. I stopped asking after the second morning if every person coming in had something wrong with their car. It turned out that Original Flavor Robbie (I hated Tanner for that) was quite popular, and Robbie 2.0 (I hated Carter for that) was barely keeping up.

They didn't ask me where I'd been, most leaning forward and whispering conspiratorially that they understood it was wolf business. Most of them knew something was off, but they didn't ask. They'd seen the missing flyers posted around Green Creek. They had bits and pieces of rumors, but they mostly left it alone.

On Friday morning two weeks after I'd arrived back in Green Creek, Gordo told me the garage would be closing early.

"Why?" I asked.

"Full moon, kid. Chris and Tanner are still newer wolves. Don't want to take any chances."

I glanced through the door. Chris was bent over an open hood. Tanner was on his cell phone calling about some parts that hadn't yet been delivered. "There been any problems?"

Gordo shook his head. "They've taken to it quicker than I ever thought they would, but it's better to be safe than sorry."

"Yeah, I guess."

"And we've got company coming in."

That was the first I'd heard about it. Granted, I didn't think the pack was filling me in on every detail, given that they were still walking on eggshells around me. "Who?"

He twirled a finger at his eyes. "Ever since Ox became . . ."

"Werewolf Jesus?" I asked.

He glared at me. "You need to stop listening to Carter."

"I'm trying," I assured him. "But he makes it hard when he won't stop talking. He's suited for politics, if you think about it."

Gordo sighed. "Point. Ever since Ox became the Alpha of the Omegas, we tend to be a bit crowded on the full moons. A few chose to stay here in Green Creek, but we've been able to place most of them in other packs. The ones that were worse off aren't more than a couple days' drive away. They come in most full moons to be around Ox. It keeps them calm when he's near."

"Their packs come too?"

"Not all of them, and never the Alphas. They understand what the Omegas need. It's not something they can provide for them. At least not yet."

"Because of your father."

He scowled. "Yes."

"Do you . . ."

"Spit it out, Robbie. I have work to do before we close up."

I thought about telling him that it was nothing, it didn't matter, because anything I asked would be like digging claws into an open wound. But I had to know. "Do you ever miss him?"

"No."

"Oh."

"Look, kid, I don't know what it was like for you. I don't know how he acted, what he said or what he did. But you know it was all a lie, right?"

I wished I'd kept my mouth shut. "I guess so."

He shook his head. "There's no guessing here, Robbie. I know . . . I know you saw some side of him and that you didn't know any better. But my father isn't like that. There was a *reason* he did what he did. He wanted something. And he took you because of it."

"What did he want?"

He said, "I don't know. But I have a feeling we're going to find out before too long. Whatever he has planned, whatever he's after, he won't stop until he has it. Or we finish it."

"Finish him," I whispered.

He looked at me strangely. "Do you . . ." He let out a frustrated breath. "Do you care about him?"

"I don't know how to turn it off." I couldn't look him in the eye. "It's this divide. I keep telling myself he's wrong, that what he did was wrong, but then I remember how he treated me. How he cared about me. And I know you all think he was using me," I added before he could interrupt. "Maybe he was. He *probably* was. But what if he wasn't? What if all of this, everything he's done, has just been because of what was taken from him?"

From the corner of my eye, I thought I saw the raven on Gordo's arm flutter its wings. "And what was taken from him?" Gordo asked. His voice was flat.

Oh, how thin the ice beneath my feet was. I could almost hear it cracking. "He said . . . he said he had a family once. That wolves took them away from him." And then, "I'm sorry."

"For what?"

I shrugged awkwardly. "Talking."

He snorted, and I shuddered when he dropped his hand on my shoulder. "Never thought I'd ever hear that from you. There's more to it than that, kid. If we'd had this conversation a long time ago, I might have even agreed with you. But I know better now. Everything my father has had done to him is because of his own actions. Wolves aren't to blame, at least not in the way you're thinking. He had a tether. It wasn't my mother. And when she found out, it didn't end well. I think he'd been manipulating her memory for years, keeping her compliant. And it fucked with her head. His tether died. My mother killed her. And then my father killed my mother and many other people. He survived somehow. His magic was stripped from him so he could never hurt anyone again. I was only twelve."

"Jesus Christ," I muttered. "How the hell did he escape?"

Gordo shook his head. "We don't know, but he did, and that's all that matters at this point because he won't stop. And neither will we. We're going to have to have a talk, kid, and soon. We've tried to give you space and time to find your bearings again, to know your place here. But we can't continue on this way. We've let it go on too long as it is. We're going to have to make a decision."

"About?"

He dropped his hand. "What we'll do in order to survive. And much of that depends upon you. I hate it, Robbie. I wish it didn't have to be this way. But you're going to have to make a choice. Either you're with us, or—"

"I'm against you." I felt sick.

"No," he said, not unkindly. "Or you stay out of our way. Because this will end one way or another. And we can't have you standing between us and them. I don't want you to get hurt."

"It's too late for that," I said bitterly.

"I know. But things could be worse."

"How?" I looked up at him.

He nodded toward the front of the garage.

Kelly was crossing the street toward us. He was in uniform. He saw us watching and gave a little wave.

"You could still not know he exists," Gordo said quietly. "And if there's one thing I've learned through all of this, it's that we need each other now more than ever. We're pack, kid."

Ox drove us home. His work shirt lay folded on the bench seat between us, the old truck bouncing on the potholes in the dirt road. He wore a loose tank top, the window rolled down, his arm hanging out the side. The air was warm, and I didn't know if there was anywhere else I'd rather be.

That lasted until we rounded the corner to the houses.

The driveway was filled with cars.

I said, "That's . . . a lot of people."

He said, "It is," but I could hear the smile in his voice.

I said, "Maybe I should just..." Go away? Stay in town? Head back down to the basement? Something other than face people I didn't know but who undoubtedly knew about what I'd done.

He stopped the truck next to the blue house, letting it idle for a moment before shutting it off. The engine clicked. The trees swayed in a soft breeze. A fat bee flew by his open window, and he watched it as it crossed over the front of the truck.

He said, "If that's what you want."

I didn't know what I wanted.

He said, "But I'd rather you stay with me, if that's all right." He was calm. Serene. He breathed in through his nose and exhaled out his mouth. He tapped the steering wheel once, twice, three times before settling his hand on the seat near his shirt. It was palm up, fingers open.

An invitation.

I put my hand in his.

He held on tightly. "You don't remember these wolves. They'll remember you. Some of them won't like it. They won't understand. But you're with me. You're with your pack. That's what I want you to focus on. Can you do that for me, Robbie?"

I could. I thought there'd come a point where I'd do anything for him, and it would happen sooner rather than later. "Yes."

He nodded. "And if there ever feels like a moment when it's too much, tell me and I'll do whatever I can to make it all go away. We'll run. Just you and me."

"I can't do that."

He didn't look angry or upset with me. "Why?"

I looked down at our joined hands. His palm was rough and callused. I wondered why they didn't heal. They felt like scars that couldn't be taken from him with a shift. "Kelly."

"Tell me."

"He's nervous. Upset, I think. About not being able to shift with the rest of us."

Ox nodded. "Did he tell you this?"

"No."

"But you know anyway."

I said, "I'm good at that. Picking out what's between the words. All the things that aren't being said. I watch."

He sounded amused. "I know."

"Oh. Right. You would know that." Then, "Did I . . ."

He waited for me to collect my thoughts.

"Was I useful? Did I contribute to the pack?" I swallowed past the lump in my throat. "Did I matter?" I hated how it sounded, like I was fishing. Like I needed his approval. I did, though. I needed to hear him say it.

He squeezed my hand, and when he spoke, there was a curl of Alpha in his voice, low and heavy. He said, "Things were . . . bad, when we were younger. I lost someone very important to me. I thought I was going to break apart."

"Did you?"

"In a way. But even when I thought I couldn't take another step, I did. I had people depending on me. People who needed me. And as it turned out, I needed them just as much. But I remember how much it hurt, like I was flayed open, all my nerve endings exposed. And when you were taken, I felt like that all over again."

I wasn't prepared for it. This truth. *His* truth. I didn't know what I expected, but it wasn't this. He meant every word.

He said, "I went to the woods. For days. I howled for you." His voice cracked, and I wanted him to stop. I wished I'd never opened my mouth, but it was too late to take it back. "I howled for you with everything I had. My father told me once that the call of an Alpha is one of the most powerful things in all the world. That it echoes through the earth and the trees and the sky. And I knew, I just *knew* that if I was good enough, if I was strong enough, that you would hear me. That you would find me and you would find your way home."

"But I didn't," I whispered.

He surprised me by laughing. It was rough and gravelly, like it crawled up from his chest through his throat. "You did, though. It just took longer than we expected. You heard us, Robbie. All of us. I forgot in those early days that an Alpha is nothing without their pack. It took longer than I'd hoped, but we came together again. We stood tall and we all howled for you. And not because you're useful or because of what you contributed or what you could tell us about where you'd been. It's because you matter. I couldn't save my mother. I couldn't save my father."

"But you could save me," I said, sounding awed.

"We could," he said. "But only because you'd already saved us. When you came, we were broken. We were lost. You couldn't fix us, but you didn't need to. You made a home in here." He tapped his chest. "And I wasn't about to let you go. That was never on the table, even if I had to go it alone. I would have moved heaven and earth to get to you." He chuckled. "Thankfully everyone came around, hardheaded though some of them may be." He glanced at me, and a hint of red bled into his eyes. "An Alpha is only as strong as his pack. And you're a part of that."

I nodded, unable to speak.

He squeezed my hand again, tilting his head back to rest against the window behind us. He closed his eyes. I'd overheard Gordo talking about Ox's Zen Alpha bullshit, and I didn't understand it then.

I did now.

He turned his head to look at me. "There are going to be rough days ahead. Are you with me?"

And I did the only thing I could.

I said yes.

And there, in the back of my mind, I heard it, louder than it'd been before.

packpackpack

· · ·

"You can run, you know," Kelly said. He sat beneath a tree at the edge of the clearing, picking at the grass between his legs. In the clearing ahead, a couple dozen wolves ran with each other, yipping, tails flicking back and forth. Clouds were starting to come in, thick and heavy, and I could smell rain in the distance, but the moon was bright, and my gums itched, my fangs wanting to drop. I forced them back. "You don't need to sit here with me all night."

He smelled so blue, I thought the weight of it would crush me. He watched Carter wrestling with the timber wolf, their violet eyes flashing in the dark.

"I'm okay where I am," I said. I sat next to him, back against the tree trunk. Our shoulders brushed together every now and then, and I was working up the courage to lay my head on his shoulder. Pathetic, really. Especially the driving urge I had to go and find the biggest animal I could and kill it so I could drag it to him. Joe had told me before we'd gotten to the clearing that Kelly wasn't a fan of bloody carcasses, and I didn't know what else to bring him. He'd refused to tell me how this had happened before, saying I'd need to hear that from Kelly when we were ready.

Carter, in his infinite wisdom, told me that I needed to be like a bird of paradise, all bright colors and prancing around a nest I'd made out of sticks and feathers and leaves in a sensual dance sure to attract the attention of a mate.

It was while I was collecting said sticks and feathers and leaves and trying to figure out what I could do about bright colors when Joe told me in no uncertain terms Carter was being a dick and under no circumstances should I listen to his advice ever again.

Which was a relief, because I didn't think I was very good at prancing or sensual dancing.

Carter assured me I was very good at it as he tried to hand me the sticks I'd dropped.

But then Joe tackled him, and that was that.

And now here we sat under a tree while wolves ran around us. Most of the Omegas had nodded toward me in greeting. One had even hugged me. Several gave me a wide berth. On them I could smell fear. It hurt, though I couldn't blame them.

It was probably best that I didn't shift.

"I don't need a babysitter," Kelly grumbled.

I shrugged. "Maybe I do. I might be dangerous."

He glanced at me. "Oh, we're joking about it now, huh?"

"Too soon?"

He huffed out a breath. "I'll get back to you on that."

"Make sure you do."

He laughed quietly. The sharpness of the blue around him faded slightly. It wasn't much, but I wanted to howl at the moon because of it. I'd done that. *Me*. And then I had to go ruin it by saying, "Maybe you can ride me."

He choked. "Holy shit."

My stomach sank to my toes. "That's *not* what I meant! Forget I said that."

"I don't know if I can," he said faintly. "That's . . . wow. Just throwing that out there, huh? Dude, my mother is here. Whatever wolfy urge you're having right now, maybe consider a little decorum."

"I mean when I shift!"

"I'm really not into bestiality, Robbie. And that has nothing to do with me being ace. I just don't want to touch your wolf dick. Please don't mount me in front of our pack. Carter would never let me hear the end of it."

I groaned, putting my face in my hands. "Why are you like this?"

"You mean amazing? I don't know. I guess I've always been this way." The blue faded even more, and now it was shot with green and something that felt almost like happiness. It was dim, but there.

I dropped my hands and banged the back of my head against the tree a couple of times. He was covering up his laughter, and I wanted to tell him to stop. To just let it out. To let me hear it. I wanted to hear it. I needed to hear it. I said, "How did we get here?"

"We walked." He squinted at me. "Did you forget that too? That's what happens when you promote sex between an animal and a human."

I bumped my shoulder against his. "I meant . . . this. Us. How did we . . ."

"Oh."

"Yeah."

He sighed, folding his hands in his lap. "You really want to hear this now?"

I nodded. "I've got time."

"Do you?"

"I think so." And because I had nothing else to give, I said, "I don't know there's anywhere else I'd rather be."

He bit back a smile, eyes on me, then away. "Gonna puff out your chest and prance?"

"I'm going to *murder* Carter," I muttered.

Kelly laughed. I puffed out my chest, oddly proud.

That only made him laugh harder.

I never wanted it to end. I wondered if it felt like this the first time. Seeing him. Really seeing him.

He wiped his eyes. "You really want to know, don't you."

"Yeah."

"Why?"

I gave in. I couldn't not. I reached over and put my hand on his knee. He tensed briefly but settled when I curled my fingers over his leg, just letting my hand rest there. I couldn't look at him. I thought my face was on fire.

He said, "That's . . ." His voice broke. He cleared his throat. "After the hunters came, something shifted. Between us. I don't know how or why exactly. You stopped being weird around me."

"Seems like I've picked that right up again."

He chuckled. "A little. It's okay, though. It's like . . . a beginning. You came to me one day. You were sweating. I remember thinking something bad had happened because you kept wringing your hands until I thought you were going to break your bones. I asked you what was wrong. And you know what you said?"

"Probably something stupid."

"You said that you didn't think you could ever give up on me. That no matter how long it took, you would be there until I told you otherwise. That you weren't going to push me for anything but you thought I should know that you had . . . intentions."

"Oh dear god," I said in horror. "And that *worked*?"

Kelly snorted, and I felt his hand on the back of mine. "Not quite. But what you said next did."

I looked over at him. "What did I say?"

He was watching me with human eyes, and I thought I could love him. I saw how easy it could be. I didn't, not yet, but oh, I wanted to. "You said you thought the world of me. That we'd been through so much and you couldn't stand another day if I didn't know that. You told me that you were a good wolf, a strong wolf, and if I'd only give you a chance, you'd make sure I'd never regret it."

I had to know. "Have you?"

"No," he whispered. "Not once. Not ever." He looked away. "It was good between us. We took it slow. You smiled all the time. You brought me flowers once. Mom was pissed because you ripped them up from her flower bed and there were still roots and dirt hanging from the bottom, but you were so damn proud of yourself. You said it was romantic. And I believed you." He plucked a blade of grass and held it in the palm of his hand. "There was something . . . I don't know. Endless. About you and me." He took my hand off his knee and turned it over. He set the blade of grass in my palm and closed his hand over mine. He looked toward the sky and the stars through the canopy of leaves. "We came here sometimes. Just the two of us. And you would pretend to know all the stars. You would make up stories that absolutely weren't true, and I remember looking at you, thinking how wonderful it was to be by your side. And if we were lucky, there'd be—ah. Look. Again." His voice was wet and soft, and it cracked me right down the middle.

Fireflies rose around us, pulsing slowly. At first there were only two or three, but then more began to hang heavy in the air. They were yellow-green, and I wondered how this could be real. Here. Now. This moment. How I ever could have forgotten this.

Forgotten him.

It had to have been the strongest magic the world had ever known.

That was the only way I'd have ever left his side.

He reached out with his other hand, quick and light, and snatched a firefly out of the air. He was careful not to crush it. He leaned his head toward mine like he was about to tell me a great secret.

Instead he opened his hand between us.

The firefly lay near the bottom of his ring finger. Its shell was black with a stripe down the middle. It barely moved.

"Just wait," Kelly whispered.

I did.

It only took a moment.

The firefly pulsed in his hand.

"There it is," he said. He pulled away and lifted his hand. The firefly took to its wings, lifting off and flying away.

He stared after it.

I only had eyes for him.

He said, "There were good days. Many good days. But they weren't all that way. Sometimes we'd fight over stupid things. You spent the night at Gordo's a couple of times. Or that's where you said you were going. But without fail, the next morning, I'd find you sleeping outside the bedroom door on the floor. Even when you were mad at me, you couldn't stand the thought of being away for long." A tear trickled down his cheek, and he wiped it away. "Sorry. I don't mean to be so—"

"No," I said hoarsely. "It's okay. It's fine. I like hearing this. I need it." That didn't seem quite right. I shook my head. "I want it."

"I should have done more," Kelly said, and his chest hitched a couple of times before he got it under control. "I wasn't... I wasn't strong enough."

I shook my head furiously. "No. Kelly, that's not—you couldn't have stopped him. I don't think anyone could have."

He was getting worked up, brow furrowing, the corners of his mouth drawing down. "That's what everyone told me. That's what I tried to tell myself." His eyes shone in the pale moonlight as he looked at me. "But how could I have let this happen?"

I squeezed his hand so tight, I thought his bones would turn to dust, the blade of grass still between us. He didn't try to pull away.

I said, "You've gotta hear me" and "you've gotta listen to me" and "Kelly, Kelly, Kelly, it doesn't matter now. It doesn't matter because no matter what happened, we're still here. We've still found our way back. I know it's not like it was, and I don't know if it ever will be, but god, look at us. Look where we are. Even after everything. I don't know you well yet, but I want to. And I don't know that I've ever wanted anything more."

He said, "You don't know that, you don't know what you want, how can you, how *can* you even know if this is—"

A peal of thunder rippled overhead.

Water splashed against my hair. Against my cheeks. The tip of my nose. Our joined hands, trickling between us, wetting the blade of grass.

I looked up to see thick clouds rolling.

The fireflies winked out.

"It's raining," I said, and I didn't know why it felt monumental. "I saw you."

"When?"

I closed my eyes against the sprinkle of rain. It was warm and cleansing, and wolves began to howl. "In Caswell. I don't know if it's a memory or a vision, but we were walking together. Just you and me. I didn't know it was you. You weren't clear. Like a haze. Fuzzy. But we were together, and you were holding my hand, and you were acting weird. You'd told me I needed to come with you, and I said you were acting all—"

"Mysterious."

I opened my eyes. "Yeah. Mysterious. And you said it wasn't bad.

That it was good. You hoped it would be good. And even though I didn't know who you were, I believed you. Because I knew you would never lie to me."

He was quiet for a moment. Then, "It wasn't a memory. At least not for you. It was . . . from me. When we found out where you were, Aileen and Patrice thought we could reach you somehow. That even though Livingstone had a hold over you, the bonds between us all were stronger than any magic he had. They said that if any of us could get through to you, it'd be either Joe or Ox."

"Or you."

He nodded. "Aileen said I needed to show you something bright. Something warm. Not necessarily the best thing that ever happened to us, but something personal and significant."

I felt like I was on a precipice. My toes were at the edge, and all I needed to do was lean over into the void and it would all become clear. "What did you want to show me? What happened that day?"

I never got an answer.

I never got an answer because the void wasn't empty.

I stepped off the edge and

(*would you hear me, dear?*)

(*of course you would*)

(*because even behind the wards*)

(*even beyond the layers upon layers of magic*)

(*i see you*)

(*and i'll never let you go*)

(*i only want what belongs to me*)

(*and i won't stop until i have it*)

I screamed as a lance of pain burst through my head, obliterating all rational thought. I tore my hand from Kelly's as he said my name again and again, voice rising in alarm. Lightning flashed and thunder rippled through the clouds as the rain fell harder.

I pushed myself away from Kelly, trying to get as far from him as I could. My claws popped and my fangs burst through my gums, and the moon, the *moon* was hidden behind the clouds, but I could still *feel* it. I turned over onto my hands and knees, digging my fingers into the earth, grass and dirt bunching up against my palms.

In front of me came an angry growl.

I lifted my head.

Omegas.

We were surrounded by Omega wolves, their black lips pulled back in quivering snarls, their fangs glinting in cracks of lightning. Their violet eyes burned brighter than any sun.

The muscles underneath my skin rippled as I half-shifted, unable to ignore the threat.

There were six of them.

Kelly screamed for Ox, screamed for Joe, but the biggest of the Omegas, a white-and-tan wolf, launched itself at me.

I knew if I fell, Kelly would be alone.

And that was absolutely un-fucking-acceptable.

I jerked to the right, rolling onto my back and over onto my feet. The Omega landed where I'd just been sitting, jaws snapping viciously, saliva dripping from its mouth. Its eyes blazed as Kelly scrabbled back against the tree.

"Don't," I warned the Omega. "You don't want to do this."

It didn't listen.

It came for me.

I grunted as its front paws landed against my chest, knocking me back onto the ground. It stood above me, lowering its head toward my throat.

Kelly whispered, "Robbie."

I kicked my knees into the Omega's stomach. A harsh breath exploded out of its mouth into my face. It mewled at me as I dug my claws into its sides, blood spilling over my hands. I roared in its face, pushing up as hard as I could. It fell off me, landing roughly at my side.

I stood slowly, the rain pounding down around us.

The other Omegas circled around me.

"Come on!" I shouted at them, my voice caught between human and wolf. "If this is what you want, *come on!*"

A gray wolf seemed braver than the others. It lunged, low and quick, and the noise it made when I caught it by the scruff of its neck was choked and surprised. I lifted it toward my face, and I wanted nothing more than to tear its fucking head off for even *daring* to come near me and my—

A second wolf attacked, knocking me off my feet. The wolf I held yelped as it crashed down with me, scratching my chest and stomach. I tried to roll away but didn't get far. I was flat on my stomach when another wolf landed on my back, pushing me into the dirt. Its breath was hot against the back of my neck as it trailed its nose against my skin, inhaling deeply.

Kelly shouted my name, and it was filled with such horror that it made my skin crawl.

Kelly.

Kelly.

Kelly.

I put my hands flat against the ground and pushed up with everything I had. The wolf on my back jumped off at the last second, landing on its feet directly in front of me. It turned slowly, and I raised my hand to tear out its goddamn throat—

"*Enough.*"

It was one word, and one word only.

But it was filled with such power, such a bright and consuming rage, that every single wolf cowered at the sound of an Alpha.

I slowly raised my head.

Ox stood before us, eyes red and violet. Rain sluiced down his nude body, his hair matted down on his head.

Elizabeth pushed by him, glaring at the Omegas. I thought she was going for Kelly.

I was shocked when she knelt at my side, hands on my arm, pulling me up to sit back on my knees. "It's all right," she whispered in my ear. "It's okay. I've got you."

"What the fuck is going on?" Gordo demanded as he approached. His tattoos shone in the dark, and Mark was loping next to him, violet eyes darting back and forth between the gathered Omegas. Then he looked at me. His nostrils flared as he inhaled sharply. He started to growl at me, but then he stopped. He snorted, lowering his head to paw at his nose.

The others began to gather around. Chris and Tanner were shifted, Rico standing between them with his arms across his chest, glowering at anyone and everyone. And it took me a moment to understand why Chris and Tanner smelled like fear.

They were scared of me.

Jessie ran up, looking like she was going to murder someone. A thin rust-colored wolf was at her side for every step she took. Dominique.

Joe was still a wolf as he came to stand next to Ox, his big paws flattening the grass. Carter and the timber wolf appeared last, and both of them recoiled as they sniffed the air.

"We were just *sitting* here," Kelly said, shoving Carter's head away as his brother tried to keep him back. "We weren't doing anything, and they just came after us. After *him*."

There was the creak of muscle and bone as Mark shifted next to Gordo. He grimaced, his eyes still alight with violet as he turned human. The wolf hair on his body was still receding when he said, "It's Robbie. Like it was with Gordo. Stinks like magic. Bad magic." He took in a deep breath before sneezing harshly. "It burns. It makes me want to hurt him."

Gordo looked shocked. "But that's . . ." He looked at me. "What happened?"

They all stood above me, watching me. I felt cornered. Trapped. One of the Omegas snapped its jaws at me, but Ox stepped in front of it. He glared at it until it whimpered and bared its neck.

Ox crouched before me, keeping his distance. "Robbie?"

I didn't know what to say.

"It's okay," Elizabeth said, rubbing a hand up and down my back. "You're safe. Kelly's safe. I promise."

I took in a shuddering breath. "I didn't . . . I didn't mean to . . ."

"Didn't mean to what?" Ox asked.

I shook my head. It was raining harder now, and I tried to think of the fireflies, of how it'd just been only minutes before, but it was lost in a fog.

I said, "I heard him."

I said, "In my head."

I said, "He could see me."

I said, "He could feel me."

I said, "And he's not going to let me go. He's not going to stop. Not until we give him back what belongs to him."

And as the rain poured down, I wondered—not for the first time—if being in Green Creek was a mistake.

NOT FAIR / FORGIVE MYSELF

They told me that it was going to be all right.

I wished I could believe them, but I couldn't take the chance that they were wrong.

Jessie sighed as she poured the line of silver across the basement, trapping me inside.

Kelly looked furious, standing near the stairs, hands in fists at his sides as rainwater dripped off him onto the floor.

"Maybe it's for the best," Gordo muttered. He looked tired. "Until we can figure this out." He shook his head. "I . . ." He'd spent the better part of an hour digging around in my head, saying he was shoring up whatever walls he could to keep his father out. I could see by the look on his face that he didn't think it'd do much. It didn't help that by the end I was snarling at him, telling him to get the fuck out of my head. The moon was pulling at me, and my emotions were all over the place. I wanted to curl up away from everyone. I wanted to lash out at all of them. I wanted them to leave me alone. I wanted to make them bleed.

"It's not his fault," Kelly muttered. "He didn't do anything wrong."

"We know," Joe told him, wrapping an arm around his shoulders. "But we can't take the chance. Not until we can be certain he won't hurt anyone—"

"Fuck you," Kelly snapped. He shoved Joe off him. "You didn't give two shits about him when he was taken, so don't act like you give a damn about any of this now."

"Kelly," Joe said, eyes wide and wounded. "That's not true. We were . . . It was hard. On all of us."

"Really?" Kelly said. He laughed, and it was such a heartbreakingly hollow thing. "Did you lift a finger to help me?" He looked around wildly. "Did *any* of you besides Gordo and Ox? Or were you too goddamn busy licking your own wounds to care that he was taken? Because I came to you. I *begged* you to do everything you could. To call everyone you knew. And do you remember what you told me?"

Joe clenched his jaw.

"You said maybe it was for the best," Kelly said. "That maybe this was the way things were going to be. That you needed to help Chris and Tanner before you could even consider helping anyone else. I didn't need my Alpha, I needed my goddamn brother, and you said *no*."

"Uh-oh," Tanner said. He inched toward the door. He didn't make it very far before Chris grabbed his arm. He looked down at Chris's hand before lifting his head again. He sighed. "I wish I wasn't so used to being naked in front of a lot of people like I am now."

"Thanks for sharing," Chris muttered. "Now shut up so Kelly can yell at us some more. I think we kind of deserve it."

"That's not fair," Joe said, sounding shocked, as if he'd never heard his brother speak to him this way before. And for all I knew, he hadn't.

"Isn't it?" Kelly asked. "Because it sounds to me like you're making the same mistakes Dad did. Out of sight, out of mind. Isn't that right, Gordo?"

"Kelly," Ox said, the warning in his voice clear.

Gordo's expression shuttered closed. "That's . . . Jesus, Kelly."

Kelly ground his teeth as he started to pace. "Aileen said we were broken. Divided. That we couldn't hope to do *anything* about this unless we fixed what was wrong with us. And you're all standing there after you've put a fucking *bandage* on a gushing wound and congratulating yourselves because of it. We can't do this. We can't keep going on this way."

Carter tried to reach for his brother, but Kelly glared at him. "Dude, I know you're upset—and it's pretty badass, if I'm being honest—and we've earned you yelling at us, but I don't know if it's fair that you say we didn't care. We did." He glanced at me. "I can't speak for everyone. But I know I did." He put a hand over his bare chest, right above his heart. "Right here. It hurt right here. And maybe we were confused, and maybe we were scared. I know that's not an excuse, but there it is." He shrugged as he dropped his hand. He looked at me again. "I'm sorry, Robbie. For everything. I should have done more for you. For him."

Kelly nodded tightly, still riled up and rigid. "This isn't working. It's a half life. It's not *real*. We're pretending like everything is as it used to be." His voice broke. "And no matter how much I wish it was, it's not. This is how we are now. This is our reality. And if we can't do this together, then we're going to die alone."

And with that, he kicked apart the line of silver and crossed over it to me. I tried to protest, but he wouldn't hear it. He sat down on the cot next to me, glaring defiantly at the pack as if waiting for them to tell him off.

They didn't.

They just stood there for a long moment.

The timber wolf moved next. He huffed out a breath, sounding annoyed, before he left Carter's side, walking toward Kelly and me. He stepped gingerly over the silver, snapping at his own back paw when it caught a small part of the powder. He came over to me. He looked me up and down, and I swore he rolled his eyes before he laid his head on my lap, blinking up at me slowly. I hesitated a moment before gingerly patting the top of his head.

"What the fuck," Carter said faintly.

Elizabeth came next. She had a thin, worn robe wrapped around her shoulders. It was far too big for her, and it dragged on the floor. Ox bent over and lifted it as she crossed the line of silver before letting it fall once she was clear.

She sat down at her son's feet, leaning against the cot. She looked out at the others, not saying a word. She didn't need to. Her silence spoke volumes.

Gordo nodded slowly. "I'll go get blankets."

Joe said, "I'll help you. I should check on the Omegas too before we settle in for the night. Make sure we won't have any more issues." He followed Gordo up the stairs.

Ox didn't say a word.

He was watching. Waiting.

Carter came next, though he was trying not to seem too eager. He told the wolf in my lap to move. The wolf ignored him. Carter tried to push him out of the way. The wolf growled at him without opening his eyes. Carter sighed and sat next to him on the floor. The wolf turned his head and pressed his nose against the side of Carter's head. "Yeah, yeah," he muttered. "I get it."

Jessie sat next to Elizabeth.

Chris and Tanner hesitated. They looked at each other, having a conversation without saying anything out loud. They nodded at the same time. They crossed the line of silver, approaching me warily, like they thought I would lash out at them.

But they came anyway.

They breathed a sigh of relief as Carter pulled them down next to him.

"Finally," Mark said. "Finally." He walked over, shorts hanging low on his hips. He ran his hand over the top of my head before settling down against Jessie, laying his head on her shoulder.

Rico remained next to Ox, scowling at the floor.

Ox looked at him.

Rico sighed. "I hear you, *alfa*. Just . . . give me a moment, okay?"

Ox nodded.

Rico took a deep breath. He raised his head, looking directly at me. He said, "Robbie."

"Yeah?" I asked, feeling overwhelmed. They were choosing me. After everything, they were choosing me. And even if Rico didn't, it was at least a start.

"You better not steal the blankets like you used to do," he said. "*Cabrón*. Always stealing blankets like you're the only one who gets them." He was still cursing me under his breath as he crossed the silver toward us. He didn't come near me, but I thought it was enough.

And still Ox didn't come.

For a moment I thought he wasn't going to.

That it'd been too much.

That *I'd* been too much.

But he knew what was in my head. Of course he did. He said, "In a moment, Robbie, I promise."

It wasn't long before Gordo and Joe returned, arms full of blankets and pillows. They were careful not to let them drag in the silver, stepping over the broken line with exaggerated steps. Chris and Tanner were yawning as they took a blanket from Gordo, standing in order to lay it on the floor. Joe threw the pillows on top of it, and Mark and Jessie were the first to lie down on it. Gordo snorted as Mark raised a hand toward him. He pulled his shirt off, leaving him in only a white tank top and shorts. Mark sighed as he curled around Gordo, fingers trailing over the stump at the end of his arm.

The others settled, leaving space for those of us who remained.

Kelly stayed beside me on the cot.

Only then did Ox cross over. His steps were slow and measured. He never looked away from me.

He said, "I dreamed of this. All of us together again. And it hurt. It doesn't hurt anymore."

I blinked rapidly.

He lay down next to Joe, kissed the side of his head.

"You ready?" Kelly whispered to me, though everyone could hear us.

I shook my head. "Just give me a moment."

He did.

But it didn't take long.

There was a space left open just for me. All I had to do was take what was offered.

Even in the face of everything, they were giving me a gift.

I stood from the cot, feeling all eyes on me. I held my hand out for Kelly. He took it without hesitation. I settled down on the blanket next to Carter. He pulled another blanket up and over us. I lay on my side away from him and barely flinched when I felt his hand on my waist. "No homo," he said. Then, "Well, maybe some homo. I don't even know anymore. And before someone says *anything*, shut up. Robbie, just so you know, my morning boner won't be for you. Mostly."

"Love," Elizabeth told her oldest, "I'd rather not hear about such things, if it's all the same to you. Though I'm glad to hear you're open to . . . new experiences."

"What?" Carter asked. "What new experiences?"

"So close," Jessie said as she yawned.

"Jesus Christ," Kelly muttered. He lay down next to me, his back pressed against Ox.

And though we weren't whole, not by a long shot, a quiet energy crackled around us. I was on the precipice again, and the void was still there, but I wasn't alone. Instead of jumping, I took a step away from it.

Carter tightened his arm around my waist.

Ox's hand was in my hair.

Kelly lay facing me. We shared a pillow. We were warm. We were safe. We were together.

Kelly reached up and pushed my hair out of my face. He was

about to pull back, but I didn't let him. I took his hand in mine and held it between us.

We watched each other without saying a word.

I was nearly asleep when Rico said, "Bambi's convinced I've slept with half of you. She wouldn't tell me which half, but since there are more men than women, that means she thinks I've sucked some dick. It's not that I'm *scared* of dick, but I don't know how I feel about balls hitting my chin, you know?"

Chris and Tanner burst out laughing even as most of the rest of us groaned.

"What?" Rico demanded. "It's a very real concern. Gordo, what do you do when you get beard burn from Mark on your balls? That has to suck. Ha. Suck. See what I did there?"

I heard him squawk as it sounded like he got a face full of pillow.

I didn't dream that night.

* * *

The day after a full moon was always a lazy day for wolves. We would be sluggish and slow, the power the moon held over us fading. It never hurt, not like the hangovers that affected humans, but the lethargy kept us from moving around too much.

Couple that with the night I'd had, and I didn't feel like moving. I didn't want to think. I was warm and sleepy, and there was an arm curled around my waist. I reached up and lazily traced my hand up the back of the hand to the arm.

"I said no homo," a voice whispered in my ear.

My eyes flashed open.

Everyone else was gone aside from the bastard behind me.

Carter burst out laughing as I tried to pull away. He held on tightly, his growl rumbling in my ear. "I know you don't remember, but you love cuddling with me. Promise. You always said as much. Pissed Kelly off to no end."

"Let me go, Carter."

"Nah," he said easily. "Just a little bit longer. Need to get my scent on you some more. Make you smell like pack. Are you into watersports? That'd make things quicker if you are. I could just whip it out and— *Oof!*"

He exhaled heavily into my neck as I elbowed him in the stomach as hard as I could. I turned to glare at him, and he was curled up, arms wrapped around his belly.

"Not cool, dude," he wheezed. "You gigantic *dick*. I was just trying to be your friend!"

Chris appeared in the doorway to the basement.

"You said you were going to piss on me!"

"Whoa," Chris said, immediately turning around and heading back upstairs. "I do not need to know that. Is that a wolf thing? No one told me that was going to be a wolf thing. Joe! *Joe!* Do I have to let your brother piss on me or what?"

"What the fuck are you *talking* about?" Joe shouted, sounding outraged.

I thought about lying back down, but Carter was only wearing boxer briefs and was scratching his junk as he yawned so widely his jaw cracked. He saw me watching and trailed a hand toward the top of his boxers, waggling his eyebrows.

Before I could murder him, Ox appeared in the doorway, completely dressed. His arms were crossed over his chest, and he looked stern.

"Crap," Carter muttered. "You were serious."

"I'm always serious," Ox said.

Carter sighed. "You know, you take this Werewolf Jesus thing a little too far." He twirled his hand in the air above him. "Take this bread, all of you, for it is my body. Eat of me and—"

"Your little brother doesn't seem to mind eating my bread."

Carter looked horrified, even as Joe screeched incredulously.

Ox grinned. "Anything else, Carter, before we begin? I could tell you about how Joe likes to—"

Carter shook his head. "Nope. In fact, I'd really rather not hear you say anything ever again. I heard enough through the walls when you and Joe started knocking buttholes, or whatever it is guys do to each other." He frowned. "Not that I care about that kind of thing, but how does that work? Do you guys just bend over and push your asses together to—"

"Get up," Ox told me.

I didn't like the sound of that. "Why? It's still early. I want to go back to sleep."

Ox shook his head. "Not this morning. We have work to do and we're getting started now. Get dressed. Everyone will meet behind the house in ten minutes. Don't make me wait." He turned and went back up the stairs.

"What are we doing?" I hissed at Carter.

He put his arm over his eyes. "Werewolf Jesus is going to work us. Took what those witches said a little too much to heart. Pack unity, blah, blah, blah." He dropped his arm and looked over at me solemnly. "When we do trust falls, I promise to catch you." He reached for me. "I'll always catch you, Robbie."

He was laughing again as I tackled him. It didn't take long before I was pinned below him, breathing heavily.

"Kelly!" he yelled. "Your mate is trying to get all up on my junk. It's unbecoming for a man of my political position. My constituents won't like this very much at all!"

I prayed the day would be over quickly.

It wasn't.

By the time we finished, I was convinced the only reason we'd done any of this was so everyone could take a turn kicking my ass. The Alphas stayed out of it, as did Kelly and Rico (though I was sure Rico itched to pull out his gun), but everyone else was fair game.

Elizabeth moved like liquid smoke, her movements so close to dancing that I thought she was toying with me. I bloodied her nose and squeaked out an apology before she flung me into a tree. That caused a hairline fracture in my arm that healed almost immediately, and she spat a thick wad of blood on the ground before saying, "Lucky hit."

I groaned as the small tree I'd crashed into fell over.

Jessie came next. She zigzagged toward me, left, right, left, and Ox said *there there there*, and I pivoted to the side as she brought the staff from over her head. It hit the ground where I'd just been standing, the tip digging into the earth. Before she could lift it, I kicked down on it, my heel striking the middle of the staff, snapping it in two. Jessie lurched forward but stayed on her feet as I hopped back.

"Oh shit," Tanner breathed.

Jessie frowned down at the broken staff. "I made that myself."

"I'll find you another stick in the woods," I said, feeling lighter than I had since I came to Green Creek. Carter choked but covered it up quickly. "Shouldn't be too hard."

She bent over and picked up the broken half. She stood slowly and banged the two pieces together twice before testing their weight. "Huh. This works too."

And then she was moving again, bringing down the staff in her right hand first. I went left. But she was there with the other staff, and I barely moved out of the way in time. She jumped back, and before I could recover, she moved in *again*. Against my better judgment, I was impressed. She flung her arm out in a flat arc and I ducked, going down to one knee.

That was a mistake.

She used my position to launch herself *off* me, her right foot on my thigh as she jumped *over* me. I didn't have time to turn before she brought down one of those fucking sticks on the back of my head. I grunted as I fell forward, stars flashing angrily across my vision. I was down on my hands and knees, and she stood above me, pointing a broken piece of her staff at my head.

She was panting, but her smile was wild and beautiful. "Not bad. Still could use some work."

I nodded, and she held out a hand to help me up.

I took it.

Ox said, "Good. That was good, both of you. Carter."

I barely had time to recover before Carter bellowed and rushed toward me.

"Oh no," I whispered before a wall of muscle knocked me off my feet.

Chris and Tanner moved as a team ("An absolute unit!" Rico announced grandly), and it wasn't hard to see that they fed off each other. They always seemed aware of where the other was, and I thought about pulling my punches with them but was convinced not to hold back when Chris picked me up over his head and slammed me down onto the ground like he was some kind of fucking wrestler. I bounced heavily and lay there, blinking up at the sky. They stood above me, silhouetted by the sun.

"You gonna just stay down?" Chris asked.

"Yes," I managed to say. "If it's all the same to you, I think I'm okay where I'm at."

"Nah," Tanner said. "I'm not done."

"Oh. Well, since you put it that way. Fuck you."

It went on for a few more minutes before Joe said, "Enough."

By then it had devolved into an all-out brawl, and Tanner had me in a headlock while Chris was trying to climb onto my back to punch my kidneys. We all stopped immediately, staring at the Alphas, breathing heavily.

Ox and Joe were watching me, arms across their chests. Chris jumped off me, and Tanner removed his chokehold. I sucked in a breath, my throat sore. "Are you sure?" I panted. "Because I could do this all day."

"You're crying," Chris pointed out.

"I'm not *crying*. My eyes are sweating!"

He patted me on the top of the head. "Uh-huh. Keep telling yourself that."

"Children," Mark said, looking toward the sky with his secret smile.

Gordo snorted. "You're just pissed off he got a hit in."

"Head back to the house," Ox said. "You're free for the rest of the day."

Thank Christ. I wanted to find a tree to collapse under and stay there for the rest of my life. I was probably going to die.

"Not you," Ox said as I tried to slink away. "Kelly, Chris, Tanner, you all stay too."

Rico frowned. "*Alfa*, maybe we should—" He stopped when Ox shook his head. He shot me a glare before spinning on his heels and stalking back toward the house.

"What a little bitch," Chris muttered.

"Don't worry about him," Tanner told me. "He'll come around. I think."

The others began to drift away, following Rico. Elizabeth and Jessie giggled with each other, looking back at me before laughing again.

Carter and the timber wolf stood next to Kelly. Carter was speaking in low tones, his hands on his brother's shoulders. Kelly nodded at whatever Carter said. Carter kissed his forehead before glancing at me. He bared his teeth and drew a finger across his throat in a clear warning. The timber wolf woofed at me, as if agreeing with Carter, before they walked after the others.

"Kelly, Robbie, with me," Ox said. "Tanner, Chris, stay here with Joe until I call for you."

And with that, he turned and started to cross the clearing, expecting us to do as we were told.

We did.

Kelly fell in step beside me as we left the others behind. "You did good."

I snorted as I rubbed my neck. "I got my ass kicked."

"You did good at getting your ass kicked."

"Gee. Thanks. Glad to know I made a great punching bag so they could work out their aggression."

Kelly stopped me by grabbing my arm. I glanced down at his hand before looking up at him. "It wasn't like that."

"Tell that to my spleen."

He winced. "Point. But Ox wouldn't have given you more than he thought you could handle. He was testing you, sure, but it wasn't *just* about that."

I looked toward the Alpha walking into the tree line, hands clasped behind his back. "Unity."

"Yeah. Ox is big on . . . well. He and Joe learned from our father. Dad was big on the pack as a team. That we had to depend on each other to anticipate what one of us might do."

"Did we do this before?"

He smiled ruefully. "All the time. You fight different. Scrappier. You used to be so worried about hurting one of us."

"I broke your mother's nose," I said dryly. "And then immediately apologized."

He shrugged. "You wouldn't have even tried before. At first when it was you against her, you refused to touch her. You said you could never hit a queen. That made her weirdly happy before she would use it to beat you up."

"What about you?"

He squinted at me. "What about me?"

I motioned between the two of us as he dropped his hand. "Did we . . ."

He laughed quietly. "We did eventually. You always tried to make excuses not to touch me. You said you didn't want to hurt me."

I closed my eyes. "It wasn't because of that."

"I know. Now. And it's endearing. But back then? I was fine with using it against you. Come on. Ox is an Alpha, which means he doesn't like to wait. He's kind of a dick like that."

I didn't protest when he took my hand, pulling me along.

Ox sat with his back against an old oak tree. His legs were crossed in front of him, his hands settled on his knees. He nodded for us to sit with him.

Kelly went first, sitting at his left, facing him. He patted the ground next to him. I hesitated before joining him.

Ox looked off into the trees. In the distance, I could hear the faint sounds of Carter bitching at the timber wolf and the wolf's answering snarl.

"You think he's ever going to figure it out?" Kelly asked Ox.

Ox's lips twitched. "One day. I just hope we're all there to see it."

I was confused. "What are you talking about?"

Ox shook his head. "Later. You did well, Robbie."

I struggled not to preen at the praise. I failed miserably, if Kelly's laugh was any measure.

"Aileen and Patrice," Ox continued. "They think we're fractured. And they're right."

"Rico needs to pull the stick out of his ass," Kelly snapped. "He's only going to make things harder if he—"

Ox held up his hand, and Kelly fell silent. "I've already talked with him. It's going to take time, but I don't know if that's something we have. And it's not just him."

I jerked my head up. Ox watched me with a calm expression.

He said, "Our father, he brought us here. Me and Joe." He looked off into the distance again as he spoke. "I thought it was mostly for Joe, because of what he would become. I thought the only reason I was there was because of what we meant to each other. But now I think he was preparing me as well. I don't know how he knew or even *what* he knew, exactly, but he saw something in me that no one else had, aside from my mother. My daddy, he . . ." Ox shook his head. "It doesn't matter what he thought. Not anymore. It hasn't for a long time, though there are days when I'm still haunted by him. But I know the difference now between ghosts and reality. And know which is true." And then he said, "Robbie, I failed you. *We* failed you."

"Oh, hey, no, you don't have to—"

"Listen."

My mouth snapped closed.

He said, "After the hunters came and tried to take over Green Creek, we were angry. We turned it into something positive. To rebuilding the town, to taking care of the Omegas and Carter and Mark." His eyes filled, a swirl of violet and red that made me sweat. "This . . . thing that I am now, this power that I have, it's more than I ever thought it could be. And I don't take it lightly. I can't. I won't. Too many people depend on me. On all of us. Thomas, he . . . he told Joe that being an Alpha was more than being in charge. An Alpha is a unifier. A protector. That he or she must be willing to give everything for his pack."

"Even his life," Kelly whispered.

Ox nodded. "Even that. And I wanted to tear down the world. My pack had been hurt. They'd been changed. Mark and Carter found control in their tethers—"

"Gordo and Kelly," I said. Ox looked surprised. "Tattoo on Mark's throat. The raven. It's the same as the one on Gordo's arm."

"Okay," Ox said slowly. "And Kelly and Carter?"

I plucked at a blade of grass. Without thinking much about it, I handed it to Kelly, pressing it against his palm. "Carter's always aware of where Kelly is. He turns to Kelly whenever he enters a room. I don't think he knows it. It's just . . ."

"Instinct," Ox said.

"Yeah. Or something close."

Ox nodded. "Good. You're observing."

"I was going to use it against you at first," I admitted. "When I thought you were all crazy."

Kelly arched an eyebrow. "We kind of are."

"Weaknesses," Ox said. "You were looking for weaknesses. What did you see?"

I hesitated. Then, "Not much. I thought about going for the humans first, but Jessie literally knocked that idea out of my head."

Ox laughed softly. "She tends to do that."

I took a deep breath, choosing my words carefully. "If there's any weakness, it's you."

Kelly gasped, but Ox ignored him. "Explain."

"You're an Alpha," I said, "which means you're willing to sacrifice yourself for your pack. But it goes further with you. With all of you. And if I . . . if I wanted to hurt you, hurt your pack, I would exploit that."

"Our pack," Ox said. "Because you're part of this too."

"Am I?" I couldn't hide the bitterness in my voice.

"Yes, Robbie, you are. We fucked up. Rage is a fire that burns bright and fierce, but it sucks all the oxygen from the air around it. In the end, it dies. I didn't expect that. I thought we would storm the compound in Maine. I thought we would force Michelle to stand down and Joe would assume his rightful place as the Alpha of all. If that meant her death, then so be it. But life is funny. We were distracted—*I* was distracted. That fire continued to burn, but it was already dying. I was still angry, but it felt distant. It didn't help that we were at one end of the country and Michelle at the other. We put all our resources into fixing what was broken here and spreading the word around to the packs who would listen about what had happened. Some believed us. Some didn't. Michelle had already begun to fracture the truth, telling those around her who would listen that we'd been infected, that we were a threat to wolves all over the world."

I tried to reconcile that with the Michelle I thought I knew, and I was troubled when I found it wasn't difficult at all. I could see her doing just that. I didn't think her cold, but I knew she could be ruthless.

Ox nodded as if he knew what I was thinking. "I didn't waste my time on those who wouldn't believe us. I may come to regret that someday, but I think it's going to come down to one simple edict. If they're not with us, then they're against us. And if they're against us, then God help them."

"What are you going to do?"

"We're working on it," he said. "Do you remember when I told you that one day I would be asking you about Caswell?"

I could only nod.

"It'll be soon," he said. "Things are in motion. Patrice and Aileen were right when they said we don't stand a chance if we're not united. But we will be, and the time will come when we will do what we must."

A chill crawled down my spine, filling me with ice. "There are children in Caswell."

"I know," he said simply. "But what I *don't* know is what's happened in Caswell since you left. What Livingstone has done, if anything."

"He wouldn't hurt them," I said, horrified, both at what Ox was implying and the fact that I was so quick to defend a man such as Livingstone.

"You can't know that," Kelly said quietly. "Not after what he did to you." He swallowed thickly, looking away. "Or to me."

"Michelle might not even be in control anymore, if she ever was," Ox said. "I don't know what he has on her or what he promised her, but he won't stop."

"At the bridge," I said suddenly, thinking hard. "He said . . ."

What do you think you could do to me? Don't you see how easy this was for me? No matter where you go, no matter what you do, I will find you, Gordo. And I will take everything until you return what belongs to me.

"What did you take? Me?" I shook my head. "Or Gordo?"

"I don't know," Ox said, sounding frustrated. "I don't know if it's a person or a thing or a place. He could mean Green Creek, though Gordo doesn't seem to think so. Too much happened to him here, and even though this is a place of power, I don't know if that's what he's after. But it won't matter if we're not together. He'll find the weaknesses. The cracks between us. And he'll exploit them." Ox laid his head back against the tree. "I can't have that happen. Not again. They were angry, Robbie. After what happened with Chris and Tanner. But when it came down to it, when we found our chance to move on you, every single person in this pack didn't hesitate. You're ours. We're all a little fucked up, and we make mistakes, but when it counts, we're together." He sighed. "I'm just sorry it didn't happen sooner. You deserved better from me as your Alpha. And as your brother."

I flung myself at him, and he caught me effortlessly. His hand came to the back of my head as he held me close, whispering in my ear that I was home, home, home, and he would never let me go again. None of them would. He loved me, he loved me, he loved me, and I squeezed my eyes shut, letting it wash over me, that little voice in the back of my head whispering *packpackpack*.

Eventually I felt together enough to pull away without embarrassing myself further. Kelly was rubbing my back, and I wiped my eyes. He was sniffling too, and I snorted when he sneezed suddenly. I heard footsteps approaching from behind us, but I didn't look up. I was worried it'd set me off all over again.

"Oh boy," Tanner said. "I understand now what Rico meant years ago when he said it smells like feelings. This is intense."

"Good?" Joe asked Ox.

Ox nodded. "We're getting there, I think."

Joe jerked his head toward Chris and Tanner. "Hey, Kelly. Can you help me with something back at the house? I probably need Ox's help too."

I wondered if anyone had ever told Joe he was subtle. If they had, they were lying.

"Sure," Kelly said, going along with it like it wasn't completely obvious what was happening. "I can do that." He glanced at me. "I'll see you back at the house?"

I didn't want him to go. I wanted him to stay and shield me from what was about to happen. But I couldn't let him do that, even though I was terrified. He squeezed my hand again before he followed Ox and Joe toward the clearing. He looked back at us once, an inscrutable expression on his face. I didn't know who he was worried for, me or Chris and Tanner. Probably all of us.

"So," Chris said awkwardly after a long silence. "What's going on?"

"Jesus," Tanner muttered. He shoved Chris, who squawked at him. "Way to make things weird."

"Hey! I'm trying! *You* do something if you think you're better than me."

"Fine," Tanner said. "I will. Just watch."

"Oh, this will be good."

Tanner looked down at me. "Robbie."

"Tanner."

"Do you want to murder us?"

Chris coughed roughly.

"Um. I don't . . . think so. No?"

Tanner looked relieved. "Good." And then he tackled me.

It took me a lot longer than I care to admit to understand he wasn't trying to hurt me. In fact, as soon as he rested his entire weight on top of me, he relaxed and sighed. "That's better. And man, if you tell anyone what I'm about to do, I will deny it and make fun of your hair behind your back."

"What? What are you going to do? And what the fuck is wrong with my *hair*?"

"It's too long and stupid," Chris muttered. "You need to cut it. Original Flavor Robbie hated having long hair. Robbie 2.0 looks like a hipster douche. I swear to God if I see a man bun at any time, Tanner will hold you down while I light your head on fire."

"Get *off* of me!" I cried, trying to shove Tanner away, but he was dead weight, and it was damn near impossible. He ran his hands up and down my sides, huffing out short, quick breaths against my neck and the side of my face. It dawned on me that he was trying to get our scents to mingle. I didn't smell like them, and I was pack, which would have irritated the wolf in him.

I sighed.

"There," Tanner said after what felt like the longest nonsexual rubdown ever. "That's better."

"You should feel bad about what you just did."

"Nah," he said, hopping up. "I mean, maybe. But nah. Chris, go for it. Make sure you *really* get it in there."

I barely had time to flinch before Chris jumped on top of me, doing the same. His movements were almost frantic, and it wasn't as strange as I expected it to be. Granted, anyone who came across us might have thought otherwise, but thankfully we were alone.

Once Chris had gotten his fill, he rolled off to the side, lying next to me on the grass. "Wow," he breathed. "That *does* feel better. Joe was right. And you can never tell him I said that."

"Trust me," Tanner said, "we're not going to talk about this ever again."

"Thank Christ," I said, scooting over slightly as Tanner lay down on my other side. He folded his hands over his stomach, and we watched the clouds go by.

I waited, not sure what was supposed to happen. What they needed from me beyond what they'd already done. I owed them everything, and I couldn't find the words to tell them as much.

Chris didn't seem to have this problem. He said, "I like being a wolf. Yeah, it took some getting used to, but all in all, it's not so bad."

I was cautious, unsure of where he was going. "Would you have . . ." I couldn't finish.

But he knew. "Taken the bite anyway?" Tanner asked. "Maybe. One day. Getting older sucks. My back always hurt from working in the garage, and my eyesight was getting pretty bad."

"I knew it," Chris said. "You were always squinting at everything."

Tanner shrugged. "Now I don't have to worry about it. Sure, I mean, I have to turn into a slobbering giant every time there's a full moon, and I accidentally hunted a deer and was eating it raw before I realized what I was doing, but I can punch through walls now, so it's pretty much a fair trade-off."

"Dude went to *town* on that deer," Chris whispered, even though it was pointless to do so. "It was so gross. Like, entrails everywhere."

"That you *ate*," Tanner retorted.

"I have a thing for guts when I'm shifted," Chris said as if it were nothing. "Don't hate."

Tanner laughed. "Don't hate. Listen to you. You're in your forties. Start acting like it."

"It's not—"

"Why are you doing this?"

They turned their heads toward me, but I stared resolutely at the sky. My hands clenched, and it was getting harder to breathe.

"Doing what?" Chris asked.

"You know what."

"Acting like nothing's wrong, and that we're your friends, and we missed you and wanted you to be there when we ate a deer?"

Fucking idiots. "Yes."

"Because it's true," Tanner said. He moved his arm over until it brushed against mine. I didn't pull away. "Maybe not the *nothing's wrong* part, but all the rest? Totally true."

"You should be scared of me. You *are* scared of me." It wasn't heavy, the scent of fear, and it bent more toward uneasiness, but it was still there.

"Well, *yeah*," Chris said. "You tried to eat us. It hurt." He sobered a little before sighing. "Look, man. We can either dance around this or face it head-on. And the longer we put this off, the worse off we'll be. Did you want to hurt us?"

"I don't remember," I reminded them.

"Oh. Right. Do you want to hurt us now?"

I shook my head.

"See?" Tanner said. "There you go."

"It's not that easy."

"Why not?" Chris asked. "Because if anyone should be having a hard time with this, it should be the two of us. Not you. If anything, you should be groveling for our forgiveness. Go ahead. Grovel. A lot. We're ready."

My throat worked. "This is serious. You can't treat this like—"

"We know it's serious," Tanner said. "It was our idea to be out here with you. Joe and Ox had nothing to do with it. We asked them for this."

That surprised me. I thought the Alphas were trying to keep the peace, shoving us together even if they didn't want to be here. "Rico—"

"Will come around in his own time," Chris said. "He's . . . he took it hard, man. Something about bleeding out in front of him, and dying, and all that junk. But he didn't see what we did. He wasn't there."

"What did you see?" I whispered.

"Blank," Tanner said. "You were just blank. Like no one was home." He poked me in the arm. "It was awful. We knew then, as we know now, that it wasn't you. It was your body, sure, but it wasn't you. Gordo's dad made you do this. Don't ever forget that. And I know this is still all new to you and that we've had time to come to terms with it, but I don't want you to think we were ever going to let you go. Chris and I, we had a long talk after. We decided to become the best fucking werewolves in the world so when it came time to drag your sorry ass back to Green Creek, we'd be ready."

"We trained like a motherfucker," Chris agreed. "I can do backflips. Which, honestly, is pretty pointless, but it looks really cool."

I was shocked into laughter. Chris grinned at me, obviously pleased with himself.

"And no," Tanner said, "we're not here because of what Aileen and Patrice said. Or at least not *just* because of what they said. We're here because you belong to us just as much as we belong to you. That's what pack is, Robbie. It's us being together. I'm not gonna lie. It's gonna be hard. I don't know what's coming, but I know I'd rather have you by my side than not. And Chris feels the same."

"Pretty much," Chris said. "We didn't . . . We were pack when we were human. I thought I understood what it meant, and maybe I did. But now? It's just . . . more. Like all the dials have been turned up as high as they can go. It sucked at first because everything was so fucking *loud*."

"Car alarms," Tanner mumbled. "The worst thing that's ever happened to anyone ever. Gordo accidentally set one off at the garage."

Chris snickered. "Tanner half-shifted and was barking at it."

I laughed again. Tanner shoved me. "You're both dicks." He sat up, looking down at me. "So. We forgive you for the whole *rawr-I'm-going-to-maul-you* thing. And in return, you can forgive us for taking so long to rescue you like the damsel in distress you are."

"It's not that easy."

"Why can't it be?" Chris asked.

"Because I don't know if I can forgive myself." I closed my eyes. "And what happens if we get my memories back? I'll have to relive what I did to you."

"Maybe," Tanner said. He grunted as he moved, twisting around before lying back down, his head on my thigh. Chris reached over and took my hand. We were connected, the three of us, by touch. It wasn't a bond. There were not threads that pulsed and pulled. But I thought it could be a start. "But I think that's a small price to pay, don't you? Because the human version of me was pretty awesome, and I want you to remember me in all my glory. Oh, and Kelly too, but let's pretend I'm what's important right now."

"You are," I whispered, and he leaned into it when I carefully put my hand into his hair.

"We'll figure this out," Chris said, and on this warm summer day, here in the middle of the woods, I knew he was telling the truth. "I know it. And when we do, and when we win, we'll be here. Together.

We'll rebuild what we had together, and no one will have to hurt ever again."

"Unless we need to fuck some shit up," Tanner added. "Because we *will*."

That sharp scent of uneasiness began to fade.

And in its place was only a vast stretch of green, green, green.

SAVE HIM / LIFE TEEMING WILDLY

Kelly was dying.
I wasn't overreacting.
Elizabeth said as much. Sort of.

"He says he's dying," Elizabeth told me the next day. I was still in the basement, not wanting to come out yet, even though everyone told me I was being an idiot. I couldn't take the chance in case Livingstone tried to get in my head again. Gordo thought it had something to do with the full moon, but he sounded dubious.

I stood abruptly, the cot scraping along the floor. "What?" I demanded. "Who hurt him? Did someone come after him? What happened?"

Elizabeth looked grave. "Perhaps you should take a look at him, just to make sure."

There was no silver keeping me in, so I flew by her, charging up the steps, sure that I was going to find nothing but blood and exposed bone when I got to Kelly.

Somehow, it was worse.

He lay in his bed in his room, surrounded by everyone in the pack. Jessie and Mark stood just inside the door, looking amused. I didn't know what the hell could possibly be so funny about this.

"Uh-oh," Rico said, glancing at me over his shoulder.

I barely had time to take in one of the few rooms I hadn't been in yet before I saw Kelly.

He was pale. His eyes were bloodshot. He coughed weakly. It was harsh and wet in his chest. He was trying to breathe, but it didn't sound like much was getting through his nose, so his mouth was open like he was panting. There was a box of tissues on a nightstand, and some were crumpled up in a trash can next to the bed.

"He's diseased," Carter said in a horrified whisper. "What's going on with him? He's . . . he's *leaking*."

Even Joe looked worried. He pressed a hand against Kelly's forehead. "He's warm. Like, *really* warm."

Ox rolled his eyes.

"Oh my god," Tanner said, wringing his hands. "Is this some kind of disease? Like the Omega infection? Are you contagious?"

"He sneezed on me," Chris whispered, eyes wide. "What if *I'm* infected now too? Why did we never call a wolf doctor when Carter and Mark started getting sick? Like a biologist? How could we have been so blind?"

Jessie sounded like she was choking, but I didn't look back to see what was wrong. I only had eyes for Kelly.

"Ugh," he said.

"What happened?" I asked. "Is this magic? Did something infect him? Why are you all just *standing* here? We have to save him!"

Now it sounded like Mark was choking too. I wondered if he'd caught whatever evil Kelly was now suffering from. How could it have spread so quickly?

I leaned over Kelly, putting my face close to his, not sure of what I was looking for but damn sure I was going to find it.

He sneezed in my face.

It was wet.

He blinked in surprise.

Silence settled.

"He's infected too!" Chris wailed. "We're all gonna die!"

"What the fuck is wrong with you?" Rico growled. "You've only been a werewolf for a *year*. Is it eating your goddamn brain? You seriously can't be this stupid."

"We're all gonna die! We're all gonna— Hey. That was mean, Rico. Now is not the time for rudeness."

Tanner nodded solemnly.

Now Jessie and Mark were choking at the same time. I hoped it would be swift and not painful for them.

"I love you," Carter whispered to Kelly. "More than anything. I wish . . . I wish we had more time. Please, Kelly. You have to fight this. You have to *fight this*."

The timber wolf howled, a long and mournful sound.

I heard Ox speaking to Elizabeth. "We really just going to let this keep going?"

"It got Robbie up and out of his self-imposed exile," Elizabeth replied. "I don't feel bad about it at all."

"It's just a virus!" Rico said, throwing up his hands.

"A *virus*?" Carter said, sounding outraged. "What kind of virus? Who gave it to him? I'll kill whoever did! I'll kill them all!"

I nodded furiously. "I'll help. I'm going to tear them apart."

"Still too soon," Chris muttered.

"I feel bad for you," Jessie said to Mark. "Seeing as how you're related to most of them. I don't have to worry about that."

"They are what they are," Mark said, and I could hear the smile in his voice.

Before I could turn around and snarl at them for being so heartless, Gordo said, "You guys are fucking idiots, I swear to God. I don't know how the hell you've survived this long. He's got a fucking cold."

Jessie and Mark burst out laughing.

Tanner and Chris were frowning. "A cold," Chris repeated.

"Yes," Gordo said, exasperated. "A cold. That's it. That's all it is."

Tanner said, "*I* knew that. I was just messing with them. Idiots, right? You guys are so dumb."

"A cold?" Carter asked. "How can he have a cold? That's a human thing. Wolves don't get . . . oh. Right. Shit. Human."

I tried to think about how to fix a cold. I didn't know. I hadn't met many sick humans. Wolves didn't get sick. Humans were weak and fragile, and even if it was *just* a cold, Kelly looked like death warmed over. His face was wet and puffy and his nose was leaking. "Soup," I decided. "I saw in a movie once that you need to give soup to sick people. It makes them feel better, especially when it has noodles in it."

"*That* you can remember?" Gordo asked. He sounded pretty much done with my shit. I wanted to snap at him that at least *his* mate was only an Omega, but fortunately my drive to stay alive overrode my mouth. That and the fact that I was slightly shocked how easy it was for me to think of Kelly as just that.

As a mate.

I knew what he was.

I had his mark on my body.

And he had mine.

"Why is Robbie sitting there with his mouth open?" Chris whispered to Tanner.

"I think he's coming to a dawning realization," Tanner whispered back. "Keep watching him."

They stared at me.

Elizabeth said, "I'm afraid we're out of soup," and I *swore* she was trying to keep from laughing like the others. "I haven't had a chance to get to the store in a few days. Robbie, perhaps you'd like to—"

"On it," I said, because goddammit, I was going to *provide*. I was going to take *care* of him. And it had absolutely nothing with wanting to flee the room in order to keep from throwing Kelly over my shoulder and carrying him away so that nothing could hurt him ever again. "I can buy soup." Then, "Crap. I don't have money." We hadn't found time to get me back into the pack finances.

"Jesus Christ," Gordo muttered. He pulled out his wallet. He fumbled with it, grunting as he flipped it open, almost dropping it. I saw him bring up his other arm, the one that ended in a stump. He glared down at it for a moment. I stepped forward to help, but Mark shook his head once, mouthing the word *wait*.

I did.

Gordo spun the wallet in his hand until he could slide a thumb up against one of the credit cards. He managed to get it out on his own. We all immediately looked away as if we were completely distracted by everything else in the room. "Here," he said, shoving the card at me. "Use this."

"Thanks." I was absurdly touched.

"I'm not going to hug you, so get that look off your face."

I had no idea what he was talking about. I wasn't even thinking about hugging him.

Much.

I turned back to Kelly. He looked up at me with glazed eyes. "I'll save you," I promised him. "Just hold on. I am going to bring you so much soup, you won't even believe it."

"Perhaps someone should go with him," Elizabeth said mildly. "I have a feeling Robbie could use the help. Kelly needs medicine too. Something over-the-counter will work just fine."

"On it," Tanner said. "I used to be a human, so I know all about this."

Chris grimaced. "You would just tell him to get clam chowder and Advil. I should go too."

"There's nothing wrong with clam—"

"It's offensive, and you should be ashamed of yourself for even *liking* it—"

"You do *not* want to talk to me about offensive. I saw you eat that mole during the full moon. That little fucker was *shrieking* as you chomped down on it—"

Gordo sighed. "Rico, go with them. Make sure they don't get into trouble."

Rico glanced at me, an inscrutable expression on his face, before he looked back at Gordo. "I know what you're doing."

"I have no idea what you're talking about."

Rico rolled his eyes. "Whatever you say, *brujo*."

"I really wish you'd stop calling me that."

"Yeah, yeah. Fine. Ox, we're taking your truck."

Ox frowned. "How are you all going to fit?"

Rico headed for the door. "I'm traveling with a pack of dogs. I'm sure one of them won't mind sitting in the back."

The wolves all growled at him, but he ignored them.

Kelly coughed roughly. And then it sounded like he was about to hack up part of his lung, so Chris, Tanner, and I decided it was probably best if we hurried.

. . . .

"It's like they're fucking five," Rico muttered as we drove into town. I looked over my shoulder to see Chris and Tanner in the bed of the truck. They were hanging off either side of the truck, wind blowing through their hair as they laughed.

"They seem to have taken to it well," I said. "Being wolves."

His hands tightened briefly on the steering wheel. "I guess. It is what it is."

The cab of the truck was warm. I was uncomfortable. I didn't know why Rico had agreed to go. I searched for something to say.

He beat me to it. "I think Chris..." He shook his head. "I think he was always going to take the bite at some point."

I nodded, trying to be as small as I could. "And Tanner?"

Rico shrugged. "Maybe. It's... intoxicating. The idea of being stronger. Faster. Able to protect those you care about."

"Is it... something you would ever want?"

Rico didn't answer.

I looked out the window.

Then, "No. Maybe. I don't know. It's... I like being human. But sometimes I think about how much easier it would be, you know?

You all can do things I can't. I can feel them, but Chris said that after he turned, it was ramped up by a lot. It took him a long time to be able to figure out how to turn it off. Or at least dampen it."

"But humans can do things wolves can't," I said quietly. "That's why humans are important in packs."

He stopped at a stop sign. "Any humans in Maine?"

"I'm sure there are. It's a big state."

He snorted. "Smartass. I'm talking about in your pack." He winced. "I mean the other pack."

It stung more than I expected it to, but I let it go. "Not really. I mean, witches, yeah. They come in every now and then. But not like . . . this. Michelle doesn't really care for humans."

"God, that woman," Rico muttered. "I can't wait to meet her face-to-face." He glanced at me. "I hope that's not going to be a problem."

"What do you mean?"

He pulled through the stop sign. "You know what I mean. It's going to come down to it one day. Us or her. Us or Gordo's dad. Things can't continue like they are. Surely you can see that."

"I know."

"Do you?" he asked, and it was a challenge. "Because I hope that's true, Robbie. I really do. I can't take the chance of needing you to watch my back only to have you go fucking feral again and become Livingstone's lapdog."

"That's not fair."

He looked like he was going to argue, but then he deflated. "You know what? You're right. That wasn't fair. I'm sorry, *lobito*. I've just . . . I've got a long memory. Always have. I'm not really used to letting things go, even when I should."

"Why do you call me that?"

"What?"

"*Lobito.*"

His jaw tightened. "It's nothing. Stupid, I guess. Just slang. Doesn't even really mean anything."

"It means little wolf."

"Yeah."

"I told you about her."

He stopped near the curb in front of a small grocery store down the road from the garage. Chris and Tanner hopped out of the back.

Rico waved at them to go on. Chris and Tanner exchanged a look before nodding and heading for the store.

Rico switched off the truck. He rubbed a hand over his face as he slumped down on the bench seat. "You did. Weirdly, you told me before you told anyone else. After the whole mess with Richard Collins." He shook his head. "We were at the garage. It was just the two of us. It was our turn to stay and catch up on all the paperwork. Gordo left us some beers, and it was late. But yeah, you told me."

"Why you?" I asked. Then, "Shit. I didn't mean that like it sounded."

"Oh, thanks," he said dryly. "That makes me feel better."

"I swear, I didn't—"

"I was a little drunk," Rico said, reaching out the open window to adjust the side mirror. "And you were laughing at me because of it. And then *I* was laughing because I . . ." He swallowed thickly. "I liked hearing you laugh. And after everything we'd been through, that entire fucking shitstorm, it was . . . good. Just to have a moment of peace. To sit back with someone else who understood and just laugh. I don't even remember how it came up. We were talking about Ox and Joe and their stupid mystical moon magic connection, and then I was telling you about my mom, may she rest in peace. And then you told me about the tree."

"Quiet as a mouse," I whispered.

"Yeah, man. That. And the thing she used to tell you. Little wolf, little wolf. And it just started from there, you know? *Lobito*. You didn't seem to mind."

"I don't. I like it. Coming from you."

He squinted at me. "But you don't remember it."

I shrugged. "No, but I know how it makes me feel now. And if it's anything like it was then, I think it's okay. I obviously told you about her because I trusted you."

He watched me a moment. "But not anymore."

"I don't really know anything anymore."

"Oh Jesus, get that look off your face. Break my heart, why don't ya?" He narrowed his eyes. "If you're trying to make me feel sorry for you, it's not working."

"I'm not."

"Goddammit. It's totally working. Look, Robbie, I . . ." He tapped his fingers on the steering wheel. "I'm trying, okay? I really am. I know shit's fucked up right now. And I don't even know what we're going to face in the days ahead. Hell, we might not even survive whatever's going to happen."

"Because it's going to be you or them."

"Yeah. It will." He frowned. "Wait a minute. When I said *us* or them, that included you. You know that, right?"

I didn't before. I did now.

He sighed. "And now you've got that dopey look on your face. I just can't with you." And then he did an extraordinary thing: he reached over and grabbed my wrist. He didn't squeeze; he didn't try to hold my hand. He just let his fingers circle the little bones. It was something small, but it felt bigger than the both of us. "I'll get there," he said. "I have to, right? Because it's the only way we're going to be able to beat them."

Oh. Fuck, that sucked to hear. That he only considered me part of this, part of this pack, out of necessity.

And then he said, "But also because I want to," and my breath caught in my chest because he wasn't lying. His heart remained steady. "I want things to go back to the way they were. I want to be able to look at you without remembering what happened. And maybe that's stupid. I don't know if things will ever be the same again, but I miss my friend."

I had to know. "What if I don't ever remember? What if I stay as I am now?"

"Then we deal with it. Together. And we remind you of who you used to be. He took you away from us, Robbie. And he took everything that we'd ever been through together. But you're here, yeah? No matter how strong Michelle is, no matter what control Livingstone had over you, you're here with us now. And that's what's important. I forgot that. And I'm sorry I did. I'm trying, okay? I swear to you I'm trying. Because I know you would do the same for me, no matter what."

I hugged him.

He grunted as I practically fell on top of him, pushing my face against his chest. And then, wonder of all wonders, he chuckled and patted my back. "Yeah, yeah. You too, *lobito*. I get it."

He let it go on for a few more moments before he pushed me away. "Enough of the feelings crap. I get enough of that with Bambi, but don't *ever* tell her I said that because I like my balls where they are. Let's go get what we need for your boy."

"He's not my *boy*—"

Rico laughed as he climbed out of the truck. "Holy shit, you should see the look on your face right now. You're Alpha red, except it's all over. Fucking dork."

He was still laughing at me as I followed him inside.

Kelly was asleep by the time we returned. The pack was spread out through the house, and no one said a word about the Mylar balloons I was struggling to fit through the front door.

They didn't need to.

I could see the amusement on their faces.

Rico shoved me toward the stairs. "We'll fix the food. Get your ridiculous ass up to Kelly. I'll let you know when it's ready. It was my turn to help with food for Sunday Tradition, anyway."

I nodded gratefully before heading upstairs.

Elizabeth was the only one still in the room with Kelly, sitting in a chair next to the bed. She looked up at me when I walked through the door. She grinned at me, wild and beautiful. "What have you got there?"

I kicked one of my boots at the floor. "Just some balloons. The woman at the grocery store said that people like balloons when they're sick."

"So you decided to buy all of them?"

"I didn't know which ones to get."

"One says 'Happy Birthday.'"

I groaned. "I may have gone overboard. Rico was pissed off when we had to try and shove all of them into the truck."

"I think Rico likes to bitch about things regardless. It's a personality trait."

I set the plastic weight tied to the balloon strings on the desk before handing her the plastic bag in my other hand. She looked inside. "And you seem to have bought every single cold remedy in existence."

"I just wanted to make sure," I muttered. I kneeled next to the bed. Kelly was sleeping, nose twitching as he sniffled. He looked warm, and Elizabeth handed me a cool cloth. I dabbed his forehead carefully, not wanting to wake him.

"He'll be all right," she said.

"I know."

"Do you?"

I shrugged.

"Well, you should listen to me, then, and believe me when I tell you so. I am a mother, after all. I know quite a bit about such things."

"He's never been human before," I reminded her.

"No, I don't suppose he has. But I've had humans in my pack." Her smile faded slightly. "I've taken care of the sick a time or two."

"If it wasn't for me, he wouldn't even be like this."

"Perhaps." She touched my back before withdrawing. "But I think you'll find it doesn't matter to Kelly. Or at the very least, he thinks it's a small price to pay. And one he would pay again and again."

"Doesn't seem that small to me."

"What if the roles were reversed?"

I looked at her. "What do you mean?"

"What if Kelly had been taken instead of you? What would you have done to get him back?"

"I don't know," I admitted. "I don't know the person I was. I can't say what I would have done."

She nodded. "Point. But let's say as the person you are now. What would you do?"

"Everything," I said immediately. I blinked. "Whoa."

"Whoa indeed," she said, lips twitching. "Memories are all well and good. They help to shape us, to make us who we are. We learn from past experiences, and they can also bring us joy in the quiet moments of reflection. But they aren't everything. Because here you are, as you are. The Robbie I knew would be doing the same thing. You're not that different from who you used to be."

"I just want to keep him safe," I mumbled.

"I know you do. And I don't know that anyone would do a better job than you. Can I ask you something, Robbie?"

I nodded.

She took the cloth from me and dipped it into the bowl on the nightstand next to the bed. She wrung it out before handing it back to me. I gently pressed it against Kelly's forehead, and he sighed in his sleep, turning his head toward me.

"What do you see?"

Kelly, Kelly, Kelly. But I didn't think that's what she was talking about. "What do you mean?"

"Here. In this room."

I looked around. I hadn't noticed when I'd burst in earlier. Aside from the bed and the nightstand, there was a small desk set against one wall underneath a window. The balloons were on top of it. There was a rug on the floor, and a closet with the door cracked open, and I could see clothes hanging inside.

But that was it.

The room was mostly blank. Like mine had been when Mark had shown it to me.

It didn't look like anyone lived here, especially not someone as bright and vibrant as Kelly.

I looked at Elizabeth, confused. "It's empty."

She was pleased, and it was all for me. I wanted to bask in it. "Yes. It is. Do you know why?"

I started to shake my head but stopped. What was it Mark had told me? "We didn't live here. We lived in the other house."

She nodded. "You did. You were so proud of yourself that day. It was as if you were both starting out on your own. And in a way, you were, even if it was right next door. You shared the house with some of the Omegas that were staying here with us, at least at first. Ox and Joe, they had been using the house, but they came back here. They knew you needed time to just . . . be together. I was standing on the porch, watching you two walk hand in hand toward the other house." Her eyes were watery, but she waved me away when I tried to hand her the box of tissues. "You made it a home. It was warm and inviting, and you were talking about starting traditions of your own. Oh, you were going to include all of us in them, but you thought it was so grown-up, so mature to invite people over for dinner. I might have helped you with that a time or two."

"I wish I could remember it."

"I know you do," she said. "But memories aren't everything, Robbie. Because here you are, starting again. And I couldn't be happier that it's you my son chose. This room, it's bare because it's not his true home. His true home was the one he made with you. He's only here because he couldn't stand the quiet. A home is a place. But it can also be a person. You're that person for him. I only wish . . ." She shook her head.

"What?"

"It's silly," she said as she sniffled. "I only wish his father could have been here to see it. To see the man he's become. To see the men they've all become. He would have loved it. He would have loved you, if only for how happy Kelly was and will be again. But I know my husband. You would have been so much more to him."

I gnawed on my bottom lip. Then, "I have something for you."

She looked startled. "You do? Oh, Robbie. I don't need anything. I—"

I shook my head. "It's not a gift. It's something that belongs to you. Something that should have been yours a long time ago. I'm only going to return it. Give me a second, okay? I'll be right back."

She nodded, taking the cloth back from me. I left her as she hummed quietly, taking her son's hand and rubbing her thumb over his palm.

As I descended the stairs, I could hear Rico, Chris, and Tanner bickering in the kitchen. Jessie was in the backyard with Dominique, setting up the table for Sunday Tradition. Mark, Gordo, Joe, and Ox were in the office on the first floor, door open. They looked up as I passed, but I didn't stop. Carter and the timber wolf stood in the front of the house, Carter telling the wolf that Kelly wasn't dying and he didn't even know why the wolf was worried to begin with. The wolf grumbled in response.

I went down to the basement.

Sitting next to the cot was my backpack.

I lifted it up over my shoulder, hoping I was doing the right thing.

Elizabeth stopped singing when I walked back into the room. I kneeled before her on the floor because she was a queen, and she deserved my respect. I placed my forehead against her leg, and her hand went to my hair. "What's this?" she asked.

I breathed and breathed and breathed.

I sat back as she dropped her hand. She watched me curiously.

I pulled the backpack around, clutching it tightly. "This is all I have."

"Is it? I don't believe that for a moment. You have so much more than could fit into such a little bag."

I shook my head. "You said that memories aren't the most important thing. And maybe you're right. But sometimes they *are* important. And these are my memories. Everything I have." I had to force myself to hand it over to her. She waited until I let it go before pulling it into her lap. "Open it."

She did without question, and I thought I loved her for it.

"Oh," she said as she peered inside. "Oh, oh. Look. Robbie. Look." She pulled out the stone wolf. Kelly's wolf. "After all this time?"

I nodded. "I thought it was mine."

"It is yours," she said. "Because it was given to you. On a bright and sunny day. Kelly was nervous. He asked me if I thought you'd accept it. I told him I believed you would with all my heart. He didn't know that you'd already come to me a few days before to ask me the same thing."

I stared at her with wide eyes. "Really?"

She grinned. "Really."

"Mysterious," I whispered.

"What was that?"

I shook my head. "It's not... It doesn't matter. Just something Kelly told me once. Did... does he still have mine? I mean, it's okay if he doesn't, I get that a lot has happened, and he doesn't have to—"

"Look in the drawer." She nodded toward the nightstand.

I did with shaking hands.

There, lying on a felt cloth, was another stone wolf. It was markedly similar to the one Elizabeth now held. The style, the pose, the stance. There were different cuts in the stone. The one in the drawer looked as if it'd been carved with a clumsier hand, but it was so close to the one I'd carried with me. They looked like a set, like they belonged together.

Elizabeth didn't say a word as I took the other wolf from her and placed it on the cloth next to Kelly's. I pushed them together. It was one thing to hear that I mattered. It was something else entirely to have evidence of it.

I closed the drawer, knowing they'd be safe there.

Elizabeth allowed me a moment to collect my thoughts. I wiped my face before motioning for her to continue.

She took out my mother's driver's license next. She smiled at the photograph. "Beatrice."

"Yeah. She... ah. She was a good person."

"I know she was. I knew her only briefly, but she was a light. I could see that even though we were both young. I'm so sorry that she's not here to see you as you are and all you've become."

I nodded and looked away.

She went through the rest of the contents of the backpack. There was a pinecone from a forest. A flower pressed between the pages of an old romance about pirates. A photograph, the edges bent, of me surrounded by cubs. She was blue when she saw it, but it didn't last. It filled with something sharper, something that felt like a great, lumbering beast.

She slowly pulled out the leather journal.

The backpack slid from her lap.

"Where did you find this?" she whispered.

"In Caswell," I said, suddenly unsure. "It was in Michelle's office. I . . . I know it sounds crazy, but I think I was meant to find it. I didn't read it," I added quickly. "At least not beyond the first couple of pages. But it didn't belong to her. I don't know why she kept it or even if she knew it was there."

"She did," Elizabeth said. "Nothing would have escaped her attention. The bigger question is why she kept it at all." She looked at me. Tears fell freely now. "You've had it this entire time, haven't you? Because of what you said that first day."

I nodded, feeling like shit. "'To my beloved. Never forget.' I didn't mean to keep it from you. I was scared."

"Why now?" She didn't sound angry, and her scent was filled with tempered grief.

"Because it's yours, and no one else should ever get to touch it unless you give them permission to do so. I don't mean to make you sad."

"I know. Thank you, Robbie. I haven't seen this in years. I don't think Thomas meant to leave it behind. But things were complicated back then." She opened the journal, and I felt like I was intruding on something private. She traced a finger over the slanted writing that filled the pages. She took in a shuddering breath as she began to flip through the journal. "I wonder . . ."

I wanted to ask, but I didn't think she would hear me.

It didn't take long until she reached the back of the journal. She looked disappointed for a moment, but then her eyes lit up. "You sneak. Of course."

She ran a finger over the back cover. There were tight black threads on one edge that I hadn't noticed before. A claw grew from the tip of one of her fingers, and she sliced through the threads. I was alarmed that she felt the need to destroy her husband's journal, but before I could say anything, she pulled out an envelope.

And then another.

And then another.

Three small squares that I hadn't known were there.

Her smile trembled. "There you are. I thought you'd been lost." She looked up at me, eyes bright. "Thank you, Robbie. You don't know what this means to me. For us. For our family. For our pack. This is a wonderful gift. And now I have something for you."

She handed me one of the envelopes.

On the front was the same handwriting from the journal. *For Kelly's Future.*

"What's this?" I asked.

"It's for you," she said. "And there's one for Ox and one for . . . well. We'll know when Carter knows."

I looked up at her. "About what?"

She shook her head. "It doesn't matter. Not now." She closed the journal in her lap, keeping the other two envelopes on the top. "My husband wrote you a letter."

I blinked. "Me? But I didn't know him."

"Hypothetical you," she said, running her fingers over the other envelopes. "Whoever Kelly chose to spend his life with. When the day came that Kelly would find his mate, Thomas planned on giving whoever it was this letter. He wrote one for each of his sons. He always planned on being here when it happened."

She stood then, bending over and kissing Kelly on the forehead. She squeezed my shoulder before heading toward the door. She paused and said, "You deserve every happiness. Remember that." And then she was gone.

The room was quiet, with only the sounds of Kelly's slow, shallow breaths interrupted by the occasional sniffle. I looked down at the envelope again. I was scared to open it. I didn't know if I deserved this, didn't know if I could be the man an Alpha king would have chosen for his son.

But it wasn't about his choice.

It was about mine.

And Kelly's.

I opened the envelope. There were two pages filled with the same script.

Hello—

I write this on a sunny day.

I think that's important.

It's a sunny day, and my son Kelly Abel Bennett has just turned thirteen years old. He's tall and gangly, not having yet grown into his limbs. He's smart, much smarter than I'll ever be. It's almost scary, if I'm being honest. He's quiet, and sometimes I worry that he spends too much time in his head. I don't always understand him (can one ever completely understand their children?), and there are times that I think him a mystery that I am desperate to solve.

Being a father isn't as I expected it to be. It's hard; there are days when I second-guess myself, days when I'm sure I've ruined them forever. This life . . . it's not easy. The Bennett name isn't quite a curse, but I sometimes think it is. We have been through much, and Kelly has seen the aftermath of what happens when someone tries to take everything away from us.

When Elizabeth was first pregnant with Carter, my father told me that I would spend the rest of my life in a constant state of fear. Even though my children would be wolves, he said, they were still fragile. Still capable of hurt and pain and suffering. It is a father's duty to protect them at all costs. He told me of the days when they would hate me, days when they would think I was the stupidest person alive. Days when I'd want to pull my hair out and question everything I'd ever done.

But those days, my father told me, would be few and far between.

Because a child is a gift.

Kelly isn't like his brothers. Carter is headstrong and blunt. He will make a fine second one day. Joe is going to be the Alpha, and will bear the responsibilities that come with the power and the title.

But Kelly...
He's something different, I think.
Something more.
I wonder about you. Who you are. What you're doing at this exact moment. Are you a man or a woman? Are you a witch or a wolf? Are you human? Do you smile and laugh and see the world for all it has to offer, for all it takes away?
Kelly is a mystery.
But he's not unknowable.
Here is what I know about my second son:
He prefers to spend time alone. If he's not alone, he'll be with Carter. Carter, as he's wont to do, will think himself Kelly's protector. It comes with being the eldest and with being each other's tether. But what he doesn't know—and what I've only recently come to understand—is that Kelly is fierce and brave, and he might be Carter's protector just as much as Carter is his.
He wonders about all manners of things. Yesterday, for example, he asked me about our territory and why it felt different there than it does here in Maine. I didn't know quite how to explain it to him. I can't even be sure I know myself. When I told him as much, he wasn't disappointed. Instead he asked me to come with him. We went outside and wandered through the forest, just the two of us. I felt guilty for a moment, not able to remember the last time we'd done this. With everything that has happened to us these last years, my attention has been elsewhere.
We went deep into the woods. He stopped after what must have been a few miles in a part of the forest I hadn't been in for years. It wasn't much different than any other part of the woods that comprise our territory. I wanted to ask why: why here, why this place, what drew him to this specific spot. But I waited.
He sat down next to a tree, his back to it. He took off his shoes, his toes digging into the grass. He patted the ground beside him, squinting up at me. His hair was too long. He had to brush it off his face. I was completely charmed by this skinny quiet boy and could only do what he'd asked.
And we sat there for almost two hours without saying a word.
Eventually he broke the silence.

Do you know what he said?

"I think any place can be special if you try hard enough."

And that was it.

Simple, really.

But the more I think about it, the more I parse through those twelve words, the more I understand he wasn't just *talking about a territory.*

He was talking about his entire world. His entire world was special because we're in it.

And this is Kelly in a nutshell: simple, at a cursory glance, but just underneath, there is life teeming wildly. In his chest beats a tremendous heart, something so vast and extraordinary that it takes my breath away. He is a light, a beacon in what can seem like a neverending darkness. A world in which he does not exist is a world I cannot even begin to comprehend. Carter made me a father by simply being born. But Kelly has helped me understand what it means to be a father, and all that it entails.

I don't know you, whoever you are. But you must be someone who knows the light he is. If he has chosen you (and you were smart enough to choose him back), then I know he'll be in good hands. Appreciate him. Love him. Never take him for granted. If you can do these things, then I promise that you will know what true love is. Kelly will never do anything to harm you, at least not intentionally. I think he would rather hurt himself than anyone else.

He's not fragile. No, that's not a word I'd ever use to describe him.

But he must be protected at all costs, because he deserves it.

I don't know you.

But I can't wait to.

I can't wait to witness what blooms between the two of you.

Knowing Kelly as I do, it might be hard, at first. But give it time, grant him patience, and you will be justly rewarded beyond anything you could possibly imagine.

I sit here on this sunny day, light streaming in through an open window, imagining what the moment will be like. When he comes to me and tells me he's met his mate (though I'll admit to never really finding that word to be entirely adequate). He'll be nervous about it, I think, and his brow will be furrowed, and he'll ask questions, so many questions, and will probably be wishing he was anywhere but here, but *he'll be fighting back a smile, and he will look as if he's burning from the inside out. I know this. I know this.*

Cherish each other. Love each other with your whole hearts. Don't ever lose sight of what's important. And that, my unknown friend, is easier said than done, and makes me a hypocrite. I can see that now clearer than ever. But if you learn with each other and grow together, then there is nothing that will stop you from becoming the people you're supposed to be.

I can't wait to meet you.

But I hope you understand that I'll be fine with waiting on that meeting for a time. Because when he gives you his heart, it will no longer be mine to hold. And I want to hold on to it for as long as I'm able.

Whoever you are, you are loved.

Never doubt that.

You are loved.

Yours,

Thomas Bennett

"Are you crying?" a weak voice asked.

I looked up at Kelly as I wiped my eyes. He blinked slowly. He was pale, and he coughed wetly, but he was concerned too, and was trying to reach for me.

I stood quickly and went to him. I pushed him gently back down on the bed, ignoring his protestations. He settled back against his pillow, frowning. His nose was running, and he had dark circles under his eyes, but I didn't know if I'd ever seen someone such as him before in my life. He was like the sun.

"What's wrong?" he asked. His frown deepened. "I'm not dying, right?"

I laughed, though it sounded broken. "No," I managed to say as I sat on the edge of the bed. "No, you're not dying. And you won't be. Not until we're very, very old."

"Oh. That's good to know."

"I think so too."

"What's that?" He pointed at the letter.

I didn't hesitate.

I gave it to him.

He sniffled as he took it, pushing himself up so he was propped against his headboard. He looked down at the writing, and his eyes widened. "This is..." He traced a finger over the words like I'd given him a great gift. "Where did you get this?"

"Your mother gave it to me."

He looked up at me. "And it's for you?"

I nodded. "For both of us, I think."

And then he began to read, eyes darting back and forth. A moment later his hands began to shake. He started to cry silently. I put my hand on his knee over the blanket. When he finished the second page, he started again from the beginning.

Eventually he set the pages aside. He leaned his head back and closed his eyes, throat working. He said, "I remember that day. When we went to the woods. Just him and me. I don't... It wasn't as profound as he was making it out to be. I was a little jealous that he was spending so much time with Joe, even though Joe needed it after all he'd been through." He coughed, and I handed him another tissue. He smiled before using it to wipe his nose. He pushed his knee up against my hand. I never thought about moving it. "It was dumb, you know? Being jealous over something like that. But I didn't know any better. So I made up something about the territory that I told him I'd been thinking about, and he didn't question it."

"Just because it wasn't profound to you doesn't mean it wasn't for him," I said quietly.

"You think so?"

"I do."

He looked down at the pages sitting on the bed. "I wish..." He shook his head. "I wish for many things. That I was a wolf again. That nothing bad would ever happen to any of us ever again. That you were..." He sucked in a sharp breath. "But I'm not a wolf. And I can't stop whatever the future has in store for us. And you are as you are. And I don't know if I can change any of that. But it doesn't matter."

"It doesn't?"

"No," he said. "Because even though I'm not a wolf, and even though shit is always flung at us, and even though you don't remember everything we had, you're still here." He smiled, and it trembled. "You said *we*."

I looked down at my hand on his knee. "What do you mean?"

"I asked you if I was dying. And you said no, and that I wouldn't until *we* were very, very old."

My face grew warm. "Oh. Um. Well. That's . . ."

"Good. That's good."

"It is?"

"Yes."

You are loved.

He burned so bright. It was all grass and lake water and sunshine, and I wanted nothing more than to have it for my own.

I said, "Kelly?"

"Yeah?"

"Can I kiss you?"

He gaped at me.

I waited nervously, forcing myself not to fidget or take the words back.

He grimaced. "Oh Christ. You're serious. What the hell is wrong with you? Do you not *hear* what I sound like? Something must be wrong with your eyes too, because I'm leaking from almost every opening I have. And I can't even begin to imagine what I must smell like to you—"

I kissed him.

Again.

For the first time.

His eyes were open, and my eyes were open, and I was drowning in him, drowning in *this*, and I didn't want to be saved. I wanted it to close over my head and pull me down until all there was in this world was him.

It was chaste, this kiss. I saw a tear trickle from his right eye before I closed my own. I was about to pull away, sure I'd gone too far, when he wrapped his hand around the back of my neck, holding me in place. He sighed against my lips, and I wondered if this was happiness, if this clawing in my chest was how I felt when we'd done this before. Because if it was, then I understood why Gordo had said I must have fought like hell. If someone had tried to take this away from me, the memory of him and the way he felt against me, I would have done everything in my power to fight back.

Even as I felt consumed by him, a low, fiery hatred burned in the pit of my stomach at the thought that it *had* been taken from me.

My pack.

My home.

My mate.

Eventually he pulled away, eyes wide. "Wow," he whispered.

"Wow," I whispered back to him.

"I'm still pretty gross."

"You are."

He snorted. "And I feel like crap."

"I know."

He looked shyly at me. "But..."

"But?"

He shrugged before jerking his head toward the other side of the bed.

It took me a moment before I realized what he was asking.

And I could barely restrain the urge to howl and shake the bones of the house.

I toed off my boots, letting them fall to the floor. I turned, carefully climbing over him so I didn't hurt him. He pulled back the comforter, and I got underneath. He was almost wolf-warm because of his sickness. He moved down on the bed and laid his head on the pillow. I did the same, our faces only inches apart. He pulled the comforter up and over our heads, surrounding us with semidarkness. Our scents mingled, and though his was human and dulled with illness, it was enough.

His eyes searched mine, and as we watched each other, I forced myself to search the furthest corners of my mind for something, *anything* that I could remember. There was nothing, of course. The void was absolute.

And I was so angry because of it.

He brought his hand between us and poked a finger against my cheek. "Stop that."

"Stop what?"

"You're thinking too hard. I can see it on your face. Just be here. Right now. With me."

And how could I refuse that?

I said, "I'm here."

"You are."

"Right now."

"Yes."

"With you."

And god, how he *smiled* at me. Here, in this little cave we'd created for ourselves, this little section of life we'd carved out, he smiled. It was bright and fierce, and I reached up to brush another tear away from his cheek before it could fall onto the pillow.

He said, "My father loved me."

I said, "He did. Very much."

He said, "I don't know why I never realized it. How deep it went."

I said, "How could he not?"

He said, "We'll fix this."

I said, "If we can't?"

He said, "Then we start again. From the beginning. It may take time, and there will be days when we both get frustrated, days when you'll wonder if I'm not better off with someone else, and I'll tell you to stop acting like such an idiot. You'll scowl at me, and I won't pay it any mind because I've had enough with the sheer amount of martyrs that we seem to have in this pack. But those days will be few and far between because every day will be us. You and me. And I won't stop. I won't ever stop. Even if I lose you again, if you somehow forget all of this, I'll do it again. And again. And again."

I was shaking. I couldn't stop. "Why?"

"Because you filled a hole in me I didn't even know was there. You make me complete. You make me happy. I see you, Robbie. I see you."

He pulled me against his chest, wrapping his arms around me. I buried my face in his neck, breathing him in as I shuddered and shook. He whispered quietly to me in that gravelly sick voice, saying, "Robbie, Robbie, Robbie, you're here. You're with me. You're safe. You're home. You're home. You're *home*."

I was breaking, collapsing in on myself. It ripped through me, tearing everything that stood in its way. In the dust and ruins of all that remained, there was only him and me hidden away from the world that moved around us. I was scraped hollow and raw, and I tried to find the words to say what it meant, what I was feeling, how desperate I was to believe every single thing he'd said.

And when I finally spoke, I spoke from the depths of everything I had left.

I said, "I'm going to love you again, okay? I promise."

He held me tighter, and his breath was warm in my ear. "I know."

Eventually we slept.

BLOOD

The end of this life hidden behind a barrier of magic began on a Tuesday in the middle of June.

This is what we saw:

I sat at the front desk at Gordo's, frowning at the appointment calendar. Chris had taken a few calls while I was at lunch, and he'd screwed something up. He'd apologized, patting me on the shoulder telling me he just *knew* I could fix it.

I scowled after him as he walked back into the garage, whistling as if he didn't have a care in the world.

My bad mood didn't last. Kelly brought me lunch again, and we sat out on the sidewalk in front of the garage, eating and talking about nothing in particular. We hadn't forgotten everything that was looming around us, but we acted like we had. If I tried hard enough, I could almost convince myself that everything was fine.

The sun was out.

The air was warm.

There wasn't a cloud in the sky. If I looked hard enough, I could see the faint sliver of the moon suspended above us. We sat close, his shoulder pressed against mine.

He said, "I don't want you to sleep in the basement anymore. You don't need to. You have a room, Robbie. You need to use it."

"I know. Ox said the same thing yesterday."

"You should probably listen to him. He usually knows what he's talking about."

"Usually?"

Kelly rolled his eyes. "He's an Alpha. You know how they are."

"I can hear you!" Ox shouted from somewhere inside the garage.

"Good!" Kelly yelled back. "I wanted you to!"

And I smiled at him because I *could*. I felt settled in my skin, and things weren't perfect, but we could *pretend*. We could pretend we were just two guys getting to know each other without worrying about everything that lay ahead.

It all came tumbling down an hour after Kelly left to head back out on patrol.

It started with Gordo.

He was saying, "Tanner, give Mrs. Warren a call. Tell her that we have to order the parts to—"

Something crashed inside the garage.

I was up before I even thought about it.

I burst through the door into the garage. Gordo was on his knees, his tablet lying on the ground, the screen cracked. He held his hand against his right ear, his stump against the other, and his face was twisted painfully. His tattoos were bright and *moving*, the roses underneath the raven twisting their barbed vines as the bird bowed its head.

Rico kneeled next to him, hand on his back, asking what was going on, what happened, are you okay, are you okay, Gordo?

Chris and Tanner's eyes were orange. I saw the hint of fangs in Tanner's mouth.

Ox stood near one of the open bay doors, eyes red and violet, hands clenched into fists as his chest rose and fell rapidly. He breathed in through his nose and out through his mouth as he got himself back under control.

"What is it?" I demanded. "What happened?"

"The wards," Gordo muttered. "Something hit the wards." He groaned as he dropped his arms, nodding at Rico, who helped him to his feet. He moved until he stood next to Ox, staring out into the street.

"North end," Ox said.

"Yeah," Gordo said, stretching his neck side to side until it popped. "It hurts, Ox. Whatever it is, it hurts."

"How many?"

"I don't know. I don't think we're under attack." He grimaced again. "But something's not right."

"Another Omega?"

Gordo hesitated before shaking his head. "No. It's more. I don't know how else to explain it."

"Do we need to sound the alarm?" Rico asked. "Warn the town?"

Ox looked to Gordo, who shook his head. "Not yet. We can let Dominique know just in case. She'll be able to turn it on if needed. The people know what to do then. I don't want to cause a panic."

"Chris," Ox said without turning around. "Tanner. Call the others. They'll have felt it. Have them meet us near the motel. Tell them to hurry. We need to move. Now."

"Don't worry about calling Mark," Gordo muttered as he rubbed his forehead. "He already knows. He felt it when it hit me. He'll know where I am."

"On it, boss," Tanner said, already tapping on his phone before holding to his ear. He began to pace, gnawing on his thumbnail.

"Shit," Chris said with a sigh, pulling out his own phone. "I hope it's nothing that wants to kill us. I really hate it when that happens."

Ox tried to tell me that I should stay behind, just in case.

It was Rico who shut him up, surprisingly, telling him that we couldn't leave anyone behind, that if we were going to be pack, we needed to act like one. That meant all of us.

Ox stared at him for a moment.

Rico didn't look away.

Ox nodded slowly. "You're right. Thank you, Rico." He glanced at me. "You up for this?"

I needed for him to believe in me. I said, "Yes, Alpha. I can do this."

He sighed, scrubbing a hand over his face. "I know you can, Robbie." He looked tired as he dropped his hand back down to his side. "Just . . . stay close. Either to me or Kelly. And if it looks as if this is a trap, I want you to run."

I took a step back. "What? I'm not going to *run*—"

"They can use you against us," Ox said, and my stomach twisted painfully. "And I can't let that happen. Not again."

I looked down at the ground. He had a point, but it hurt more than I expected it to. He was the Alpha. He had to think of the safety of his entire pack.

He put a finger under my chin, tilting my head back so I would look directly at him. He towered over me, and I bared my neck. His eyes flared as he trailed his finger along the line of my jaw and the skin of my throat. "I need to keep you safe," he said. "I don't know if we'd survive if we lost you again. I won't let anyone take you, but if I tell you to run, you *run*. Do you hear me?" And underneath, hidden in the swirling storm amassing itself inside me, I heard his voice, faint but strong.

packpackpack
I nodded, helpless to do anything but.

Rico came back across the street from the diner. I could see people standing in the windows, staring out at us. Dominique was in the doorway, watching Rico's back as he jogged back to the garage. "She'll wait to hear from one of us," Rico said. "And she'll keep the others here too." He shook his head. "They want to come out all guns blazing. Remember when it was this great big secret? Now everyone knows, and everyone wants to shoot something. Fucking humans, man. Now, where are my guns? I want to shoot something."

Kelly pulled up outside the garage in his patrol car. The light bar across the top was dark, and there was no siren. It was easier to keep things quiet for as long as possible.

He opened the door and climbed out, nodding at me before looking to Ox.

"Robbie, you're with Kelly," Ox said. "Rico too. Tanner, with me. Gordo, you follow in your truck with Chris. The others?"

"On their way," Chris said, putting his phone back in his pocket. "Jessie wants me to tell you that she's on summer break and that she's not pleased you're making her leave the house. But no worries!" he added quickly as Ox turned to stare at him. "She's just kidding. I think she wants to hit someone with a crowbar." He frowned. "We're really violent. I don't know why I'm just realizing that now. Huh." He shrugged. "Eh, what can you do? Let's go fuck some shit up."

"Fucking werewolves," Ox muttered, but I could hear the pride in his voice.

· ·

"Bambi," Rico said into his phone in the back seat, "I can't talk long. I'm in the back of Kelly's cop car and— What? No, I haven't been arrested. I didn't *do* anything! Would you just— Oh. Right. Yeah, I guess that was illegal. But that was one time, and no one knows about it except for you and every person in the pack, which, now that I think about it, is a lot of people. I'm with Robbie and— Oh *man*, you know I love it when you get all hard-core. Yes, baby, I've got my guns. If there's shooting, I'll make sure it counts just for you. Your man is gonna take *care* of shit— You are *not* a better shot than me! You just got lucky— You're right. That was uncalled for. I'm sorry. You're the best thing that's ever happened to me. If I was a wolf, you would be my moon."

"Does he know we can hear him?" I whispered to Kelly.

"Yeah," Kelly said. "He just doesn't care. He says it's part of his charm, but that can't be right."

I bounced my leg, shifting in my seat. Ox and Tanner were in front of us, Gordo and Chris behind us. We quickly left the main thoroughfare of Green Creek behind, but not before I saw people in the shops watching us through the windows. Ox said they'd be ready if it came down to it, but that didn't go very far toward making me feel better. They were all human, and I didn't know if they could stand up against wolves or witches or whatever fresh hell was heading toward us.

It didn't help that I was distracted thinking about what Ox had said. About the hold that was over me, how a few uttered words could strip everything away and make me turn against them. The very idea made me fear for all those around me. I would fight it as hard as I could, but I remembered being in Caswell, all those times Ezra had stood near me, whispering his poison in five simple words.

Would you hear me, dear?

I didn't want that to happen again.

Kelly settled his hand on my bouncing knee, and I sighed.

"We'll be fine," he said.

He couldn't know that, but I thought it was for him just as much as it was for me. It wasn't a lie when I said, "I know."

Kelly squeezed my knee. "We're together. All of us."

"It's not the same."

"No, it's not. But that won't stop us."

"You're carrying a gun."

He pulled his hand away. "Saw that, huh?"

"Yeah."

Kelly's hand tightened on the steering wheel. "Ox and Joe thought it was a good idea. I can't fall back on being a wolf. I need a way to protect myself."

I didn't like the sound of that. "Know how to use it?"

He glanced in the rearview mirror. "Rico taught me."

"That . . . doesn't exactly inspire confidence."

"Oh, fuck you, *lobito*," Rico said. "I'll have you know that I'm *amazing* when it comes to shooting—yes, my love. I know. But being humble has never been in my nature. You can't tame me, no matter how hard you try. I am a *man*, and I— Bambi, I swear to God, if you don't stop laughing, I'm going to hang up on you."

"If it comes down to it, stay behind me," I said to Kelly.

His eyes narrowed. "I can take care of myself."

"I know, but I—"

"I did the entire time you were gone. So don't think you can tell me what to do. Not now. Not about this. Not when it comes to pack."

"I think they're about to fight," Rico whispered into the phone. "I gotta go. *Yes*, I'll call you back later. Jesus, woman, would you get off my—and she hung up on me. I deserved it."

"It's not *about* that," I snapped, suddenly and unnecessarily angry. It was weirdly vicious, this need to impress upon him that he could *break*, that he could break so easily, and we wouldn't be able to save him. If he got hurt, the bite wouldn't work. Not with what Livingstone had done to him. "I'm just trying to keep you safe."

His hands tightened on the steering wheel until his knuckles were bloodless. "I don't *need* you to keep me safe, Robbie. Everyone helps everyone else. That's how a pack works. Just because I'm human doesn't mean I'm going to stand on the sidelines."

"He's got a point," Rico said, and I turned in my seat to glare at him. He held up his hands to placate me. It didn't work. "Take it from one of the dwindling members of Team Human. We can hold our own. And I've trained your boy. He knows what he's doing. Give us some credit, huh? We may be human, but we're still part of this pack. We've made it this far."

That didn't help as much as he seemed to think it did. "There's more to life than just surviving."

Kelly looked grim. "Not for us. Not now. Maybe one day, but right now, survival is all we know."

* * *

The motel on the outskirts of Green Creek looked better than I expected. It'd had a recent coat of paint, and the doors had electronic locks. The sign sitting above the motel promised free wi-fi and some bagels.

I recognized the man in the office as having been in the diner when I first escaped from the Bennett house. His eyes were wide as he walked toward the vehicles pulling up in the gravel lot.

"Is it happening again?" he asked as Ox climbed out of the truck. "Are we under attack? Let me go get my gun, and I'll—"

"No, Will," Ox said. "I want you to stay inside until we come back."

The man—Will—frowned as he looked out at the rest of us. His gaze settled on me for a few seconds before he turned back to Ox. "You sure about that, Alpha? There's strength in numbers. You said so yourself."

I wondered what Ox had done to inspire such devotion, but I didn't have to think too hard. I thought he'd done so by simply existing. This town held a great secret and kept it hidden away from the rest of the world, all while turning to the wolves and offering what amounted to their lives.

It only took me a moment to realize I was doing the same.

I watched as Ox settled his hands on Will's shoulders. "I know. But we don't know what's happened. It might be nothing."

"Or it might be more of those hunters," Will said. "Or Omegas. Or some other manner of shape-shifters. Or vampires."

"Christ," Rico muttered. "I *told* you there's no such thing as vampires. That's ridiculous."

Will rolled his eyes. "Says you. You belong to people who turn into wolves the size of horses, and you want to lecture me on what's ridiculous?"

Rico opened his mouth, but no sound came out. Then, "I've never thought about it that way. Oh my god, what if there are *vampires*?" He yelped when Gordo smacked him upside the head. "Asshole."

"Go back inside," Ox told him. "Close the security gates. Don't leave until you hear from one of us."

Will nodded as he took a step back. "You call me if you need me. I may not be as young as I once was, but I know how to take care of things. I've got your back, Alpha. All of us do. Don't forget that."

He left Ox staring after him as he went back to the office. He locked the door behind him and then reached up to slide a metal grate over it. He did the same to all the windows.

Kelly saw my nose twitching. "The motel rooms have the same safeguards. We made the changes after . . . well. Long story. Let's just say Will knows firsthand what wolves can do. I'll tell you about it later."

Before I could respond, wolves came out of the tree line beyond the motel.

Mark was first, coming at a run, eyes violet, chest rising and falling rapidly. He skidded in front of Gordo, kicking up dust and gravel. He pressed his muzzle against Gordo's chest, breathing him in.

Gordo put his hand between his ears. "We're okay," he said quietly.

Mark growled, lips pulling back.

Gordo sighed. "I hear you. I've got this. I'm in control." He brought up the stump at the end of his arm. The tattoos were swirling, crawling over scar tissue. I felt his magic, enormous and untamed. It caused the air around him to stutter, but he took a deep breath, and the symbols carved into his skin stopped moving. "I'm good. You're with me, so I'm good."

Mark huffed a breath against him before stepping back.

Elizabeth came next, just as a little car pulled into the parking lot. Jessie jumped out, crowbar in hand. "What happened?" she demanded, looking at Ox. Elizabeth rubbed up against her, and Jessie settled a hand on her back. "It's the wards, isn't it? I felt that. God, I'll never get used to it."

Joe came, followed by Carter and the timber wolf. Joe's eyes were red, and he stopped in front of Ox. Ox reached under his chin, grasping his jaw, and pressed his forehead against Joe's.

Carter went to Kelly and sat at his side, head cocked, ears twitching. The timber wolf circled them both slowly, growling low in the back of his throat, his ears flattened against his head. Carter *whuffed* at him, and the timber wolf nipped at his shoulder.

I was thunderstruck. I didn't know why I hadn't seen it before or why no one had told me. "Holy shit, Carter, is the wolf your—"

A bright flash of pain rolled through me as Rico kicked me in the shin. "Your *friend*," Rico cried. "Is that wolf your *friend*." He glared at me as I rubbed my shin. "Isn't that right, Robbie?"

Carter looked confused, glancing back and forth between the two of us.

"Later," Rico muttered. "Focus, okay? We've got bigger things to worry about than Carter's . . . friend."

As Will closed the grate over the last window, Ox turned toward all of us. He let his eyes fill, and the power that emanated from him settled over me. It almost felt like it'd been with Ezra, dreamlike and peaceful, but I didn't think Ox was the type to exert his will over others. Not unless he was forced to.

I had to believe that.

He said, "We stick together. Always within sight. Listen. Be ready for anything." He glanced at me. "Robbie, with me. Kelly, behind him. Everyone else, you know what to do."

"And here's where my childhood friends take off their clothes in public," Rico said with a sigh just as Chris and Tanner began stripping.

"Don't be jealous of my rocking werewolf bod," Chris said.

"I hope it's not bad wolves," Tanner muttered. "I still have PTWD." He winced and looked at me apologetically. "No offense, Robbie."

"Post-Traumatic Werewolf Disorder," Rico explained at the look on my face. "It happens when things get all bitey."

"Chris," Jessie said, staring up at the sky, "if you could shift so I don't have to see your junk again, that'd be great."

Chris didn't argue. The muscles and bones underneath his skin began to move, and he grunted as he fell to his knees. His shift was slower than a born wolf's, as was Tanner's. But it wasn't long before two wolves stood before us, eyes orange.

"Dominique?" Ox asked Jessie.

"She knows what to do. Don't worry about her. Focus on what we need to do, Ox. Let's get this over with." She tapped the crowbar against her shoulder. "And don't get in my way."

He nodded before looking at Gordo wordlessly.

Gordo was staring off into the trees, his hand still on Mark. "It's hurt," he whispered. "There's blood. Whatever it is, it's been injured."

"Don't take any chances," Ox said.

Rico cocked his gun. "My kind of *alfa*. Shoot first, ask questions later. Let's rock 'n' roll, motherfuckers."

There was no shooting.

There was no fighting.

But *oh*, was there blood. I could smell it the closer we got to the wards, heavy and thick and filled with so much anguish, I thought

I would drown in it. It was a wolf, but not one of ours. It wasn't an Omega.

It was an Alpha.

Ox stopped, raising his snout, nostrils flaring as he inhaled deeply. Joe stood at his side, a yin and yang of black and white. I was struck then by a ferocious memory of being in Caswell, standing in Michelle's office, phone ringing, computer beeping, as black-and-white wolves haunted me like ghosts.

"All right?" Kelly whispered, hand brushing against mine.

"Yeah," I muttered. I shook my head, trying to clear my mind. "Just . . . I'll tell you later. There's blood. A lot of it."

"Do you need to shift?"

I couldn't tell him that I was afraid to. That I didn't want to scare Tanner and Chris. That I thought I could stay more in control as a human. I said, "No. Not yet. Gordo was right. Someone has been hurt. Badly."

He nodded as Gordo stepped between Ox and Joe, the Alphas pressing against him. Mark came up behind him, bowing his head and pressing it against Gordo's back. Gordo inhaled deeply, exhaling slowly before he raised his hand and began muttering under his breath.

My skin prickled as his magic rose and the wards before us lit up. They were familiar, and my gums itched as my fangs threatened to drop. The timber wolf growled at Gordo, but Carter bumped against him to distract him. Gordo paid them no attention as he pressed his hand flat against the ward. There was a pulse of light and the distant chime of what sounded like bells, and then the ward collapsed in on itself—but only the one. It created an opening, and Gordo dropped his hand. He looked back at us. He was sweating, the sheen on his forehead flashing in the sun. "Okay," he said as he panted. "We should be good. Christ, that takes a lot out of me. Patrice and Aileen put too much into it. Fuck."

The stench of blood grew stronger, and Ox shifted back. The muscles in his back rippled as he stood. He said, "It's Alpha Wells." He took a step beyond the wards.

We followed him single file before spreading out on the other side of the barrier.

Kelly saw it first, a splash of blood against a green bush, the deep red dripping onto the forest floor. He touched the leaf before rubbing his fingers together. "It's not tacky. She's got to be close."

She was.

Fifty yards beyond the wards, the trail of blood came to an end. There was a large boulder, and on the other side of it was a woman I'd last seen on a forgotten bridge in Virginia.

Shannon Wells didn't open her eyes as we came before her. I didn't even know if she was conscious. Her chest rose and fell quickly, her breath shallow and sounding painful. She was naked, as if she'd shifted with the last of her strength.

Her numerous wounds weren't healing. I saw the wet white of bone through a gash on her forearm, which hung uselessly at her side. Her chest was a mess of deep slashes. Her face was bloodied and swollen, and her mouth hung open. She looked as if she were missing teeth.

"Oh no," Jessie whispered, pushing by me and crouching before her. She reached out but hesitated, like she was unsure of where to touch the wounded Alpha and not hurt her any further. She whipped her own shirt over her head and settled it carefully over the Alpha's lap as if to preserve her dignity. "Ox, you have to help her."

Elizabeth shifted next to Jessie. She was still half-wolf when she reached out and cupped Shannon's face in her hands. "Shannon. Can you hear me?"

Shannon groaned but didn't open her eyes.

"What happened to her?" Rico asked quietly. "She looks like she's been ravaged. Why isn't she healing?"

"It's too much for her," Ox said, crouching down on Shannon's other side. "Her body is weakened."

Shannon Wells opened her eyes.

They flickered red. Then to her normal green. Then red again.

And then violet.

She began to scream.

It burst out of her, a sound of pure horror, eyes wide but unseeing. She tilted her head back against the boulder and screamed like she was never going to stop. Birds took flight from the trees around us as her voice echoed through the woods. I felt the terrible song of despair down to my bones.

Jessie fell back as Shannon jerked forward, still screaming. Joe stepped in front of Jessie, allowing her to pick herself up while he stood guard. But Shannon didn't go for her. She didn't go for any of us. All she did was scream as her life's blood dripped from her body onto the forest floor.

Ox's eyes filled again, and he half-shifted before roaring in her face.

Her screams cut off like her throat had closed.

Clarity leaked back into her eyes.

And it was horrible.

She was *aware*, and I felt the sharp pieces of her breaking off.

When she spoke, her voice was choked. She said, "I . . . I . . . I came. I came. Because. I have nothing. I have no one. It's all gone. It's all gone. They . . ." And, her voice a growl, "Alpha. Alpha, Alpha."

Then her eyes rolled back into her head, and Elizabeth caught her before she could fall to the ground. She looked up at us, face pale. "Her eyes. They're . . . Gordo?"

He shook his head. "I don't think so. It's not like the others. It's . . ."

Ox nodded solemnly. "We need to get her back to the house. Make her comfortable." He looked stricken as he bent over her, putting a hand against her forehead. He grimaced as he closed his eyes. "I don't . . . She doesn't have much time." He dropped his hand before leaning forward and kissing her cheek. "I'm so sorry, Shannon."

And then he picked her up in one smooth motion. She didn't make a sound as her head hung back off his arm, her hair like a wet flag slick with blood that splashed onto the ground as Ox moved slowly through the forest.

We stayed quiet as we followed him back the way we'd come.

. . .

Will threw the grate up over the door as we returned to the motel. He burst out, talking a mile a minute, demanding to know if he needed to gather the town to defend Green Creek. He stopped when he saw Ox and who he carried in his arms.

"Is that one of you?" he whispered. "A shape-shifter?"

"It is," Jessie said, going to him as Ox walked to the truck. "Tell everyone who asks that there was no threat. There never was. It was only her. She's one of the good ones. Gordo's repairing the wards, so nothing else should be able to get in."

Will nodded. "Can do." Then, "She looks rough. Is she going to make it?"

No one answered him, which was answer enough.

Ox climbed carefully into the back of the truck, making sure not to jostle Shannon. She groaned but didn't open her eyes as he sat with his back against the cab, Shannon bleeding into his lap. Jessie's shirt was already soaked through. Tanner reached into the truck and pulled out an old towel, handed it over to Ox, who laid it on Shannon. Blood immediately bloomed like roses against it.

Joe stood on his hind legs, looking at them both, propped up against the side of the truck. Ox's face was blank, waves of blue, blue, blue pouring off him. He said, "Get to the house. We need to make her comfortable for the time she has left."

Joe nodded, stretching his head toward Ox, licking his cheek before he dropped back down on all fours. He growled, and Carter, Elizabeth, and the timber wolf ran after him as he took off toward home.

Chris and Tanner had already shifted back and were getting dressed. Gone was the bravado they'd felt just a short time before when we'd stood in the parking lot.

Kelly nodded toward his patrol car. "Come on. Let's go home."

I glanced back at Ox to see him brush a slick strand of hair off Shannon's face. He whispered, "What have I done?"

* * *

The ride back to the house was almost completely silent. It was just me and Kelly, Rico opting to drive Ox's truck.

We pulled back onto the dirt road when I said, "What did he mean? Gordo. He said it wasn't like the others."

Kelly was tense. His shoulders were stiff, and his brow was furrowed. "Carter. His wolf. Mark. It was because of the infection. Because of whatever Livingstone tried to do, spread to the wolves. It's magical. They only have control because of Ox and what he is. Shannon . . . she's not like them. But she's still an Omega."

I closed my eyes. "Which means her tether was ripped from her."

"Yeah."

"Her pack. Are they . . . ?"

"I think so."

"They had kids. Three of them. Brodie. John." And even though I hated myself for it, it took me a moment to think of the last one. "James. Jimmy."

"You remember them?"

I shook my head. "She told me over the phone. On the bridge. That I'd met them. That I'd been in their house. That I'd sat at their table. That I *ate* with them. Is this him? Is this Ezra?" And *that* was a lie, wasn't it? All of it.

Every single piece.

Every single part.

The way he'd pretended to care for me.

The way he'd loved me.

The way he'd made me feel safe.

"I don't—"

"Fuck!" I cried. "Fuck! God*dammit*." I roared as I smashed my fist into the dashboard again and again. It cracked under the force of it, bones in my fingers breaking.

Kelly slammed on the brakes, and I threw open the door and stepped out onto the road. I screamed up at the sky, and everything I felt, all the anguish and rage and fear of what had been done to me and all that lay ahead poured out of me. I had known the truth weeks ago, the weight of it heavy on my shoulders. But only now did I let it crack me open and fill me up.

There was a tree just off the road. An old elm. The trunk was thick and solid.

Little wolf, little wolf, can't you see? my mother whispered from somewhere through the fire scorching the earth. She sounded like she was dying.

Quiet as a mouse.

I punched the tree again and again and again.

The branches shook as the trunk split, bark breaking off in large clumps. Leaves fluttered down around me. Sap leaked from the tree, mixing in with my own blood, and I didn't stop. I couldn't.

But there was a voice through the fire, through the storm in my head. It was saying my name, saying "Robbie" and "please" and "don't do this, please don't do this," and wasn't *that* just the thing? Because hadn't Chris or Tanner said the same thing at one point? Hadn't they begged me to stop?

They had.

And I hadn't stopped.

A hand fell on my shoulder, trying to pull me away.

I spun on my heels, snarling, ready to lash out.

Kelly didn't move.

He wasn't afraid, at least not of me.

His hand wasn't on his gun, ready to pull it in case he needed it.

"Why didn't I know?" I shouted at him. "Why did he do this to me? What the fuck does he want?"

"I don't know," Kelly said carefully, like he was trying to calm a cornered animal. And he was, foolish though it should have been. I wanted to shove him away. "We don't even know if he had anything to—"

"Don't," I growled. "He did this. He *did this*. You know it as well as I do. And I laid my head in his lap and thought he hung the moon. I thought he was my friend. I thought he was my *family*. And you all just let me go."

"Fuck you," Kelly snarled, angrier than I'd ever seen him. "You want to make this about you? Fine. Let's go. Let's go home and stand above Alpha Wells and you can tell her how much this hurts you, how *angry* you are for something you had no control over. I'm sure it'll make her feel better before she dies. Come on. Come *on*. What the hell are you waiting for? Isn't this what you want?"

Oh Jesus. I couldn't breathe. I deflated, the ruins of my hands already stitching themselves back together. I bent over, wrapping my arms around my stomach as I gagged. A thin line of spit hung from my lips. I retched, but nothing came out. Kelly stayed where he was, and I was grateful for it. I didn't want to be touched. He was right, of course. About everything. And here I was, throwing it back in his face.

I spat onto the ground, my throat working as I struggled to catch my breath. "Shit," I muttered.

A car came down the road. It stopped next to the truck. Jessie and Chris. I heard Chris roll down the window. "Everything all right? What are you— Holy *shit*, Robbie! What the hell happened to your hands?"

"Leave it," Kelly snapped. "Go. Get to the house. We'll be there in a minute."

"You good?" Jessie asked, and I knew what she *wasn't* saying.

Are you safe from him?

"Yes," Kelly said. "Go."

She didn't argue. They pulled away, the sounds of the car fading as they headed down the dirt road toward the house.

The cuts on my hands were closing, the skin knitting itself back together. All that remained was the blood.

"You done?" Kelly asked.

I nodded, spitting onto the ground once more before pulling myself upright with a groan.

"Good," Kelly said. "Now I'm going to talk, and you're going to listen."

"You don't need to—"

"I swear to God, if you say another fucking word, I *will* shoot you. You'll heal, but it's going to hurt."

I nodded, looking down at the ground.

He stepped in front of me, our knees bumping together. He tilted my head up so I looked him in the eyes. I tried to turn away, but his grip on my jaw was firm. I could have easily broken his hold on me, but I didn't want to. Not really. His blue eyes were bright, and I thought I could watch him forever, if only he would let me.

He said, "You know I didn't leave you. I've told you that before, and I wasn't lying. Yes, we fucked up, and *yes*, it's taken a long time for everyone else to come around, but we're here with you. *I'm* here."

"It's not the same—"

"Shut. *Up.*" His hand tightened around my jaw, applying pressure against my skin. "You don't think I know that? Because I do, Robbie. Better than anyone else. Because I know you. Because I have loved you for *years*. And I love you still. No matter what. But this isn't about us. This isn't about you. And even if it *was*, it's not your fault. If Robert Livingstone has anything to do with this, that's on him, much like what he did to you. You didn't ask for it. Alpha Wells didn't either. Everything he said to you, everything he whispered in your ear, was a *lie*. All he cares about is destroying everything we've made for ourselves, and you're fucking helping right now. Pull yourself together. This is going to get rough, and I need you, okay? I need you by my side, because I don't know how I'll get through this if I don't have that. So man the fuck up."

I collapsed against him. He wrapped his arms around me. I did the same, clutching his uniform as I shook. I took in great gasping breaths, and he never let me go. He didn't speak, but he didn't have to. Just having him close was enough.

"I'm sorry," I muttered against his throat.

He sighed. "I know you are. This sucks, I know that. But you're . . . Christ. I need you to be strong with me, because I don't know if I can be strong for both of us. I've tried, Robbie. Through everything, but I can't keep going on like this." His throat clicked as he swallowed. "It's killing me."

I pulled away, but not enough that either of us needed to drop our arms. We stood there, in a forest in the middle of nowhere, on a dirt road that led to home, and I knew that I'd do everything I could to keep this. To hold on to it with everything I had.

His eyes searched mine.

I said, "I can do that."

"Will you?"

"Yeah," I said hoarsely. "Anything for you. It's—"

He kissed me there, in the bright, bright sunlight. He breathed into me, and I thought he was giving me life, warm and all-consuming. Our noses bumped together. My hands went to his elbows. He sighed into my mouth, and all I ever wanted was a place to call home.

And here was home, in a person so fierce and wild that I wanted him to tear me apart.

He kissed the corner of my mouth.

My cheeks.

My forehead, his hand coming up and gripping my neck.

"We'll figure this out, okay?" he whispered, lips still pressed against my skin. "And no matter what happens, no matter if we stay as we are or get back all that was taken from us, it'll be you and me."

I believed him, even as I wondered if this was going to be one of the last moments we ever had like this.

Eventually he pulled away, but not before he reached up and fixed my glasses. His hands lingered on the sides of my face. "I see you. For all that you are. For all that you're not. And I never want to lose sight of you again."

I turned my head and kissed his palm.

"Good?" he asked when he dropped his hands.

I shrugged, then nodded.

"I'll take it," he said. "Come on. I don't think she has much time."

She didn't.

BROTHER

Shannon Wells died later that night, but not before she told us what she could.

She was in Elizabeth's room, the one she'd shared with her late husband. I hadn't been inside since I'd returned to Green Creek, not wanting to intrude on a wolf mother's sanctuary. It was bright and airy, and the walls were a soft yellow, like sunlight on a spring morning. And though Thomas Bennett was nothing but ash, I swore I caught the scent of an unknown wolf embedded into the walls and floor and ceiling.

We didn't want to crowd Shannon, but we needed to hear what she had to say, if she could say anything at all. She was awake, and her eyes flashed violet. She spoke in a low voice, but not to any of us. At first I didn't think she even knew we were there.

She said, "Of course we can go, Jimmy. We'll just have to wait for the weekend."

She said, "Oh, why are you bleeding? What's happened? Who did this to you?"

She said, "When I'm with you, I feel like I can breathe."

She said, "*Mom, look out! Look out for the—*"

She said, "There was this song I heard on the radio. It's old. Peggy Lee singing about Johnny Guitar, and it made me *ache*."

The Bennett brothers all made wounded noises as if they'd been gut punched. I didn't understand why.

And then Shannon laughed a terrible laugh, humorless and sounding almost like a scream. It went on and on until I thought I would go mad.

She fell silent eventually, hands twitching at her sides.

Elizabeth sat next to her, cleaning her wounds as best she could. The gashes were red and angry looking, and though the blood had slowed to a trickle, it wouldn't be enough. Death has a stench, low and sickly sweet, like rotted meat. It surrounded her like a black cloud, thick and overpowering.

Chris and Tanner stood just outside the room, heads bowed as they leaned against the wall. Rico was with them, muttering quietly about how they didn't have to go in, they didn't have to see this, to just stay where they were.

I wanted to be with them, but I couldn't.

I had to witness it. The full extent.

She deserved as much.

Jessie moved in and out of the room, bringing fresh towels and bandages, though it was almost pointless.

Gordo stood on the other side of the bed, Mark behind him, his forehead pressed against the back of Gordo's neck. The witch held his hand out over Shannon, lips moving but no sound coming out. His tattoos were vibrant as they shifted, and there was a sheen of sweat on his upper lip. His stump was shaking, and the raven was curling into the roses on his arm.

Ox and Joe stood at the foot of the bed, each with a hand wrapped around one of Shannon's ankles. At first I thought they were keeping her from jerking her legs, but I felt their energy rolling off them in calming waves, pouring down onto Shannon. Joe's eyes were red, Ox's mixed with Alpha and Omega.

Carter stood at the window, looking out at the forest behind the house. The timber wolf sat next to him, as if on guard.

Kelly and I were out of the way in one corner of the room, watching, waiting, though for what, I didn't think we knew.

We didn't have to wait long.

I saw the moment clarity returned to Shannon, the violet fading away, leaving only eyes like frosted glass. She took in a deep breath, her chest rising and causing her wounds to stretch. They made a wet sucking sound that even magic wouldn't be able to make me forget.

A tear fell down her right cheek.

Elizabeth wiped it away before it could fall onto the bed. In its place, she left a streak of blood. It only made things worse.

Shannon said, "This isn't a dream."

"No," Ox said, and it was blue. "No, Alpha. It's not a dream."

Her bottom lip trembled. She squeezed her eyes shut. She exhaled heavily, and her face twisted into a rictus of agony that I didn't think had anything to do with her injuries. Her throat worked, and her hands clenched. "I'm really here?"

"Yes, Alpha."

She nodded. "I made it. They tried to follow me, but I lost them. I don't know how."

"Who?" Joe asked.

She laughed again, grating and harsh. "Suffer the little children and forbid them not. I never understood that. Not until now."

"Where is your pack?" Ox asked, even though he knew the answer as well as the rest of us.

She chanted, "Gone, gone, gone. They've gone away, and I didn't even have a chance to say goodbye. I tried, Alphas. I tried to save them. But I couldn't. It was too much. And I couldn't hurt them. I couldn't bring myself to hurt them."

"Of course not," Joe said kindly. "You would never hurt your pack."

She shook her head. "Not them. They were already hurt. They were already... Oh god. John. Jimmy. They were... they were... Mother! Where are you? I can't find you! It's dark, oh my god, it's so dark. Please, Mother. Please don't go."

I bowed my head as Kelly grabbed my hand. I held on for dear life.

Shannon continued, speaking to phantoms only she could see. She spoke of flowers and dragonflies. She said she was chasing them, but she would never catch because she didn't want to hurt them. She just liked their wings, she said, so pretty, so thin and bright.

Gordo sighed as he took a step back, arms trembling. He shook his head. "There's nothing I can do. It's... She's too far gone." He looked spooked as he turned to his Alphas. "This wasn't just one wolf."

"They were many," Shannon whispered. "So many. Like ants. Swarming. I went on a picnic once. It was lovely. I wore a pretty dress. I spilled juice on it. I felt bad, but my mother said not to worry about the little things, that stains would wash out and all would be well."

"We'll keep her safe and warm," Elizabeth murmured. "It's the best we can do. She will have that, at least." She nodded at Jessie, who handed her another cloth. Jessie took the red-stained rags that had piled next to the bed from the room. It didn't help. The scent of blood was sharp. I didn't know if it would ever leave.

And then Shannon said, "Robbie. Robbie. Robbie."

They all looked to me.

I blinked rapidly.

I thought about leaving. Just heading for the door and running as fast as I could for as long as I was able.

Kelly squeezed my hand as I stepped toward the bed.

"Robbie," Shannon said again.

"I'm here," I told her as Gordo and Mark stepped back. I took their place next to the bed. I knelt on the floor, unsure if I should touch her. That decision was made for me when she lifted her hand toward me. Her grip was stronger than I expected. For a moment I had hope, but her blood was smearing into my skin, and it was a desperately futile thing. "I'm right here."

"Are you?" she asked.

I looked to Ox and Joe. Joe was furious, though he was trying to maintain control. Ox nodded at me, and I turned back to Shannon.

"Yes."

"You were lost."

"Yes."

"And then you were found." She chuckled. It crawled from her throat and died as soon as it left her mouth. "You were blind, but now you see."

"Yes."

"Did you know?"

I started to shake my head but stopped. "About what?"

"What he would do. What he was capable of." She winced, her body tensing suddenly before relaxing again. "What he would bring upon my pack."

Ezra.

Robert Livingstone.

I hung my head, unable to look at her any longer. "No, Alpha. I didn't know."

"Because he took that from you."

"Yes."

"We're almost the same. He took everything from you. And he took everything from me. But you're lucky. Because you got yours back. Why can't I have mine?"

"I don't know," I told her. "I don't know why."

She nodded as if that was the answer she expected. "I heard him. I don't know how he found us, but he did. He was in the walls. In the ceiling. He was everywhere, and he wasn't happy. He wasn't laughing.

He sounded *sad*, Robbie. Like he didn't want to be doing what he was doing. But he did it anyway. I heard his voice. He said that all this pain, all this suffering wasn't something he wanted, but it was necessary. And I *believed* him. I *believed* him when he said he didn't want this, but he did it anyway. What kind of person does that make him?"

"A beast," I whispered.

She said, "Malik died protecting John and Jimmy. I told them to stay back, but it was too much because I couldn't... I couldn't hurt them. I couldn't stop them because I couldn't hurt them."

"Who?"

She turned her head slowly to look at me. Her skin was sallow and stretched tight, like she was made of wax. I thought I heard her neck creak. "The children. Brodie. He...something changed in him. Something flipped. He turned on us. But it wasn't just him. We were in the middle of nowhere. Nebraska. Waiting until we received word that we were safe. We never heard. *We never heard.*"

Joe growled as he shook his head, lips in a thin line.

Shannon only had eyes for me.

She said, "They came through the fields. I didn't know what I was seeing at first. I thought there'd been an accident. A bus, maybe. But they didn't answer me when I asked what was wrong, and there were *so many of them*. Their eyes were empty, and I had time to shout for my pack. Time to tell them to run, please, just run, but they *swarmed*. They fell upon me, and I tried to fight back, I tried to stop them, but they were *kids*."

Her words were like ghosts dragging their chains as they haunted me. "He's using the children?"

"*Yes*. And I begged for them to stop, I *pleaded* with them to listen, to just listen, that I could help them, that I could keep them safe, but they didn't hear me. They couldn't shift, not all the way. But they had their claws. They had their fangs. Just like Brodie." She moaned, and it sent a chill down my spine. "Brodie. Malik... he was shouting inside the house. I heard him even as they tore into me. Even as his voice came from the fields, telling me this was a warning to all who would stand against him. We weren't the first. I could feel it when their mouths were on me, biting and tearing. Transference. Like memory. We weren't their first, and we weren't going to be their last."

Oh no. Oh please no. "He's killing packs?"

Ox swore as he took a step back from the bed. His eyes were fiery, and it looked as if he was barely hanging on.

"Yes," Shannon whispered. "The ones that took in Omegas. We defied him, and he is making us suffer for it." Her hand tightened in mine. "I couldn't hurt them. You have to believe me. I couldn't hurt them. I couldn't hurt them because they were only kids. They didn't know what they were doing. I wish I had. I wish I'd slaughtered them all. Maybe then . . . maybe my pack would be . . ." She turned her face toward the ceiling again. "Malik died. John died. Jimmy died. He liked you. Even if you don't remember him. He talked about you for days. You liked monster movies. It was simple. But it was enough for him."

Kelly's hands settled on my shoulders. His presence was soothing.

"I shifted," Shannon said in a dead voice. "And ran. I left my pack behind and ran because I didn't know what else to do. He let me go. He knew where I was running to. He knew where I'd go. And he gave me a message. For you. For all of you."

"Tell me," Ox said hoarsely.

"He wants what belongs to him," Shannon whispered. "You've taken that which is his, and he wants it back. He won't stop until this is done. And everything that has happened or will happen . . . it'll be on you until you give him what is his. You can't beat him, Alphas. Not as he is now. Not with all that he has. He has a hold on them, all the little cubs. They aren't feral. They aren't hunters. They're children. And he is using them as weapons. You have to help them. You have to save them. Promise me."

Spin me! they'd cried as they'd surrounded me in Caswell. *Spin me! It's my turn, Robbie! Spin me!*

Was Tony one of them? The little boy with wide eyes and question after question, the little boy who had told me that he didn't like it when I was sad, that he didn't like it when I was blue, that he wanted me to be happy. Was I happier when I'd been there before? He'd asked me that behind the house after we'd run together. A secret just between us.

"Ease up," Kelly whispered harshly in my ear. "You're going to hurt her more."

I looked down in horror to see I was squeezing Shannon's hand so tightly, it was a wonder her bones weren't splintering. I let her go and fell back, bumping into Kelly's legs.

"We promise," Elizabeth said quietly.

Shannon barely noticed. She was talking to her phantoms again, begging her mother to tell her this was all a nightmare, that she would wake up from this and nothing would hurt. She asked about a boy, a beautiful boy she had a crush on, and she giggled when she said it. "He's so handsome." Her voice had a dreamlike quality. "I know he's older and he probably doesn't even know I'm alive, but I can't stop thinking about him. Can I tell you a secret?"

"Yes," Elizabeth said, hand going to Shannon's brow. "Of course you can."

"He's a human," Shannon whispered. "He's a human, but I don't care about that."

"Good," Elizabeth said. "It doesn't matter if he's human or not."

"Really?"

"Yes."

"I—" Her eyes were wide but unseeing, and her chest rose and fell rapidly. She reached up toward the ceiling, her hand shaking. She said, "Mother? There you are. Where have you been? I've looked for you for so long. You left me, and it was endless. The dark. But I've found you again, and I can see the stars. Do you . . . do you remember when we played in the snow? That was my favorite day."

And then her hand dropped. Her eyes slid unfocused. There was another exhalation that sounded like wind over water. Her chest didn't rise again.

Her heart, her Alpha heart, continued on for another beat, and then another, and then another.

And then it too fell silent.

No one spoke.

No one moved.

Elizabeth broke the spell that had fallen over us. She pressed her fingers over Shannon's eyes, sliding her eyelids shut. The wolf mother had a strange look on her face, and I felt a conflagration rising in her. She stood slowly, staring down at Shannon.

Joe started for her, but Ox held him back, shaking his head.

Elizabeth Bennett said, "All this pain. All this death. Everything that has been brought down upon us. For what? What is the reason?

What is the purpose of all of this? To make us suffer? To make us break? And for *what*?"

No one answered her.

"I'm tired of all of this," she said, and her voice was low and wolf-like. "We give everything we have, but it's never enough. It's a curse. A curse upon us all." Her eyes were wet as she lifted her head, looking at each of us in turn. "And I've had enough."

She moved then, pushing past her Alphas. They didn't try to stop her. They looked at each other before turning to follow Elizabeth out of her bedroom. Rico asked what was happening, what was going on, but she ignored him. I made it out of the room in time to see her vault over the landing above the first floor. She landed on her feet below us and turned to head deeper into the house.

"Holy shit," Rico breathed.

"Go," Jessie said from the doorway. "See what she's doing. I'll stay with Shannon."

The Alphas were already down the stairs, Joe calling after his mother. We hurried after them, Chris and Tanner nearly tripping over each other and falling down the stairs. Rico caught them by the backs of their shirts.

I heard the sound of a door flying open and crashing into a wall, the wood cracking.

Elizabeth was in the main office. She stood in front of her husband's old desk. Her hands were pressed down on it, claws digging into it, leaving divots in the surface. "No more," she muttered. "No more. No more. This ends. This ends *now*."

"Mom," Kelly said. "What are you doing?"

She looked at him, eyes blazing. "What should have been done a long time ago. We let ourselves become complacent. We told ourselves that since there were thousands of miles between us, there were bigger things to worry about. That others needed us more. First the Omegas. Then Robbie. We give and we give and we give, and for *what*? To be repaid in blood and death? I'm sick of it. I have had my pack taken from me. I have had my sons taken from me. I have had my *husband* taken from me. And all because of a name. Because of who we are. Because of where we come from. All we have ever wanted was peace, to exist and live and love like everyone else, but we *can't* because of who we are."

Joe looked uncomfortable. "We have a duty. We're Bennetts—"

Her eyes flashed, and Joe closed his mouth. "Don't you think I know that?" she demanded. "Don't you think I *understand*? Because I do. More than you could possibly know. And it's time we accept our place. It's time we finish this once and for all. Because we will never know peace unless we take it for ourselves. Unless we *fight* for it. For too long we've stood idly by. No more. I'm done." She rounded the desk until she stood in front of the computer.

"What are you doing?" Carter asked.

"What we should have done a long time ago."

The large TV mounted on the wall lit up, the screen a deep and calming blue. I almost immediately recognized the little icon in the middle of the screen.

"Oh shit," I breathed. "You're going to call Michelle Hughes."

"You're damn right I am," Elizabeth snapped. "I want to see her face. I want to see the look in her eyes when I tell her I'm coming for her. That she and Robert Livingstone are not long for this world if they don't stand down immediately. She needs to hear it from me. This is the end, one way or another. It's time."

"You know they won't stop," Ox said. "They might not even listen."

And oh, how she *smiled* at him, feral and twisted. "I'm counting on it."

Ox looked at all of us. I wondered what he saw. Fear? Resolve? Defeated acceptance? I was more scared than I could ever remember being, which was fucking *ridiculous*, given everything that had happened over the past few weeks. But there it was, clawing at my chest. It was getting harder to breathe, but Kelly was there, always Kelly, and he took my face in his hands, forcing me to look up into his eyes. "We can go," he whispered. "You don't have to be here for this. Just say the word and we'll go."

"Where?" I asked, and I hated the way my voice broke. "There's nowhere we could go. Nowhere that they won't find us."

He sighed. "We'll figure it out. Just . . . let's go, okay? Come on."

But I couldn't. As much as everything in me was screaming to listen to him, to do exactly what he was saying, to run, run, run, I couldn't. I was terrified, yes, and I wasn't prepared to see Alpha Hughes again, but it was overridden by something primal and fierce, a sharp tug of *packpackpack* that was pouring off Ox. He was scared too, but it was such a *small* thing in the face of his pack. He was strong and powerful, and I thought maybe I loved him.

I thought maybe I loved them all.

And I said, "No." I stepped away from Kelly. He dropped his hands, looking resigned. "No. If we do this, then we do it together." I squared my shoulders, trying to look braver than I felt. "Those kids, Kelly. All those kids in Caswell. If what Shannon said is true, then I have to be here. I have to hear it from her myself. You don't—you don't *know* them like I do. These kids, they didn't do anything. They don't deserve this. They're innocent. And if he's using them, if they're both using them, then someone needs to stop them."

"Hoo boy," Rico said. "I got chills, *lobito*. Actual chills. Goose bumps and everything. But let's be clear on one thing. If you try any martyr bullshit, I swear to God I will shove my gun down your throat until it reaches your intestines and then I will pull the trigger. You get me?"

Carter snorted. "I don't know if that's anatomically possible— You know what? That look you're giving me right now makes me realize that you would certainly try, so I'm just gonna let you have this moment."

"Damn right," Rico said. "I'm sick and tired of the fucking people in this pack who think that self-sacrifice is a legitimate way to go. We do this together or we don't do this at all. And Ox, don't you dare say a goddamn word, because you're the worst. Don't think we've forgotten about what you did with Richard Collins. You aren't going to be able to so much as *breathe* without one of us noticing. You thought a hand through your stomach was bad? Try it again and see what I do to you."

"I wouldn't expect anything else," Ox said mildly. "I've got the most aggravating pack in the entire world."

"But you love us," Chris said without artifice.

"Yes," Ox said simply. "More than anything."

"Maybe she won't answer," Tanner said, sounding as if that was a fantastic idea. "I'm under the impression that being a dictator hellbent on wolfy domination is a lot of hard work."

"Then we keep trying until we get ahold of her," Elizabeth muttered as she glared down at the computer. "And if we can't, then we show up on her doorstep. She'll know we mean business one way or another. But I have a feeling that she knows this moment is coming." She looked up at me. "Doesn't she, Robbie?"

I couldn't speak.

But that was answer enough.

"Be careful what you say to her," Gordo said. "We don't know who else is going to be listening in." He was pale, his tattoos flickering. Mark pressed his nose against Gordo's ear, breathing in slowly. "My father... he... if he's there, he'll hear everything." He glanced at me. "And I don't know how far his reach will extend. If he'll be able to do anything to... you know."

I felt terrible when Rico sucked in a breath and took a step away from me. But before I could say anything, Rico shook his head and moved toward me again. He looked me up and down before turning back to Gordo. "Chance we'll take, *brujo*. He's part of this. No one gets left behind. Not again."

Gordo rolled his eyes. "I told you not to call me that, you ass. I just... It doesn't matter. You're right. Be ready for anything. Don't underestimate my father. Chances are he'll be there, hearing every word."

Elizabeth's expression tightened. "I know. I want him to. Ready?"

No. I wasn't. I didn't know if any of us were. We were angry, and it was like a fire spreading between all of us, this burning rage, but it felt like it was growing too big too quickly. I didn't know how much longer we could control it, or if it would be snuffed out the moment all the air was gone.

"Hold on," Ox said, and I exhaled explosively. If we were going to do this, I wanted to get it over with. We looked at Ox. "Chris, Tanner. I want you to leave." They started to protest, but he held up his hand and they quieted. "I need you to do something for me. Get on your phones. Start calling around to all the packs we've sent Omegas to. See who answers. If anyone does, tell them to get to the safe houses we've set up. They know what to do if that call ever came. I need to know who else Livingstone got to. If it's just Alpha Wells or if there are others."

They nodded and headed for the door as they pulled out their phones. Rico stopped them both before they could leave and hugged each of them. After, they closed the door behind them.

There was nothing left to wait for.

"Do it," Joe said.

The TV began to beep as the call went out.

Kelly took my hand.

It went on so long that I began to think no one would pick up. Sweat trickled down the back of my neck into the collar of my shirt. I pushed my glasses back up on my nose, and I heard my mother whispering *little wolf, little wolf, little wolf.*

The beeps from the TV cut off as the picture filled.

The office thousands of miles away looked as it did the last time I'd stood in it: the books in the background, the chair, the desk—all of it was the same. I remembered the first time I'd sat in it, but my resolve strengthened when I realized what I was thinking of *wasn't* the first time. I'd been in there before, and they had taken it from me.

Alpha Michelle Hughes sat in the chair. She looked cool and calm, and if it was anyone else, I might have thought she was in control. That she *had* expected this and still thought she had the upper hand.

But I'd spent close to a year knowing her. Watching her. Working by her side. I could see the cracks in the steely façade. It was in the little things, the way she tapped her fingernails against the desk, the way her eyes widened briefly at the sight of all of us, the flaring of her nostrils, as if she thought she could get our scent from the other side of the country.

And there, for a split second, her eyes shifted away from the screen.

Like she was looking *beyond* it.

She wasn't alone.

It was brief, and then she looked straight at us again.

It felt like she was looking straight at *me*.

She was.

She said, "Robbie. I see you're—"

And Elizabeth Bennett said, "No. You will *not* say his name. Any hold you've had over him, anything you've done to him, it's over. You are finished. If I ever hear you speak his name aloud again, I swear to you it'll be one of the last things you do. I'll see to it myself. It's my turn to talk, and you're going to listen."

She flinched. "Elizabeth, I don't know what you think—"

"No," Elizabeth said coldly. "You don't. You never have. And that's always been to your detriment. You underestimate those you see as beneath you. I was only the wife of the Alpha to you. Someone to appease to get what you wanted but never to take seriously. That was one of your many mistakes. And it will prove to be your undoing. Because I am *done* with diplomacy. Hear me, Alpha Hughes, and hear me well. You tried to murder my pack with hunters. We survived. They didn't. You tried to take Robbie away from us. And yet here he stands, with us as *one* of us. He is a Bennett, and he always will be. Your time is over. Stand down and stand down now. I will take your unconditional surrender. You'll be held responsible for your treasonous crimes against my pack because of your alignment with the hunters, and against the wolves as a whole. My son will assume his rightful place as the Alpha of all, as he was always meant to. And before you even think of speaking, know that this isn't a negotiation. You do not have a choice in the matter."

"Haven't we been here before?" Michelle asked, shaking her head. She sounded aloof, almost airy, but there was something *just* off in her voice. I was sure most everyone else in the room missed it, but I didn't. "You, the Bennett pack, threatening me from the safety behind your wards in Green Creek, while the rest of us live out in the real world. You think yourselves so high and mighty, so much better than all of us. And your husband was no different. He didn't see the way things were supposed to be, and it cost him his life."

"Maybe it did," Elizabeth said. "But Thomas believed in the greater good. He believed in the strength of the pack and all that it was comprised of. You have forgotten what it means to be an Alpha, if you ever even knew at all. Thomas was infinitely more an Alpha than you could ever hope to be."

"He trusted humans," Michelle said, claws digging into the surface of the desk. "And look where it got—"

Elizabeth laughed, grating and harsh. "You don't get to talk to me about trusting humans. Not after Meredith King. You trusted her enough to send her to do your dirty work. She and her people paid the price for coming after my family. You're going to find yourself in a similar position unless you *stand. Down.*"

Michelle narrowed her eyes. "Are you threatening me?"

"You're damn right I am," Elizabeth growled. "And it would do you well to listen. There's been enough bloodshed, enough good people giving their lives in the name of the wolves. But I will not hesitate to add to the body count. I will come for you, Alpha Hughes. And nothing you can do will stop me."

She nodded slowly. "If that's the way it's going to be."

"It is."

She looked grave. "Then it is my unfortunate duty to inform you that the Bennett pack is now considered an enemy of the wolves. I'll ask for your surrender. Your Alphas will be stripped of their power and Green Creek will be turned over to me. You caused the deaths of over thirty witches, slaughtered by Omegas under your control. You harbored these Omegas even though they should have been put down the moment they lost themselves to their wolves. Carter and Mark Bennett still breathe, though you were under explicit order to end their lives for the greater good. For all I know, whatever bonds that stretch between you all are infected and rotting because of them."

"Rude," Carter said, and the timber wolf woofed in agreement. "I think we're doing fine. Why don't you come here and I'll show you just how much?"

She ignored him. She was getting worked up, though she was still trying to stay in control. "These are the crimes of the Bennett pack, and ones you will need to answer for. You will be tried for said crimes, and I will mete out your punishment as I see fit. Do you understand the terms as I've relayed them to you?"

"Yes," Ox said. "And we decline."

Her eyes narrowed. "What?"

"We decline," Ox said. He stepped toward the screen. "Can he hear me? Is he there with you? I think he is. And I think he scares you. You've found yourself drowning in something you thought you could control. But you can't, Michelle. You're already too far gone. And for that, I'm sorry. I thought . . . I thought once I could save you. That deep down, there was still good in you. That was a mistake, and one I won't make again." His eyes filled with red and violet, and I could hear him howling in my head. His voice was deep when he said, "Robert Livingstone. You took from me. You took from my pack. Show yourself."

At first nothing happened.

I thought we had it wrong.

That he wasn't there at all.

Then I heard him sigh from somewhere in the office, and I was hit with a wave of agony, biting and tearing, thinking of how I'd lived with him. How I'd laughed with him. How I'd *loved* him when he smiled at me, when he put his hand in my hair and made me believe that he wanted nothing more than to have me by his side. He had found me, taken me in, given me a home, and it was all a lie.

Robert Livingstone stepped into view. Whatever glamour he'd used to disguise his true nature was gone. All that remained was the man from the bridge, the one who'd tried to kill my pack, the one who'd taken my mate's wolf away from him.

Oh god, how I hated him.

And oh god, how I loved him still, knowing everything he'd done. It was a small part of me, twisted and gasping, but it was still there. I didn't know how to turn it off. It made me feel like I was dying.

My skin crawled as he motioned with the flick of his hand for Michelle to vacate the chair, as if she were nothing but a little lapdog. It was extraordinarily disrespectful to do to an Alpha, and something I never would have thought him capable of when I'd been in Caswell. And she *listened* to him. She didn't question it. She stood up quickly, as if it were the easiest thing to do.

Livingstone settled himself in her chair, hands folded on the desk in front of him. I could see flashes of Ezra in every part of him. It felt as if my vision was blurring, trying to see him for who he'd been and who he was now.

"Robbie," Robert said, voice even as if this was a normal conversation. "I wish that we were seeing each other under different circumstances. I have so much to tell you, things you should've heard from me a long time ago. But time has gotten away from me." He leaned forward. "How are you, dear? Are they treating you well? I expect they are. They always did care for you, just as I came to."

I cowered. I hated it, but I couldn't stop. I had a full-body twitch, and my shoulders hunched as I lowered my head. Kelly's grip tightened on my hand, but it wasn't enough. It would have been easier had Ezra spoken harshly, making grand proclamations about how he was going to destroy us all. Maybe that would still come, those threats, but here he was, sitting at the Alpha's desk, and he sounded fucking *hurt*, like he had any right.

"Don't," Kelly snarled at him. "Don't talk to him. Don't even *look* at him. He's not yours. He never was. And he'll never be again."

Robert simply nodded and said, "I understand. Kelly, isn't it? How do you find being human? You may not understand this, but I know what it's like to have something ripped from you, something important. I know more than you possibly think. I could have snuffed out the little thing you call your life. I didn't. I showed you mercy. Could Richard Collins have said the same? Elijah?" He shook his head. "I think not. I gave you a chance."

"Richard Collins was *because* of you," Kelly retorted. "Elijah was *your* doing."

He arched an eyebrow. "Really. Elijah was *my* doing." He chuckled ruefully. "I'm flattered how Machiavellian you're making me out to be, but I had nothing to do with the hunters. I wouldn't have been so inelegant. One could argue that I was indirectly responsible, given the spread of the Omegas, but I'm offended you would think I'd be so brutish as to enact a group as unrefined as *hunters*." He sat back in his chair. "Richard, on the other hand, well. When a beast is caged for so long, you can't expect it to be as forward-thinking as one would hope. Live and learn, I suppose."

"How dare you," Elizabeth breathed. "How *dare* you think—"

"Elizabeth," he said with a grave nod. "Do you remember what we once had? Because I do. The Bennetts and the Livingstones have a long history, one that goes farther back than even you could imagine. We're tangled together, these little snips and snarls that connect us all. We were pack. We were harmonious. There was a synchronicity that I don't regret. Abel Bennett was a good man. I was saddened to hear of his passing. But you managed to survive. Even after everything that's happened to you, you survived. You *flourished*. In the face of everything thrown at you, you still managed to be the queen you are."

"I am," Elizabeth said. "And it's my burden. I know why I do what I do. I have lost many. But I carry them with me always. And if you think fear of what could be will stop me, then you've made yet another mistake."

"Of what *could* be?" Livingstone asked. "Oh, my dear. This isn't going to go how you think. What do you hope to achieve? I expect you'll storm the compound, your misplaced indignation filling you with justification for your cause. There will be casualties, you'll all tell yourselves, but it'll be for the greater good. You'll wash the blood on your hands away as if it's nothing, and then the future will be bright and shining as the little prince becomes a king. Is that right? Am I close? Please. Tell me."

"Yes," Joe said bluntly. "That's exactly it."

Livingstone nodded. "As I expected. Foolish, but then you're animals, so I'm not surprised. You think with fang and claw but neglect to consider that I care not for the fate of wolves. I only want—"

"What you did to Alpha Wells says otherwise," Ox said, rage simmering just underneath the surface. "I was with her when she took her last breath. Don't tell us you don't care what happens to the wolves, especially since everything that has happened to them falls upon you."

Livingstone looked incredulous. "Everything? Alpha Matheson, how can you be so blind? Oh, the stories I've heard about the boy who ran with wolves. The human Alpha who led a fractured pack. The boy who became a man even though his daddy thought he would amount to nothing. Look at you now. The Alpha of the Omegas. I am *fascinated* by you, by everything that you are. And yet you stand where you are, spouting the things you do as if you think I'm some kind of monster. I know mercy. I know kindness. I know love. Isn't that right, Robbie? Tell them how much I love you. I kept you safe. I gave you a home. And it took over a *year* for your pack to remember they give a damn about you. Why is that? Why didn't they love you enough to—"

"They did," I said through gritted teeth. "They do."

He shook his head sadly. "I wish I could believe that, but I know better. When I found you, you didn't fight me. You wanted it. You were *begging* me to take you away, and how could I ignore such desperate pleas? I couldn't. Though I should have realized just how much of a hold the Bennett pack had over you. How deep their claws had sunk into your flesh."

"I didn't give in," I said weakly. "I wouldn't . . . I wouldn't *do* that." I could feel the others looking at me, but I only had eyes for the man on the screen.

"You did," he said gently. "I can show you. I can give you your memories back. I can give Kelly back his wolf. I'm asking you to think, to *really* think about this. Any element of surprise you had is gone. Come tomorrow, next week, a *year* from now, it doesn't matter. You, in your righteous fury, and me knowing the real truth. It'll all end the same. Or . . ." His expression softened. "Or we can finish this now, and all it would take is to give me back what belongs to me. I know mercy. I allowed Alpha Wells to crawl her way to Green Creek to show you just how serious I am and how far I'm willing to go to make sure you understand the importance of what I'm asking of you. This could all be over so easily. No one else will have to suffer. Who is missing from your pack currently? Jessie? Tanner? Chris? Are they reaching out to your little network? You're going to find some of those calls going unanswered. While you were wrapped up safe and warm in your territory, pretending you haven't stolen from me, I've done my due diligence to make sure I have your undivided attention, and I think you'll find you're very much alone."

"What do you want?" Ox asked.

Livingstone smiled. "Ah. Thank you, Alpha Matheson. It's simple, really. I want Robbie. I've grown fond of him." He took a deep breath. "And I want my son."

Mark snarled as my skin turned to ice. "Fuck you. You're never going to lay your hands on Gordo ever again. I won't—"

"Down, boy," Livingstone snapped, and *there* was the anger I'd been expecting. His face twisted into something dark. "Your threats mean nothing to me. Gordo has made his choice, and as much as it pains me to say, I know nothing will change that. Gordo was lost to me a long time ago. No. I don't want him. This isn't about *him*. It's about his brother. My second son. I will have him and Robbie. Give them to me and all of this will end."

An absolute, stunned silence followed. It was as if all the air had been sucked from the room. Mark looked thunderstruck, and Gordo gaped at the screen. Ox and Joe turned to him, eyes wide.

"What the fuck are you talking about?" Gordo asked hoarsely. "I don't *have*—"

Robert sighed. "Of course you don't know. Yet another little secret the Bennetts have kept from you." His smile was cold. "Your mother didn't understand. I did love her, in my own way. But she wasn't my tether. Wendy Walsh was different, unlike anyone I had ever met. She enchanted me. And when she became pregnant, I thought I could make it work. I thought I could have this. I was already a father, but this was a way to ensure my line would go on in the event of . . . complications." His smile curved down as if his mask was slipping. "Abel Bennett found out, and he acted quickly. He went behind my back. He told her things she shouldn't have known. Things I'd kept from her to keep her safe. About all of us. It scared her. And she *listened* to him. Abel, who only cared about his precious pack. He forced her to leave, to give up our child, and I *railed* against him. I told him he was making a mistake, that he would live to regret this." His eyes widened dramatically. "But he didn't, did he? Not for long, anyway. But by then it was already too late for all of us."

"You're lying," Gordo whispered.

He shook his head. "I'm not. I swore to myself that when I was finally free, when I escaped my prison, I would find my children. I would bring them back into the fold and make everyone who had stolen from me suffer. And when Michelle found the strength within herself to free me from my captivity in exchange for the only thing she wanted more than anything else, I knew I would stop at nothing to get what I wanted. She became the Alpha of all. And I was free to search for my son."

He ignored the roars of anger. The sounds of fury. The howls of betrayal. I couldn't see Michelle, but I knew she was still there, I knew she was still listening. If she'd been standing in front of me right then, I would have torn her apart. Everything that had happened, all that I'd learned about the history of the Bennett pack, all that they'd—*we'd*—lost had been brought upon us because of Robert Livingstone's escape.

Richard Collins.

Thomas Bennett.

Maggie Callaway.

The Omegas.

Kelly.

Me.

And now this.

Livingstone waved a hand at the screen in dismissal. "Yes, there it is. Such useless anger, hollow and empty. This was all *because* of the Bennett pack. If Abel had just let the chips fall where they may, we wouldn't be here. All the death that followed would never have happened. But it has, and there's nothing you or I can do to change that. I told you. I care not for the fate of wolves. I only want what's mine.

Wendy would have insisted upon it. I know it. Give Robbie to me." The mask slipped further, and I saw the feral animal underneath. "*Give me back my son.*"

Gordo was enraged. "Who the hell are you *talking* about? We don't have anyone! This is just another game to you, another trick to try to—"

Livingstone leaned forward. "Gavin. I know you can hear me. I can see it in your eyes. I don't know what's happened to you. I don't know how you came to be as you are now, but I can help you. I can fix you. I can give you back your life so long as you return to your rightful place at my side." His voice cracked, and his eyes were wet. "You are my son, and I have searched for you for so long."

Nothing happened.

And then the timber wolf next to Carter rose to his feet. His claws clicked on the wood floor. Carter reached out for him, but the wolf shook him off. He stepped toward the screen, tilting his head as he looked at Livingstone. His muscles were tightly coiled, and his tail was stiff behind him. His shoulders shifted as he snorted, pawing at the floor.

"Yes," Livingstone whispered. "You are a Livingstone. And it's time you remember that."

It wasn't the Alphas who spoke.

It wasn't the queen.

It wasn't Gordo, who was staring at the timber wolf as if seeing him for the first time.

It wasn't Rico.

It wasn't Kelly or me.

It was Carter.

And he said, "No."

Whatever spell had been cast over Robert Livingstone broke. He sucked in a sharp breath, and he narrowed his eyes as he looked at Carter. Carter, who stepped forward next to the timber wolf, Carter, who had a fiery look on his face, eyes shining violet, teeth bared, claws out. Carter, who looked as if he were ready to eviscerate the man on the screen if only given the chance.

Carter Bennett said no again, in such a deadly growl that I shivered. Carter was easygoing, aloof, cocky, and quick to smile. He loved his pack, and in the weeks since I'd come back, I had never seen him like he was now. Rage rolled off him in palpable waves, and though I was cut off from the bonds that stretched between him and the rest of the pack, even I could *feel* it. It wasn't unlike what I'd felt from his mother, a great fire that threatened to burn everything down until nothing but charred bones remained.

He put a hand on the wolf's back, fingers curling into its hair, holding on tight. He glared at the screen.

I saw the moment Gordo realized what it meant. He paled, looking between the two of them, an expression of utter disbelief tinged with awe on his face.

"You can't have him," Carter said, and his voice was *quaking*. "I don't know who the fuck you think you are, but I will *never* let you touch him. Not while I'm still standing. You want him? You have to go through me."

The wolf growled from deep in his throat and snapped at Carter, teeth missing him by inches. It was meant to be a warning, but Carter wasn't having it. "Oh, fuck you, man. You're in so much shit, you don't even know. And you can bet I'm going to deal with you later, you dick." He looked back at the screen. "He doesn't belong to you. He never has. He has a pack. He has a place. It's here. With us." His hand tightened in the wolf's hair. "With me. And if you think you will ever take him away from us, then you're out of your goddamned mind. I am *done* with this. With you. You're no different than Richard Collins or Elijah. Than any other motherfucker who thinks they can come for us. You're going to regret ever crossing the Bennetts. And I'm going to make sure of it. You want a war? Guess what, asshole. You've got one."

Livingstone sat back in his chair, closing his eyes as he tilted his head toward the ceiling. He took in a deep breath and let it out slow. He opened his eyes again. The mask was gone. All that remained was barely contained fury. "Do you speak for your pack?"

"He does," Ox said. He stepped forward on the wolf's other side, putting his hand on top of Carter's. The wolf hung his head, lips pulled back over his teeth. His nostrils were flaring, and his tail curled underneath his back legs. "But in case that's not good enough for you, then hear me. I am the Alpha of the Omegas. I am one of the Alphas of the Bennett pack. And you can't have Robbie. You can't have this wolf. They're *mine*."

Livingstone nodded slowly. "I want you to remember this moment, Alpha. Everything that will follow, everything that comes to pass, all of it could have been avoided had you just given me what I wanted. The blood of your pack will be on you and no one else. You've played your hand too early."

Ox Matheson said, "I'm going to kill you."

And Livingstone replied, "You will try. Come, then. Bring your war. Let us end this, once and for all."

The screen went dark.

No one moved.

We jumped when the door to the office flew open, Chris and Tanner barging in. They came to a stop, looking around wildly at all of us. "What happened?" Chris demanded. "What did we miss?"

WE SURVIVED / NEVER AGAIN

Shannon Wells burned.

Elizabeth insisted on it. We brought the wood ourselves, building a pyre on the other side of the clearing. Kelly told me quietly it was on the opposite end from where they'd said goodbye to Thomas Bennett, that the ground there was sacred to them and they wouldn't ever build another fire in that spot.

I could only nod.

Gordo was doing as Gordo did and ignoring everyone and everything, including Mark. I could see the frustration on Mark's face as he tried to talk to the witch but didn't get a response. Mark shook his head at me when I tried to approach them, waving me off.

As for Carter... well. The roles seemed to have reversed. Wherever the wolf went, Carter followed, as if he thought the wolf was going to take off the moment he looked away. He muttered unintelligibly under his breath. It sounded vaguely like ominous threats, but I couldn't quite make them out. Kelly stood near them, wringing his hands like he wanted to reach out for comfort but hadn't quite worked up the courage. My heart ached for him. For both of them.

"This is so fucked up," Rico grunted as he carried an armful of wood. "Just when I think I'm starting to get my feet on solid ground again, there's a fucking secret brother. I swear to God, witches and wolves are the most dramatic bitches I've ever known in my life. Like for *once* can we just have a normal day without stupid shit happening?"

We were outside of the clearing. Chris and Tanner were off to our left, gathering more wood for the pyre. Elizabeth said it didn't need to be large, but it needed to be enough. I understood what she meant, and she'd nodded gratefully at me before disappearing with Jessie back up the stairs to ready Shannon for her final journey.

"You guys had no idea?" I asked. Then, "*We* had no idea?"

Rico snorted. "Nice save, *lobito*. And no. We didn't know shit. How could we?" He frowned. "Though I suppose there were little signs, but we didn't know what we were looking at. The damn wolf came with Elijah. When they first attacked us, there was a moment when the wolf caught Gordo's scent, and I swear it hesitated, but I always thought I was seeing things. Then there was gunfire and explosions and it just slipped my mind. And after, it was all about him and Carter and how Carter's a fucking moron who can't see what's right in front of him."

"He's figuring it out," I muttered.

Rico sighed. "I know. And it couldn't be coming at a worse time. What happens if..." He looked distant as he stared off into the woods. Eventually he shook his head. "It doesn't matter. We survived the beast and the hunters." He paused, considering. "We survived *you*. We'll survive this too."

"Gee, thanks, Rico."

"Yeah, yeah. Let's go. I think we've got enough."

The pyre was crude and shapeless, more a pile of wood than an actual structure. But it was enough. As the stars began to appear overhead, as the sliver of moon peered through the fading light, we laid the Alpha to rest.

Elizabeth carried her from the house, her face stoic, her strides slow and sure. Shannon was wrapped completely in a white sheet, her head lolling against Elizabeth's shoulder. I could make out the shape of her nose, and at one moment her arm slipped down, swaying with every step Elizabeth took. But Jessie was there, lifting Shannon's arm back under the sheet.

Elizabeth carefully placed her on top of the pyre. Once that was done, she leaned forward and kissed Shannon's forehead, lips moving but no sound coming out. She stayed hunched over her for a long, long minute, but eventually she stood upright and took a step back.

The wood was slick with lighter fluid and oil.

It caught quickly.

The flames burned bright as they leapt up into the dark sky, sparks and smoke rising toward the stars.

We were all silent, lost in our own thoughts as she burned.

Rico spoke first. "She was an Alpha."

"Yes," Elizabeth whispered, eyes reflecting the dancing fire.

"What happens to her power if there's no one to give it to?"

We all held our breaths.

Elizabeth said, "An Alpha, strong of heart and mind, mated to one they love most, can give their power away in order to save a life. To a Beta they return, never again to hold the power of an Alpha. Just a story, of course. Wolves pass along the Alpha power to their successors constantly, though usually not under the threat of death. I've never heard of bringing someone back from the brink in such a way. Regardless, it was too late for her. And stories are just that—stories." She sucked in a sharp breath. "We come from the moon. And to the moon we return. Her line has ended. All that she was is becoming smoke and ash. It will rise, and she will hear her pack howling her home. There will be no more pain. There will be no more sorrow. She'll run free and know only peace."

She bowed her head, a tear trickling down her cheek.

It took only a moment before she was surrounded by her sons, all of them hugging her and each other. Kelly laid his head on her shoulder, but his eyes were on me.

I wondered if this was how it'd been for them when they'd said goodbye to their father.

If they believed her words.

I didn't know if I did.

Gordo stood away from the rest of us. He wasn't watching the fire.

He was watching the wolf.

· · ·

When the pyre was nothing but smoldering embers, the pack began to drift away in pairs. Jessie and Elizabeth, Carter and the wolf, Ox and Joe, Chris and Tanner. Kelly looked at me, but I told him I'd meet him back at the house. He glanced at Mark and Gordo on the other edge of the clearing before nodding. He trailed after Rico, looking back at me over his shoulder only once before he disappeared into shadows.

I waited and watched.

Mark stood in front of Gordo, holding on to his elbows. Gordo was looking away as Mark spoke. He shook his head once, and Mark all but threw up his hands. He sighed before leaning forward and kissing Gordo's cheek. "I love you," I heard him say.

Gordo winced. "I know. I love you too. I just . . ."

"I get it, Gordo. But don't shut me out, okay? Not about this."

Mark stepped away from him. He headed toward me. He checked the pyre to make sure it was dying before he said, "It's hard on him.

He doesn't know what to think. It's like a large part of his life has been a lie."

"I know."

Mark looked at me. "You do, don't you? Don't push him, Robbie. It'll only make him close up more." He patted me on the shoulder before leaving the clearing for the house.

I took a deep breath before I walked toward Gordo. I didn't think I could add anything Mark hadn't already said, but something pulled me toward Gordo. He didn't seem surprised to see me. His shoulders slumped, and he shook his head before I could open my mouth. "Look, I don't want to hear it, okay? Ox already tried, and Mark did too. I don't need anything else right now."

"Okay," I said. "We don't have to talk. Sometimes, it's okay to just be, you know? Without saying a word."

He glared at me. "And you think you need to *just be* near me right this second?"

I wasn't intimidated. "I think so. If you want me to go, I will."

His shoulders slumped further. "Goddammit. God*dammit*."

"Come on." I grabbed him by the arm, careful of the stump at his wrist. I led him away from the pyre in the opposite direction of the house. I thought he would protest and pull away, but he didn't. His head was down, and he didn't speak, but he followed me willingly.

I found the perfect tree a little ways into the woods. It was old, the trunk wide. There were green leaves on it, and the grass underneath was springy and soft. I pushed him down to the ground before settling next to him, our backs against the tree.

"What are we doing?" he asked.

"Just being."

"This is stupid. We've got things to do. We need to—"

"It can wait."

"It *can't*," he retorted, but he didn't try to stand. "Chris and Tanner said they could only reach five out of the ten packs they called. *Five*, kid. Which means that there are five packs who've been torn apart by—"

"You can't know that."

"Patrice and Aileen have already confirmed one. They said it was a bloodbath. And the children in that pack were gone."

I hadn't heard. I'd been caught up in everything else. "Shit."

"Succinct as always."

"I suppose I shouldn't even try to say that we could just give him what he wants." I looked down at my hands. "What he's asked for."

"Yeah, that'll go over well," he said dryly. "Let me know when you're going to do that so I can make sure to be there."

"Worth a shot."

He shook his head. "We can't . . ." He shifted, stretching his legs out in front of him, crossing them at the ankles. "I didn't know."

His brother. I nodded.

"How did I not know? They hid it from me. All of them. Another secret." He knocked the back of his head against the tree. "Elizabeth said she didn't know."

"Do you believe her?"

He didn't hesitate. "Yeah. She and I, we have an understanding. But that doesn't mean Thomas didn't know. Abel did, at the very least. But I . . . I should have known. When I saw him. When he saw *me*. He's been here this entire time, and he just— I tried a couple of times, to help him. To see if I could break him out of his shift. It never worked." He flexed his hands in the grass. "He was more wolf than anything else. But I could tell he didn't like it when I was in his head."

"He may not even remember who he was, Gordo. How long has he been shifted? Years? That has to take a toll on him. Maybe it has to do with being an Omega. Or maybe he's just lost."

Gordo glanced at me. "You sound like you know what that's like."

"I do," I admitted. "Even though I didn't *know* exactly, when I was in Caswell, I always felt off. Like the lines of who I was were blurred or the colors inverted. Like a photo negative, I guess. I didn't know what it was. I do now."

"It's weird, right?"

"Yes," I said promptly. Then, "What?"

He shrugged. "That even through all my father's magic, part of you knew. That you didn't belong there. That you already had a home and you just needed to find your way back to it."

I hated what I was about to say, but he needed to hear it. "And maybe that's the same for your brother. For . . . Gavin."

Gordo tensed. His fingers dug into the earth.

"Why do you think he's here? Why do you think he's stayed?"

He spoke through gritted teeth. "Because he's got it in his head that Carter is—"

"It's not just about Carter, Gordo. That's part of it, and maybe a big part, but I don't think that's all it is. I think part of him knows. Like part of me knew. And you never gave up on me. You never let me go."

"I couldn't," he whispered.

"You fought for me. All of you."

"Yeah, kid."

"I don't know what's going to happen. I don't know if we'll even make it out of all of this alive. But don't you think the wolf needs to know we're fighting for him too? Because he's part of this. Just as much as you are. Just as much as I am. You wouldn't let me go. You didn't forget me, even after all of you were taken from me. We don't give up on pack. We never have. And we never will."

"He's not pack," Gordo said harshly.

I waited.

"Fuck," he muttered. "Felt that, did you?"

"The lie? Yeah. But that's okay. I don't need to hear your heart to know you don't mean it."

We were quiet for a long time after that. I wanted to get back to the house, but I didn't want to leave him here by himself. Even though he wouldn't say it out loud, I thought he needed me here just as much as I needed him.

So I stayed.

Eventually he lifted his arm and put it around my shoulders, pulling me close. I laid my head on him, and he didn't even try to shove me off.

"I'm happy you're here," he said quietly, as if it was a great secret just between the two of us. "It wasn't the same without you."

I nodded against him. "Can we beat this?"

He didn't answer right away. And that seemed to be answer enough until he said, "I don't know. After everything we've been through, all those we've faced, this should be just another thing."

"But it's not."

"No. It feels different. It's not just about me. It's about Mark. It's about Carter. It's about all the other Omegas who have had their lives stolen away because of him. And you. It's about you, because I'll be damned if I'll let my father keep the memories from all the times I made fun of you because of your stupid fucking glasses."

I laughed. It was shockingly loud here in the forest, and it echoed through the trees.

He held me tighter.

And then he said, "I made Kelly a promise. A long time ago."

"What?" I whispered.

"I told him I would find you. That I would do everything I could to bring you back. And I did, but not all the way. And I aim to keep that promise all the way through to the end. No matter what."

I felt cold.

They knew we were coming.

Livingstone was right when he said the element of surprise was gone, if we'd even had it at all. Rico and Tanner and Chris wanted to move *now*, but Ox turned his focus on the wolves who'd sided with the Bennetts, the ones who'd taken in Omegas. He began to move them into hiding, instructing them to stay that way until they heard back from us.

"And what if we don't hear from you?" one Alpha asked, voice crackling through the phone.

"You will," Ox said simply.

I almost believed him even as I wondered if it was already too late.

But I kept that thought to myself, especially when Ox came to me on a sunny afternoon toward the end of June. I knew what he wanted. I knew what I would give him.

He said, "I told you once that the day would come when I'd ask you to tell me everything you know. About Caswell. About the wolves there and where their loyalties lie. Do you remember?"

I could only nod.

"You didn't trust me when I told you this. Do you trust me now?"

Yes, yes, yes.

"Because I am your Alpha."

Yes, yes, yes.

He stood above me, eyes filling with a swirling mix of red and violet. He leaned forward until he pressed his forehead against mine, and I said, "*Oh.*"

Green Creek knew something was happening.

They were wary in ways I hadn't seen before, and at first I thought it was because they were scared of us.

But it turned out they were scared *for* us.

They stopped us in the streets, asking us what was happening.

What was going on.

If something was coming.

If they needed to fight.

Will seemed to spearhead the rising concern. He came to the garage even though it was closed, banging on the door until Gordo unlocked the front door. "What's coming?" he asked. "And don't tell me *nothing*, boy. That's shit and you know it."

"Nothing," Gordo said. "Because we're going to it."

Will's eyes widened. Then, "You're all coming back, right?"

"We're going to try."

Will nodded. "That's not very reassuring." He glanced at me before looking back at Gordo. "Has to do with shape-shifters?" He wiggled his fingers in Gordo's face. "Magic stuff?"

"Yeah."

"Okay," Will said, puffing out his chest. "Then you all go do whatever it is you need to do. I'll set up a patrol around the town until you get back and Carter and Kelly can take over again. It's what we pay them for. Don't want them to shirk their responsibilities."

Gordo gaped at him as Will turned and marched back out of the garage. "Don't you worry about the town," he called over his shoulder. "I'll shoot anything that looks at us funny, be it vampires or beasts or another religious nut sack who takes the Good Book way too literally. I promise you that. Just make sure you come back, Gordo. We need someone to fix our cars for cheap." He crossed the street, heading toward the group of townsfolk gathering in the diner.

"Jesus Christ," Gordo said irritably, though I could hear the pride in his voice.

· · ·

"Gordo's pretty pissed, huh?" I told the timber wolf on the final Sunday in June. The wolf followed me as I walked down the dirt road away from the houses. Ox, Joe, and Gordo had spent the morning grilling me about the compound: the wards, the walls, how many people, wolves, witches, the layout. Whether I'd ever used any hidden way in or out of Caswell. I told them there were good people there, innocent people who would want nothing to do with whatever Robert Livingstone had done. And if what we'd heard was true, if he had taken control of children, we'd have to be careful. This wasn't like what they'd faced before. They couldn't just kill indiscriminately. Kelly had told me what happened with Richard Collins and the hunters led by Meredith King. This thing we were doing, this absolutely crazy thing, couldn't be like what they'd done before.

Ox looked grim when he said we would do everything we could not to hurt any of the children.

That should have made me feel better.

It didn't.

And it didn't help when Ox and Joe announced they wanted Kelly and me to stay behind.

Before I could snarl at them, demanding to know what the fuck they were thinking, Kelly said, "No."

Joe frowned. "Kelly, I don't . . . I know you think you need to be there. But you're human. You could get hurt."

"So could I," Jessie said. "Are you going to tell me to stay behind?"

"That's not—"

"Me too," Rico chimed in. "Go ahead, *alfas*. Say it to my face. Say, 'Rico, you handsome devil, you're staying right here in Green Creek while the rest of us ride off to kick some ass.' Say it. I dare you."

Joe threw up his hands. "I'm not trying to piss anyone off. But Kelly can't—"

"Maybe don't worry about what Kelly *can't* do and focus on what he *can* do," Jessie retorted. "He's not a wolf anymore, but that doesn't mean he's weak. He's one of us."

"Motherfucking Team Human," Rico agreed. "We had to open up enrollment since *lobito* here tried to eat up half of our membership." He kicked me in the shin. It hurt. "No offense, little wolf."

I glared at him as I rubbed my leg. "None taken."

"And you need me," Kelly reminded them. "We go as a pack. All of us. That's the way it's supposed to be. Stronger together, remember?"

"What about Robbie?" Joe asked, sounding apologetic as he glanced at me. "We know what Livingstone is capable of. What he'll do. What he's already done. Can we really take the chance that he won't try to trigger Robbie? If we're in the middle of a fight, we can't be worrying about whether or not we'll literally get stabbed in the back." He winced. "Sorry, Robbie."

I tried to keep a straight face, even though it hurt to hear. He had a point. We didn't know just how far Livingstone's reach over me extended.

Gordo stepped in, though he sounded unsure. "We'll shore him up as best we can. Patrice and Aileen are coming back to Green Creek with as many wolves and witches as they can. I can't make any promises, but we might be able to keep my father from triggering him."

That wasn't the ringing endorsement I'd been hoping for.

"And he'll be with me," Kelly said fiercely. "I won't let Livingstone anywhere near him."

"That won't matter if he gets to you again," Joe argued. "Kelly, I love you so goddamn much. All of you. I don't want to risk losing you. I can't. What if Livingstone *does* get to Robbie? What if he forces him to turn on you? What do you think that would do to him?"

"Everything is a risk," Elizabeth said quietly. "All that we do. And yet we do it anyway, knowing it's for the greater good."

And Joe said, "I can't believe this. I can't believe you'd all take this chance." His chest was heaving. "We . . . we're so close to ending this. And you're all getting hung up on this one detail. This one *thing.*"

And on and on it went, spinning in dizzying circles.

They were talking around me. Talking *for* me as if I wasn't even there. I turned and left the room, struggling to breathe.

The timber wolf followed.

Gavin.

I'd barely stepped off the porch when I heard something behind me. I glanced over my shoulder to see him coming down the stairs, trotting toward me.

I waited until he was next to me before continuing on.

It felt strange. Talking to the wolf without knowing if he could understand me. Ox said he was an enigma, that trying to connect with him through pack bonds wasn't unlike what was going on with me. There was an empty space, a void. He was an Omega, but Ox didn't have control over him as he did the others. And yet he didn't seem to be feral, not completely. There was a spark of intelligence in his eyes, but that didn't mean he knew what we were saying. What *I* was saying.

And there was something weirdly cathartic about it.

"And Carter's pissed off too," I said as we walked. "Though I don't think he knows why, exactly. He's good, Carter. And brave. Smart. But not about this. How the hell can he not see what's right in front of him?"

The wolf snorted, and I took it for what it was.

"Did you know? About him? About Gordo? Before you came here?"

He cocked his head at me, ears twitching.

"You had to stay for a reason, right?"

He growled.

I sighed. "Right." The houses were out of sight behind us, the road stretching out before us, and I was struck, then, by just how easy it would be to take this decision out of their hands. To put an end to all of this, just as Livingstone had said. I was under no illusions that I could trust a single word that came out of his mouth, but what if? What if he was true to his word? What if all he wanted was the two of us and he would leave everyone else alone?

"We could just go," I said suddenly, and the wolf stopped. I did too. I didn't look at him, but I knew he was listening. "You and me. We could just leave. Head east on our own. Because that's what people do for those they care about. They do anything they can to keep them safe. I don't think I had that in Caswell." I paused, considering. "Either time. I was sent here to keep tabs the first time, and I never left. If I'd had a home before, I wouldn't have stayed. These people. This pack. They made something for me here. They allowed me to stay." I closed my eyes. "It would hurt them, but it would be a gift in the long run. They could see it in time. They might even forgive us someday."

I opened my eyes as the wolf rounded in front of me, hackles raised. He bared his fangs as he growled at me, pawing the dirt and gravel. He took a step toward me, and I took an answering step back. His eyes were alight, and the air was hot and hazy around us. It almost felt like I was dreaming.

Before he could take another step, a voice spoke behind me. "You can't."

I turned.

Joe stood in the middle of the road. He looked impossibly young for one so strong, here in these woods that thrummed with the blood of all those who had come before him. He had a complicated expression on his face, part anguish, part irritation. And there was blue too, rippling off him like he had no control over it.

He said, "You can't. You just can't."

I hung my head. "Why? It'd be easier—"

"I don't give a *fuck* about easy," he snapped, Alpha filling his voice, creating a deep and unwavering timbre. "If I did, I wouldn't be here. We never would have made it this far. Look at me, Robbie."

I did. I was helpless not to.

The irritation was gone, though the anguish remained, filling in the cracks. He looked stricken, hands jerking at his sides like he wanted to reach out for me and thought better of it. The wolf stood next to me, tail swishing, waiting to see what the Alpha would do. What he would say.

Joe shook his head. "I let you down."

I barely kept from rolling my eyes. "I think you were justified—"

"No," he said, taking a step toward me. I was frozen in place. "That's not fair. That's an excuse. An easy one. And one I've taken before." He took another step. I could see his mother in him. His brothers. He felt like the wolf from my dreams, the one I knew now to be his father. And in this haze of green and blue, he was a king without a crown. I thought he could save us all if only given the chance. "My father . . ." His chest hitched. "He told me that an Alpha couldn't be absolute. That I would need to listen. He said the measure of an Alpha isn't the power he holds over others but what he does with it. I would need to know kindness as well as strength. I would need to put pack above all others, even myself. An Alpha without a pack isn't an Alpha at all. Richard Collins didn't understand that. He only wanted the power. To use it to twist everything until it lay in ruins. He wanted to destroy. He almost took everything. Do you know why he failed?"

The wolf nuzzled my palm, nipping lightly at my fingers.

"He failed because he didn't understand the lessons of my father. He didn't understand what it meant to be pack. And neither did I. Not until you taught me."

I was alarmed when he fell to his knees in front of me. I was horrified when he bared his neck, a sign of submission I'd never seen from an Alpha before. His eyes were wet and pleading. His voice was broken when he said, "I let you down, Robbie. I should have done more. I should have listened. To Ox. To Gordo. To Kelly most of all. I forgot the words of my father. You were—are—part of my pack, and I—I just let you go."

"Get up," I said roughly. "Get up, get up, *get up—*"

And he said, "No. Not until you hear me. Not until you understand. You are important to me. When you were gone, I tried to ignore this hole in all of us. I told myself that we had other things to worry about. I closed ranks, and that was a mistake."

I saw movement behind him, and there, standing down the road, was Ox. He watched. He waited.

Joe never took his eyes off me.

"If you leave," Joe said, "if you decide to give up, to give *in*, then what the hell are we fighting for? What's the point of all of this?"

"It'd be easier," I whispered.

"It would," he agreed. He tried for a smile, but it shattered. "But I don't want that. Not if it means losing you. You're my brother's mate. But more than that, you're *my* brother, just as much as Kelly and Carter. You can't go, because without you, we're incomplete. And if we're incomplete, then we're nothing."

"You survived," I said, surprised at how bitter it sounded.

"We did. But there's a difference between surviving and living. And I want to live, Robbie. I want to live for you. For all of you. Because we deserve it. We deserve to exist in a world where we only know peace. We deserve to be happy. *You* deserve it. And I forgot that. If you'll forgive me, I promise I'll never let it happen again."

I wiped my eyes. "You can't promise that. No one can."

"*I* can," he said.

"Why?"

He reached out for my hand, hung on as if I were a lifeline. "Because pack is family. And family is everything. An Alpha is only as strong as his pack. And you are my strength."

He brought my hand up to his throat, wrapping my fingers around his neck. I felt him breathing. I felt the steady pulse of his heartbeat.

He spoke only truth.

His truth.

I sank to my knees before him, his hand still pressing my own against his throat. He swallowed thickly, his Adam's apple rising and falling against the webbing between my thumb and pointer finger. The wolf circled around us, brushing against the both of us, eyes still brightly violet.

I said, "Joe."

He said, "Robbie."

And I said, "Alpha, Alpha, Alpha."

His eyes filled with fire. His claws prickled my skin. There was a moment, a brief and shining moment, when I thought I heard his voice in my head, when I thought I felt the thrum of bonds connecting us, and though they were tenuous, they held.

And in this whisper, I heard

pack

pack

pack

Then it was gone, as if it'd never been there at all.

But it was enough.

The road behind us stretched on, but it wasn't meant for me. Not now. Not yet. And when I put feet to it, I wouldn't be alone.

"Never again," Joe whispered. "I promise."

And for the first time since I returned, I believed Joe Bennett.

•   •   •

We stayed until the full moon, though it felt dangerous to do so. The longer we waited, the more time Livingstone had to prepare. Help was coming, Ox told us, and we needed all we could get. And it was better to be on the other side of the full moon. The wolves in Caswell wouldn't be as strong. Neither would we, but that was left unsaid.

July 5, 2020.

A Sunday.

It started with Tradition.

We laughed a lot that day. There was food, more than even a pack of wolves could eat. And stories, so many stories, told by each member of the Bennett pack.

Elizabeth spoke of a dream she'd once had. Of her husband and how he brought her stone wolf back to her.

Joe told us about a time when it'd been just him and his father.

He'd been little, sitting atop his father's shoulders as they wandered through the forest.

Rico regaled us all with a story of how he, Chris, and Tanner had gotten Gordo high for the first time when they were thirteen, and how all the lightbulbs in his house had burst at once. They'd chalked it up to a power surge at the time, but now he knew it was because Gordo had been talking about Mark in a disgustingly dreamy voice. We all laughed at that, even as Gordo glared at Rico.

Mark said how full his heart had been the first time he'd seen Gordo after the Bennetts returned to Green Creek, that even though Gordo was yelling at him to stay the hell away, Mark had wanted nothing more than to hug him and never let him go.

Chris and Tanner took turns, almost giggling, as they reminisced about when Jessie had first come to Green Creek and how Ox had acted like an idiot at the first sight of her, following her around like a creepy stalker.

Not to be outdone, Jessie reminded them of how the same would probably happen to them one day now that they were wolves—that they would most likely succumb to the mystical moon magic. Chris and Tanner were outraged.

Gordo, on his third beer, seemed loose and easy when he said he never would have expected that he'd actually *like* having wolves around again. He had a goofy grin on his face, and he laughed without reservation when Mark tugged him close, his nose in Gordo's hair, beard scratching Gordo's cheek.

Carter spoke of seeing Joe for the first time after he was born, and how he told his mother he didn't think something so small and wrinkled and *loud* could ever be an Alpha. I didn't think he realized that his hand never left the timber wolf's head, rubbing between his ears.

And Kelly, always Kelly. Kelly, who was only halfway into his *first* beer and yet was talking loudly and snorting in quiet laughter, even as Carter tried to get him to drink more. Kelly, whose eyes were wide and bright, Kelly who looked at me as if I were the moon itself, Kelly who said we were where we were supposed to be, *with* who we were supposed to be with. And seemingly without thinking about it, there, in front of everyone, he leaned forward and kissed me, a loud smacking thing that caused Rico and Tanner and Chris to hoot and holler, demanding we get a fucking room.

I was dazed, my head spinning, my heart thundering in my chest. I tried to find the words to tell him, to tell them all, what this moment meant. What I thought we could be. That it almost didn't matter if I never remembered the life I'd once had because I knew I could make a new one out of the bones that remained.

It was Ox who spoke last.

He said, "I love you," and we all fell silent. He looked at each of us in turn. "More than I could possibly say. And I've never been prouder of who you've all become. Remember this. Here. Now. If there ever comes a time when all seems dark, when all seems lost, remember this moment. Because this is who we are. This is who we're supposed to be. It's time. It's time to run."

He tilted his head back as the sky filled with stars, as the moon shone down around us. He howled, and it echoed throughout Green Creek, shaking it to its very foundation. It rolled through each of us, and as we sang our songs in response to the call of our Alpha, I told myself nothing could stop us.

"Jesus Christ," Rico muttered as Chris and Tanner took off their clothes. "Chris, you really need to do something about your bush, man. It's like an old-growth forest down there. What the fuck. Learn to manscape." But he was laughing when Chris threw his shirt into Rico's face.

We ran that night.

Through the woods to the clearing.

The humans kept up with us, light on their feet and breathless.

In my wolf head and in my wolf heart, I knew that no matter what happened, I would have this moment.

And no one, not even Robert Livingstone, would be able to take that away from me.

· · ·

We slept together that night as a pack, curled together safe and warm.

I thought everyone was asleep. I was about to drift off when I heard whispers from my left.

I opened my eyes.

Carter and Kelly lay facing each other. My arm was around Kelly's waist, and Carter was holding on to my hand, but I didn't think they knew I was awake.

Carter said, "We've got this, man. You'll see."

"What if we don't?" Kelly asked, and I ached at the worry in his voice.

Carter sighed, reaching up to flick Kelly on the forehead. "Stop being so pessimistic. You gotta *believe*."

Kelly huffed. "You're so stupid."

"Yeah, probably. But I've got my looks still, so I'm not too worried about it."

They were quiet for a moment. Then, "Carter?"

"Yeah?"

"I'm scared."

"I know, Kelly. Me too. But as long as we're together, we'll be all right."

"Really?"

"Yeah. Really. You stay with me and Robbie. You protect us, and we'll protect you. I've got your back, okay?"

"Always?"

"Always." He sighed. "Can I tell you something?"

"Yes."

"I really hope we fucking straight-up murder Gordo's dad. I'm sick and tired of this Omega bullshit. I want my tether back."

Kelly laughed, though it sounded closer to a sob. "I'm right here. I'm right here."

Carter squeezed my hand. He knew I was awake. "I know you are. It's just . . . I miss it. Having you always in my head. I didn't realize just how much I'd miss it until it wasn't there anymore. It's like this . . . this vacuum, you know? I get it now. How you must have felt when Robbie was gone. I never want you to feel like that again, so we're going to fucking *destroy* Robert Livingstone, and then we'll come home, and it'll be like it used to be."

"You promise?"

"Yeah, Kelly. I promise."

They slept soon after, curled together.

I stayed awake for a long time.

. . .

The sky had barely begun to lighten when I shook Kelly awake. His eyes opened slowly, unfocused and blinking. He saw me, and he smiled. I knew right then and there that I would do anything for him.

"Hey," he said. "What's going on?"

"I need your help," I whispered.

He unwrapped himself from his brother, who smacked his lips and grunted in his sleep before turning over, burying his face in the timber wolf's stomach. The wolf flicked its tail once before breathing deeply.

Elizabeth opened her eyes in the low light. She didn't speak. She smiled before closing her eyes again.

I led Kelly by the hand up the stairs to the second floor. We passed by his room. He yawned, jaw cracking as he rubbed his eyes. "Okay?"

"Yeah. Okay."

I pushed open the door to the bathroom. I let go of his hand, and he stood in the doorway. I went to the sink and stared into the mirror. It was the face I'd seen for as long as I could remember, but it wasn't the right one. Not yet. Parts of myself were still hidden away, lost in the grip of magic behind an unbreakable door.

I shrugged my shirt up and over my head, dropped it to the floor. I opened one of the drawers beneath the sink. The electric razor was still there, where I'd seen it a few weeks previous. I hadn't been ready then.

I was now.

He took it from me wordlessly, looking down at it, then back at me. I closed the lid to the toilet and sat down on it. I reached back and grabbed a towel hanging from the wooden rack. I spread it over my shoulders. I took a deep breath.

He said, "You don't remember. But sometimes you act like you do. It's almost like muscle memory. A reflex."

I blinked. "What?"

He closed the bathroom door. "Before. You didn't like people you didn't know touching you. That included getting a haircut. You weren't mean about it, it was just . . ." He shook his head. "It was just one of your things. You said it made you nervous."

"I've always been that way."

He smiled, though it faded almost immediately. "I know. You did it, though, because none of us knew how to cut hair. When we were on the road going after Richard Collins, we shaved our own heads. I told you about that once and you all but demanded I do the same for you." He laughed. "You told me later that you just used it as an excuse to get my hands on you."

I groaned. "Jesus *Christ*."

"Yeah, I pretty much saw right through you. Mom always used to do it for you, but then you asked me and I just . . ." He shrugged. "I couldn't say no."

I looked down at my hands. "Couldn't?"

"Wouldn't," he said. "It was such a little thing, but it felt so big. I was pretty bad at it at first, but I got better at it. You trusted me, and so I made sure I knew what I was doing."

"I want it all gone," I told him. "All of it. You don't need to . . . It doesn't need to look like it was before. I just . . ."

"I know. Here. Sit on the edge of the bathtub. It'll make things easier."

I moved. My hands were shaking, and I wasn't sure why.

He watched me for a moment before motioning for me to spread my legs. I did, my feet flat against the white bath mat. He stepped between my legs, and I sighed as the scent of him enveloped me.

Grass.

Lake water.

Sunshine.

He ran a hand through my hair. I leaned into the touch. He gripped it slightly, pulling my head back to look up at him. My pupils felt blown out, my hands shaking as I curled them into fists on my lap. "You sure about this?" he asked.

"Yes."

"There's no going back."

"I know."

He hummed a little under his breath. He slid the switch of the razor up, and it started to vibrate.

There was something extraordinarily intimate about what followed. We didn't speak. We only breathed. He put his hand around the back of my neck, holding me in place. I followed the sound of his great heart, a minor drumbeat in the grand scheme of things, but something so terrifyingly precious in this fractured reality. He started at the front, and hair began to float down around me, onto my shoulders and back, individual strands clinging to my cheeks. It felt like we were the only people in existence. It didn't take long, and there were times when he stepped back, gripping me by the chin, turning my face side to side. My eyes never left his. I couldn't look away. I didn't think I ever wanted to. And it filled me with a staggering fury, knowing I'd been torn away from this.

From him.

If I wasn't in love with him yet, I knew I would be soon.

It was inevitable.

I needed him to understand.

I did the only thing I could. I gave him back the words he'd once gifted to me.

I said, "There was something . . . I don't know. Endless. About you and me. We came here sometimes. Just the two of us. And I pretended to know all the stars. I would make up stories that absolutely weren't true, and I remember looking at you, thinking how wonderful it was just to be by your side."

He gripped the back of my neck tighter.

I could smell the sharp sting of salt and knew he was crying.

I leaned forward and pressed my face against his stomach, breathing him in.

He held me there for what felt like hours.

Eventually I pulled back, and he continued.

He slowly stepped into the bathtub so he could finish what he'd started.

By the time he was done, the sky outside the open window was brightening. He stepped out of the bathtub and switched the razor off, set it on the back of the toilet. He ran a hand over my prickly scalp, brushing off the last few hairs.

He put his finger under my chin again, tilting my head up.

His eyes were bloodshot, but he was in control.

"There you are," he whispered. "Hey. Hi. Hello."

"Here I am," I croaked back.

He knelt before me slowly, hands resting on top of my thighs, the tips of his fingers under my sleep shorts. I shrugged until the towel slid off me, falling into the bathtub.

Kelly's eyes were shining, so human, but with the undercurrent of a born wolf.

I cupped his face.

I leaned forward until our foreheads pressed together.

My thumbs brushed over his cheeks.

His expression stuttered.

And I kissed him with everything I had. I put everything I was feeling into it, my anger, my despair, my hope and dreams that one day all of this would be behind us and we could be as we once were. That all would be well and nothing could ever hurt us again.

I pulled away, but only just, our lips still brushing together. I lifted one of his hands and pressed it against my chest, right over my heart. I needed him to feel it. I needed him to know. "I'm going to love you," I whispered to him. "I'm going to love you, and I'm never going to let you go."

My heart remained steady and true.

He laughed, though it cracked, and then he kissed me again and again and again.

* * *

The others were waiting for us as we descended the stairs, hand in hand.

They were still in the living room, curled together, though they were all awake.

Rico, of course, spoke first. He whistled. "Looking good, little wolf. Still got a weird-shaped head, though." He rolled away, cackling as Elizabeth threw a pillow at his head.

Gordo stood, Mark's fingers trailing along the raven in the roses on his arm. He stepped over the others until he stood before us. His gaze searched my face. And then he grinned, and my god, it was blinding. "Good to see you, kid," he said. "Missing something, though." He reached up, and I didn't even flinch when he carefully put my glasses on. He tweaked the tip of my nose before stepping back. "There. That's better. You look ridiculous with those on."

Something settled within me, and it was warm.

We all turned toward the front of the house a moment later at the sound of an engine coming down the road.

Many engines.

"That'll be them," Gordo said. "We ready?"

Kelly squeezed my hand as I said, "Yeah. We're ready."

UNTIL THE END / SHARP STING

I bit back a scream as I shot up, covered in sweat, looking around wildly.

"It's okay," a voice whispered. "You're okay. You're here. You're here."

Kelly. At my back, breath hot against my ear. I nodded, rubbing my hand over my face.

"Jesus," Aileen said as she slumped into Patrice. He wrapped an arm around her, though he too looked on the verge of collapse. Gordo was panting, as were two other witches whose names I hadn't learned before they'd invaded my head. The others stood at the edge of the clearing, watching us with concern but coming no closer. Patrice had warned them to stay away. This wasn't a matter of pack. It was magic. "That was harder than I expected. You feel that? It wasn't like it was before. Something's shifted."

Patrice grimaced. "He's fighting it. Learnin' his place. It's big. Dat ol' magic Livingstone put on 'em is warrin' with who he is. Pack. Duality. Split."

"Is that good or bad?" Kelly asked, and I was grateful for his voice, seeing as how I couldn't find my own.

Patrice shrugged. "For Robbie? Good. For Livingstone? I don't know. Just might make him try all dat much harder."

"We did the best we could," Gordo said, his hand on his lower back as he stretched. "Put as much distance between him and the door as we could. How you feeling, kid?"

"Like you've all just fucked with my head," I grumbled. I pressed my hands against my temples, trying to force away the painful fog.

"It's a stopgap," Aileen warned as the other two witches stumbled away. They held on to each other, both of them looking back at me with wide eyes as they headed toward the others. "Won't last forever. Especially if Livingstone gets his hands on you. If we had more time, maybe we could—"

"No," I said. "We've waited long enough. We don't know what he's done to the wolves in Caswell. The kids. We don't *have* more time.

You did what you could, and I'm thankful for it. Even if you've dug around in my brain again." I couldn't keep the bitterness from my voice.

Aileen knew what I wasn't saying. "We aren't like him. Our magic is white. His is black."

"Worse," Patrice said. "Absence of color. Sucks all da light in. And he'll use it ta his advantage. Can't forget dat."

"He won't," Gordo said.

Aileen glared at him. "That goes for you too, boyo. I know you're in this up to your neck. Hell, we all are. But it's more for you, given that it's your daddy and what he did to your Robbie here. Don't lose sight of what's important. It's not about revenge. It's about the greater good and bringing an end to all this madness. It's personal. I get that. But don't make it about *just* that."

"I don't know what you're—"

"Dale."

Gordo ground his teeth together. "Yeah, well. Maybe that one's personal. But if he's as gone as Robbie told us he is, then it doesn't matter."

Aileen sighed. "Be that as it may, you shove that down as far as you can, Gordo. We can't have you going off half-cocked because you're pissed at your mate's ex."

"It's a little more complicated than that," Gordo retorted. "He betrayed us. He *used* Mark to—"

Aileen held up her hand. "I know. But we've got bigger fish to fry here. Remember that. Your father will use it to distract you. Don't let him."

Gordo looked like he was going to argue further, but instead he scowled. I wanted to reassure him, tell him that I didn't think there was any coming back for Michelle's former witch, but my mouth was dry, my tongue like thick sandpaper.

Kelly stood up behind me, helping me up as he did so. He came around and stood in front of me, searching my face as if he was looking for evidence of what the witches had done to me.

Before he could say anything, Ox was there, looking at all of us. "Did it work?"

"Yes, Alpha," Patrice said. "Tink it did. Robbie is . . . you have found harmony again. Unity. It's fragile. But it's holding. If we're to move, it must be now."

"Can you do anything for Kelly?"

Aileen hesitated before shaking her head. "I thought we could. But it's beyond us. The only way to break the magic is to destroy it. And the only way to do that is . . ."

"To kill my father," Gordo muttered. Ox grabbed his arm, but Gordo pulled away. "I'm fine. You don't have to worry about me. I've known it would come to this for a long time." He looked at Mark at the edge of the clearing, standing next to Elizabeth. "I promised him I would fix this. Make things right. And I'm going to do just that."

"*We* are," Ox told him quietly. "Because we're in this together."

Gordo laughed hollowly. "Until the end."

Ox nodded. "Until the end."

It was strange, really.

Leaving this place behind.

Which is why I felt a mournful tug in the middle of my chest when we gathered in front of the Bennett house for the last time.

We had a dozen wolves. The strongest fighters. Two additional Alphas. Eight Betas. The two Omegas who had the most control. They were itching for a fight. One of the Alphas said that he'd known Malik for years. He wanted blood.

We all did.

It was a pulse just underneath our skin.

In addition to Aileen, Patrice, and Gordo, there were three other witches. Two of them had dug around in my head. The third was young, a boy who assured me he was twenty, though he barely looked like he'd started high school.

And there was our pack. All of us. Standing together.

I thought Ox would give a grand speech, tell us all that we were stronger together than we'd ever be alone. That it was time for us to fight back, to bring an end to those who would do us harm. That we would return victorious. Every single one of us.

He didn't.

Because he knew, as we all did, that there was a chance none of us would return. That this would be the last time we all were together.

He said, "It's almost time." Then he stepped away toward the blue house, hands in his pockets, shoulders slumped. We watched as he stood near the porch, head bowed. I heard him whispering and made out the words *hey, Mom*, and I tuned him out. It wasn't meant for me.

Elizabeth was staring up at the pack house. Carter and Joe stood on either side of her.

"You know," she said, "your father would be proud of us."

"You think so?" Carter asked.

She smiled at him. "I know so."

Rico stood away from the others, hands on Bambi's waist. She was poking his chest, her words curt. "You don't do anything stupid," she said. "You get there, you kick some ass, and then you come *back*. I swear to God, Rico, if you die, I will have one of these witches bring you back to life just so I can murder you myself."

"I don't think that's how it works, *mi amor*— Ow! Would you stop *hitting* me?"

"Then you fucking *listen* to me!"

And then they were trying to eat each other's faces. Humans were so confusing.

Jessie made a noise as another car appeared down the road, an old junker I'd seen Dominique driving. The car had barely come to a stop before she jumped out, a determined look on her face.

Jessie looked confused. "Hey, I thought we already said goodbye."

"We did," Dominique said, eyes flashing violet. "But I need to do something before you leave."

And then she kissed Jessie.

"Whoa," Tanner said. "That is . . . huh."

"That's my *sister*," Chris growled at him, elbowing Tanner in the stomach. "Stop staring!"

Jessie looked dazed as Dominique pulled away. Dominique nodded, satisfied. "There. Now you have even more of a reason to come back. You owe me a date, Alexander."

Jessie nodded as she blushed. "Ah. Yeah. I can . . . I can do that."

"Finally," Bambi muttered. "Now I won't have to hear them both pining after each other. It was getting pretty awful."

"We are literally the gayest pack that has ever existed," Rico said to no one in particular. "I see no problem with this."

Ox finished his business at the blue house. He walked back toward us quickly. His eyes were red and violet. We all turned to him.

And the Alpha said, "Let's go."

Our caravan slowed as we reached the main street through Green Creek.

"What the hell?" Carter asked as he leaned forward against the steering wheel. "What are they doing?"

"Holy shit," Kelly whispered, taking my hand in the back seat without looking.

I had no words.

The people of Green Creek had lined the sidewalks. They stood in front of the shops, in front of their houses. Will was in front of the diner, surrounded by a group of men and women.

He was the first.

He tilted his head back and howled.

It was... well. It was a human trying to sound like a wolf. His voice was hoarse with age, and it came out as more of a yell than anything else.

But then the others joined in, their voices mixing together.

I saw a boy and a girl beating their chests as they sang the song of the wolves.

It went on and on and on as we drove down the road.

They filled the streets as the last car in our caravan passed by, walking slowly after us.

The last sight I had of Green Creek was its people, its strange and wonderful people, letting us know how to find our way home.

We drove without stopping for as long as we could, switching out drivers so everyone could get a chance to sleep. We avoided major cities. We stopped briefly in the middle of nowhere Wyoming, mountains rising up around us. We stretched our legs and ran under stars that seemed infinite in the black sky above us. We spotted a few bison, and though I knew we felt the urge to hunt, we let them be.

Carter sang along with the radio. Elizabeth joined in with Dinah Shore and Peggy Lee.

Once, at near three in the morning, when Kelly was driving and Elizabeth sleeping soundly, her head resting on her son's jacket against the window, I looked out the back to the bed of the truck. The timber wolf lay on a blanket, head raised. Normally he was hidden in the back of a van that Aileen had brought, but he'd started growing irritated. We were on back roads in Iowa, so we weren't too worried about someone seeing him. Carter slept next to him, head lolling side to side with the movements of the truck, the wolf's tail curled over his lap. The wolf must have felt me watching, because he turned to look at me. He flashed his eyes in acknowledgment before laying his head on Carter's chest.

"He's close, isn't he?" I whispered as I turned back around. "To figuring it out."

Kelly looked at me through the rearview mirror. "Carter?"

"Yeah."

"I think so."

"You never thought about telling him?"

Kelly snorted. "All the time. Mom said he needs to figure it out on his own. But I think part of him already knows."

"Why?"

"I haven't smelled another person on him in a long time."

We drove on.

Close to dawn of a summer day in early July:

"We're close."

Ox glanced at me from the driver's seat. "I know."

Gordo and Mark were in the back. "How much longer?" Gordo asked.

I stared out the window at familiar sights. "Less than an hour." I glanced at him. "You ever been here?"

"No." He narrowed his eyes. "Never had a reason."

This was it. I'd never have another chance. "There are good people here. Innocent people."

"We know," Mark said quietly. "But if they're not with us, then they're against us."

I swallowed thickly. "They may not have a choice. I know it's stupid. And if it comes down to it, if we have to make a decision, then we need to do what we have to."

"But," Ox said.

I shook my head. "But we have to save as many of them as we can. Those kids, Ox. We can't hurt the kids. No matter what. They don't deserve this. And he will use that against us. He knows we're coming. This isn't like Green Creek. This isn't our territory. It's his."

Gordo sighed as he sat back in his seat. "Maybe we'll get lucky and they'll just give up."

"Yeah," Mark said. "Maybe."

Forty-seven minutes later, I saw the sign.

CASWELL
EST. 1879

I closed my eyes.

CHAOS

Caswell looked no different. The buildings were the same. The trees were the same. Even the birds sounded the same through the open window.

But there was a change, one I didn't even realize until Gordo spoke. "Stop the truck."

"What?" Ox asked. "We're not—"

"Ox. Now."

He pulled over to the side of the road near the movie theater and parked against the sidewalk. Gordo was out of the cab even before Ox turned off the engine. He stood on the sidewalk, head cocked.

Ox glanced at me and shrugged before climbing out himself.

Mark and I followed. I looked back to see the others pulling up behind us, cars and trucks shutting off. Wolves and witches began to fill the sidewalk. Aileen and Patrice went to Gordo, eyes wide.

"You felt it too?" Aileen asked.

Gordo pressed his hand against the front door of the movie theater. "Yeah."

"What is it?" Joe asked as he stretched, arms above his head. "Is this it? I thought there were walls."

I shook my head. "This isn't the compound. It's still a little ways off."

"Then why are we—"

"Wards," Gordo muttered before stepping back from the movie theater. "There are no wards."

I blinked. "Wait, what?" I stepped up next to him even though I already knew he was right. I hadn't even realized as we'd crossed into Caswell, but we should have hit Livingstone's wards already. "Shit."

"They should be here, right?" Gordo asked.

I nodded. "We should have run into them a mile back."

Patrice muttered under his breath in a foreign tongue, fingers twitching, eyes oddly vacant. There was a soft burst of color in the air in front of him that faded as quickly as it'd appeared. He said, "Dey were here. Dey've been dismantled."

A murmur went up around us. "Why?" one of the Omegas asked. She shifted nervously. "Why would he do that?"

"Because he's inviting us in," Aileen said. "He wants us to come. He knows he has the upper hand."

"Great," Rico muttered. "That's just great. Hey, guys. Idea. Let's *not* walk right into the trap the crazy witch has set up for us. Huh? Right? Any takers? Anyone at all?" He sighed when no one spoke. "Fucking werewolves." He crossed his arms and glared at the sidewalk.

"It is what it is," Aileen said. "We knew it would be this way. We planned for it. It's why you waited for us to come to you." She glanced at the other witches. "We'll use containment magic as best we can. Ox will attempt to gain control over the Omegas. The rest of us are support. Stick with what we know. No deviations."

"Is it always this empty?" Kelly asked me, looking at the buildings. Others were uneasily peering in through the windows. "It's like this place has been abandoned."

I shook my head. "There's normally people here already. These businesses should be getting ready to open. It's mostly for the people in the compound. Something's off."

"Understatement," Chris said. He looked spooked. His nostrils flared as if he were trying to chase a scent. I had done the same, but there was nothing in the literal sense. It was like an *absence* of smells. "Do you think they know we're—"

Someone laughed. It was high and sweet and caused my stomach to clench.

We spun around.

There, standing in the middle of the empty two-lane road, was a child.

He was dressed in shorts and a T-shirt with a graphic of a cartoon character on it. His feet were bare and dirty. But the way he held himself made a chill run down my spine.

His head was cocked, his hair falling over his forehead. He held his arms down at his sides, his fingers flexed. Claws grew slowly and shrank back. Grew and shrank. Grew and shrank. He twitched like a low current of electricity was running through him.

And his eyes were violet.

"What the fuck?" Rico whispered.

I pushed through the crowd. Kelly tried to pull me back, but I shook him off. I stepped off the sidewalk into the street, crossing behind Ox's truck, losing sight of the boy briefly before seeing him again.

"Tony," I breathed.

He smiled around a mouthful of sharp little needles.

The smile faded as I said his name again and stepped toward him. "Hey, cub. It's me. Robbie."

"I don't like this," one of the wolves said.

I took another step toward the boy. He didn't move, never looking away from me.

"I've come back," I said. "I missed you. Did you miss me?"

Tony growled in warning.

I stopped, spreading my hands wide to show him I wasn't going to hurt him. "It's all right, cub. I'm here now. You're safe."

The violet in his eyes faded slightly. "Robbie?" he whispered. He sounded lost and unsure, and it made my heart sore.

I nodded. "Yeah, cub. It's me. What happened?"

A tear slid from his eye onto his cheek. "I had a bad dream."

I took another step. "You did? About what?"

"Monsters," he whispered. "Monsters who want to eat me."

"You're awake now. And if there are monsters here, I won't let them hurt you."

"You won't?"

I shook my head. "Never."

"You promise?"

"Yeah, Tony. I promise." I was almost to him. One more step and I could reach out and touch him. I still couldn't smell him. I couldn't smell *anything* other than the sour road sweat of the group of people I'd come with.

He looked up at me with wide, wet eyes. "You left."

"I know."

"You left," he repeated, his voice taking on a strange lilt. It was almost like a song. "You left. You left. You left. You *left*. You. *Left*. You. *Left. You*—"

He tilted his head back and screamed.

I rushed forward even as Ox shouted for me to stop.

I scooped Tony up in my arms. He didn't struggle, only continued to scream. It tore from his throat, and I didn't know how someone so small could make such a terrible sound. His claws dug into me, and

I grunted as they pierced my skin, blood welling, the sharp coppery tang shocking in the void. He stopped screaming immediately, sitting back in my arms, wrapping his legs around my waist. He stared down at my arms, where blood was spilling.

He grunted.

Ox said, "Robbie, put him down. Now."

Tony bent over, almost in *half*, and I felt the wet slide of his tongue against my skin, lapping up the blood from the wounds that had already healed. He grunted and snorted as he sucked it down his throat, and I let out a cry of revulsion. I pulled my arms away, meaning to drop him, but he tightened his legs around me and looked up, eyes glowing, a bright smear of blood on his lips. His tongue flicked out, chasing it, coated red. He grunted again before he inhaled deeply, fangs snapping together, jaw clicking.

Kelly was behind me, shouting at Tony to let me go, to get the fuck off me. Tony reached up, digging his claws into my shoulder, glaring at Kelly and hissing.

Kelly took a stumbling step back. "What the fuck is wrong with him?"

"He's feral," Aileen said. "Oh my god, he's *feral*—"

"Holy shit," one of the wolves breathed. "Look."

I turned, still trying to hold Tony back, following the wolf's shaking hand as he pointed above us.

There, standing on top of the buildings, were children.

Many, many children.

The wolves and witches tried to scatter as one vaulted over the edge of the movie theater, claws extending from her hands and feet. She landed on a witch, the man who'd helped Aileen, Patrice, and Gordo shore up my mind. He screamed when she dug her claws into the flesh of his face. Rico pulled out his gun, but before he could raise it, magic began to gather around the witch. He screamed as the girl sliced through his face again and again, spinning around. There was a sharp crack as a flash of light burst from his hand. It struck Ox's truck on the passenger side, causing the frame to crumple, the metal shrieking as the truck flipped over with a jarring crash, the windows blowing out, shards of glass flying out and refracting the morning sunlight.

The witch fell, but the little girl never stopped. Her hands rose and fell, rose and fell, feet kicking into the soft flesh of his stomach. She snapped her head up, her face dripping with blood as she snarled at two wolves who were rushing toward her.

The other children followed, jumping off the buildings, raining down around us with claws and fangs, their eyes all violet.

I jumped away from the sidewalk, Tony still holding on to me. Wolves around me shifted, clothing tearing as muscle and bone tore and broke. The timber wolf knocked Carter out of the way before a child could land on his back. The wolf yelped as the boy, who couldn't have been more than six or seven, lowered his head, burying his teeth into Gavin's neck. He bent forward, trying to knock the kid off him. I recognized the child. His name was Ben. His mother was a sweet and quiet Beta who lived in the compound. Ben fell off the wolf, landing on his back on the ground, blinking up toward the sky, body twitching.

Ox's eyes blazed in shades of violet and red, and he *roared*, the sound shaking the ground beneath our feet. The Omegas with us whimpered.

The children did not.

They didn't stop.

"Do I shoot them?" Rico shrieked. "Oh my god, do I *shoot them*?"

"They're fucking *kids*," Jessie snapped at him. She ducked, her crowbar trailing along the ground as another boy sailed over her, landed roughly on the ground, and rolled along the pavement. The boy was up and moving even before he came to a stop, bits of gravel stuck into his arms as he rushed Jessie again.

A great black wolf landed in front of her, eyes a mix of red and violet. He roared at the boy so loudly that one of the windows in the movie theater shook and cracked. The boy skidded on the road, feet tearing and leaving bloody streaks behind him. He jerked back, mouth hung open.

Aileen stepped forward, reaching into a pouch that hung on her hip. She pulled out a bluish powder and muttered into it. It flared like gunpowder, and she threw it at the boy, sparks dropping onto the ground with a hiss. The boy screamed as the powder struck him in the face, and he bent over, trying to wipe it away, tears streaming down his cheeks.

I shoved Tony off me and he landed on the road, my blood still dripping from his mouth. He glared up at me, feral and pissed off. He came for me again, loping on his hands and feet, but jerked back when a sharp crack of gunfire exploded around us and a divot appeared in the pavement in front of him.

"Don't make me shoot you," Kelly said, finger tightening on the trigger again. "Please."

Tony growled at him, muscles coiling in his legs as he prepared to jump, but he stiffened before I could step between him and Kelly. His back arched like he was having a seizure, the cords in his neck sticking out.

It was happening to all of the children. Every single one of them stood as Tony did, like they were being electrocuted. The wolves growled as we regrouped, unsure of what the hell was happening. I saw the witch who'd been hit first lying on the sidewalk, eyes open and unseeing. His chest didn't rise.

"What's happening to them?" Rico whispered.

"I don't know," Gordo said, panting. There was blood on his face, but I couldn't see where it'd come from. I didn't think it was his. "It's like they're— Look *out!*"

But his warning was for nothing.

The children moved as one, but they didn't come for us. They took off across the road, heading east toward a line of trees that led to the top end of the Aroostook National Wildlife Refuge. If they were returning to the compound, they'd cut north once they hit the trees. They didn't stop once they disappeared into the forest.

"Jesus *Christ*," Rico said, sounding breathless. "What the fuck was *that*?"

Ox's face was twisted as he shifted back. "They ... they didn't hear me. They—"

"Livingstone's stronger," Aileen said, crouching down next to the dead witch. "His magic is deeper. He knows we're here." She shook her head as she reached up and closed the witch's eyes. Elizabeth paced around them, growling low in her throat. Carter was licking at the blood on the timber wolf's back. Aileen stood slowly, hands curled into fists. "Alphas, if we're going to do this, we have to do it now."

Joe tilted his head back and howled. Ox shifted to a great black wolf once more, joining in with his mate. The other wolves sang with them.

Kelly grinned at me, crazed and beautiful. He said, "Shift. Lead us."
"You stay with me. You stay by my side."
"Always."
He kissed me then, and I tasted blood.
I called on my wolf.
My skin rippled.
I was angry.
So fucking angry.
My clothing shredded and I—
breathe
just breathe
ox
alpha
kelly
mate
i am wolf
i am pack
i am bennett
sing
sing this song of war

I was above myself, like I was floating and attached by a tether, my wolf holding on to me tightly. I led the way through the reserve, ignoring the familiar sights and scents of the refuge. The others followed closely behind, the humans and witches running at our sides. Kelly was there, always there, the scents of grass and lake water and sunshine filling my lungs with every breath. I was stronger because of his presence, his need to hunt combining with my own.

There was a twist of green shooting through me, the sweet power of relief as my Alphas followed me, trusting me to lead the way. I could hear the faint voice of Ox in my head, louder than it'd ever been, saying *go go go PackBrotherLoveFriend show me show me.*

The trees should have thinned as we got closer to the compound. The trees should have fallen away. Instead the forest grew *thicker*, the brambles and underbrush overgrown and wild like they hadn't been just a few months before. I was going to ignore it, hell-bent on getting to the compound, but I was shocked out of my shift when a recognizable scent filled my nose.

Kelly nearly tripped over me but managed to stay upright. "What are you doing?"

I couldn't answer.

The other wolves stopped. Ox tilted his head, asking a question without making a sound.

I ignored him.

I took a step toward a tree I didn't recognize. It looked like it was rotting, its trunk black and leaking sap like blood.

Some of the other wolves shifted behind me, demanding to know why we'd stopped, what the hell I thought I was doing.

I pressed my hand against the tree trunk, my palm immediately coated with a viscous fluid. I recoiled as the trunk seemed to *breathe*, the wood expanding and contracting, the bark split.

"What is this?" I whispered. I inhaled again, and I swore it smelled like Sonari, the teacher from the compound. The one who'd once tried to court me with the carcass of a bear.

Patrice said, "Robbie, *don't*," but I didn't listen.

I tore at the tree, digging into the bark. It peeled away like flesh and muscle. Each piece I pulled off snapped wetly. Sap leaked in thick streams. I was about to dig further when the stream of sap parted and a finger stuck out from the tree.

"No," Aileen whispered.

I stared as the finger twitched as if beckoning me. I heard Jessie say there were others, that *all* of these trees looked like they were breathing, but I couldn't look away. I reached up above the finger and broke off another large section of tree bark. The tree bled, and through its lifeblood, a face appeared, the mouth opening and closing soundlessly, lips coated in sap, eyes blinking.

Sonari.

She was *in* the tree.

I cried out as I stumbled backward. Kelly caught me around my bare waist, saying, "Robbie, Robbie, Robbie, listen to me, *listen* to me," but all I could see was Sonari, her finger jerking, her mouth opening and closing over and over and over.

Gordo pushed by us, tattoos flaring brightly. Mark was there too, still a wolf, pressed against his side. The raven on Gordo's arm looked like it was screaming, the roses closing into tight red buds, vines and thorns twisting.

"Is she alive?" Jessie asked, voice shaking. "Are they all alive?"

I looked around at the sound of her voice. There were dozens of similar trees, their branches leafless and dark, their trunks groaning. The sound reminded me of when Kelly was sick, that wet *thickness* in his chest. The trees stretched out ahead of us toward the compound, though I couldn't see the walls, given how many there were.

"I think so," Gordo said. He sounded grim. "I've never seen anything like this."

Patrice stepped forward, palms together in front of his chest. He turned them until his fingers pointed in opposite directions toward his elbows. He dragged his hands apart, a brief moment where his fingertips touched before they parted. There was a beat of nothing, and then his skin seemed to glow preternaturally, the spots of rust that covered his face standing out in sharp relief.

The trees moaned, Sonari's most of all. Their branches shook, sounding like the rattling of bleach-white bone. Sonari's tongue stuck out from her mouth, sap dripping off the tip. Patrice caught it before it hit the ground and rubbed it between his fingers. He brought it to his face and inhaled deeply.

"Dere alive," he said quietly as he wiped his fingers on his jeans. "He's contained dem. Trapped dem here."

"Can you help them?" Jessie asked. Chris and Tanner, still shifted, pressed against her sides.

Patrice shook his head. "Not now. Take more time den we have, if I could even do it at all. Dis is deep magic. Deeper den I ever seen. Dis is black. All black. If we remove dem, we might kill dem."

Gordo looked like he was going to touch Sonari's face, but Mark took his shirt in his jaws, pulling him back. Gordo barely put up a fight, still looking at Sonari. "He did this," Gordo whispered. "He did this."

Ox went to him as a human, stepping carefully in front of him. "Gordo."

"Ox," Gordo said in a fractured voice.

Ox nodded. "I know. And we'll fix it. All of it. But we have to finish this first. Focus. I need all of you. Can you do that?"

For a moment I thought Gordo was in shock, but he closed his eyes, taking a deep breath. When he opened them again, they were clear. "Yeah. I can do that."

"Good," Ox said. He looked at me. "You with me?"

I tore my gaze away from Sonari, whose tongue still hung from her open mouth, dripping sap. "Yes."

"Are we almost there?"

"Yes."

"Show us."

I pushed through the trees, Ox's voice in my head a low and constant thrum.

I knew them, these trees. Those encased inside. I could feel them. There were no children, though that knowledge didn't bring any relief. It only meant they were inside the compound.

The air was thick and heavy. It rested on my chest, making it harder to breathe. I wanted to tear into the trees, to rip apart the bark and pull them out, but I knew that Livingstone would expect that. He *wanted* that. The wolves' blood would be on our hands.

It took longer than it should have to reach the compound, the trees getting thicker the closer we got. We had to push aside branches, and every time we touched the wood, there was a low, dark pulse from inside the tree, a moan, a quiet scream. They were *aware*.

I was devastated.

Kelly knew. He whispered, "We'll take care of them. I promise."

I wished I could believe him.

We reached the wall at the south end of the compound. The others gathered behind Ox, Joe, and me. Ox looked up, brow furrowed. "I know you told us about this, Robbie, but it's bigger than I thought it would be. Have these always been here?"

Elizabeth shifted, pulling herself to her full height. She stepped up between Ox and Joe, pressing a hand against the wall. "No. Thomas, he . . . always believed that this place should be open and free to anyone and everyone so long as they came in peace. He learned that from his father. This isn't like it was before. This is Michelle. Yet another thing she's taken from the wolves."

"Maybe it was Livingstone," I said before I could stop myself. "Maybe she didn't have any other choice. Maybe she—" I closed my mouth, almost biting my tongue.

"We can't take that chance," Joe said quietly. "If she's here, if she's with him, then she has to be dealt with. We don't have a choice. You heard what he said. That she was the one who let him out."

"Yeah," I muttered. "But he lies about everything. He could be controlling her just like he did to me."

"I dunno," Rico said. "I'm all for shooting first and asking questions later. Seems safer that way." He grimaced. "Except for the kids. Fuck him for using kids."

Ox looked up at the top of the wall again. He raised his voice so all could hear him. "We don't kill the children. No matter what. Subdue them. Contain them. Use force if necessary. But keep them alive at all costs."

Kelly sighed. "This is such a clusterfuck." Carter nosed at his hand, and Kelly rubbed the top of his head between his ears.

"How do we get inside?" Jessie asked. "March through the front gate?" She looked at me. "Unless you know of another way inside."

I shook my head. "Two entrances, one in the front and back. They'll know."

"He already does," Gordo said. "He knows we're here."

"We go up and over," Ox said.

Rico groaned. "I knew you were going to say that. And I should point out the walls are concrete and at least fifteen feet high. Some of us are human." Then, "Oh god, you have an idea I won't like, don't you?"

"Chris," Ox said, "you've got Rico. Kelly, you're with Robbie. Elizabeth, Jessie. Gordo, Mark. Patrice and Aileen, with me and Joe. Tanner, Carter, bring up the rear. Gavin, you stay with Carter." He turned to look at all of us, this group of wolves and witches and humans who all knew full well what we were about to walk into. "Stick to the plan like we discussed. Spread out. Smaller groups. You leave Livingstone to the Alphas and Gordo."

Chris pulled out of his full shift to a half-shift. He grinned at Rico through a mouthful of fangs. "Climb on, buddy."

"I hate all of you," Rico mumbled. "So, so much. I'm a man in my forties. I should *not* be getting a piggyback ride from my naked friend." But he moved toward Chris.

"Ready?" I asked Kelly.

He nodded.

I reached out and touched his cheek, fingers trailing to his jaw. He turned his face and kissed my palm. His eyes were bright, and I knew that if this was it, if this was the last moment we'd ever have together, I was loved.

"Now," Ox growled. "Move now. It's time to finish this once and for all."

Kelly jumped on my back, arms around my neck, knees digging into my hips. His breaths were light and quick in my ear. I half-shifted, claws sprouting from my fingers and the tips of my toes.

Kelly whispered, "Pack. Pack. Pack."

We leapt toward the wall. Ox and I hit it first, our claws digging into the stone with loud cracks.

We began to climb, muscles straining as we pulled ourselves quickly up the side. The others followed, and by the time I reached the top, everyone was moving.

The sight of the houses around the lake caused my heart to twist. For a moment I thought nothing had changed—that it looked like it always did, an idyllic scene of houses surrounding a lake.

But it was a lie.

Even as I pulled Kelly and me over the top of the wall, I could see the signs of battle. One of the houses had been burned to its foundation. Whatever had happened to it hadn't spread to the other houses, though they hadn't made it out unscathed. Windows were broken. The porch of one house had been destroyed. Doors hung off their hinges as if they'd been kicked in.

I jumped from the top of the wall, the air whistling around us as we hurtled toward the ground. Kelly grunted in my ear as I landed in a crouch. He slid off my back, wobbling a little before shaking his head.

"Good?"

"Yeah. Good."

The others landed around us.

I was ready to follow through with Ox's orders, to spread out and see what we could see, when Rico said, "Where is everyone?"

All of us stopped. The wolves tilted their heads, listening for any movement.

There was none.

"Maybe they've gone," one of the Omegas said, eyes flashing. "Run away."

A child laughed, the sound carrying across the lake.

"Goddammit," Rico said. "This is why I never want kids. They cost too much money and also can be taken over by a dick of a witch and turned into killing machines. Fuck kids. Fuck them all."

"Layout the same?" Joe asked me.

"Yeah. As far as I can tell."

"Go, then," Ox said, and I felt his power rolling through me as his eyes filled with that familiar swirl of red and violet. "Don't stop until it's over."

We went.

We spread out through the compound, breaking off into smaller groups. Kelly and Rico and Chris fell in behind me. Chris shifted back into full wolf, while I stayed half-shifted. I couldn't cut myself off from Kelly, needing him to be able to hear me. Rico and Chris were tuned in with the pack. Kelly wasn't. I couldn't stand the thought of him stumbling blind.

They stayed close as we moved between the houses. The quiet was eerie, the only real sound coming from the lake lapping on the rocky shore. Kelly stayed close, his hand grazing my bare back. He and Rico had pulled their guns, eyes narrowed and darting side to side.

The houses on either side of us were empty. The one to our left had holes in its side, ragged and small, and it took me a moment to recognize it for what it was. It looked like they'd been *chewed* open, leaving a space wide enough for a child to slip through.

Rico was right. Fuck kids.

"What the hell?" Rico whispered, looking around wildly. "This is some goddamn horror movie shit. I don't like this. I'm a minority. Everyone knows minorities die first in horror movies."

"No one's dying," Kelly snapped at him.

Not while I could help it.

We rounded the lake, making sure to keep enough distance between us and the water so we wouldn't be trapped if suddenly surrounded. I could see the others moving behind us and across the lake. Elizabeth and Jessie were quick, going from house to house, stopping only for Elizabeth to check to make sure each house was empty before moving on.

It took nearly ten minutes before we joined up again on the northeast side of the lake.

Elizabeth was staring up at the largest house, prowling before it, a low growl in her throat.

The wolves looked confused. The Omegas were shifting from side to side. The other Alphas were snarling quietly, lips pulled back over their fangs.

I knew why.

I felt her too.

I stepped toward the house. Kelly tried to stop me, but I shook him off as his brother and the timber wolf came to stand on either side of him.

"Michelle!" I shouted up at the house. "Come out now! You're surrounded!"

Nothing happened.

I balled my hands into fists. "You fucking come out!"

Still nothing. I was about to storm into the house and drag her out when Ox put his hand on my shoulder. I glared at him, but he was serene and calm, sending waves of it washing over me.

He squeezed my shoulder before dropping his hand. He turned to the house and raised his voice. "It's over, Alpha Hughes. Or at least it soon will be. This has gone on long enough. This can end peacefully. Surely even you want that. Your people have suffered enough. You are an Alpha, and an Alpha always puts their pack above all else."

I thought it wasn't going to work.

I thought she would ignore us.

Instead, the door opened.

Michelle Hughes stepped onto the porch.

She wore a long, flowing dress, the hem swirling around her bare feet. Her shadow stretched behind her in the morning sun. Her hair rested on her shoulders, and her eyes were red.

I felt a pull when she looked at me, quiet and soft. A whisper of what once was and would never be again. She frowned at all of us, taking us in. The porch creaked underneath her. Her mouth twisted at the sight of humans. At Carter and Mark, their eyes flashing violet. She glanced off toward the trees, a complicated expression crossing her face.

"Alphas," she said as she looked back at us. "You came."

"You knew we would," Joe told her.

"I did, little prince," she said. "I wouldn't expect anything less from the Bennett pack. Always sticking your noses in the business of others. You never learn from the past." She shook her head. "Thomas understood. He would never have—"

Carter managed to stop his mother as she rushed forward, teeth snapping, eyes ablaze. Michelle barely flinched as Elizabeth snarled at her, claws creating divots in the grass and dirt.

"I seem to have struck a nerve," Michelle said mildly. "My apologies. I never . . ." And for a moment her countenance split. She seemed lost. Confused. But then it was gone. She squared her shoulders, and regardless of what else she was, regardless of all she'd done, she was still an Alpha, and a powerful one at that.

The Alpha of all.

"Stand down," Ox said, voice even. "Stand down now and this can all be over."

"If only it were that easy," Michelle said. "You shouldn't have come here. You could have stayed in Green Creek and we would have—"

"Jesus *Christ*," Jessie said. "Lady, I don't know what kind of power trip you're on, but if you think we'd just let packs be destroyed, then you don't know the first thing about us."

Michelle cocked her head as Jessie glared defiantly. "Human. I never understood the attraction. What could you possibly bring to a pack of wolves? You're so . . . breakable."

"Yeah? Why don't you come down here and we'll see who's breakable." Jessie tilted her head side to side, popping her neck as she smacked the end of her crowbar against her hand. "I think you'll be surprised."

Michelle laughed bitterly. "I'm sure I will. You have a warrior's heart. I can see that. It won't be enough, but I see you. Jessie, isn't it? The schoolteacher. And Rico. The roughneck from the garage."

"Fuck you too, bitch," Rico growled.

Her gaze crawled dismissively over the rest of us until it fell upon Kelly. I stepped forward, but it wasn't enough. "And you. Kelly Bennett. This is because of you. You just couldn't let him go. You just couldn't let things be."

"You stole from me," Kelly said coldly. "And I'm going to make sure you never touch him again."

"Are you?" Michelle asked. "And just how are you going to do—"

Kelly moved, almost quicker than I could follow. He stepped

around me, raising his gun. A sharp crack of gunfire caused my ears to ring and my eyes to water.

Had it been anyone else, the headshot would have been true.

But he was dealing with an Alpha.

She jerked her head to the side and the silver bullet embedded itself in the door behind her.

The sound of the gun rolled over the lake and echoed throughout the compound.

Michelle's expression twisted, her face elongating. "You shouldn't have done that."

"*Behind you!*" Aileen cried.

I glanced over my shoulder.

There, standing on the path that led away from the Alpha's house, was a thin man.

He stood stiffly, as if all his muscles were tensing at once. His mouth hung open. A line of spittle fell from his bottom lip onto his chin. His eyes were completely white. He breathed, but it was harsh, chest heaving. He took a step toward us, but it was unnatural, his knees barely bending. He looked as if he were attached to unseen strings, like a puppet.

And I knew him.

Once he'd given me the truth, though I hadn't known it then.

You. Are. Wolf.

You. Are. Pack.

You. Are. Bennett.

"Dale," Gordo snarled. Mark roared as he stood next to his mate, tail curling around Gordo's waist.

Dale didn't respond. I wasn't even sure he *was* Dale anymore.

He raised his hands, fingers twitching.

"*Move!*" Patrice shouted.

There was a beat where nothing happened.

Then all hell broke loose.

Michelle leapt from the porch toward the Alphas, dress tearing as she shifted. Joe shoved Ox to the side, and Michelle landed on the ground where they'd been standing, the tatters of her dress falling off her back and onto the ground. Her wolf was larger than I remembered, rivaling Ox and Joe and the timber wolf. Her eyes were on fire.

Before she could move again, Elizabeth jumped onto her back, claws digging in. Her head moved viper-quick, and Michelle yelped when fangs sank into the back of her neck, Elizabeth's head jerking side to side.

Gordo shouted in warning as the ground underneath our feet began to break apart. I looked back in time to see bright colors swirling in front of Dale as magic gathered at his fingertips. His mouth was still open and his eyes were still white, but he fell to his knees, slamming his hands onto the ground.

There was a deep rumble as the ground split, columns of dirt and rock shooting up around us. The people around me cried out as some of them were knocked off their feet. Kelly raised his gun and fired again, this time aiming for Dale, but the bullet ricocheted off an unseen barrier in front of Dale with a sharp whine.

I grabbed Kelly by the hand and pulled him out of the way just as another column rose where he'd been standing, dirt and grass and rock showering down around us.

Then the children came.

They ran out from between the houses.

They fell from the rooftops.

A couple of them crawled from the lake, water dripping from their little bodies, eyes alight in Omega violet. They weren't shifted, but hair sprouted and receded along their faces, and their claws were wicked sharp, like little needles.

We broke apart, our group moving in opposite directions. I turned in time to see Michelle knock Elizabeth off her back, the wolf mother landing on the ground with a terrible crash. Joe and Ox both shifted, black and white, yin and yang, and charged Michelle.

Gordo's tattoos were as bright as I'd ever seen them as Mark charged Dale. For a moment, I thought he'd get there and tear out his throat, but Dale raised his head, eyes wide. Mark stopped in his tracks with a surprised whine before he rose off the ground, levitating a few feet in the air. His body contorted painfully before he slammed into the side of a house, the siding cracking before giving way.

"Oh," Gordo breathed, "you should not have done that."

I grabbed Kelly by the hand and pulled him away from the house as Rico followed us, gun raised. "Who do I shoot?" he was screaming. "*Who do I shoot?*"

I didn't know.

Rico couldn't shoot the children as they swarmed the wolves. Patrice cried out in pain when a little girl sank her claws into his leg. One of the Alphas lifted a child—a boy named Caden who'd smiled brightly whenever he'd seen me—and hurled him into the lake. He landed with a splash and breached the surface, sputtering, already moving back toward the shore.

Rico couldn't shoot Michelle, as she was tangled up in a drag-out fight with Joe and Ox, each of them moving in a blur, drawing blood. Joe's white fur was splashed with it. Michelle was savage in her attacks, going low, and Ox whined when her teeth closed around his right back leg and bit down.

Rico couldn't shoot Dale, as there was a barrier in front of him.

It was chaos.

The timber wolf was furious when a little girl landed on top of Carter, stabbing at the back of his neck. Gavin went for her, looking feral, but Carter snapped himself to the side. The girl fell off him and landed on the ground, slowly blinking up at the sky.

"We have to help them," Kelly panted, sweat dripping off his forehead. "We have to—"

There, standing near the back of the Michelle's house, was Tony.

Next to him was Brodie, the boy whose pack had been so cruelly taken from him.

They were holding hands, their eyes violet. Tony looked at me blankly. He didn't recognize me. Neither did Brodie.

I took a step toward them.

They turned and ran.

I chased after them.

"Robbie, *no!*" Kelly screamed as I shifted and hit the ground running as a

wolf
i am wolf
i am
pack
i am
bennett
cubs

little cubs
stop
hear me
listen
fight
you must fight this
you must stop
i will help you
i will save you
i

cried out as my shift was torn from me as I passed through a ward unlike anything else I'd ever felt. I hit the ground and rolled, a sharp rock cutting into my back. I felt it start to heal, though slower than normal.

I stood up in time to see Tony and Brodie disappear down a familiar road.

The sounds of battle came from behind me, but they seemed distant.

I took a step forward and—

A hand grabbed my arm, tugging me sharply.

I whirled around to see Kelly and Rico, looking scared. "What are you doing?" Kelly demanded.

"Tony. Brodie. They're *here*. And I know where they're going."

Rico looked beyond me down the dirt road. "Where?"

"To my old house. The one I shared with Ezra. With Livingstone." I jerked my arm out of Kelly's grasp. "We have to help them."

"Maybe we should—"

"We *promised*," I snarled at Rico. "We told Shannon we would help them."

"You're going where he wants you to," Kelly said quietly. "You have to know this. You have to know he's waiting."

I nodded. "I know. But we don't have a choice. We can't let him have them. We can't let him win."

"Shit," Rico groaned. He turned his face toward the sky and inhaled deeply. "Well. We were fucking crazy to come here in the first place. What's another bad decision or two?"

And then this man, this ridiculously wonderful human, howled at the sky, the cords in his neck standing out. It echoed in the forest around us, and there came the sound of answering howls from back in the compound.

"I've been practicing," Rico said with a shrug as we stared at him. "Pretty good, right? And fuck me, you're naked and we have guns and we're going to go face an evil witch. Let's do this thing."

He took off down the road.

There was a pulse of *something* in my chest, something I couldn't remember feeling before. A tug that almost seemed familiar.

And it was connected to Rico.

We followed him down the road.

* * *

The house stood no different than when I'd left it.

I ached at the sight of it.

We came to a stop a few yards away.

Brodie and Tony stood on the porch, hands still joined. They watched as we approached, growling low in their throats, heads cocked.

"Okay," Rico whispered, gun drawn. "Now what? They're trapped, right? I mean, we probably are too, but still."

I took a step toward the boys. "Tony."

There was no recognition there.

"You know him," Kelly said.

I nodded, never looking away from the boys.

"He doesn't know you. Not anymore."

"Tony," I said again, and the boy bared his fangs. "It's okay. It's me, Robbie. I'm here. I'm—"

"Would you hear me, dear?"

I fell to my knees, clutching my head as a terrible wave of magic assaulted me. It rolled over me, obliterating every thought I had. I screamed at the ground, struggling to stay in control even as my mind filled with a dense, heavy fog. It was calming. Soothing. I wanted nothing more than to let it take me away.

And then Kelly said, "Robbie, Robbie, *please*," and I gritted my teeth as his hand came down on my bare shoulder, covering the mark he'd put there with his fangs. The mark I didn't remember receiving.

The mark that meant *mate*.

I raised my head, the fog pulling at me with long tendrils.

"No," I managed to say in a guttural voice. "No. You can't. You *can't.*"

Livingstone stood on the porch behind the boys, his hands on the tops of their heads. "I think you'll find I can. And I will."

Rico and Kelly spun around me in a practiced move, guns raised. They opened fire at the house, and though their aim was spot-on, the bullets sparked against a barrier in front of Livingstone's face and ricocheted off into the porch.

Livingstone slowly shook his head. "All this bloodshed. And for what?"

"Yeah, I don't know if you're in any position to talk about bloodshed," Rico said as he reloaded. "You know, seeing everything you've done and all."

Livingstone looked at me, and his expression turned pleading. "I am giving you a chance, Robbie. To give me what I want. All of this could be avoided. Everything."

"You *stole* him," Kelly snarled, pointing the gun at Livingstone again, though it was useless. "You're never going to touch him again. Not while I still stand."

"I see that," Livingstone said. "Maybe you shouldn't be standing anymore, then."

I couldn't stop him.

I wasn't fast enough.

He raised his hand.

I reached for Kelly.

He was hurled off his feet as the air sparked and crackled around him. He flew across the dirt road and slammed into a tree. I heard the sharp crack of bone as his leg broke. He screamed, and I screamed with him as he fell to the ground at the base of the tree. He turned himself over and began to crawl toward me, leg dragging behind him.

"Such perseverance," Livingstone marveled. "I see what you found in him, Robbie. I understand now. Mates. It's a shame, really. Would you hear me, dear?"

I cried out again as the fog wrapped itself around my head.

"Fight it!" Kelly shouted. "Robbie, you fight it, goddammit!"

"He can't," Livingstone said. "I see what the witches have done to him. How they've locked him down. It's only a matter of time.

Robbie, dear, listen to me. Listen to my voice. There is a human next to you. He is a threat, much like your father was. Do you remember what your father did? This human will do the same. You can stop him."

I turned my head toward Rico.

Rico took a step back. He raised the gun toward me. "Robbie. Please. Don't make me do this."

I stood slowly.

Rico stumbled back even as Kelly tried to push himself up, screaming again in pain as his bad leg gave out. But it was a distant thing, a faraway thing, lost in the fog.

I growled at the man before me with a gun.

This human.

I took another step toward him.

The barrel of the gun shook.

"No," Kelly whispered. "Rico, *don't*—"

I slapped the gun out of Rico's hand before he could get off a shot. It landed on the ground, bouncing away from him. He raised his hands to ward me off.

It wouldn't stop me.

It wouldn't—

Kelly said, "I see you, you know?"

Kelly said, "I see you."

Kelly said, "And I will *never* let you go."

And I—

It was good between us. We took it slow. You smiled all the time. You brought me flowers once. Mom was pissed because you ripped them up from her flower bed and there were still roots and dirt hanging from the bottom, but you were so damn proud of yourself. You said it was romantic. And I believed you. There was something ... I don't know. Endless. About you and me. We came here sometimes. Just the two of us. And you would pretend to know all the stars. You would make up stories that absolutely weren't true, and I remember looking at you, thinking how wonderful it was to be by your side. And if we were lucky, there'd be—ah. Look. Again.

"Fireflies," I whispered.

"What was that?" Livingstone asked, his voice a whipcrack of warning.

"Fireflies," I said again, louder, as the fog burned away. "It's all fireflies and—"

Time slowed around me.

I tilted my head toward the sky.

She whispered, *Little wolf, little wolf, can't you see? You are the master of the forest, the guardian of the trees.*

Quiet as a mouse no longer.

It started in my chest. This great bloom of fire.

It consumed me, and I *burned* with it as these strings so much like tethers exploded out from me. They struck Rico first, and I heard *lobito lobito lobito*, and then they moved on to Kelly, and it was *i love you i love you i love you*, and it went on and on and on until there were Jessie and Elizabeth, Chris and Tanner, Gordo and Mark, Carter and the timber wolf, faint though it was, and then, oh, *and then* it was the Alphas, their voices bright and strong, and I heard them all. I heard them all when they sang *BrotherLoveFriendMatePack we see you we feel you we will never let you go because we're packpackpack and pack is love pack is home pack is—*

"Pack is everything," I said.

"What is this?" Livingstone demanded. "What have you done?"

I looked at him, the bonds of my pack writhing within me, giving me strength. I'd never felt so alive. So vital. So present, here, in this moment. I took a step toward Livingstone. "I don't need you. I don't love you. You can't control me. Not anymore."

He said, "Would you hear me, dear?" but it was such a *small* thing, such a *negligible* thing when it plucked against the strings so vibrant and fibrous.

And I said, "*No.*"

He narrowed his eyes. "So be it. Remember, when all you love is gone, I gave you a chance."

He shoved the boys forward.

Tony and Brodie ran, claws raised.

I took a breath and braced for impact.

And I was hit, but not from where I expected.

I fell to the side when Rico crashed into me.

I stumbled. I would remember that always.

I turned in time to see Brodie sink his claws into Rico's chest again and again and again.

Blood spilled as Rico said, "Oh. Oh. Oh."

The claws raked down into his stomach.

Birds took flight from the trees.

Kelly said, "No. Oh god, no."

Tony hit Rico, who took a step back, somehow managing to stay standing. Tony climbed onto his back, knees hooked around his waist, and he raised his claws to sink them into the back of Rico's neck.

Rico looked at me. He grinned. His teeth were bloody. He said, "Worth it. All of this. You. Them. I—"

Tony brought his claws down.

Rico grunted and fell to his knees.

The boys jumped off him and landed on their feet, hissing as they backed away, covered in Rico's blood.

I caught him before he fell.

His eyes were open and glassy. His breath was ragged in the ruins of his chest. His blood smeared onto my skin, and I couldn't stop the bleeding, I couldn't make it stop.

"Rico, Rico," I chanted. "Look at me, stay with me, *stay with me*."

Livingstone stepped off the porch. Tony and Brodie huddled at his sides, burying their faces in his stomach.

I looked up at him, eyes wet. "Why?"

Livingstone said, "Because it's the only way."

He raised his hand, and his tattoos flared to life.

I tilted my head back and howled a song of horror, needing our pack to hear me, needing them to know all we had lost. It echoed in the forest around us, and in the distance I heard an answering roar that sounded like a scream.

Magic wrapped itself around us, and I held Rico close to my chest. I whispered, "I've got you. I've got you. I've got you."

We were lifted up off the ground. I couldn't fight it.

"I thought I could be enough for you," Livingstone said. "I really thought I could. I should have known that the wolves would never let you go."

And then we were flung up and *over* Livingstone, and the moment before we crashed into the house, causing it to collapse around us, I heard Kelly cry out my name, and I had a second to think that at least it would be quick for him, and we would enter the clearing together, and we would run and run and run under a full moon and nothing, *no one* would hurt us ever again.

It felt like a kiss before dying.

Rico and I smashed into the house and it all went dark.

· · ·

I wasn't unconscious very long.

I opened my eyes, dust and shards of wood falling on my face.

I was confused, unsure of where I was and what had happened. I hurt all over.

I groaned as I tried to sit up. I didn't make it very far.

A large beam lay on my chest. Bones were broken, and when I coughed, it felt like I was drowning.

The remains of the house surrounded me. A second beam above me, sticking up at an angle, created a small pocket, holding up the debris, though it creaked dangerously as I tried to free myself.

I laid my head back down. I was tired.

"Hey."

I turned my head.

Rico lay a few feet away, bloodied, body at an awkward angle like he too had been broken. He blinked slowly at me. His eyes were red, and for a moment I thought he was an Alpha. And then it dripped down his cheeks.

He smiled. "Sucks, huh? Got our asses kicked." His voice was low and rough, words exploding from him with each quick exhalation.

"Rico."

"Little wolf," he whispered. "Legs. Can't feel them."

I roared in anger, trying to push the beam off me again. The house shifted once more, and more wood fell around us.

"Wouldn't do that if I were you," Rico grunted. "Bring it all down. Smash us like bugs."

"I'm going to save you," I promised him. "I'm going to get us out of here."

"Yeah. Sure."

I looked around, trying to find something, *anything* that would help me. Help us.

There was nothing.

"It's okay," Rico said. His breaths were easier, and he had a vacant look in his eyes I didn't like. "I . . . I always knew this could happen."

"Rico, listen to me. We're going to get out of here. We're going to get out of here. We're going to go home."

"Home," he whispered. He coughed, and a bubble of blood burst from his mouth. "Bambi's going to kick my ass."

"*Yes*. Yes, she is. And I'm going to fucking *laugh* at you when she does."

"I love you, you know."

Tears fell from my eyes. "I love you too."

He nodded. "It's good. To be with someone who feels the same way. At the end. I always . . . I never wanted to be alone. It was my biggest fear. And look." He smiled. "I'm not alone."

"Rico. *Rico*."

His chest rose and fell. Rose and fell. Rose and fell.

I waited for it to rise again.

It didn't.

He stared at me, unseeing.

I howled. As loud as I ever had before.

The house shifted above me.

I—

I can't wait to meet you.

But I hope you understand that I'll be fine with waiting on that meeting for as long as possible. Because when he gives you his heart, it will no longer be mine to hold. And I want to hold on to it for as long as I'm able.

Whoever you are, you are loved.

Never doubt that.

You are loved.

A white wolf was with us. Not pure white, though. He had a smattering of black on his chest. His back. He lay down next to me, his massive head near my face. His eyes were red, and when he pressed his nose against my forehead, I said, "*Oh*."

The pack bonds within me stretched tight, and I searched through all of them, finding Jessie and Chris and Kelly and Carter and Gavin and Tanner and Gordo and Mark and Joe and Ox, and there, there there there, faint and breaking, was Rico.

I grasped on to it, holding it tight, pulling it into my chest, wrapping it around my heart.

The Alpha huffed in my face.

And he said, *packpackpack pack is hope pack is family pack is love you are my pack you are my hope you are my family and i love you i love you i love—*

I screamed as I pushed on the beam with the last of my strength. It shifted easily, almost torn from my grasp.

The white wolf was gone.

Above me, the sun shining behind him, was Oxnard Matheson, eyes blazing red and violet.

He said, "I've got you."

I believed him.

He lifted the beam above his head and threw it off behind him. I heard it crash on the ground somewhere in the distance. I took in a gasping breath, the bonds of the pack shining brightly.

I rolled to my side, spitting out a thick wad of blood. "Rico," I managed to say. "You gotta help Rico."

He nodded, moving toward our brother.

I pushed myself up off the ground as my bones began to knit back together. I groaned as my ribs snapped back into place. "He's—is he—"

Ox brushed a bloody lock of Rico's hair off his face. "I can't lose you. I won't."

Ox tilted his head back, neck popping as his face elongated. His fangs dropped, reflecting the morning sunlight.

And then his head snapped forward, fangs sinking into Rico's shoulder.

The bite of an Alpha.

And as Rico's shoulder *crunched*, I heard Ox in my head saying *you are pack you are brother you are mine.*

you

are

wolf

At first nothing happened, and I thought we were too late.

Ox pulled away.

Rico's bond, his tenuous string, faded.

"No," I whispered. "No, no, *no—*"

The string vibrated as if plucked.

Again.

And again.

And again.

Rico jerked as Ox held on to him. His mouth fell open as he began to seize, feet kicking out, causing motes of dust to rise and catch the sunlight.

Rico's dark eyes snapped open.

The blood in the whites of his eyes receded.

And then, there, in this house, in this place so far from home, came the bright flash of orange.

BEAST

"Kelly," I said.

Ox nodded. "Led Robert away. Gave me time to get to you."

"Is he all right?" I was frantic, trying to parse through the bonds, but they were all so loud and bright that I couldn't focus.

"No. None of us are. It's time to end this."

"Oh, fuck *me*."

We turned.

Rico was bent over, hands on his knees, hair hanging down around his face. He was covered in blood, but the wounds were closed. He lifted his head, nostrils flaring, eyes shining. "Is this what it's always going to be like?" he demanded. "I can hear everything. I can *smell* everything. And *lobito*, I have to say, you do *not* smell good to me right now." He stood upright with a grimace, hands going to his lower back.

"You get used to it," Ox said.

"*How?*"

"We don't have *time* for this," I snapped at them. "We have to get to the others before—"

"Yeah, yeah," Rico muttered. He raised a hand in front of his face. "How do I make my claws come out?" He flexed his fingers. Nothing happened. "Huh. That's disappointing. When this is all over and we're regaling everyone with stories of our victory, we're going to say that I made my claws come out right away. Deal?"

"Deal," Ox said. He looked down the road. Above the trees in the distance, a thick black column of smoke was rising. "We have to hurry."

I began to run down the road. A black wolf appeared at my side, eyes red and violet. I looked over in surprise to see Rico running *past* me, moving faster than I expected. His eyes were wide when he looked back at me. "How the fuck am I moving so fast?" he yelled. "What kind of nonsense *is* this?"

We ran on.

We hadn't been gone very long.

Fifteen, twenty minutes at most.

But the compound was changed as if a lifetime had passed. Some of the houses were on fire. A couple of others had been razed to their foundations.

Elizabeth and Jessie were locked in battle with Michelle Hughes near the Alpha House. Elizabeth had a large gash on her side, but she wasn't letting it slow her down. Michelle was snarling, tail twitching, jaws snapping. Elizabeth crouched like she was going to attack. Instead, Jessie ran up behind her, jumped *onto* her back, and ran three steps along her spine before leaping toward Michelle, crowbar raised above her head. Michelle moved to the right, but she was too slow, and Jessie brought the crowbar down on Michelle's side, the silver burning the Alpha's skin. Michelle whined and tried to bite Jessie, but she was too quick, landing and rolling away before getting to her feet again. She saw us, eyes widening, before turning back toward Michelle.

Gordo's tattoos glowed as bright as the sun. He scraped his fingernails down his right arm, drawing blood over the raven and roses. He flung it at Dale, who stood on the beach near the water. The blood hit Dale in the face and began to sizzle, Dale's skin peeling back. Dale didn't seem to notice, and from behind him a large boulder rose out of the lake. Mark tackled Gordo just as Dale *hurled* the boulder at them. It smashed into the ground where Gordo had been standing. Even before Gordo stopped rolling, Mark was up and moving, eyes violet as he charged toward Dale. I thought he was going to make it, going to tear his fucking head off, when Dale's fingers twitched. The ground underneath Mark's paws seemed to *bend* upward before it exploded in a grinding flash of dirt and rock. Mark was thrown to the side, yelping as he landed wrong, his front right leg breaking. My stomach twisted as I saw the shiny wet knob of bone jutting out at the knee.

The sky above seemed to grow dark as Gordo rose to his feet. He reached up with his only hand and wiped the blood from his mouth, flicking it to the ground.

He said, "You shouldn't have put your hands on my mate."

The raven spread its wings.

The roses bloomed.

Gordo slammed the stump of his arm into the ground. Thick vines burst from the earth, wrapping around Dale's arms and legs, black thorns piercing his skin. Wild roses bloomed along the vines as they lifted Dale into the air. He didn't struggle, the same blank look on his face. Gordo grunted, twisting his stump in the dirt, and the vines flung Dale into the lake. He landed with a large splash a few yards offshore.

Gordo was already running toward the water. Without slowing, he stepped up onto the writhing vines, which flung him into the air above the lake. For a moment, he hung suspended above the water, above Dale, who breached the surface. And then Gordo was falling.

"Gordo!" Rico screamed.

But Gordo didn't hit the water.

There was a terrifying *snap* as the temperature seemed to drop a hundred degrees in a single instant. One moment Dale was floundering in the water, head sinking below the surface, and the next the entire fucking lake turned to ice.

Gordo landed roughly on the ice, limbs flinging out in different directions as he slid along the surface.

He came to a stop near Dale's hand, which was the only visible part of him. Gordo pushed himself to his feet before he spat down at the hand. He turned toward us. He started to grin, but then his face twisted. "Look *out!*"

We whirled in time to see Michelle hurtling toward us. Elizabeth was struggling to rise to her feet with Jessie's help.

Michelle didn't slow, and she only had eyes for me.

She jumped.

And then Ox was there in front of me, half-shifted, catching her by the throat. She grunted as her legs flew forward with the momentum. Ox brought her face close to his, roaring the call of an Alpha. He didn't wait for a response, instead flinging her back where she'd come from.

Elizabeth and Jessie ducked as Michelle flew over them and crashed into her house. The porch shuddered and collapsed as Michelle hit the doorway. The door cracked under her weight before it was torn off its hinges. Michelle landed inside the house and didn't move.

"Where's Kelly?" I shouted at Gordo.

Before he could respond, I heard Tanner's furious howl from the other side of the lake.

I ran toward him, Rico bellowing after me.

Nothing else mattered but getting to Kelly.

I flew past Aileen and Patrice. They had a group of feral children in front of them. The kids were snapping their teeth, trying to get at the witches but unable to get past the barrier Aileen and Patrice had created.

I saw dead wolves, at least three that had come with us. One of them had been an Alpha, and one of his Betas looked up at me, confusion mingled with fear on his face, eyes suddenly flashing red.

I ignored it.

There wasn't time.

I felt my pack behind me as I ran.

What I found made me stop cold, my breath catching in my chest.

The earth on the south end of the lake was scorched, blackened and cracked.

Tanner stood above Chris, who lay panting on the ground, ribs exposed from a deep cut on his side.

The timber wolf—Gavin—was snarling, sounding angrier than I'd ever heard him.

Robert Livingstone was dragging Carter and Kelly toward us by their hair. He looked no worse for wear. Kelly was struggling weakly. Carter's eyes were closed, body looking as if it'd suffered a repeated assault. His face was bruised heavily along his jaw, eyes swollen. He wasn't healing.

"This," Livingstone said. "This is what you've done. This is what you've brought upon yourselves. Do you think I *want* this? Do you think this is *necessary*? All I asked, all I *ever* asked for is what was mine, what was owed to me. And you refused. All of you refused, and it has come to this. How dare you."

"Let them go," I snarled, Gavin at my side.

To my surprise, he did. Kelly and Carter fell to the ground. Carter groaned as Kelly tried to raise himself up. He looked at me, face ashen. He was bleeding from a cut on his forehead, and it ran in rivulets down his face.

Livingstone stood between them. Instead of angry, he looked *weary*, like he was exhausted. There were shadows under his eyes, his pupils blown out. He raised a hand toward us. "Gavin," he said, voice soft, "I can fix this. I can make it all go away. Come with me. Let us leave this place behind." He looked down at the brothers at his feet, then back up at us. His gaze trailed behind us to Tanner and Chris, to the rest of the pack coming at a run. He sighed as he shook his head. "Wolves. With them is only death. Suffering. I know. I *know*. They turned Gordo against me. They poisoned my wife, filling her head with falsehoods. They drove her to take my tether from me, and then, when all was lost, they tried to contain me. They took my magic from me. They *ripped* me in half like it was *nothing*. Abel Bennett. Thomas Bennett." His lip curled. "The princeling. The human Alpha who cannot stay out of my *goddamn way*."

My pack gathered around me, wild and strong. Ox and Joe stood on either side of me, their anger boiling over through the pack bonds between us.

"This is *over*," Gordo growled. "The children are contained. Dale is dead. You have nothing left. You've *lost*. Let them go."

Livingstone turned his face toward the sky. He took a deep breath, let it out slow. "So it would seem. But that's the thing about appearances, my son. They can be an illusion."

"My grandfather chose to spare your life," Joe said, shoulders squared. "He knew what you'd gone through. What had happened. He showed you mercy."

Livingstone laughed bitterly. "And where did that get him? He's nothing but dust. Like the pack that once was. Like Thomas."

Elizabeth shifted. "You don't deserve to speak his name."

Livingstone nodded. "You think you've won. And I can see why. But you are sadly mistaken. Gavin. Don't make me do this."

Gavin took an uncertain step forward.

Carter groaned as he raised his head. "Don't," he managed to say. "Gavin, he's . . . lying. Don't . . . listen . . ."

And Gavin stopped.

Cocked his head, ears pricking.

Livingstone narrowed his eyes. "What's this?"

"He's with us," Ox said. "He's pack."

"Pack," Livingstone spat. "*Pack*. Fine. Remember, this is on you." He looked down at Carter. "You made me do this."

He raised his hand toward us, tattoos bursting brightly.

A wave of magic bowled over us in a great storm, rocking us off our feet. We landed roughly on the ground as it continued to push against us. It tore at our skin. Jessie tried to pick herself up but was thrown back toward Tanner and Chris.

Ox gritted his teeth as he pushed himself up, fighting against the rising winds. Joe rose behind him, pressing against his back, pushing them both forward. Mark curled around Gordo to keep him from flying back. Rico held on to my leg as I dug my fingers into the earth.

Livingstone reached down and grabbed Carter by the hair again, pulling him up as if he weighed nothing. Carter was too weak to fight him off. Kelly struck at Livingstone's legs, but it did nothing.

Above the raging winds, I heard Livingstone say, "I am sorry for this, child. But this is the price you must pay for all that your family has done to mine. Your sacrifice will not be forgotten."

The markings on his arm began to move, and Carter screamed, body jerking as if electrified. The tattoos crawled up Livingstone's arm, and they were dark, the magic black and wicked.

Elizabeth cried out for her son as the tattoos hit Livingstone's hand and moved toward Carter's open mouth.

Something shot past me, quicker than I could follow.

Carter fell to the ground as the storm ceased.

I blinked slowly.

Livingstone kicked as he was raised into the air, a large hand covering his face, claws cutting into his skin.

A man stood before him, the white and gray and brown hair of a timber wolf receding from his neck and shoulders as he shifted toward human. He was almost as tall as Kelly, his dark hair long and ragged as it fell on his shoulders. The thin muscles in his arms and legs quivered. His face was twisted in fury. It took me a moment to realize what—*who*—this was. He looked like the man he held writhing in his grasp, like the witch lying on the ground next to me, albeit a younger version.

Gavin snarled, "Don't. Touch. *Him.*"

And then he threw his father as hard as he could. Livingstone flew backward, and the moment before he struck the remains of a smoldering house behind him, I saw the look on his face.

Betrayal.

He hit the house, sparks and flames rising up as the house collapsed.

Impossibly, *ridiculously*, Carter whispered through a mouthful of blood, "Oh shit. I think I'm bisexual."

Before anyone could react to *that*, or this new wolf-turned-human who had saved us all, the remains of the house Livingstone had crashed through exploded, debris whipping out around us.

Gavin fell on top of Carter and Kelly, shielding them from the blast.

Livingstone rose from the fire.

"You've taken them from me," he said, stepping back out onto the ground. "Gordo. Robbie. Gavin. All now with the Bennetts. Everything that was mine, you've *taken from me!*" He raised his hands toward us, the storm beginning to build again.

I looked to Kelly, wanting the last thing I saw in this world to be his face.

lovelovelove, he whispered to me, *my heartsong*.

Livingstone took a lurching step forward as a wolf reared up behind him, claws digging into his neck and back, eyes burning red.

Michelle Hughes.

She opened her mouth wide, and then her jaws closed over his shoulder.

The bite of an Alpha.

To a witch.

She jerked her head side to side.

Livingstone's mouth opened wide, but no sound came out.

Michelle pulled away, dropping down behind him.

Livingstone took a stumbling step forward.

His tattoos started to flicker.

He gasped as he looked around, confused.

He raised his hand to his neck, fingers bloodied as he pulled them away.

"No," he whispered. "Not . . . not like this."

The marks on his skin began to burst. They twisted angrily on his arms, and his skin started to burn as each symbol flared, the skin blackening.

He raised his bloody hand toward Gavin.

Toward Gordo.

Toward me.

He said, "Please."

He said, "Please help me."

He said, "Please don't let me die."

And Gordo said, "Fuck you."

Livingstone fell to his knees in front of us as we pulled ourselves up. He tilted his head toward the sky as I rushed toward Kelly, lifting him up and pulling him close. He wrapped his arms around me.

"Hold on to me," I whispered.

"Always."

Robert Livingstone howled toward the morning sun, a song of anguish and rage that rattled my bones. I gritted my teeth against it, and in my head, in the deepest part of me, there was only *packpackpack*.

The tattoos crawled up Livingstone's arms, disappearing under his shirt and reappearing on his neck. They rose up his throat to his jaw and into his open mouth. He choked as they forced their way inside. His throat bulged as he swallowed them down.

An unseen shock of magic detonated over us.

Kelly cried out, tensing against me.

I held on as tightly as I could.

Mark's shift melted away as he collapsed to his hands and knees, panting toward the ground, eyes flicking ice blue, violet, ice blue, violet.

Carter lay on the ground on his back, limbs skittering in the dirt, chin jutting up toward the sky.

And then it was gone.

Robert Livingstone looked old and faded. His skin was sallow. His eyes were closed. He took a breath. And then another. And then another.

He said, "This isn't the end."

He fell face-first onto the ground.

His heart stuttered in his chest.

And then he died, quiet as a mouse.

Silence fell over the compound, the only sounds coming from the shifting and cracking of the ice on the lake.

"Robbie," Kelly whispered.

I pulled away, but only just.

And Kelly's eyes were the bright Halloween orange of a Beta wolf. He grunted as the fracture in his leg repaired itself with an audible *snap*.

I kissed him with everything I had.

And I could feel him, I could feel him, I could *feel* him in my head and heart, his voice a wolfsong.

I heard a choked sob coming from next to us, and I looked over, shocked to see tears running down Gordo's cheeks. He was cupping Mark's face in his hands, demanding that he do it again, do it again, goddamn you.

Mark did.

His eyes flashed orange.

He hugged Mark as hard as he could.

Which meant—

"Carter," Kelly said, pulling away from me. He turned and ran toward his brother, who had just sat up, head in his hands. Carter barely had time to brace himself before Kelly tackled him back onto the ground. Carter grinned up at him as his eyes filled with the same orange as the rest of the Betas. They laughed and clutched at each other, Kelly babbling that he was going to *murder* Carter if he ever did something like that again.

It was Elizabeth who figured out what the rest had missed.

"Robbie?" she asked.

I looked toward her. She approached me slowly. Joe and Ox came next to her. Chris and Tanner were behind them, wounds healing. Jessie had her arms slung around Rico, his head on her shoulder. They were all watching me.

"Yeah?" I said hoarsely.

"Do you remember?"

I was taken aback. I hadn't even—

And then my heart sank to the pit of my stomach.

Because the void was still there, vast and black. Oh, it had light in it now, the threads of the pack stretching across it, but it was still wide open and gaping.

I hung my head.

She rushed toward me, gathered me up in her arms. "It's okay," she whispered. "It's okay. We'll figure it out. I promise."

A wolf growled.

I spun around, pushing Elizabeth behind me, baring my fangs.

Gavin stood above Kelly and Carter, lips pulled back over his teeth, eyes still violet. And he was staring at Michelle Hughes.

She had shifted back to human, her nude body streaked with blood.

She was pale as she looked at us.

She said, "I . . . did what I could."

She said, "You have to believe me."

She said, "I never wanted this."

She said, "I never wanted this to happen."

She said, "I was under his control."

She said, "Like Robbie. I was just like Robbie. I couldn't fight him off. I couldn't stop him. I swear to you. On my life. I only wanted for the wolves to survive. I never—please. Please believe me. I'll do whatever you want. Joe." She took a step toward us, and Ox snarled at her. She stopped again, hands up to placate. "Joe," she said again, voice stronger. "Alpha Bennett. I've . . . done so much. For the wolves. I'll step down. You will become the Alpha of all. Just . . . spare me. Please."

"What the hell?" Gordo muttered. I glanced over at him. He was looking down at his arm. The raven was twisting furiously.

Joe stared at her for a long moment. "You stopped him."

"Guys," Gordo said. "Something's wrong. Something's—"

She nodded furiously. "I did. I waited for the right moment. I knew if you came—*when* you came—that it would be our only chance. I had to make him think I was still on his side. Until I could finish this. Finish *him*. A witch can't live through an Alpha bite. The wolf magic and witch magic are incompatible." She smiled shakily. "He's dead. And *I killed him*. I saved you. I saved all of you—"

She jerked forward, eyes widening.

I screamed for her as a hand burst through her chest, blackened, the fingers ending in long, glistening hooks.

Blood poured from her mouth as Robert Livingstone rose behind her, black hair growing along his face, eyes blazing orange. He roared at us over her shoulder as he pulled her heart out through her back.

She was dead before she hit the ground.

Livingstone held her heart in his hand as Kelly and Carter scrabbled away from him. Ox and Joe stepped forward, half-shifted, roaring.

Livingstone's eyes filled with red.

Michelle had been an Alpha. And now Livingstone had taken it from her.

"*You did thissssss,*" he hissed at us, and impossibly, he began to grow, his body contorting, muscles rippling as his bones creaked. His shift overcame him, but he wasn't like any wolf I'd ever seen. His clothes shredded and fell to the ground, but he remained on his hind legs, which were bent at the knees, feet turning into long black paws shot with white hair across the tops. His chest expanded, ribs breaking and reforming. His arms were bulky with muscle, and the claws on his hands and feet were at least six inches long. His face *stretched* into a savage mockery of a wolf, his head bigger than any I'd ever seen. He towered above us.

A beast.

He tilted his head back and howled. It rolled over us, the ground shaking beneath our feet.

"*What do we do?*" Rico shrieked. "*What do we do?*"

"We finish this," Ox growled.

"*Yessss,*" Livingstone said, jaws snapping.

But he was stronger than us.

Than all of us.

And here, at the end of all things . . .

We lost.

Oh, we gave it everything we had. Ox and Joe charged at him, and we all shouted when Livingstone swung his massive arm out, striking them both in the chest, knocking them back. I barely had time to take a breath before Joe crashed into me, slamming us both to the ground.

He rolled off me as gunfire erupted above us. I looked up to see Jessie walking toward the beast, Rico's guns in her hands. She kept on shooting, and the bullets were *silver*, but they barely made a mark, bouncing off Livingstone's face and chest, only pissing him off even more. The guns dry-clicked and Jessie threw them to the ground, pausing only to scoop up the crowbar before charging. Livingstone swung at her, and she ducked, falling to her side, her momentum carrying her *underneath* him between his legs. He started to turn, but she was already on her feet behind him, bringing the crowbar down onto his back.

It broke, the end snapping off and falling to the ground.

"Well, shit," Jessie said.

Before Livingstone could put his claws on her, Chris and Tanner and Rico shouted in unison, these brave men who had carried the hearts of wolves in their chests even before they'd been bitten.

They were no match for Livingstone. He knocked them away easily. Chris and Tanner landed on the ground near a burning house. Rico flew out onto the lake, sliding along the ice.

I had to end this.

I had to stop him before he hurt anyone else.

I ran toward him, claws popping.

"Robbie, *no!*" Gordo cried, but it was too late.

I would do this for him.

For Kelly.

For my family.

For my pack.

I jumped.

And Livingstone caught me by the neck.

"*You,*" he growled, pulling me close to his face. He opened his maw, and I could see endless rows of teeth. I struggled against him, beating on his hand and arm, but it was useless. "*I gave you life. I gave you a home. I gave you everything. And thissss is how you repay me?*"

"Fucking die already," I managed to say, and sank my claws into his right eye. It was almost as big as my palm, and I *yanked* on it, feeling it pop underneath my fingers.

Livingstone howled in pain, his grip around my neck tightening until I thought my spine would break.

Instead, he threw me to the ground. My breath was knocked from my chest as my arm broke. I turned my head slowly to see what remained of his eye still in my hand.

Joe and Ox pulled themselves to their feet.

Carter and Kelly stood before the beast, next to their mother.

Jessie circled Livingstone, keeping a safe distance.

Chris and Tanner helped me to my feet as my arm healed.

Rico slipped over the ice before hitting the beach, eyes orange.

Mark stood next to Gordo, their ravens' wings stretched wide.

"Stop. Please."

Two words, grunted with what sounded like great hardship.
The beast looked down.

Gavin stood before him, looking up at his father. It was discordant, seeing his face, so like his brother and father. But it was harder somehow, darker. It was in his eyes.

Feral.

"Leave," Gavin grunted. His face twisted like he was struggling to form words. "With you. I'll. Go. With you. Don't. Don't touch. Them."

Livingstone craned his neck toward his son. "*Leeeaave?*"

"Yes," Gavin said. "Us. We go."

Livingstone snapped his teeth at Gavin. "*Whyyyy?*"

And Gavin said, "You're. My father."

The beast reared back, nostrils flaring.

"No," Carter said, taking a step forward. "You can't—"

Livingstone jerked his head toward Carter. He roared, his remaining eye flashing in warning.

"Here!" Gavin shouted. "Here! I. Will *go*!"

Livingstone looked back down at him. And extended his hand, claws flashing in the sunlight.

Gavin took it without hesitation.

"Joe!" Carter cried. "You have to stop him. You can't let him—"

"*No*," Gavin snarled at him, eyes violet. "Stay. *Back*. Don't want. This. Don't want. Pack. Don't want. Brother. Don't want. *You*. Child. You are. A *child*. I am not. Like you. I am not. *Pack*."

And his heart never stuttered.

But he lied. Because he *was* pack. They were faint, the threads that stretched from him toward us, and just as we began to pull on them, just as we began to tug them, to sing to him, to remind him where he belonged, Gavin broke them.

Carter sounded as if he'd been punched, bending over and gagging.

The others were distracted.

They didn't see what I saw.

The look on Gavin's face, brief though it was.

It was heartbreak, real and devastating.

And then it was gone.

Livingstone roared again, and I covered my ears.

By the time my head cleared, Gavin and Livingstone were running.

They didn't stop when they hit the wall. Livingstone leapt up and *over* it, and Gavin clawed his way to the top and jumped to the other side.

He never looked back.

They were gone.

Carter took a step forward, hand raised, fingers trembling.

And when he turned toward us, gone was the bravado, gone was the man I'd come to know. In his place stood a lost boy, eyes wide and wet, lip trembling.

"Mom," he croaked as a tear spilled down his cheek, chest hitching. And ah, god, there was so much blue pouring off him, I thought it would drown us all. "He . . . left. Mom? Why—why did he go? Why did he leave? I didn't know. *I didn't know.*"

Elizabeth went to her son, holding him close as Carter broke apart, shoulders shaking. She whispered in his ear, telling him it would be all right, that it would be all right, my love, I promise you. I promise you. I promise you.

There were cries of joy as the people of the compound poured through the gates, whatever magic had held them in the trees now gone. The kids screamed for their parents, eyes clear but confused. Tony's mother and father swept him up, each of them kissing his cheeks, his chin, his forehead as he babbled at them, telling them he'd been asleep for a long time and had the strangest of dreams, but he was awake now, and why were they crying? Why were they sad?

Brodie looked lost and unsure, but Ox was there, crouched before him, hands on his shoulders. Brodie's face crumpled as he collapsed into Ox, sobbing against his chest.

Elizabeth led Carter away from the rest of us, his head bowed, hands in fists at his sides.

Kelly watched them leave. "What are we going to do?" he whispered to me.

I wrapped my arms around his shoulders. "I don't know."

"We can't beat him. Not like we are now."

"I know."

He turned his head toward me. "Gavin didn't want to go."

I sighed. "You saw that too?"

He nodded and looked back at his mother and brother. "He sacrificed himself. To save us."

"We'll figure it out."

"We have to. For all of us. But for Gordo and Carter most of all. They deserve to know the truth. And he's part of this. Gavin is part of this. Of us."

"He's pack," I said quietly.

"Yes. And we don't leave pack behind. Ever."

"Ever," I said, hugging him closer.

He put his face in my neck, breathing in deeply. "You don't remember."

I closed my eyes. "No."

"It's okay."

"I don't—"

"Grass. Lake water. Sunshine."

I sucked in a sharp breath.

"That's what I smell like to you. Isn't it?"

"Yeah," I said hoarsely. "It is."

"I never told you what it was like for me. How I knew that day. When we came back. How I knew you were my mate."

"It's—"

"Home," he whispered. "You smell like home. You always have. And that's the only thing that matters. You don't need to remember because I remember for the both of us."

I swallowed past the lump in my throat. "Are you sure?"

He nodded.

I kissed the side of his head. "Then we won't worry about it. We won't—"

"I tink we can help with dat," a voice said from behind us.

We turned to see Aileen and Patrice standing there, looking dirty and worn but otherwise unharmed.

They were both smiling.

* * *

There were questions. So many questions. The residents of Caswell were scared. They demanded answers, wanting to know what had happened and what was going to happen next. They didn't have an Alpha, they cried. They didn't have anyone to lead them.

They didn't want to turn into Omegas.

They gathered in front of the remains of the house that had once belonged to Michelle Hughes. We stood in front of it, a wave of anger and sadness bowling over us from all sides. I didn't blame them. After everything we'd all been through, after everything we'd seen, I understood their fear.

Ox was trying to calm them down, but they weren't listening.

It wasn't until Joe Bennett spoke that they quieted.

He was staring off at the lake, a strange look on his face.

He said, "My father... he stood here once. I remember it. Clear as day. He was crying. I found him. He tried to hide it from me, but I found him. I couldn't talk. I couldn't... My voice had been stolen from me by a man named Richard Collins." Joe turned to look out at the crowd. He took a deep breath. "I did the only thing I could. I put my hand on his hip, putting my scent on him. I bared my neck, wanting him to know that no matter what had happened, no matter what I'd gone through, I knew him. My Alpha. My father. And he was *shocked* by the display, so much so that I think he forgot he was crying. He asked me what I was doing. But I couldn't answer him. I didn't know how. So I hugged him."

Elizabeth wiped her eyes, Carter standing stonily at her side.

"I hugged him," Joe continued, voice growing louder, an undercurrent of *AlphaAlphaAlpha* behind his words. "Because I needed him to understand he didn't have to hide his sadness. That he didn't have to be tough and brave all the time. That he was my father and it was his job to protect me, but as his son, I loved him no matter who he was or what he was capable of. That we were stronger together than we would ever be apart." He looked around at the crowd of wolves and witches and the last of our humans. "And I *will* be strong for you. But I can't do it alone. I need you. I need all of you. If you'll have me. If you'll allow me to be your Alpha, I promise you, I will do everything for you. Because pack is everything."

At first no one moved.

No one spoke.

We waited.

And then Tony stepped forward—little Tony who had blood on his hands but would never know of it as long as I still drew breath. His mother tried to stop him, but his father grabbed her arm, shaking his head. She didn't argue.

He looked at all of us, the Bennett pack.

He smiled at me briefly before he looked to Joe.

"Are you a good wolf?" he asked.

"I try," Joe said quietly. "And if I ever fail, I have people to remind me of who I am."

"Your pack," Tony said.

"Yes."

He reached up and tugged on Joe's hand, pulling him down, their faces inches apart. Tony touched Joe's cheek, dimpling his skin. He laughed when Joe snapped at him playfully with a low growl.

And then Tony bared his throat.

Joe blinked rapidly, breathing heavily through his nose.

He trailed his fingers along Tony's neck, flashing his Alpha-red eyes.

Tony scrunched up his face.

His eyes flickered orange.

The crowd sighed. It sounded like the wind.

"I did it!" Tony crowed.

"You did," Joe said, smiling warmly. "And I'm so very proud of you."

"Thanks, Alpha!" He ran back to his parents. They scooped him up in their arms as he laughed.

Joe rose, taking Ox's hand in his.

He said, "I am Joe Bennett. My father was Thomas Bennett. My grandfather was Abel Bennett. I have their strength within me, and that of all those who came before me. We are pack. I know you're scared. I know that uncertainty lies ahead. We have much to do. But we'll do it together because we're the goddamn Bennett pack, and our song will always be heard."

The people of Caswell, Maine, all bared their necks to him.

His eyes filled with fire again, and when he howled, I knew things would never be the same.

In the ruins of the compound, we howled with him.

Joseph Bennett.

The Alpha of all.

HEARTSONG

On a normal day toward the end of September, I knew it was time.

Or at least Gordo knew for me, and didn't seem to have a problem telling me as much.

"You're being fucking stupid about this," he growled as he closed the door to his office in the garage. He pointed to the chair in front of his desk. I thought about arguing, but the look on his face made me keep my mouth shut. He wasn't here for my shit.

I sat down, refusing to look at him.

He sighed as he sank back down into his own chair. "Kid, I don't know why you want to drag this out."

"Yeah, well. Who wants to remember the time they almost killed two members of their pack?"

He grunted as he scratched the stump of his arm. "It's more than that."

I grimaced. "That's not—"

"What are you so scared of? Aileen and Patrice said it has to be—"

"I *know* what they said," I snapped. I took off my glasses and scrubbed a hand over my face. "I just . . ."

"You just . . ."

I didn't want to say it out loud. It sounded ridiculous even to me. But I didn't think Gordo was going to let me out of here without saying something. And if I couldn't talk to him about it, I probably wouldn't ever say anything at all. I gnawed on my bottom lip before saying, "What if I don't like the person I was?"

He blinked. "What?"

I tried to keep my frustration down. "I've got this . . . this life. I've made it for myself, even after everything. What if I get my memories back and everything changes? What if I don't like who I was and who I'll become? There's no going back after this." I looked at him hopefully. "Unless you could take it all away again if I—"

"Yeah, that's not gonna happen. I wouldn't do that to you, kid."

I deflated. "It's hard."

"I know. But you're being a dick about it."

"Hey!"

He sat forward, elbows on the desk. He looked grumpy as fuck, and I felt a surge of affection for him. This ridiculous man who for some reason loved me like a brother. Which, of course, I didn't necessarily talk about out loud, given how touchy the subject of *brothers* was at the moment. I knew Gordo talked to Mark about Gavin, though not the specifics. Other than that, Gordo didn't mention him at all. But I knew he was hurting, maybe almost as much as Carter was.

After the fight, Joe had decided to stay in Caswell for a while to give everyone there time to get used to him, to help them rebuild their homes and lives. He also wanted to make sure that no one was still under Livingstone's hold. Michelle had been their Alpha. Livingstone had taken that power away from her, but he hadn't asserted control over the compound. He'd just left. He'd gotten what he wanted. Mostly.

A few of the wolves had left, not wanting anything to do with the Bennetts. Santos, the one who'd been guarding Dale and who'd gone after Alpha Wells and her pack, had been one of them. I didn't know if he went looking for Livingstone, but he was there one day and then gone the next, without so much as a note left behind.

I had a feeling we'd see him again.

But Joe's favor with his new pack rose when he honored Michelle Hughes with a pyre worthy of an Alpha, regardless of all that she'd done. She'd burned, and when she was nothing but smoke and ash, I felt a weight lift off my shoulders. I allowed myself a few tears over her, but that was all.

There was brief discussion of trying to get everyone moved to Green Creek, but packing everyone up and bringing them cross-country wasn't in the cards. There wasn't room, at least not yet. I thought Joe and Ox were making plans, preliminary though they were. Elizabeth, Carter, and Tanner had stayed with him in Caswell initially, with Ox going back and forth, but they'd come back a week before, just as they had the previous full moon at the beginning of the month. I hadn't been ready then. I didn't know if I was now.

I told myself we had bigger things to focus on.

Healing.

Putting our lives back together.

Looking for Livingstone and Gavin, though they had all but disappeared.

But...

It was on me, Aileen and Patrice had informed us. It was all on me. The reason I hadn't snapped back like Carter and Mark had after Livingstone had initially died, the reason my door hadn't shattered like theirs, was because I didn't *want* it to.

I was holding it closed.

"You're frightened," Aileen said quietly, "of what you'll find. Of remembering all that has happened. And that fear is stronger than any magic Robert Livingstone ever had. Until you conquer that fear, you'll remain as you are."

I didn't want to believe her or Patrice, but I knew they were right.

Kelly didn't push. I didn't know why until he told me that he would support whatever decision I made. But I thought there was something in his eyes, something in his voice that proved him a liar, even though his heart remained steady.

I loved him fiercely.

What if that changed? What if nothing was ever the same?

It didn't hurt that he was distracted too, trying to get Carter to open up. Carter, who had turned surly and gruff, who rarely smiled or spoke. I heard their many one-sided conversations as Kelly pleaded with him over the phone to no avail. It upset him, but I didn't know what else could be done aside from finding Gavin and bringing him back.

Carter had nearly bitten Kelly's head off when he said as much. I heard the anger in his voice when he snapped that Gavin had made his choice, and he didn't give a fuck about it.

Elizabeth said Carter spent a lot of time alone in the refuge outside Caswell. I hoped he was finding peace in the trees like I had.

"This isn't just for you," Gordo said now, voice soft. "I... look, kid. I won't pretend to know what it's like between you and Kelly, but I do know what it's like to be mated to a wolf. And all the baggage that comes with it. Things are better now with Mark, but we've had to fight tooth and nail, fang and claw to get where we are. Loving a wolf... it's hard. Especially when one of those wolves is a Bennett. We don't have normal lives."

I snorted despite myself. "That's an understatement."

He ignored me. "But you'll never know just how deep that love goes until you give in to the truth. You may think you can continue on as you are now, and maybe you will, for a little while at least. But you'll know deep down that it isn't everything. That you're still holding a part of you back. And Kelly doesn't deserve that. Not after everything. Not after all he did to get to you."

I hung my head.

"I'm not trying to make you feel bad, kid. Just wanted to lay it all out for you. Give you something to think about."

I nodded, listening to the sounds of Rico and Chris in the garage, shitty rock music playing from the old stereo.

Gordo's chair creaked as he sat back. "We have a fight on our hands. One day, and one day soon, we'll find him. And when we do, it's either going to be him or us. And we'll need everyone that we can get by our side at their full strength."

I looked up at him. "Your dad."

"Yeah."

"And your brother."

His expression tightened. "I don't give a fuck about—"

"Don't lie, Gordo. Not to me. Not when you're giving me shit about the truth."

His knuckles popped as he curled his hand into a fist. "I . . ." He shook his head. "Goddammit. I don't know what to think about . . . him."

"Gavin."

"Yeah."

"He looks like you."

"The fuck he does," Gordo growled. "Mangy-ass motherfucker."

I laughed.

Gordo looked surprised, and his lips quirked. "Bastard."

I sobered, putting my glasses back on.

Little wolf, little wolf, can't you see?

"I'll make you a deal."

He looked wary. "What?"

"I'll go through with this. What I need to do. To get my memories back. But you have to promise me that when we find Gavin, when we bring him back, you'll treat him like you treat me."

Gordo scowled. "And how's that?"

"Like I'm your brother."

Gordo's expression stuttered. He opened his mouth but closed it. "Fuck. Kid. Robbie, you *are* my brother."

"I know. But so is he. And he deserves to know it. From you. From all of us."

Gordo closed his eyes, breathing through his nose.

He didn't even give me shit when I rose from my chair and rounded the desk, then leaned over and hugged him. He brought his hand up and gripped my arm. "Yeah," he eventually said. "Okay. I . . . I'll do what I can."

"I know you will," I mumbled into his hair.

"So, deal, then?"

"Deal."

"Good." He shoved me off him. "Because the full moon is tomorrow, and everyone's coming back from Maine. I already told them you'd do it. Now get the hell out of my office. You have work to do, and I don't pay you to fuck around."

"You *what!*"

He ignored me, squinting at his computer, typing with one hand in that hunt-and-peck method I'd come to know.

"Gordo!"

"Get out."

I went.

Gordo offered me a ride home, since he was headed to the pack house anyway, but I waved him off. I wanted to walk. Clear my head. Put my thoughts together.

He hesitated before nodding.

Out on the street, people waved at me.

I waved back, but I didn't stop to talk to them. I didn't have the words yet.

The people of Green Creek had been relieved at our return, though they'd been scared at first when they saw some of our pack missing. They'd calmed when Gordo and Ox explained (leaving out some of the more violent details) that Joe and the others would be away for a little while longer.

I'd felt guilt at the look on Bambi's face when she'd come running toward Rico.

He grinned at her, but she stopped in front of him, eyes wide.

"You're different," she whispered.

Rico's smile faltered. "Uh. Yeah." He scratched the back of his neck. "I guess... I guess I am. Got myself a little full moon problem." He glanced away.

And I said, "He saved my life. I wouldn't be here if it wasn't for him. And he came back to you because he knew you'd murder him if he died."

They both stared at me.

And then Bambi launched herself at him, wrapping her legs around his waist. He held her up by her thighs, and she cursed him, telling him he was fucking *stupid*, and how *dare* he scare her like that, and show me your eyes, show me your damn wolf eyes, and then he'd *growled* at her, and I realized I probably didn't want to witness what was going to happen next, so I left them to it.

But when I turned around to walk away, I almost walked smack into Dominique and Jessie, and *that* wasn't any better, given how Jessie was getting her own welcome home.

I left the town behind, heading for home. There was a crispness to the air, the leaves beginning to change colors and dropping to the ground. Every now and then a car passed me by, but I didn't look up from the road.

At least not until I heard the *woop woop* of a siren as a car pulled up behind me, tires crunching in the gravel on the side of the road.

"Sir, I need you to stay right where you are," a voice announced from a speaker. "I've had reports of a wild animal on the loose."

I grinned and shook my head as I turned around.

Kelly Bennett climbed out of his cruiser, straightening his duty belt before closing the door. The light bar was flashing red and blue.

"Wild animal? Sounds serious."

He arched an eyebrow. "Oh, it is. You gotta be careful 'round these parts. Things in the woods like you wouldn't believe. Mountain lions. Maybe even a bear or two."

"Is that all?" I asked.

He shook his head. "Heard stories."

"About?"

His eyes flashed orange. "Wolves."

"I think I can handle myself."

"That right? Well. Might put me at ease if I could escort you wherever you need to be."

"I don't know where that is."

His smile faded slightly. "You sure about that?"

Shit. "Gordo called you."

He shrugged.

"Fucking witches," I muttered.

"Didn't say much," Kelly said. "Just that you were walking home. He thought you could use some company."

"And that's all he said." It wasn't a question.

"He *might* have said a little more," Kelly admitted. He leaned back against the front of his cruiser, crossing his legs. It was strange, really, this simple act of him being here as he was. He made it hard for me to breathe in all the best ways. And I understood what Gordo had been saying in his office. About me. About Kelly and what he did or didn't deserve. About all of us. It made sense in ways it hadn't even a few minutes ago.

Because there was this guy. This man. This wolf. And he was looking at me like he never wanted to see anything else. I knew as sure as I knew anything else that if I said no, if I said I wanted to stay as I was now, he'd be fine with it. He'd be okay. He'd support me, and he wouldn't push.

But I owed him more.

I owed him everything.

I moved toward him as he leaned against his cruiser in the autumn sunlight. He spread his legs, allowing me to step between them. His hands went to my hips, fingers tugging on the hem of my work shirt, my name stitched in red on my chest.

He said, "Hey," and "Hi," and "Hello," and I knew I would do whatever it took. He never stopped fighting for me. I needed to do the same. For him. For myself.

For us.

I pressed my forehead against his, breathing him in, and it was grass and lake water and so much goddamn sunshine.

"I'm scared," I whispered.

He said, "I know you are. But I'm going to be with you every step of the way. No matter what."

He kissed me, warm and sweet.

Which, of course, was ruined a moment later when Chris and Tanner drove by, honking the horn, hollering out the open window. They slowed but didn't stop. I flipped them off but never stopped kissing Kelly. I heard them laugh as the truck sped up, heading for the houses at the end of the lane.

"We got this," Kelly said. "All right? We got this."

I sighed. "I know. I just . . ." I shook my head. "What if this changes? You and me?"

"Then we adapt," he said. "We grow. We learn. And we do it together. The two of us. I love you, Robbie. No matter who you are."

We stayed there for a time.

Eventually we moved on.

That night we lay curled together in our bed in the blue house. He fell asleep first, and I watched him as the night stretched on.

"Okay," I whispered to him. "Okay."

Nightfall on an autumn evening.

The moon was full and bright.

The pack was together again.

We ran through the woods.

Into the clearing.

Bambi was there, laughing and trailing after a black wolf with white paws like socks (much to Rico's dismay and Chris and Tanner's delight). He was still learning, apt to stumble, not quite used to four legs. I thought Bambi would be pack, and soon. Jessie was making rumblings of needing to open up membership for Team Human, seeing as how the numbers had dwindled. Ox and Joe were going to talk to her in the coming weeks. I didn't think they had anything to worry about. It probably didn't hurt that Bambi was pregnant, though I didn't think Rico knew. Elizabeth was the first to figure it out, given how her scent had changed. We were all waiting to see how long it would take Rico. Chris and Tanner had a bet going. Chris said it'd be another month or two. Tanner thought he wouldn't know until he was actually holding the kid in his arms.

And since it'd happened before Rico had been turned, the kid would be human.

A child.

In the Bennett pack.

Carter trailed after Kelly, rubbing up against him at every chance he got. I watched them from the sidelines, sitting with Patrice and Aileen. Carter was thinner than he'd been even a few weeks before. He had a haunted look in his eyes that never seemed to fade. Kelly was worried. I was too.

"You can run with them," Aileen said quietly. "There's still time, boyo."

I shook my head, the itch of the full moon maddening. "It's okay."

"In your head," Patrice said. "Stuck. What are you afraid of?"

"Most things."

"Ah. I see."

I looked at them. "You think this will work?"

"If you want it to," Aileen said. "There's only so much we can do, Robbie. Magic isn't... it's not the be-all and end-all. It's not wish fulfillment. It can be a dangerous thing depending on the user."

"Livingstone?"

She shook her head. "Nothing. I don't know how he's done it, but he's turned ghost."

"Gordo says we need to be together in order for us to beat him."

Aileen and Patrice exchanged a look that I couldn't decipher. "He's right."

"Do you think it'll be enough?"

Patrice sighed. "It has ta be. He won't stop. He's wolf now. And he's tasted blood."

"How?" I asked helplessly. "How the hell did he survive the bite? It should have killed him."

"It should have," Aileen agreed. "But it didn't. And we can either waste time speculating, or we can actually *do* something about it. Look, Robbie, I'm not going to lie to you and say this will be easy tonight, or whatever we'll face come tomorrow. Ox is special. The fact that he has remained as he is, the Alpha to the Omegas, even after the destruction of Livingstone's magic, is a testament to that. But he cannot do this alone. Neither can the Alpha of all. I may not be a wolf, but

I know the importance of pack. They need you as much as you need them."

I looked out at the others. Ox lay as a black wolf at the other edge of the clearing, watching his pack run. Joe was beside him, resting his head on Ox's back. Chris and Tanner and Rico were wrestling while Jessie and Bambi rolled their eyes, Dominique sitting next to them, eyes flickering between Beta orange and Omega violet. Gordo sat with his back against a tree, Mark's head in his lap.

Elizabeth nosed Carter as Kelly yipped, tugging on his tail. I thought he was going to snap at the both of them, but he sagged, giving in. He howled, and it was tinged with blue, though he began to chase after his brother.

"We're not whole," I said. "Not yet."

"Gavin."

I looked at Patrice. "He's part of this."

He rubbed his jaw. "I didn't—" He shook his head. "Bennett pack. Just when I tink I have you figured out."

"We need to find him."

Aileen patted my knee. "We will."

I wished I could believe her. And not just for Carter. For all of us.

I turned my thoughts to better things. "How's Brodie?"

"As well as can be expected," Aileen said. "He's hurting, of course. But your little friend Tony refuses to let him sleep anywhere but in his room."

"He'll be safe with Tony and his parents," Patrice said. "We'll make sure of it."

"We're heading back in the morning," Aileen said. "We just came out here for—"

"For me."

She shrugged. "You weren't ready before."

"Am I now?"

"Are you?"

I looked back at this pack of mine. This ridiculous, wonderful pack. At the way they moved in the moonlight, the way they sang together, the way they loved each other with their whole hearts.

I had known that love once, or so I'd been told.

I knew it now, yes, but I thought it could be different.

I thought it could be more.

I said, "Okay."

Aileen nodded, satisfied. "Then we'll begin."

"You're going to spit on dirt and leaves and make me eat it, aren't you."

Patrice chuckled. "Someting like dat."

It was exactly like that.

I left them in the clearing.

I walked through the woods, knowing I wouldn't be alone for long.

My path was lit by the moon and stars.

I trailed my hands along the trunks of trees, the bark rough against my skin.

I thought of my mother, so fierce and wild, telling me that I was the guardian of the forest.

I wondered what she would think of me. Of who I'd become. Of what I'd made for myself.

I heard footsteps behind me, and I fought back a smile.

I was being hunted.

I took off running.

A howl rose up behind me, and the chase was on.

I ran as fast as I could, branches slapping against my arms and chest, the wind whipping through my hair. I didn't shift. I didn't need to. I was alive, alive, alive, and in this place, in this magical territory, the blood of all those who'd come before me sang in my veins.

I burst through the tree line, the lights of the houses bright.

I barely made it halfway to the blue house when a great weight landed on my back, knocking me to the ground. I hit the ground with a crash, a growl at the back of my neck, the breath hot. I gasped as a wet nose pressed into my hair. "Asshole."

There came the grind of muscle and bone, and I closed my eyes.

"Got you," Kelly whispered. "Got you, got you, got you."

"You did."

He rolled off me, panting at my side. I turned my head, grass poking against my ear. His eyes burned orange as he looked at me, searching for something.

I nodded.

He sighed. "You're sure?"

I was. Now more than ever. "Yeah. For you. For them. For myself."

He grinned, wild and beautiful. His teeth were sharp.

It was so simple, wasn't it?

This.

Him and me.

So I said, "I love you. No matter what happens."

His expression stuttered and broke. He turned his face toward the sky. His chest hitched, but he got it under control. "Me too."

I rose slowly, pushing myself off the ground. I looked down at him spread out on the grass, naked and comfortable.

I held out my hand.

He didn't hesitate.

I led him toward the house.

- - -

He followed me up the stairs to our bedroom. It was just as we'd left it. His duty belt hung off the back of a chair near the desk. The closet door was open, our clothes hanging together, our scents mingling. Two stone wolves sat on the windowsill, pressed together.

It was here. Us. The evidence of a life lived together. I was scared, but fear only strengthened my resolve.

He closed the door behind us, shutting us away from the world. He leaned against it and looked at me.

I let my gaze trail over him, stopping at the mark on his neck.

My mark.

A fiery sense of satisfaction rose within me, seeing it there. Knowing what it meant.

"Like what you see?" he asked.

"More than you know," I said honestly. Then, "Are you . . . okay with this? I know sex isn't—"

"Asexual people have sex," he said quietly.

"I know. But I don't want to force you to do something you don't want to do. I need you to be okay. That's more important."

He pushed himself off the door. "Strange."

"What?"

He chuckled. "You said the same thing to me the first time we had sex. That you were worried that you were making me do something I didn't want to do. I loved you for it then, and I love you for it now."

"Oh," I said, face growing warm. I scratched the back of my neck. "I guess some things don't change."

"I guess they don't," he agreed, taking a step toward me.

I stepped back. My legs bumped into the edge of the bed. I sat down.

He stood in front of me, miles and miles of skin on display.

There was heat here, rumbling within me, low and warm, almost like fire.

He lifted my shirt up and over my head, then let it fall to the floor.

He pressed a hand against my chest, pushing me back on the bed.

He crawled on top of me, hands on either side of my head, knees against my hips.

He leaned down and kissed me, long and slow. He deepened the kiss slightly, his tongue swiping against my lips, but he didn't push further.

I brought my hand to the back of his head, holding him in place.

He hummed against my mouth. I opened my eyes to see orange up close.

My fangs itched in my gums.

"You'll see it," I whispered. "Aileen said you'll see it all when I do. You'll see everything."

He said, "I know," and he kissed me again and again and again.

It wasn't fierce, the way he loved me. It wasn't the burning fire of passion. It was heavy and soft. It was love unlike anything else I'd felt. My hands tightened in the comforter as he kissed my chest, hands on the button of my jeans. He pulled the zipper down, reaching inside and holding on to me, his hand hot as he caressed me.

He didn't take me in his mouth, but he didn't need to. Instead he brought his hand to his lips and, while he knew I was watching, licked his palm slowly. And then his hand was back on me, slick and hot, moving up and down, squeezing *just* right.

And later, much later, when we were both slick with sweat, our pupils blown out, me above him, his legs over my shoulders, his cock half-hard against his stomach, he said my name like a whispered prayer. In my head a rattling metal door shook in its frame as I thrust into him with a snap of my hips. His claws scratched my back, and it was almost here, it was almost time, and I couldn't stop, I *wouldn't* stop, not for anything.

Right before I came, he whispered, "Use the memory of my fangs in your skin."

And then he reared up, face elongating, and I cried out as he bit down, as he loved me, as he loved me, as I—

I

I

I

I am standing in front of a wooden door. My stomach is in knots. I'm nervous, so fucking nervous, but this is important. I calm my heart, even though they have to hear it. Hear me. Alpha Hughes's voice is still whispering in my head, telling me to keep my eyes open for anything and everything and to tell her all I see, no matter how small, no matter how minute.

I knock.

The door opens.

"Wolf," this strange and wondrous human says.

I grin at him. "Ox. I come in peace and bring tidings of great joy. My name is Robbie Fontaine. You may have known my predecessor, Osmond."

It's the wrong thing to say.

Wolves snarl just out of sight.

"Yeah, probably not the best idea to mention that name. That's my bad. Won't happen again. Well, I—"

I

I

I

I want him. I don't know why. I'm supposed to watch them and report back east, but I'm starting to leave little details out, starting to keep things hidden, and it's dangerous, it's wrong, but I can't bring myself to stop it. He's here, Ox, and he's unlike anyone I've ever known before. I tell myself it's just a crush, I tell myself it's just infatuation, but there is this pulse in my chest, this light, and I think it's because of him, and I—

I

I

I

I kiss him.

He pushes me away.
He tells me no.
It's not a broken heart I feel.
But it's close.
I run, I run as fast as I can, howling under the moon, and I—
I
I
I
I am standing on the porch of the house, and there are people *coming, people I don't know, and Ox is there, he's saying be ready, be ready, and Elizabeth's eyes are more alive than I've ever known them to be, and Mark is frowning, and Rico and Chris and Tanner are moving side to side, nervous, unsure of what's happening, what's coming for us.*

Men.
Four of them.
Heads shaved.
One's a witch.
Three are wolves.
I don't know them.

But my pack does, and I stutter over that thought, I almost break *at it, because this is* my *pack, these are* my *people, these are the ones who I would do anything for.*

One is an Alpha.
Two Betas.
One witch.

And there's something about one of the Betas I can't quite put my finger on, can't quite grasp. It's like a little bird, wings fluttering in the back of my mind, but then it flits away, gone before I can stop it. I don't like this, I don't like this, I—
I
I

I'm moving faster now. I'm like a comet trailing light and stardust behind me. I can't stop, and it hurts, oh my god it hurts, *but there's a voice from somewhere deep inside me, and it's saying* here here here look here look here LoveMatePack see me see me very well *and I—*
I
I

I
I open my eyes.
Kelly Bennett says, "What are you doing out here?"
I squint at him. The sunlight is bright, and I smell grass and what seems like lake water, which is strange, given there's no lake nearby. "I'm thinking."
"About what?" He sounds suspicious, but I tell myself it's because he doesn't know me very well yet. Richard Collins is dead, and Joe and Ox are mated, and we're breathing.
I shrug. "Things. Nothing too important."
"You're weird." He says this, but he isn't leaving. I don't know why. But it doesn't bother me. He's . . . well. He's Kelly. He's a little cold, but sometimes I catch myself watching him when he smiles.
"I was reading," I tell him. "And then I just decided that I wanted to think."
"What were you reading?"
I waggle my eyebrows. "A pirate story. He was plundering some booty."
He grimaces as I show him the cover, a woman in a frilly dress pressed against the bare chest of a pirate with the terrible name of Captain Peter Longhook. "Ox said you read those books."
I snort. "Those books. Wow. That was a lot of disdain in just two words. Congrats, I guess."
And then he laughs.
In the scheme of things, it should be nothing.
It's small, and it surprises him as much as it does me.
Later, when I'm trying to sleep, I'll replay it over and over again in my head, this moment, these few seconds, as it's the first time I ever made Kelly Bennett laugh.
He doesn't leave.
He sits next to me.
He doesn't talk much, but that's okay. I talk enough for the both of us. I—
I
i
i am wolf
i am wolf and kelly
needs food

kelly must have food
deer i will kill him a deer
biggest deer
there you are deer
i will kill you
deer is faster than me
stupid deer
i hate you deer
something else
i run back to house
i find a box
crackers
kelly likes crackers in yellow box
i bring them
i bring them to him
he isn't taking box
why
moon is bright and he won't take crackers
i put them down
push them
he growls at me
i growl back
he
he
takes box
shakes head
box breaks
crackers in grass
not deer but okay
he eats crackers
better than deer
i
i
I

"I need to tell you something," I say, my voice strong. "And I know it might be surprising to hear from me, but I think . . . I think you're amazing. I think you're wonderful. I don't know if there's anyone like you in all the world, Kelly. And I know you probably don't think of *me the same way, and that's okay. I don't want to put any pressure on you. I would never do that. I just . . . I look at you, sometimes, and my heart is in my throat and I can't* breathe. *I guess that means you take my breath away, ha, ha, but . . . goddammit. This is fucking awful."*

I shake my head in disgust.

My reflection in the mirror in my bedroom does the same.

I sigh as I drag my feet toward the door. I'm late for training, and Ox will kick my ass if I take any longer. It's probably for the best, anyway. Kelly doesn't see me like that. There's no scent of arousal when I'm around him. And Kelly . . .

. . . is standing on the other side of the door, arm raised as if to knock, but he's frozen, his eyes wide.

Well, fuck.

"Please tell me you didn't hear anything just now," I beg him.

He drops his hand, blinking slowly. "Um."

I put my face in my hands and groan.

He says, "I take your breath away?"

I drop my hands. "All right. Have at it."

"Have at *what*?"

I grind my teeth together. "Laugh it up. Make fun of me. I know I'm being stupid. I know I'm—"

"You're *serious*?" he demands.

"Ye-es?"

He takes a step back. It's like he's stabbed me right in the chest.

"I won't bother you," I mutter, looking down at my shoes. "Just . . . forget it."

I start to push by him when he says, "No."

I stop. "No what?"

"I'm not going to forget it."

"Um, why?"

He nods. "I'm . . . okay. With it."

I gape at him, unable to form words. Okay with it *isn't* exactly a ringing endorsement, but I have to stop from howling for everyone to hear.

His nostrils flare, and he rolls his eyes. "I'm not going to have sex with you. Stop it."

I have no fucking idea what he's talking about.

He says, "Look. I . . . might like you. At least a little bit."

I say, "Oh. Yeah. Cool. Cool, cool, cool. Uh. Me too. A little bit."

He says, "I figured."

I say, "What gave it away?"

He says, "The crackers. You brought me crackers."

And I say, "I tried to kill you a deer but it was too fast and oh my god, are you for real *right now*?"

And it happens again. That little laugh, and I swear to God I never want to hear anything but that sound ever again.

He smiles at me.

I smile back.

I—

I

I

I

I don't see it coming. The first moment. And that's what makes it so extraordinary; it means so much because it's so small. One moment I'm telling Kelly a story about how I once got fleas as a wolf, and he's laughing, laughing, laughing, and then he *stops* laughing, looking at me with a curious expression. I'm about to ask him what's wrong, about to tell him I don't still *have* fleas, if that's what he's worried about, when he leans over, light and quick, and kisses the corner of my mouth.

He pulls away just as fast, cheeks darkening as he leans back against the tree we're sitting under.

"What was that for?" I ask him quietly.

He says, "Because I wanted to."

"Oh."

"Yeah."

"Can you maybe do it again some time?"

He smiles. "Yeah. Maybe."

I—

I

I

I

I ask, "What is this?" as we walk through the woods.

He laughs, taking my hand in his. "It's nothing. Just . . . why do you ask so many questions all the time?"

I bump his shoulder against mine. "I need you to come with me.

That's what you said. You have to know how that sounds. All mysterious."

"It's . . . goddammit. I'm not trying to be mysterious."

I don't believe him. But it doesn't matter. Because there is nowhere else I'd rather be.

He says, "I know," like he can hear my thoughts. Maybe he can. It wouldn't be such a bad thing. Having someone know me like that. It's not the same as hearing the wolf thoughts through the bond. That's a matter of pack. This is a matter of the heart.

I go with him, because even if he's being mysterious, I would follow him everywhere.

He takes me to the tree where he kissed me for the first time.

(And where I kissed him the second time a few days later.)

He's working himself up toward something, and I think I should be nervous, think that something's wrong, but he's green, he's so green like he's relieved, and I don't know what it could be.

And then he says, "I have something for you." He slides the backpack off his back, putting it between us. He leans back against the tree.

I look down at the bag. "Like a present?"

"Sort of. I . . . just . . . ugh. This shouldn't be so hard."

I take his hand again, squeezing his fingers in mine. "It's okay. Take your time. I'm not going anywhere."

He looks at me. "You mean that, don't you?"

I blink. "Of course I do. Why wouldn't I?"

He shakes his head. "It's not—it doesn't matter." And then he says three words he's never said to me before, three words that I know in my heart he feels but never had been spoken aloud.

He says, "I love you."

My eyes are wet as I smile at him. I don't care about that. "I love you too."

He exhales. "Good."

"Good," I agree, itching to tackle him, to cover him with my entire body, to let him know that I've got him, I've got him, I've got him.

I wait, because he's not finished.

He reaches down for the backpack and unzips it, and right before he opens it, right before he takes out the object inside, I realize what this is.

What this means.

"My father gave this to me," he whispers as he pulls a stone wolf out of the bag. *And even though I should be surprised that it looks so much like my own, I'm not. It fits because we fit. There's something infinite about us, and I tell myself I will never forget this moment. The way he looks. The way he smells. The sunlight on the back of my neck and the grass beneath us. Every piece and part of it I memorize, storing away to keep it safe. To keep it whole.* "He told me one day I would know who it belongs to. Who I would want to give it to."

"And you want to give it to me," I whisper back.

He nods.

He holds it out to me.

And it's that simple.

I take it from him, and then *I tackle him. He's laughing, and I'm laughing, and I'm kissing every inch of him that I can get my mouth on, promising him all the while that I'm going to love him forever, that I'm going to be the best mate, just you wait and see, Kelly, I promise you, you're never going to be disappointed for choosing me, you're never going to think you've made a mistake, because I will do* everything *for you, and I will never, ever forget you, I—*

I

I cry out as he bites into my shoulder before I sink my own *teeth into his flesh, and it all snaps into place, this bond between us, this thread of shining light that wraps itself around my heart and tightens. There's blood in my mouth, and it's all grass and lake water and sunshine and he's summer-warm and I know what's next, I know what's going to happen next, and I don't want it, I don't want to see it, I don't want to remember. I want to stay here with him, stay here in this moment where everything is wonderful and nothing hurts. And I—*

I

I

I

I can't.

Because it's not who I am.

I see that now.

I see all that I am and all that I've become.

Who these people have made me into.

I am good.

I am loved.
I am wolf.
I am Bennett.
I am packpackpack.
There's a door.
In the middle of a clearing.
It's metal.
But when I touch it, I realize it's an illusion.
It's not metal at all.
It's glass.
There's a wolf next to me.
White with a splattering of black.
His eyes are red.
He presses his nose against my forehead, and I say, "Oh."
And then he's gone.
But others have taken his place.
All of them.
Here. With me.
Gordo says, "Kid, it's time."
Elizabeth says, "We've got you."
Jessie says, "We're here for you."
Rico says, "Until the end."
Tanner says, "It's gonna hurt, but then it'll be over."
Chris says, "And we aren't going anywhere."
Mark says, "Because you belong with us."
Carter says, "You've always belonged with us."
Joe says, "We love you."
Ox says, "And we will never let you go."

And Kelly is there, bright and beautiful Kelly, and I'm scared, I'm so goddamn scared, but he takes my hand in his, and he leans over and kisses the skin beneath my ear.

He says, "I love you, I love you, I love you, and do it, do it, Robbie, break down the door, shatter it like glass and come back. Come back to me."

For him, for them, I would do anything.
I press our joined hands against the door.
It begins to vibrate.
It cracks right down the middle.

BrotherLoveMatePackFriend we're here we're here we're here and we're the goddamn bennett pack hear us hear our song
And I—
I
I
I

I am a couple of hours from home in the middle of nowhere, Oregon. The radio is low, some shitty rock music that plays in the garage that I constantly give the guys crap for. But it reminds me of them, reminds me of home, and even though it's only been a few days, I miss them.

I miss all of them.

My phone vibrates, and I look down briefly. A text from Kelly.

Don't stop for food. Mom's cooking for you.

I grin as I send back some hearts.

I look down the lonely stretch of road in front of me. It winds through an old-growth forest, and I haven't seen another car in either direction in almost twenty minutes. It's like I'm the only person left in the world.

I think about the Omega I dropped off with her new pack. She seemed nervous, but the smiles on the pack's faces showed me we made the right decision. They'll take care of her. They'll make her part of them. She will have a home and a place in this world. And if she ever needs us, ever needs Ox, we're only a phone call away. I made sure she knew that before I left.

There's a sign up ahead, yellow with a black arrow. The curve is sharp, and I ease up on the gas pedal. I'm reaching down to turn up the stereo, the song coming on one of Gordo's favorites, though he tries to deny it. I'm singing along terribly about being hungry like the wooooolf when I hit the curve. I'll be home by lunchtime.

There's a man standing in the middle of the road.

I grunt harshly and spin the wheel. My reflexes are on point, and there's a second that feels like it stretches out for years and years when I miss him by inches, his head covered in a hood and bowed, hands pressed palms together in front of his chest as if in prayer.

The car hits the steel girder and jerks roughly, metal squealing, sparks flying. The right front tire blows out, and the steering wheel shakes under my hands. I remember what Gordo has taught me, and I fight the urge to slam on the brakes. I wasn't going fast to begin with, and the car starts to slow, the shredded tire thumping roughly. My backpack, which was sitting on the passenger seat, falls to the floor.

I come to a stop yards down the road, my heart thundering. I take in a deep breath and then another and then another. "Fuck," I mutter, rubbing my hand over my face. "Jesus Christ."

I turn off the car as I look in the rearview mirror.

The man is still in the middle of the road, facing away from me.

I'm pissed off.

It could have been worse.

It could have been so much worse.

I could have died.

I open the car door.

And immediately know something is wrong.

The forest around me is silent, but not because there's nothing there. It's an absence of sound, like I'm trapped inside some kind of bubble. I frown as I shut the door behind me, immediately on guard. There's nothing to him. No scent. I can't tell if he's a wolf or a human or—

"Hey." I take a step toward him and

(no no nononono please no please don't make me please don't make me see this)

he lifts his head, though I can't see his face. He's tall, his hands pale against the black cloak he wears. I'm acutely aware I'm far from home with no one around. I glance back at the car. The engine ticks.

"Hey," I say again as I look back at the figure. "Are you all right? Man, you can't be standing in the middle of the road. Someone could get hurt."

The man doesn't respond.

I'm getting pissed off. "I'm talking to you. What are you doing? Are you okay? I'd ask if you needed a ride, but you've fucked up your chance for that. Gordo's going to kill me. The car belongs to the shop."

And the man says, "Gordo."

I stop, a chill arcing down my spine like lightning.

The man says, "When I gave him his tattoos, he screamed. Did you know that? I can't blame him. It hurts like you wouldn't believe. But pain is edifying, teaching one the ways of the world. If there was ever a lesson I could have imparted to him, it would have been that wolves aren't the only things with teeth that tear and rend."

I take a step back, not knowing it's already too late.

The man lifts his head. His hands rise to the hood, sliding it back. His hair is white and wispy, fluttering in the cool breeze. The sleeves of his cloak slide down his wrists to his forearms, and I see the tattoos carved into his skin.

He turns his head.

He's smiling.

"No," I say. "You can't—you can't be here. You can't—"

He chuckles. "Oh, Robbie. I think you'll find that I can. Would you hear me, dear?"

I know I can't win.

Not against him.

Not against this witch.

I can't beat him alone.

I turn and run, starting to shift. My clothes are tearing as I reach the girder, planning on vaulting over it and disappearing into the woods. The trees will keep me safe. They always have. I'll be quiet as a mouse, hiding away until it's safe. I've done it once before. I can do it again.

Except I don't make it.

The air around me starts to burn ozone-sharp. I'm frozen, muscles tensing, caught halfway between human and wolf.

"Robbie," he says from behind me. "I'm afraid you're not going anywhere. Look at me."

"No," I say through gritted teeth.

"Look. At. Me."

I turn. I try to stop it, but I don't have control.

He's standing closer now. I can see the lines on his face, a face so familiar that it takes my breath away. I think wildly that *this is what Gordo will look like when he's older, this is the face of my friend,* but it's a lie, because there's something in his eyes, something dark and twisted.

He's still smiling.

He says, "You know me."

"Fuck you," I manage to say.

He shakes his head. "You're going to help me."

"The hell I will. We're going to kill you, we're going to—"

"We," he says. "We. Your pack? Yes. I suppose you think you will. But your pack isn't here, Robbie. They can't help you now."

I try to move, try to get away as he walks toward me slowly, but I can't. My feet are stuck to the ground like they've taken root.

His tattoos are so bright.

"All I want is what belongs to me," he says quietly. He's only a few feet away, and I think about Kelly waiting for me back home. Kelly, Kelly, Kelly. The last thing I sent to him was a fucking heart emoji. If only I'd known what was about to happen. If I had, I would have told him I loved him. I would have told him I never loved anyone like I love him. I would have thanked him for making me whole. For giving me hope. For giving me a home. I would have told him that even if this was always going to be my ending, if given the chance, I would do it all over again. For him. For my pack.

"You're going to help me," Robert Livingstone says. "It's time that I take back what is mine."

"I won't," I snarl at him. "I won't. I won't. I—"

I can't breathe.

His hand is wrapped around my throat and I can't breathe.

"You will," he whispers, and the tattoos on his arm are moving, oh my god, they're *alive* and *moving*, and I scream because they're coming for me, they're coming for me, they're—

(grass and lake water and sunshine)

(i see you)

(i'll never let you go)

The first symbol hits my tongue, and I'm being torn apart. It hurts like nothing ever has. It's a shock wave that obliterates almost everything else. I don't know how long it goes on, how long I hold out, because I'm fighting, oh Jesus, I'm fighting as hard as I can, but it's too much, it's too strong, and a second symbol crawls into my mouth, and it feels like dying, it feels like death, but I'm thinking about *him*, thinking about how he looked in sunlight, in the shadows late at night, how he laughed, how he whispered in my ear sweet words that meant nothing to anyone but us.

"Would you hear me, dear?" Robert Livingstone asks. "Would you hear me?"

And I'm laughing.

Here, at the end.

I'm laughing.

It's choked and terrible, but I can see the moment it hits him. There's fear on his face, though he tries to cover it up. And it only makes me laugh harder.

"I love you!" I scream into the cool morning air, a heartsong like I've never sung before. "Kelly! I love you! I love you! I love you!"

And then everything I am is gone.

* * *

I prowl through the trees.

Voices ahead.

My ears flatten against my skull.

I am wolf.

I growl.

"What the hell?" one of the voices says. "Did you hear that?"

"What? No, Tanner. I didn't hear that."

"I swear to God I heard something, Chris. What if it's an Omega? Er. Sorry, dude. Another Omega?"

"Then we run like hell and let the wolves save us like always."

Three of them.

Two humans.

One Omega.

There's a tiny voice whispering in my wolf brain, telling me no, telling me to stop, but it's buried under bloodlust.

I go for the Omega first.

He hears me coming at the last second, but he's still caught off guard.

I tear out his throat, the blood gushing over my snout.

The other two—

(chris and tanner that's CHRIS AND TANNER NONONO)

(would you hear me dear don't kill them you need to stop you need to STOP)

But there is blood on my tongue, blood down my throat, and I want more, I need more.

"What are you doing?" the one called Chris is screaming. "Robbie, what are you doing?"

I turn toward them.

They try to run.

They don't get far.
(what are you doing
robbie
robbie
please don't
please don't do this
oh my god what's wrong with you
you're not
please please please i don't want to die
please you're hurting me robbie you're hurting me
oh god no
no
let me go let me go LET ME GO LETMEGOLETME)
"Robbie!"
I lift my head.
There, standing with a stricken look on his face, is a man.
I start toward him.
And that little voice in my head whispers MateLovePack, but then it's gone.
I do the only thing I can.
I run away, away, away.

* * *

Later, much, much later, I open my eyes.
For a moment I don't know who I am.
And then—
"Hello, Robbie."
I look over. A kindly old man is sitting on a tree stump. His hands are liver-spotted and shaking, and he smiles at me. It's sweet and lovely, and I think how it's been a long time since anyone has looked at me in such a way.
"Who are you?" I ask. I push myself up off the ground. I don't remember how I got here, but it's shortly after a full moon, so I'm not surprised. Those nights can be taxing when a wolf doesn't have strong bonds with a pack.
"My name is Ezra," he says. "And I come in peace, bringing tidings of great joy. We have been watching you for a long while. My Alpha finally decided it was time. She would like to offer you a place in her pack."

And oh, are those words like a song I never expected to hear. It's too good to be true. "What?" I croak out. "Who is your Alpha?"

"Why, it's the Alpha of all," he says. "Michelle Hughes. She knows you're a good wolf. And she wants to put you to work. To give you a home. A place to belong."

I can't believe what I'm hearing. Hope rises within me. "She does?"

He nods. "She knew your mother, Robbie. She knew Beatrice Fontaine. A wonderful woman, she told me. Those were her exact words."

My eyes sting, but I can't do anything to stop it.

"You should know how rare such an offer is. You're important, Robbie. To her. To me. To all of us. Please. Would you hear me, dear?"

He says, "The Alpha of all needs you, Robbie."

He says, "It is a great honor to be summoned before her."

He says, "She has heard about you. We all have. The solitary wolf."

He says, "Would you come with me, dear? I have so much to show you."

It is too good to be true. "Are you sure? Are you sure it's me she wants?"

"Oh yes," he says. "There is no one else."

"Please," I pant. "Please, please, please."

Ezra smiles. "Good boy. Now. Take my hand. Let me guide you home."

I do the only thing I can.

I take what is offered.

He pulls me up. He's stronger than he looks.

And then he says, "Kelly."

I blink at him. "Who?"

He shakes his head. "Never mind. You remind me of someone I once knew. Slip of the tongue. Come, dear. I have much to tell you. Oh, and don't forget your backpack. I've often learned that those who travel light treasure what they have more than others. I wouldn't want you to leave anything behind."

A rush of affection roars through me at this man I don't know.

I lift my backpack from the ground, hoist it over my shoulder.

Ezra squeezes my hand. "Come, dear. It's time to go home."

He leads me away, and I don't look back. I—

I

I
I

    . . .

I opened my eyes.

Kelly was staring down at me, eyes wide and wet.

He said, "Robbie?"

I went for a smile, but it broke immediately. I tried to be strong, tried to let him know that all was well, that I remembered everything, remembered *him*, but instead of words, I started to cry.

It crashed over me, and before long my entire body was shaking as I sobbed.

He was there, right there, holding on to me like he was never going to let me go.

"It hurts, it hurts, Kelly, it *hurts*, I can't breathe, I can't—"

And he said, "I know, I know, oh, Robbie, oh, I know. But it'll pass, I swear, it'll pass, and I'll still be here, *we'll* still be here."

But I couldn't stop.

He said, "Ox! Oh my god, *Ox*, I can't—"

And the door to our bedroom crashed open, and Ox was there, and without a word he scooped me up in his arms, whispering to me that they were going to take care of me, that they were going to make it all right again.

I couldn't stop shaking as he carried me down the stairs, Kelly trailing after us.

The others were waiting for us in front of the blue house. Just when I thought I was getting under control, I saw Chris and Tanner and I *remembered* the way their blood had felt in my mouth, I *remembered* how their skin and muscles had torn, their bones breaking as I bit down, I *remembered* their screams for me to stop, to please stop, please, please, please.

But they weren't afraid of me.

They didn't cower back.

No.

Instead they put their hands on me, on my face, in my hair, telling me they loved me, they loved me and they wouldn't let anything happen to me again.

They followed us to the other house.

Joe opened the door, and Elizabeth led us to the living room. The furniture had been pushed out of the way, and there were blankets and pillows on the ground. Ox laid me down in the middle, and the others filled in the spaces around us, always touching.

Kelly was there, fierce and protective. He pulled me from Ox, and I collapsed against his chest. He ran his hands up and down my back, saying, "You're okay. You're okay. You're okay. I've got you."

I believed him.

I was safe.

I was warm.

A hand pressed against my leg. Another wrapped around my ankle. There was a kiss against the back of my neck and the scrape of fingernails against my side. Chris and Tanner shoved Ox out of the way and lay on the other side of me, wrapping themselves around me from behind, clutching me tightly. They whispered words of hope, of love and peace. I took everything they said and filled the emptiness of the void until it overflowed.

And in the middle of it all, bright as the sun, was a tangle of threads.

Of bonds that stretched between us all, stronger than they'd ever been.

They whispered *packpackpack*.

And I was home.

Eventually I quieted.

Eventually I calmed.

My chest stopped hitching.

My eyes stopped leaking.

I was very tired.

I opened my eyes.

Kelly was watching me, a worried look on his handsome face.

I reached up and touched his cheek. "I see you."

He smiled a trembling smile. "You do?"

"Yeah."

"You remember?" *You remember me?*

"All of it. Everything."

A tear fell from his eye. I wiped it away.

He grabbed my hand. "You can't ever leave me again."

I couldn't promise that. None of us could.

I said, "I won't. Never again."
He kissed me.
I closed my eyes.
And here, at last, I followed the wolfsong and found my way home.

BREAK

We should have seen it coming.
 Some days, he smiled.
 Some days, he laughed.
Some days, he looked alive, his eyes bright and shining.

But there were nights too, nights I'd hear Kelly climb out of bed. I'd listen as he went down the stairs onto the porch, where his brother waited.

I didn't want to listen.
I couldn't stop myself.
Kelly spoke.
He said, "Hold on to me."
He said, "As tightly as you can."
He said, "I know it hurts."
He said, "I know what it feels like."
He said, "But we'll find him."
He said, "We'll find him and bring him home."

Carter never spoke, but I could feel the sharpness of it along the bonds, though he tried to keep it from us. In these moments, alone with his brother, with his tether, he allowed himself to grieve.

Those nights were few and far between.
We thought he was getting better.
We thought he, like the rest of us, was recovering.

It was the beginning of December before we realized how wrong we were.

· · ·

It was a Friday, and Gordo was demanding to know why I'd thrown up Christmas all over his garage.

I waited until he was done ranting and raving. I was used to it. He would get all riled up and have a good snit and then would deflate and let me do whatever I wanted.

I just had to wait it out.

"I am drawing the line at the inflatable waving snowman," he growled at me. "I don't even want to know how the hell you got it on the roof, but I want it taken down now."

"Tanner and Chris helped me," I said, throwing them under the bus without a care in the world.

I ignored their shouts at my betrayal. Outside, flurries fell with the promise of more on the way. We were supposed to get at least eight inches overnight, something that Rico had immediately made dirty to all who would listen until Bambi told him *he* was going to get eight inches again if he didn't shut up. He'd closed his mouth immediately. I really didn't want to know. But Rico was pretty much wrapped around Bambi's finger, especially now that he'd figured out what that strange smell around her was. They were in the break room, and he was massaging her feet, telling her he was going to be the *best* daddy, just you wait and see, he was going to *rock this shit*.

I thought he would too.

But he wasn't here to save me from Gordo's wrath.

I had to face it on my own.

"It makes us look more festive," I countered. "More inviting. Gets more business. As your office manager—"

"That's not a thing."

"*As your office manager*, I made an executive decision in order to brighten the place up. Speaking of, I want to talk to you about painting next year, both interior and exterior."

Gordo scowled at me as he crossed his arms. "No. And in case you need reminding, we're the only garage within thirty miles. People come here because they don't have a choice."

I snorted. "Jesus. How the hell did you ever survive without me?"

His expression softened, and I knew I had him. "That's . . ." He narrowed his eyes. "Are you *playing* me?"

Goddammit. "Uh. No? I'm just reminding you that last Christmas, I was alone in Maine with your father while the rest of you were here, and how sad I was, even though I didn't remember any of you, and it's just so heartbreaking to think—"

He threw up his hands. Well, one hand at least. "Fine. But no more."

"Maybe a little more," I countered. "I found these lights in the attic of the house. They blink. I'm going to hang them around the front."

"No."

"Gordo. So sad. So alone."

"Ox!" he yelled. "Do your Alpha thing and make him stop!"

"Can't!" Ox called back. "I promised myself to never use my power for evil!"

I grinned at Gordo. "See? You lose. And while I'm at it, I want to talk to you about the office Christmas party we're going to have."

"The office *what*?"

"We'll—"

And it hit us.

Glass shattering in our chests.

Gordo grimaced, the raven folding its wings, the roses shriveling.

I gasped, bending over the desk, claws digging into the wood.

Rico snarled even as Bambi asked him what was wrong.

"What the fuck?" I muttered. "What the hell was that?" I blinked rapidly, trying to understand the wave of blue that washed over me.

Ox burst through the doorway, eyes red and violet. The others were close behind him.

"Home," he growled. "We have to get home. Something's wrong."

. . .

Kelly pulled in front of us as we were leaving the garage, the bar on top of his cruiser lit up, siren wailing. Ox was on the phone with Joe as Gordo drove, the others in a truck behind us. Ox was saying, "You felt it, he wouldn't, no, please tell me he wouldn't, is he—"

The snow was falling harder by the time we reached the house at the end of the lane.

Kelly had barely put the car in park before he jumped out and ran toward the house, the rest of us on his heels.

We followed the sound of a breaking heart to the office.

Elizabeth Bennett stood in front of her husband's old desk, hand over her mouth, eyes wet. In her other hand was a piece of paper.

She looked up at us as Joe roared and punched a hole in the wall. Mark was looking off into nothing, his mouth in a thin line.

"What is it?" Kelly demanded. "Where's Carter, why can't I feel him, what happened, what happened, *what*—"

She dropped her hand. She whispered, "He's gone."

Joe slumped against the wall, sliding down to the floor, face in his hands.

"No," Kelly said, stepping forward. "No, he wouldn't, he wouldn't leave, he wouldn't do that to me, he wouldn't—"

Elizabeth held up the paper in her hand.

Kelly didn't take it, a haunted look on his face.

Ox moved around him. He took the paper from Elizabeth even as Jessie burst into the house, breathless. "What happened?" she asked as she pushed her way into the office. "Is something coming? Are we under attack?"

"It's Carter," Rico muttered, rubbing the back of his neck. "He left."

We all looked to Ox. He was staring down at the paper in his hands, eyes darting back and forth. He was pale when he looked back up at us. "He's gone after Gavin. He says he's sorry, but he has to do this. He has to find him." He swallowed thickly. "And that he was going to cut himself off from us. From the pack. He doesn't want anyone coming after him. He doesn't want anyone else getting hurt."

"No," Kelly said, shaking his head. "He wouldn't—he wouldn't do that to me." Anger like I'd never felt from him before filled his voice, tinged with the deepest blue. "He wouldn't. I'm his *brother*. I'm his *tether*. He wouldn't—" His voice broke.

"There's a message for you," Elizabeth said quietly as she cried. "He made a video."

Ox turned on the TV hanging from the wall.

The screen was blue.

Ox pressed Play.

Carter Bennett filled the screen, sitting behind his father's desk. His face was pale. He took in a stuttering breath and shook his head.

Then:

Kelly, I . . .

I love you more than anything in this world.

Please remember that.

I know this is going to hurt, and I'm sorry. But I have to do this.

You see, there was this boy. And he's the best thing that ever happened to me. He gave me the courage to stand for what I believe in, to fight for those I care about. He taught me the strength of love and brotherhood. He made me a better person.

You, Kelly.

Always you.

You *are the best thing that's ever happened to me.*

You're my first memory. Mom was holding you, and I wanted to take you for myself, hide you away so no one would hurt you.

You're my first love. I knew that when you would always smile when you saw me, and it was like staring into the sun.

You're my heart.

You are my soul.

I love Mom. She taught me kindness.

I love Dad. He taught me how to be a good wolf.

I love Joe. He taught me that strength comes from within.

But you were my greatest teacher. Because with you, I understood life. What it meant to love someone so blindingly and without reservation. To have a purpose. To have hope. I have been a big brother for most of my life, and it's the best thing I could ever be. Without you, I would be nothing.

I know you're going to be angry.

But I hope you understand, at least a little bit.

Because I have this hole in my chest.

This void.

And I know why.

I do.

It's because of him.

I have to find him, Kelly. I have to find him because I think without him, there's always going to be part of me that feels like I'm incomplete.

I should have listened to you more when Robbie was gone.

I should have fought harder.

I didn't understand then.

I do now, and I'm sorry. I'm so sorry.

Maybe he'll want nothing to do with me. Maybe he'll . . .

I have to try. And I know Ox and Joe and all the others are looking for him, for the both of them, but it's not enough. Kelly, he saved us. I see that now. He saved us all.

And I have to do the same for him.

I have to.

I made you a promise once. I told you that I would always come back for you. I meant it then and I mean it now. I will always come back for you. No matter where I am, no matter what I'm doing, I'll be thinking of you and imagining the day I get to see you again. I don't know when that's going to be, but after you kick my ass, after you scream and yell at me, please hug me like you're never going to let me go because I won't ever want you to.

Fuck. I can't breathe. I can't—

Kelly stepped forward and pressed his hand against the screen, the tips of his fingers covering Carter's throat. He hung his head, shoulders shaking.

Remember something for me, okay?

When the moon is full and bright and you're singing for all the world to hear, I'll be looking up at the same moon, and I'll be singing right back to you. For you.

Always you.

I love you, little brother, even more than I can put down in words. You've got to be brave for me. Keep Joe honest. Give Ox shit. Teach Rico how to be a wolf. Show Chris and Tanner the depths of your heart. Hug Mom and Mark. Tell Gordo to lighten up. Have Jessie kick anyone's ass who steps out of line.

And love Robbie like it's the last thing you'll ever do.

I will come back for you, and nothing will hurt us ever again.

I'll be seeing you, okay?

The video ended, Carter's face frozen on the screen.

No one spoke.

Eventually Kelly turned toward us, and for a moment, I was reminded of his brother standing in the ruins of the compound like a lost little boy, asking why, why, why did he go, why did he have to leave?

I felt cleaved in two.

He walked by us without speaking.

The others parted.

I followed him.

He went out the front door and down the porch. He looked around, his breath like smoke pouring from his mouth as the snow fell. "He'll come back," he muttered. "He'll come back when I call for him. He said he always would, he promised me, he *promised* me."

Kelly tilted his head back and howled.

It was an aria of blue.

It echoed in the forest around us as it died.

He waited.

There was nothing.

He did it again.

And again.

And again.

By the fourth time, his voice was hoarse and cracking.

He stumbled forward. "Carter! *Carter*!"

Winter birds took flight from the trees.

"CARTER!"

I caught him before he fell to the ground. I went down with him, holding him against my chest. He laid his head back on my shoulder and howled again, the air splitting around us. But this song wasn't about calling his brother home.

It was a hymn for the missing.

For the lost.

I tightened my hold around him.

"We'll find him," I whispered. "I promise. We'll find him."

The snow continued to fall.

ELEVEN
MONTHS
LATER

PROMISE

In the middle of nowhere, an old truck pulled into a gravel parking lot in front of a small, squat building. The town around him looked as if it'd died a long time ago, and all that remained was dust and bones.

The door to the truck opened and a tall man stepped out, boots crunching in the gravel. He squinted up against the afternoon sun. Deep lines formed around his eyes and mouth, and the bones in his cheeks were prominent. His hair curled around the collar of his jacket, shaggy and unkempt. He rubbed a hand over a scraggly beard, scratching his jaw. His jeans were torn, his right knee poking through.

He rubbed a hand over his face as he sighed.

It'd been a long day.

A threadbare flag fluttered.

He didn't see anyone else on the road.

He walked toward the building.

An old flyer in one of the windows, the paper yellowed with age, the edges worn, advertised a potluck from four years before.

He pushed open the door. Cool air washed over him.

A woman looked up from behind the counter. Her eyes widened at the sight of the man, and she glanced over her shoulder as if looking for someone to save her.

He ignored it. He knew how he looked. He couldn't do anything about it. He wasn't going to hurt her. He just wanted what was his. What he'd come for.

He *knew* it was here too.

He could smell it.

Faint, but still there.

He sucked in a greedy breath, tasting the last lingering scent.

The woman said, "Help you?"

The man said, "I think you have something for me."

"That right? Don't know what that would be. Never seen you before in my life. You're not from around here."

The man chuckled tiredly. "No. Definitely not. I'm not even sure where here is."

Her gaze narrowed. "Bedford. Kentucky."

"Huh," the man said. "Never been to Kentucky before. How about that." He took a step toward the counter and was surprised when he found he couldn't move. He should have seen this coming. Stupid mistake.

He looked up.

Above him, etched into a beam on the ceiling, was a glyph he didn't recognize, pulsing green.

"Wolf," the woman whispered.

"Witch," he replied. "I'm not here to hurt you. Or anyone in this town."

"You really expect me to believe that?"

"You have something for me."

"I don't know what you're—"

"A week ago, another wolf came in here," he said. "Give or take a day or two. Left a message. Probably told you I'd be coming." He sighed. "Probably bitched about it too."

She stared at him for a moment.

Then she nodded. "I might remember something like that. I didn't believe him when he told me who it was for. Name like that doesn't come around these parts."

"Lived here long?"

"All my life."

He looked out the window. "There used to be a pack around here, right? Probably before you. Who was their witch? Your mother or your father?"

"Why?"

He shrugged. "Humor me."

"My mother. She's dead. Long time. Wolves are long gone." She frowned. "I like it better that way. Don't care much for wolves. You'd do best to move on."

"I will. Just as soon as you give me the message."

She hesitated before she turned around and disappeared through a door.

She was back even before it stopped swinging.

In her hand was an envelope.

She placed it on the counter and stepped back before she held up her hand, fingers twitching as she muttered under her breath. There was another pulse of green, and the glyph above faded.

"Take it," she said. "Take it and leave."

"How long?" he asked as he stepped up to the counter. He stared reverently down at the envelope. He was almost scared to touch it for fear this was nothing but a dream. "How long ago did you get this?"

"Six days."

"And which way did he head after he left?"

A pause. Then, "North."

"Did you see anyone else? Don't lie to me."

She shook her head. "I think he was alone."

The man picked up the envelope. "Oh, I doubt that." He closed his eyes as he brought it up to his nose, inhaling deeply.

Yes.

Yes.

Yes.

He turned to leave.

He was at the door when the woman said, "Is it true?"

He stopped, but he didn't look back. "What?"

"What they're saying. About the Alphas. About the wolves. About a beast that can't be killed."

He looked back at her, eyes flashing Beta orange. "Oh, he'll die. I'm going to make sure of that. Forget you ever saw me. I was never here."

And then he pushed open the door and stepped out into the parking lot.

For years, after all was said and done, the woman would remember this man.

She would remember how all she felt from him was blue.

But if pressed, she would say that underneath everything, she felt the green of relief.

Of hope.

It was small, but there.

And it was enough.

And though now she didn't recognize it for what it was, she still followed him out the door.

She said, "Wait."

She said, "I think..."

She said, "He didn't recognize me. But I recognized him."

She said, "And I think I know where he's going."

The man climbed back into the truck, the bench seat creaking under his weight. He tapped the envelope against the steering wheel, trying to gather his courage.

A flutter in the back of his mind, an old memory hidden away. A little thing his father had told him. A bit of a poem. He couldn't remember it exactly, never having been one for poetry, but it'd always stuck with him. Something about promises to keep, and miles to go before he could sleep.

He opened the envelope carefully, almost lovingly.

He set it aside as he unfolded the piece of paper.

Six words in large, blocky letters.

But it was enough. He traced his finger over the words, already committing them to memory, as he had the ones that'd come before.

STOP FOLLOWING ME. GO HOME ASSHOLE.

He stared at it for the longest time.

Eventually he put it with the others in the glove compartment.

He looked down at the dash.

There, resting against the odometer, was a photograph.

Three boys with blond hair and bright blue eyes, all smiling widely.

Brothers.

He reached out and touched the faces of the younger two.

"Soon," he whispered, and it was a promise he would keep.

A moment later the truck started up.

He pulled out of the parking lot.

Before he headed north, he turned on the radio.

An old rock song was just beginning.

He thought the band was called Rainbow.

The song was "Run With the Wolf."

Carter Bennett laughed until there were tears in his eyes.

And then he drove on.

Read on for an exclusive

Heartsong

SHORT STORY

The wolf mother. A queen. A survivor. A wife, a partner.
Elizabeth Bennett thinks about memory and the power it has. To lift, to destroy, reminders of what was and what will never be. Strong memories: Thomas, a teenager. Cocky, with a half smile with enough power to light up a small city, and he *knew* it. The first time she'd met him she'd been unimpressed, even if his scent was unlike anything she'd experienced before. The second time had gone about as well as the first, though hazy now, lost to time and age.

It's the third time that has stayed with her all these years. Both young, both powerful, but trapped in a bubble where nothing hurt, where everything felt like it should be. That bubble would burst, and devastatingly so, but not then. Not the third time.

His father had insisted upon the meeting, and what Abel Bennett wanted, he got. As the Alpha of all, when he spoke, people listened. Her mother had been in a tizzy over it, Elizabeth rolling her eyes at the thought of such a fuss over a silly boy. She would rather be running through the forest, her shift coming easier for her now. Yes, Thomas was handsome, and he could be funny in unexpected ways, but he was also a Bennett: full of himself, his name an immovable crown that would always be part of him.

This third time started off the same as the other meetings: Elizabeth curious, but not letting it show on her face; Thomas posing even though he'd deny it when called out for it. He had muscles, which . . . okay. So did she; did he think it would impress her?

Later, when it was just the two of them, he said, "I'm going to be the Alpha one day."

She snorted, sunlight filtering in through the kitchen window, motes of dust floating in dizzying dances. She looked at him across from her, popping his knuckles again and again. Bemused, she realized he was nervous. He should be. She knew her worth.

"I don't actually care about that," she said, just to see what he would do.

"Oh." He deflated. "That's . . . fair. It's not *that* big of a deal. I guess."

"But good for you," she said. "That's what our world needs, another man in charge."

He blinked at her, mouth agape.

She watched him as she sipped her tea.

Thomas stared at her for a long moment. Then he asked a question she did not expect, a question that changed everything. Years and years later, she would look back upon this moment as the time when she began to believe. That he was something . . . special. That he could be something more.

He asked, "What would you do differently?"

No one had ever asked her that question before. No one had sought out *her* opinion. Not about being human, not about being a wolf, *anything*. And here he was, a king-in-waiting, the closest thing to a prince the wolf world would ever know, and he wanted to know what *she* would do.

Never one to let an opportunity go to waste, Elizabeth Bennett spent the next two hours outlining everything she would change. For his part, Thomas never once tried to interrupt her. Instead, he nodded every now and then. Other times, he rubbed his jaw thoughtfully. Still others, he laughed, a sunny sound that crept into her bones and made a home for itself.

When she finished, her throat was parched, her eyes a little gritty. But she did not regret it, not for a moment. If Thomas Bennett thought anything was going to happen with them, then he needed to understand that she was *not* a demure, passive partner. She had seen the way her mother constantly gave in to her father's wants and whims—even to her own detriment—and she had long ago promised herself that she'd never be put into the same position. She had a voice and she planned to use it, regardless of what others thought.

She was about to tell him as much when he reached over and laid his hand on top of hers, a warm weight that she could pull away from if she chose.

She didn't.

Because Thomas Bennett said, "I've never met anyone like you before."

He said, "Where did you come from?"

He said, "Why can't you be the Alpha? You'd be better at it than all the rest of us put together."

And with that, she was lost to him.

In the clearing, the boys seated before her, Elizabeth thinks she hears a warm, familiar chuckle from somewhere behind her. A brush of fingers through her hair. She doesn't turn; she doesn't need to. There wouldn't be anyone there.

But she knows.

She says, "Sen knew something was wrong. The cat was dead, but its bite had pierced her flesh. Before long, she could feel it inside, the rot. The blackness. It ate at her, sticky little tentacles reaching, reaching for every part that made her human."

"Omega," the youngest boy whispers, eyes wide.

Yes, she thinks as a low tremor rolls through her. *Yes*. Time heals, but it's not a cure-all. It can't be. Not after all she's seen. Not after all she's done.

She says, "She was running out of time."

She says, "It grew harder to breathe, and she felt so *angry*."

She says—

It pulled at her, the infection, the disease, the darkest parts of her whispering, Give in, let it wash over you, let it take you away. You tried. You did. More than anyone else. Isn't it easier to just . . . stop?

She shoved the voice away, and it laughed, a twisted approximation of her own.

Nights became days which became nights again, all melting together. It was the sun, then the moon, then both at the same time. Stars during the day, gone at night, leaving only a black shroud covering the world.

Sen was no longer sure if she was heading in the right direction. Once, during daylight that seemed to never end, she'd become distracted by an animal. A marmot, uninfected by the rot. She hunted it, chasing it through trees and shrubs that left scratches on her arms and face. The wood dissolved around her in streaks of wet paint, and she snapped and snarled at it, wet chokes turning into gibbering howls.

Days—weeks? months? years?—later, she found herself at a small pool of water with nary a ripple. She leaned over it, her reflection staring back at her. She panted; her reflection smiled—teeth bloodied with bits of hair stuck in them—and violet eyes flashed brightly.

Hungry, always hungry. The fruit, dried meats, bitter, dead. Alive, she needed something alive with hot flesh and molten blood. Sink her teeth into it. Tear, rend, destroy.

Feed. Feed. Feed.

At some point, she began to run. She did not know why. Something chasing her? Or was she the pursuer? A thin line between hunter and prey. Her head jerked side to side at every sound. Distractions, and dangerous ones at that.

She ran and ran through the woods, through the ancient forest, blind to the fact that the rot reached for her at every step, begging her to let it consume her, let it have her, let it taste her. She felt it nipping at her heels.

Faster and faster and faster until she—

Until she came to a clearing.

She burst through the tree line, lines of rot snapping out around her. As she hit the ground hard, she rolled onto her back, knife held out in front of her.

Nothing came.

The trees closed, branches and vines moving to close the path.

She stood slowly as a deep and rumbling voice spoke from behind her.

"Human," it said.

Heart jackrabbiting in her chest, she turned.

In the center of the clearing, a god. It lay on its stomach, paws stretched out in front of it, each longer and wider than the woman before it. The creature—the wolf god—defied logic, defied reason, but then gods often do. With a coat of pure white, the wolf towered above her, its massive head bigger than even the largest home in the village. The tip of one of its twitching ears blocked out the sun. Its nose—the same black as the blade of her knife—leaked rot down the front of the wolf's maw, the hair coated, glistening. Its tail did not move, curled around its left side, bushy, limp.

Sen stared at the god with a mixture of terror and awe. She could not speak, her throat closed, tiny whistling breaths falling from her lips.

"**You do not belong here,**" the God of the Forest said. "**A child of man is not fit to stand before me. Leave, or I shall eat you as I have all the others.**"

"Not all of them," she said. "Stories, tales, whispers about people coming to you on two legs and leaving on four." She shook her head as the rot fought for control of her voice. "No. I have traveled far for an audience. I will not be denied."

The God of the Forest snorted, shaking its head. Splashes of rot fell from its nose, landing on the ground. Each bit of black oil appeared sentient, crawling for the tree line. "**Humans,**" it said angrily. "**You take and you take and you take, and even when you've taken all there is, you still want more. Selfish.**"

"It's killing us," she cried, and it was only then she realized how angry she was. "The infection is spreading through the forest. Everything is affected. If it doesn't stop, nothing will survive."

"**Perhaps it's for the best,**" the God of the Forest said. "**It was only a matter of time before man gave in to his true nature. You think yourself better than all of creation even though as a species, you have barely learned to walk upright. Younglings. That's all you are.**"

"I am not afraid of you," Sen said. "I—" She coughed roughly, hand to her mouth. When she pulled it away, her palm was coated in black. She could feel it on her teeth, her tongue.

The old god laughed, a low, throaty thing. "**It seems as if you have something else to be afraid of. Can you feel it? Tugging at you. The insistence. The corruption. You are not immune.**"

"What is it?" she whispered, wiping her mouth with her sleeve.

"**Balance,**" the wolf said. "**Where there is light, there is darkness. One cannot exist without the other.**" It blinked slowly, eyes a cold blue one moment and violet the next. "**This is . . . inevitable.**"

"No," she said, shaking her head. "I refuse to believe that. You're sick, and it's spread through the forest. The only way to save everything is if you help us."

The wolf rose, the ground shaking underneath the weight of its body. It towered above her, a bird flying between its ears, and as she took the beast in, she saw something she had missed: in the center of its chest, a barbed spine jutted out, the hair around it matted with shining black liquid.

"What is that?" she asked.

The wolf god grinned, its fangs on full display, gums black and dead. "*What you have done to me. A penance because of the hubris of your kind. I created the ground, the trees, the wind. I made the air and the stars and the berries you pick in summer and autumn. I made the food and the water. I gave you life, gave the magic of my kind to your people, and this is how I am repaid? You make demands of me as if your people aren't filled with malice and fear and destruction. You claim the poison is killing the world as if you haven't already started to do the same.*"

"If you made us, then how is this our fault?" Sen asked angrily. Then, without waiting for an answer, "We pray to you. You choose to ignore us."

"*I am a god,*" the wolf said. "*What I do with my time is my business. I should eat you now and be done with you, ungrateful little child.*"

Sen raised her knife. "You can try."

The god chuckled as it lowered its head toward her. Its immense size was almost impossible for her to quantify. Its nose—now near the ground—was almost as tall as she was. "*You are a curious creature. The others who have come before you cowered in fear. Why are you different?*" He inhaled deeply, her clothes rustling, strands of hair lifting from her head. "*Do you feel it inside? The way it pulls, the way it yanks at every single part of you. Wouldn't it be easier to just . . . let it? Why would you continue to fight what you cannot stop?*"

"Because someone has to," she said, skin slick with sweat. She was burning from the inside out. Angry at the god. Furious that it would not listen. Her hand itched to lash out with the knife, to cut into the wolf and see what kind of blood spilled out. Perhaps it would contain all the secrets of the universe that would become hers if she drank of it. Or maybe, just maybe, she would become the God of the Forest. Cut its heart from its chest and eat away at it until she had her fill.

This did not go unnoticed by the wolf. It said, "*It's in you. It's not changing you but revealing what has always been there: a destiny of pain and death. That is all humans are capable of. It's all you've ever been.*"

"We are more than that," Sen said, though it felt like a lie. "And you can't see that because you've been blinded to what you've become."

"*And what is that, child?*" the god asked dangerously. It lifted its head away from her, moving toward the other side of the clearing. As

Sen looked on, black rot fell from its body, splashing on the ground. The god stopped, snuffling the top of one of the trees.

"A monster," she said. "You say you created the world. Why would you want to be the one who destroys it?"

"**Because it is my right,**" the god thundered, looking back at her over its shoulder. "**If humanity is a disease, then I must be the cure.**" Its eyes began to fill with violet. "**I grow weary of you. Be a dear, won't you? Start running. I do love a good chase.**"

And with that, it spun around quickly, charging toward her, the ground rolling beneath its paws. Jaws hanging open, the wolf god lowered its head toward her.

Sen didn't move.

The god skidded to a stop in front of her, dust billowing in thick clouds, the wolf's paws leaving long divots in the ground. It opened its mouth wide and roared at her, the stench from its throat meaty, sickly. Rotten.

"You don't frighten me," she said, skin vibrating.

"**Lies,**" the God of the Forest said, nostrils flaring. "**Perhaps others would believe such a thing, but I am a god. I see you, Sen. I see every single part of you.**" It inhaled again. "**You dreamed of it, didn't you? What you will become.**"

"No," she said, and for a moment, she could taste her grandfather's blood on her tongue. "I would rather die than let that happen."

"**Then allow me to be of service,**" the god said. "**After all, I am a benevolent god when I want to be. It will be over before you know it, and then all of this will just fade away.**"

She eyed the spear in its chest. "That," she said, pointing at it. "Where did that come from?"

"**It does not matter. It is of no concern. Stalling isn't going to save you.**"

"I can remove it. Help you. Free you from it."

"**What if I don't want you to?**" the god asked. "**It is mine. And it's not as if it'd do you any good. Be it here, now, or sometime far, far away, humans will spread an infection of their own, one without a cure. You cannot stop it.**"

And she said, "I can try."

She was moving even before the God of the Forest could react, her footsteps light, quick, almost as if she were floating. As she approached its right paw, the god snapped at her, teeth like spikes as she dove out of the way, somersaulting before leaping to her feet and jumping.

Sen landed on the wolf's right paw. Clenching the knife between her teeth, she began to climb the wolf's leg, pulling at the long hair for purchase.

The wolf attempted to shake her off, jumping up and down, flicking its paw back and forth. Its massive head dove toward her, and she leapt up the limb, fangs missing her legs by mere inches, the heat of its breath like a flash fire against her skin.

She continued to climb, muscles quivering with exhaustion. The rot inside her told her to bite, to sink her teeth into the god's leg and chew her way into the wolf.

She ignored it, but barely.

As she climbed higher and higher toward the barb in its chest, the wolf tilted its head back and howled, its song as loud as anything Sen had ever heard. She gritted her teeth against it, looking up. As she watched, the sky split apart, sunlight giving way to the black of night, and stars appeared, so many stars that did not exist, forming constellations that flickered and fluttered across the sky.

The sun sank quickly, and in its place, a full moon rose from the curve of the world, its ethereal shine bright and cold.

Climbing higher and higher, she reached the top of the leg. Above her and off to the left, the barb, the spine, the spear: it stuck out from the wolf's chest, quivering. The wolf lifted its leg once more—to try to shake her off again?—but it only brought her closer to the thing in its chest.

As the wolf howled again—longer, louder, filled with rage—she jumped with all her might . . .

. . . and crashed into the spine stomach first, bent over it awkwardly. The impact knocked the breath from her lungs, and as the wolf howled in pain, she began to slide off the barb, hands coated with rot. She caught herself at the last moment, feet dangling into nothing, the thin muscles in her arms burning.

"Little flea," the god muttered. "**After I finish with you, I'll find your village. Nothing will remain once I'm done. Your people, your life, your history will only be smoldering ruins. Humanity deserves no better.**"

Yes, *a dark voice whispered in her head.* Consume. Eat. Destroy. Blood in the soil. Flesh in the teeth.

"No," Sen said, panting. "No. I won't let you."

Swinging her lower body back and forth, she managed to press both feet flat against the wolf. With the last of her strength, she gripped the spear, sludge coating her fingers, crawling across her knuckles to the back of her hands to her wrists, her forearms. It felt heavy, alive, her skin crawling.

She pulled, gritting her teeth.

The god howled again as the barb gave just a little, rot pouring from the wound in a gush that slapped against her torso, her hips, her legs. It dripped down to the ground beneath her and still she pulled, hands sliding, the cords in her neck jutting out in sharp relief. Through a tiny sliver in the cracks of her eyelids, she saw the moon begin to spin, followed by the stars, all swirling as if caught in a tornado.

The spear slid out another inch, and the wolf screamed, a sound that tore through Sen, but not enough to make her stop. In a clearing so far from home and under an alien sky with a feral god, Sen sent a prayer up into the endless void, one free of rot and violence.

The spear pulled free in a wet squeal of grinding bone, and Sen fell, black infection raining down around her.

She landed roughly, awkwardly, her left leg folded at an odd angle. It snapped immediately, bone bursting through skin. She screamed, her chest feeling like she'd swallowed sharp glass. A bubble of blood burst from her mouth, coating her cheeks and nose and chin in a fine mist.

She tried to rise, but the pain proved to be too great.

Turning her head slowly, her vision failing, she saw the thing that had pierced the god: embedded into the earth, the spine. The barb.

The spear.

She recognized it. It had come from her village. Wood from an oak. Feathers at one end from an eagle, painted blue and green. At the other, sticking partway up from the earth, a pointed end carved from black stone, the same stone that formed the blade of her knife.

"We did this," she whispered.

The sky above—stars and moon fixed in the sky once more—disappeared as a great shadow appeared above her.

"Yes," the god said. "**You did. They came. They did not see a god, but a monster. And in their fear, the humans acted as they're wont to do: rather than allowing mysteries to exist in an unknown world,** they allowed their terror to rule them. A spear to the chest of the god they came to worship? To make demands of? Their fear—their hatred—spread to me, and they paid for it with their lives."

"They didn't know," she said weakly. "You can't blame them for that."

The wolf snorted. At the edges of her awareness, Sen saw the wound in the wolf's chest had closed, all evidence of infection gone. Even its eyes were different, a swirl of red and orange that looked like the sun.

"**You are broken**," the god said, lowering its head farther, the exhalations from its nose like a warm breeze across her skin. "**Your body is dying. The infection may yet delay the inevitable, but it will matter little to you. All that you know will be gone.**"

"So long as you are free," Sen whispered, "I will greet death with open arms."

The god's eyes narrowed. "**Why?**"

She coughed, her chest on fire. Blood dribbled down the side of her cheek. "Because everything deserves a chance. Even you."

The god said, "**I do not understand you.**"

The god said, "**But I don't know that I need to.**"

The god said, "**You have done me a great service this day. A gift, then, in recompense. Perhaps you are the one who can change the fate of your kind. Or perhaps you'll squander it, and those who come after you will only know darkness. What will you do, I wonder?**"

She didn't have any strength left to fend off the god. Her limbs were numb, cold, lifeless. Her heart stuttered in her chest as the wolf opened its mouth, an endless maw that looked as if it could swallow the world.

It did not.

Instead, it bit down gingerly onto her left hand, the palm caught between two fangs: one from above and one from below. Warmth, then, not from blood or infection, but from the breath of a god, and as she exhaled, it breathed in and bit down, the fangs piercing her hand.

Sen opened her mouth, but no sound came out. She felt the pain from the bite—bright, like a shooting star—but then it was gone, gone, gone as her body began to seize. Her legs jerked, her right arm flailed, her left still caught in the teeth of the wolf. Unable to stop it, her back arched painfully, spine cracking, teeth tearing into her bottom lip.

The bone in her leg pulled back into the skin, the flesh knitting itself together, smooth and unmarked. Her vision sharpened until she could see the grain of the wood of a broken tree limb lying on the ground on the other side of the field. She sat up as the wolf released her hand. Lifting her palm in front of her face, spinning it this way and that, she watched the holes from the wolf's fangs close.

And then her gorge rose swiftly and without warning. She barely had time to turn her head before she vomited a noxious black stream onto the ground. She gagged around it, feeling it pull against her tongue, her teeth, the roof of her mouth. The mess quivered as she wiped the back of her hand across her mouth, before it hardened, turned gray. The wolf lowered its head toward it and blew a stream of air from between its lips. The rot fluttered, flaked, and then flew away until there was nothing left.

Sen rose unsteadily to her feet. She felt . . . different. Stronger. More powerful. Alive in ways she'd never experienced before. She breathed in, and the scents that flooded her nose should have been overwhelming, but she could parse through them with the greatest of ease. The forest. The undergrowth. Moss and lichen and sap and fungus. Her hearing, elevated. A herd of deer moving unseen, the blood flowing through veins and arteries. The flap of a hawk's wings as it circled overhead. A boulder tumbling down the opposite side of the mountain.

In wonder, Sen asked, "What have you done to me?"

"*A gift*," the god said. "**A curse. I alone cannot free the world of infection. It is beyond me now. It may appear to recede, even for lifetimes, but it will never truly disappear. It cannot, for as long as humans exist, there will be darkness.**" It looked up into the night sky. "**Bound to the power of the full moon, you will spread my gift to your people as others have done before. It will be up to you to lead them. Will you be their savior? Or will you be their ending? That remains to be seen.**"

"How?" she asked.

The wolf lowered its head toward her until they were face-to-face. She could see herself reflected back in its eyes, and for a moment, she thought her own eyes flashed red.

"**Alpha**," said the God of the Forest.

Elizabeth Bennett says, "Sen returned to her village. Weeks had passed, and her people had thought her lost to the forest. When she emerged, a great celebration occurred. They sang and danced and ate until they could eat no more. And once the revelry had died down, Sen told them the truth. She showed them what she had become."

"An Alpha," the youngest boy says in awe.

"Yes," Elizabeth says. "An Alpha, made to fight the infection that now existed in the world. And though her people were rightfully scared, they listened, they learned. They accepted the gift from the God of the Forest, and Sen became their leader. A pack. Just like ours."

"And the infection?" the oldest boy asks. "The rot. The thing that turns us into Omegas?"

"Not gone," Elizabeth says carefully. "It never can be. Where there is fear and hatred, an infection finds a home. It can spread unchecked until the wolf is feral. But worry not, little ones. Our bonds are strong, our tethers right where they need to be, which is the point of the story. If we take what Sen learned, and use it to—"

"There you guys are," a voice says. "Dad said it's almost time."

Elizabeth looks up from her grandsons and finds her granddaughter standing a few feet away, hands on her hips. Callie—with short brown hair and the sardonic smirk only found on fifteen-year-old girls—taps her foot impatiently. "I'm starving, and Dad said we can't eat until everyone is there. Up, up!"

Elizabeth smiles. "Of course. It's tradition, after all. Come, my cubs. Callie has spoken, and you know what happens when we stand between her and a meal."

The boys rise to their feet, jostling each other. The oldest two, brothers: Caleb, freshly turned eleven, and Zane, a newly minted teenager. Zane helps Caleb up from the ground, brushing grass and dirt from his shorts, a bittersweet echo of her oldest sons at that age.

Liam, the youngest at seven, decides he needs to do somersaults in the grass. "Three more," he begs even as Callie grumbles about being late for burgers.

Before Elizabeth can answer, Zane scoops Liam up and throws him over his shoulder. "Dinner," he tells Liam above his complaints. The boy sighs, deflates, and then says he can walk *just* fine, and that he doesn't need to be carried. Zane sets him down with a warning. Liam, of course, immediately performs a series of serviceable somersaults, leaping to his feet and howling at the sky, his arms above his head.

They move through the woods, her grandchildren chattering excitedly around her about First Wolves and Alphas and gods that lived in the forest. Liam holds her hand, swinging it back and forth. Ahead, their heads pressed together, Caleb and Zane, whispering.

Callie walks with Elizabeth and Liam. She's distracted, as if something's on her mind. Elizabeth bumps her shoulder and says, "All right?"

Callie blinks, looking a tad sheepish. "Just . . . thinking."

"About?"

"Being Alpha."

"Ah," she says. "I see. Have you talked to your fathers about it?"

She shrugs. "You know how they are. Lessons. Instructions." She makes a face. "Long walks in the woods where barely anyone talks because I'm supposed to be feeling up trees or whatever."

Elizabeth barely holds back a laugh. "That sounds about right, though don't let them know I said that."

Callie rolls her eyes. "I know I'm supposed to be a certain way because of what I'll become, but what if I suck at it?" She looks away. "What if I make things bad for everyone?"

"I have known many Alphas," Elizabeth says slowly. "Some good, some . . . not. You will be one of the good ones, Callie. I know it."

"Yeah," Liam says. "And I'll get to be a Beta in your pack, and we'll go on adventures and be like Sen!" He tugs on his grandmother's hand. "Is there really a gigantic wolf in the forest?"

"I don't know," Elizabeth says. "Perhaps you and Callie and Zane and Caleb will be the ones to find it again."

"I'll make it sing with me," Liam says firmly. "I bet I can howl louder than it. And it'll be all, like, *Whoa. Maybe you're the best wolf.*"

"You're so special," Callie says.

"Thanks!" Liam says cheerfully.

"See?" Elizabeth says, glancing at her granddaughter. "You won't be alone. Never again."

Callie takes Elizabeth's hand in her own and squeezes. Then she says something so preposterous that Elizabeth almost chokes.

"Mark told me that we should start calling Gordo *Guncle.*"

She laughs, the wolf mother. She laughs loud and bright. It causes Zane and Caleb to look back at them, Zane's eyebrow arched, Caleb looking confused. She waves them off as she laughs and laughs.

When she has some semblance of control, she says, "I agree. If you'd like, I can record it when you do. I'm sure his reaction will be . . . proportional."

"That just means he's going to get red in the face and yell about *fuckin' werewolves*," Liam says sagely.

"Language," Elizabeth scolds. "You don't get to say such things until you're far older."

"Guess what else you can't do until you're older?" Callie asks. "Watch!"

And with that, she runs away from them, her shift coming quickly. Muscles groan and expand, clothes tear—honestly, do they think money grows on trees?—and then a tan-and-black wolf is barreling through Caleb and Zane, knocking them to the side. They yell after her before they too shift, running, running, paws kicking up dirt and leaves.

Elizabeth sighs as she picks up the remains of their clothes. When she glances back at Liam, he's frowning hard as he scuffs his shoe against the ground. "What is it, little wolf?"

He sighs in that way only children can, as if the entire weight of the world is upon his tiny shoulders. "I want to shift too."

"Ah," she says. "You will, one day."

"But why not today?" he asks, crossing his arms in a tremendous pout.

She kneels before him, forehead pressed against his. He breathes her in. Perhaps not able to shift quite yet, but a wolf through and through. "I have no doubt that when the day comes, you will be one of the greatest wolves I have ever known."

A cautious smile, a thin sliver of hope. "The biggest too?"

My love, my wife, a voice whispers. Memory or ghost, it does not matter.

"The biggest," she agrees. "Come. Let's go home."

Turn the page for a sneak peek
at the final book in the Green Creek series

BROTHERSONG

A Green Creek Novel

"Complex and startling... Green Creek is the perfect setting."
Charlaine Harris

TJ KLUNE

NEW YORK TIMES BESTSELLING AUTHOR

Available now from Tor Books

Copyright © 2019 by Travis Klune

GONE

"A wolf," my father told me once, "is only as strong as his tether. Without a tether, without something to remind him of his humanity, he'll be lost."

I stared up at him with wide eyes. I thought no one could ever be as big as my father. He was all I could see. "Really?"

He nodded, taking my hand. We were walking through the woods. Kelly had wanted to come with us, but Dad said he couldn't.

Kelly had cried, only stopping when I told him I'd come back and we'd play hide-and-seek. "You promise?"

"I promise."

I was eight years old. Kelly was six. Our promises were important.

My father's hand engulfed my own, and I wondered if I would be like him when I grew up. I knew I wasn't going to be an Alpha. That was Joe, though I didn't understand how my two-year-old brother would be the Alpha of *anything*. I'd been jealous when my parents told us Joe would be something I could never be, but it'd faded when Kelly said it was okay, Carter, because that means you and me will always be the same.

I never worried about it after that.

"Soon," my father said, "you'll be ready for your first shift. It'll be scary and confusing, but so long as you have your tether, all will be well. You'll be able to run with your mother and me and the rest of our pack."

"I already do that," I reminded him.

He laughed. "You do, don't you? But you'll be faster. I don't know if I'll be able to keep up with you."

I was shocked. "But . . . you're the *Alpha*. Of *everyone*."

"I am," he agreed. "But that's not what's important." He stopped under a large oak tree. "It's about the heart that beats in your chest. And you've got a great heart, Carter, one that beats so strongly that I think you might be the fastest wolf who ever lived."

"Whoa," I breathed. He dropped my hand before sitting on the ground, his back to the tree. He crossed his legs, motioning for me to do the same. I did so, and quickly, not wanting him to change his mind about how fast I would be. My knees bumped his as I mirrored his pose.

He smiled at me as he said, "A tether to a wolf is precious, something guarded fiercely. It can be a thought or an idea. The feeling of pack. Of home." His smile faded slightly. "Or of where home should be. Take us, for example. We're here in Maine, but I don't know if that's our home. We're here because of what's asked of us. Because of what I must do. But when I think of home, I think of a little town in the west, and I miss it terribly."

"We can go back," I told my dad. "You're the boss. We can go wherever we want."

He shook his head. "I have a responsibility, one I'm grateful for. Being an Alpha isn't about doing whatever I want. It's about weighing the needs of the many. Your grandfather taught me that. An Alpha means putting others above yourself."

"And that's going to be Joe," I said dubiously. When I'd seen him last, he'd been in a high chair in the kitchen, Mom scolding him for putting Cheerios up his nose.

He laughed. "One day. But not for a long time. But today is about you. You're just as important as your brother, as is Kelly. Even though Joe's going to be the Alpha, he'll look to you for guidance. An Alpha needs someone like the two of you who he can trust, who he can look to when he's uncertain. And you'll need to be strong for him. Which is why we're here. You don't need to know what your tether is today, but I'll ask you to start thinking about it and what it could be to you—"

"Can it be a person?"

He paused. Then, "Why do you ask?"

"Can it?"

He stared at me for a long time. "It can. But having a person as your tether can be ... difficult."

"Why?"

"Because people change. We don't stay the same. We learn and grow and, from new experiences, are shaped into something more. Sometimes, people aren't ... well. They aren't who they're supposed to be or how we think of them. They change in ways we don't expect, and while we want them to remember the good times, they can only focus on the bad. And it colors their world in shadows."

There was a look on his face I'd never seen before, and it made me uneasy. But it was gone before I could ask after it. "Is a tether a secret?"

He nodded. "It can be. Having a tether is . . . it's a treasure. One that is unlike anything else in the world. Some even say it's more important than having a mate."

I grimaced. "I don't care about that. Girls are weird. I don't want a mate. That's stupid."

He chuckled. "I'll remind you of that when the day comes. And I can't wait to see the look on your face."

"What's yours? You can tell me. I won't say anything to anyone."

He tilted his head back against the tree. "You promise?"

I nodded eagerly. "Yeah."

When my father smiled for real, you could see it in his eyes. It was like a light shining from within. "It's all of you. My pack."

"Oh."

"You sound disappointed."

I shrugged. "I'm not. It's just . . . you always talk about pack and pack and pack." I scrunched up my face. "I guess it makes sense."

"I'm glad you think so."

"Is it the same for Mom?"

"Yes. Or at least it was. Tethers can change over time. Like people, they evolve. Where it once might have been the idea of pack, it's become more pointed. More focused. For her, it's her sons. You and Kelly and Joe. It started with you and grew because of Kelly and Joe. She would do anything for you."

Fire burned in my chest, safe and warm. "Mine won't ever change."

My father looked at me curiously. "Why?"

"Because I won't let it."

"You sound as if you already know what it is."

"'Cause I do."

He leaned forward, taking my hands in his. "Will you tell me?"

I looked up at him, too young to understand the depths of my love for him. All I knew was that my father was here and asking me something that felt important, something just between us. A secret. "You can't tell anyone."

His lips twitched. "Not even Mom?"

I frowned. "Well, she's okay, I guess. But not anyone else!"

"I swear," he said, and since he was an Alpha, I knew he meant it. I said, "Kelly. It's Kelly."

He closed his eyes. His throat clicked as he swallowed. "Why?"

"Because he needs me."

"That's not—"

"And I need him."

He opened his eyes. I thought I saw a flash of red. "Tell me."

"He's not like Joe. Joe's gonna be Alpha, and he'll be big and strong like you, and everyone will listen to him because he'll know what to do. You'll tell him. But Kelly is always going to be a Beta like me. We're the same."

"I've noticed."

I needed him to understand. "When I have bad dreams, he doesn't make fun of me and tells me everything is going to be okay. When he hurt his knee and it took a long time to heal, I cleaned it up for him and told him it was okay to cry, even though we're boys. Boys can cry too."

"They can," my father whispered.

"And I think about him all the time," I told him. "When I feel sad or mad, I think about him and I feel better. That's what tethers do, right? They make you happy. Kelly makes me happy."

"He's your brother."

"It's more than that."

"How?"

I was frustrated. I didn't know how to put the thoughts in my head into words. Words that would show him just how far it went. Finally, I said, "It's . . . he's everything."

For a moment I thought I'd said the wrong thing. My father was staring at me strangely, and I squirmed. But instead of a rebuke, he pulled me toward him, and it was like I was a cub again as I turned around, settling between his legs, my back against his chest. He wrapped his arms around me, his chin on the top of my head. I breathed him in, and in the back of my mind, a voice that had once been weak whispered as strong as I'd ever heard it.

packpackpack

"You surprise me," my father said. "Every day you surprise me. I'm so lucky to have someone such as you as mine. Never, ever forget that. And if you say your tether is Kelly, then so it shall be. You'll be a good wolf, Carter. And I can't wait to see the man you'll become. No matter where I am, no matter what has happened, I'll remember this gift you've given me. Thank you for sharing your secret. I'll keep it safe."

"But you're not going anywhere, right?"

He laughed again, and even though I couldn't see him, I knew he was smiling all the way up to his eyes. "No. I'm not going anywhere. Not for a very long time."

We stayed there, under a tree in the refuge outside of Caswell, Maine, for what felt like hours.

Just the two of us.

And when we finally went home, Kelly was waiting for us on the porch, gnawing on his bottom lip. He lit up when he saw me and almost tripped as he ran down the stairs. He managed to stay upright, and he tackled me into the grass as our father watched. He threw his hands up over his head as he howled in triumph, a cracked thing that didn't sound anything like the other wolves.

I grinned up at him. "Wow. You're so strong!"

He poked my nose. "You were gone for*ever*. I got bored. Why did it take so long?"

"I'm here now," I told him. "And I won't leave you again."

"Promise?"

"Yeah. I promise."

And as I hugged my tether close, listening to him talk excitedly in my ear about how Joe had stuck *two* Cheerios up his nose and how Mom had gotten mad when Uncle Mark had laughed, I told myself it was a promise I'd always keep.

"Jesus fucking Christ," I snapped. "Do you have to follow me everywhere? Dude. Seriously. Back off."

The timber wolf glared at me.

I tilted my head, listening.

Everyone was in the house. I could hear Mom and Jessie laughing about something in the kitchen.

I jerked my head toward the woods.

The timber wolf huffed out a breath.

I ran.

He followed.

I laughed when he nipped at my heels, urging me on, and in my head, I pretended I could hear his wolf voice saying *faster faster faster must run faster so i can chase so i can catch you so i can eat you.*

We went deep into the forest, bypassing the clearing, heading for the furthest reaches of our territory. The wolf never ran ahead, always staying at my side, his tongue lolling out of his mouth.

We ran for miles, the scent of spring so green I could taste it.

Eventually I stopped, chest heaving, muscles burning from exertion.

I collapsed on the ground spread-eagled as the wolf paced around me, head raised, sniffing the air, ears twitching. When he decided there was no threat, he lay down beside me, head on my chest, tail curled over my legs. He huffed out an annoyed breath in my face.

I rolled my eyes. "Have to keep up appearances. I've got a reputation to maintain. You know how much shit I would get if anyone found out?" I flicked his forehead.

He growled, baring his teeth.

"Yeah, yeah. And I wasn't exactly lying. You do follow me everywhere. A man has got to be able to shit in peace without an overgrown dog scratching at the door. You don't see me staring at you when you're squatting in the backyard."

He closed his eyes.

I flicked him again. "Don't ignore me."

He opened one eye. For something that wasn't exactly human, he certainly could get his exasperation across.

"Whatever, man. I'm just saying."

He sneezed on me.

"Fucking asshole," I muttered, wiping my face. "Just you wait. You'll get yours. Kibble. I'm going to make sure you only get kibble from here on out."

Thick clouds passed by overhead. I laughed when a dragonfly landed between his ears, causing them to flatten. The translucent wings fluttered before it flew away.

He was a heavy weight upon me.

Once I thought it crushing.

Now it felt like an anchor holding me in place.

It should have bothered me more than it did.

He grunted, a question without words, his breath hot on my chest through my thin shirt.

"Same old, same old. Who, how, why. You know how it is."

Who are you?

How did you come to be this way?

Why can't you shift back?

Questions I'd asked over and over again.

He grumbled, lips pulling back over his teeth.

"I know, dude. It's whatever, you know? You'll figure it out when you're ready. Just . . . maybe that could be sooner rather than later? I mean, would it be so bad if you—stop growling at me, you dick! Oh, fuck you, man. Don't take that tone with me."

He moved his head, nosing at my arm.

I ignored him.

He pressed harder, more insistent.

I sighed. "You're spoiled. That's what's wrong here. You think you've got it good. And you do. Maybe too good." But I did what he wanted, resting my hand on top of his head, scratching the backs of his ears.

He closed his eyes again as he settled.

We were drifting, just the two of us. The world around us turned hazy, the edges like a dream. Hours passed by, and sometimes we dozed, and sometimes we just . . . were.

I said, "You can, you know?"

I said, "If you want to."

I said, "I don't know what happened to you."

I said, "I don't know where you came from or what you had to deal with."

I said, "But you're safe here."

I said, "You're safe with us. With me. We can help you. Ox . . . he's a good Alpha. Joe too. They could be yours, if you wanted."

I said, "And then maybe I could hear your voice. I mean, totally no homo, but I think it'd be . . . nice."

He was shaking.

I looked at him, thinking something was wrong.

It wasn't.

The motherfucker was *laughing* at me.

I shoved him off me. "Asshole."

He rolled over on his back, legs in the air, body wiggling as he scratched himself on the ground. Then he fell to his side, mouth open in a ferocious yawn.

"Would it be so bad?" I whispered. "Shifting back? You can't stay this way forever. You can't lose yourself to your wolf. You'll forget how to find your way home."

He turned his head away from me.

I'd pushed enough for the day. I could always try again tomorrow. We had time.

I sat up, stretching my arms above my head.

His tail thumped on the ground.

"Okay, so where did we leave off last time? Oh. Right. So, Ox and Joe decided it was time for them to mate. Which, honestly, I try not to think about because that's my little brother, you know? And if I *do* think about it, it makes me want to punch Ox in the mouth because *that's my little brother*. But what the fuck do I know, right? So, Ox and Joe . . . well. You know. Bone. And it was weird and oh so gross, because I could *feel* it. Oh, shut up, I didn't mean like that. I meant I could *feel* it when their mate bond formed. We all could. It was like this . . . this light. Burning in all of us. Mom said she's never heard of a pack having two Alphas before, but it made sense that it happened with us because of how crazy we already are. Ox is . . . well. He's Ox, right? Werewolf Jesus. And then he and Joe came out of the house, and I *never* want to smell that on my little brother ever again. It was like he'd *rolled* in spunk, and Kelly and I were gagging because what the *fuck*? We gave him so much shit for it. That . . . that was a good day."

I glanced down at him.

He was watching me with violet eyes.

"And that's how it ended. At least the first part. There's still Mark and Gordo to—"

His tail twitched dangerously. His body tensed.

My hand stilled. "Why do you get like that every time I bring up Gordo? I know you're an Omega and all and you've probably got evil Livingstone magic in you, but it's not his fault. You really need to get over whatever the hell is wrong with you. Gordo's good people. I mean, yeah, he's a dick, but so are you. You guys have more in common than you think. Sometimes you even make the same facial expressions."

He snapped at me.

I laughed and fell back against the grass, hands behind my head. "Fine. Be that way. We don't have to talk about it today. There's always tomorrow."

We stayed there, just the two of us, until the sky began to streak with red and orange.

* * *

As I sat behind my dead father's desk for the last time on a cold winter morning, I wondered what he would think of me.

He told me once that difficult decisions must be made with a level head. It was the only way to make sure they were right.

The house was quiet. Everyone was gone.

My father was a proud man. A strong man. There was a time when I thought he could do no wrong, that he was absolute in his power, all knowing.

But he wasn't.

For someone such as him, an Alpha wolf from a long line of wolves, he was terribly human in the mistakes he made, the people he'd hurt, the enemies he'd trusted.

Ox.

Joe.

Gordo.

Mark.

Richard Collins.

Osmond.

Michelle Hughes.

Robert Livingstone.

He had been wrong about all of them. The things he'd done.

And yet . . . he was still my father.

I loved him.

If I tried hard enough, if I really tried, I could almost smell him embedded in the bones of this house, in the earth of this territory that had seen so much death.

I loved him.

But I hated him too.

I thought that was what it meant to be a son: to believe in someone so much that it caused blindness to all their faults until it didn't. Thomas Bennett wasn't infallible. He wasn't perfect. I could see that now.

Days ago, I was on a ledge.

Below me was a void.

I hesitated. But I thought I'd already been falling for a long time. I just hadn't realized it.

That final step came easier than I expected it to. I'd already prepared. Drained my bank accounts. Packed my bags. Prepared to do what I thought I had to.

Which led me to this. Now.

This moment when I knew nothing would ever be the same.

I looked at the computer monitor on the desk.

I saw a version of myself staring back, one I didn't recognize. *This* Carter had dead eyes and black circles underneath them. *This* Carter had lost weight, his cheekbones more pronounced. *This* Carter had bloodless skin. *This* Carter knew what it meant to lose something so precious and yet was about to make things worse. *This* Carter had taken hit after hit after hit, and for what?

This Carter was a stranger.

And yet he was me.

My hand shook as I settled it on the mouse, knowing if I didn't do this now, I would never do it.

And that's the point, my father whispered. *You are a wolf, but you're still human. You give all you can, and yet you still bleed. Why would you make it worse? Why would you do this to yourself? To your pack? To him?*

Him.

Because it always came back to him.

I thought it always would.

Which is why when I hit the little icon on the screen to start recording, his name was the first thing from my lips.

"Kelly, I...."

And oh, the things I could say. The sheer *magnitude* of everything he was to me. My mother told me when I was young that I would never forget my first love. That even when all seemed dark, when all was lost, there would be the little pulsing light of memory stored deeply away.

She'd been talking about a faceless girl.

Or boy.

She hadn't known that I'd already met my first love.

My throat was raw.

I was so very tired.

"I love you more than anything in this world. Please remember that. I know this is going to hurt, and I'm sorry. But I have to do this."

I looked away, unable to watch this broken man speak any more than I had to.

"You see, there was this boy. And he's the best thing that ever happened to me. He gave me the courage to stand for what I believe in, to fight for those I care about. He taught me the strength of love and brotherhood. He made me a better person."

I tried to smile to let him know I was okay. It stretched wide on my face, foreign and harsh, before it cracked and broke.

"You, Kelly," I said hoarsely. "Always you. You're the best thing that's ever happened to me."

I looked out the window. There was frost on the glass. Snow was beginning to fall. "You're my first memory. Mom was holding you, and I wanted to take you for myself, hide you away so no one would hurt you." It was fuzzy, the edges frayed like it'd been nothing but a dream. My mother was wearing sweats, her face free of makeup. Her skin looked soft and glowing. She was speaking quietly, but her words were lost to me, a quiet murmur that disappeared at the sight of who she held.

A tiny hand reached up, the fingers opening and closing.

And there, in the recesses of my mind, I heard her speak four words that changed everything about who I was.

She said, "Look. He knows you."

I didn't understand then the earthquake this caused within me.

I poked his fat little cheek, marveling at the way his skin dimpled.

He blinked up at me, eyes bright and blue, blue, blue.

He made a noise. A little squawk.

And I was reborn.

"You're my first love," I said in this empty room, lost in the memory of how his hand had wrapped so carefully around my finger. "I knew that when you would always smile when you saw me, and it was like staring into the sun."

I swallowed thickly, looking away from the window.

"You're my heart," I told him, knowing there was a chance he'd never forgive me. "You are my soul. I love Mom. She taught me kindness. I love Dad. He taught me how to be a good wolf. I love Joe. He taught me that strength comes from within."

My breath hitched in my chest, but I pushed through it. He needed to hear this from me. He needed to know why. "But you were my greatest teacher. Because with you I understood life. What it meant to love someone so blindingly and without reservation. To have a purpose. To have hope. I have been a big brother for most of my life, and it's the best thing I ever could be. Without you, I would be nothing."

It hurt to breathe. "I know you're going to be angry. But I hope you understand, at least a little bit." I looked back at the screen. "Because I have this hole in my chest. This void. And I know why. It's because of him."

Leave. With you. I'll. Go. With you. Don't. Don't touch. Them.

"I have to find him, Kelly. I have to find him because I think without him, there's always going to be part of me that feels like I'm incomplete. I should have listened to you more when Robbie was gone. I should have fought harder. I didn't understand then. I do now, and I'm sorry. I'm so sorry. Maybe he'll want nothing to do with me. Maybe he'll. . . ."

No. Stay. Back. Don't want. This. Don't want. Pack. Don't want. Brother. Don't want. You. Child. You are. A child. I am not. Like you. I am not. Pack.

"I have to try," I pleaded in this empty room. "And I know Ox and Joe and all the others are looking for him, for the both of them, but it's not enough. Kelly, he saved us. I see that now. He saved us all. And I have to do the same for him. I have to."

Blood rushed in my ears. My vision was narrowing. There was a heavy weight on my chest, and I couldn't catch my breath.

I said, "I made you a promise once. I told you that I would always come back for you. I meant it then and I mean it now. I will *always* come back for you. No matter where I am, no matter what I'm doing, I'll be thinking of you and imagining the day I get to see you again. I don't know when that's going to be, but after you kick my ass, after you scream and yell at me, please hug me like you're never going to let me go because I won't ever want you to."

I tried to say more, tried to continue, but the weight was crushing me, and I bowed my head, claws digging into the surface of the desk. "Fuck. I can't breathe. I can't—"

My shoulders shook.

I gave in to it. My eyes burned as I choked on a sob.

I had to finish this while I still could.

It already felt like it was too late. For me. For him.

For all of us.

"Remember something for me, okay? When the moon is full and bright and you're singing for all the world to hear, I'll be looking up at the same moon, and I'll be singing right back to you. *For* you. Always you."

I wiped my eyes. The screen was blurry, and the stranger staring back at me looked haunted and lost. "I love you, little brother, even more than I can put down in words. You've got to be brave for me. Keep Joe honest. Give Ox shit. Teach Rico how to be a wolf. Show Chris and Tanner the depths of your heart. Hug Mom and Mark. Tell Gordo to lighten up. Have Jessie kick anyone's ass who steps out of line. And love Robbie like it's the last thing you'll ever do."

And ah, god, there was still so much I had to say, so much I'd never told him, so much he needed to hear from me. That the only reason I was a good person was because of him. That our father would be proud of who he'd become. That when I'd been lost to the Omega, feeling it clawing at me, threatening to pull me down into an ocean of violet, I'd held on with all my might to the ragged remains of my tether, refusing to let it go, refusing to let it be taken from me.

I am alive because of you, I wanted to say.

But I didn't.

I said, "I *will* come back for you, and nothing will hurt us ever again."

I said, "I'll be seeing you, okay?"

And that was it.

That was all.

A lifetime broken down into a few minutes of begging my pack to understand the terrible choice I was about to make.

I stopped the recording.

I thought about deleting it.

Just . . . deleting it and forgetting about all of this.

It would be so easy.

I'd delete it, and then I'd stand up. I'd leave the office. I'd sit on the steps on the porch until someone came home, and I'd tell them what I'd done and what I was about to do. Maybe it'd be Mom. She'd be smiling at the sight of me, but that smile would fade when she saw the look on my face. She'd rush forward, and I would tell her everything. That I thought I was losing my mind, that I hadn't known what Gavin was, not until it was too late. That I should have fought harder for him, that I should have told him that he couldn't leave with Robert Livingstone, he couldn't leave with his father, he couldn't leave *me*. Not when I understood. Not when I knew now what I should have known a long time ago.

Or maybe it'd be Kelly. Maybe he'd know something was wrong.

Dust would be kicking up from the tires of his cruiser, the light bar across the top flashing, the siren wailing. He'd throw open the door, the look on his face a mixture of worry and anger.

"What are you doing?" he'd demand.

"I don't know," I'd reply. "I'm lost, Kelly. I don't know what's happening, I don't know what's going on, please, please, please save me. Please tie me down so I can never leave you. Please don't let me do this. Please don't let me leave. Scream at me. Hit me. Destroy me. I love you, I love you, I love you."

I saved the video instead.

I stood up.

It was now or never.

Before I left the office, I looked back once.

For a moment I thought I saw my father standing behind his desk, hand stretched toward me.

I blinked.

There was nothing there.

A trick of the light.

I closed the door for the last time.

And yet. . . .

I hesitated on the porch, duffel bag at my feet.

I told myself it was because I was taking it in. This place. Our territory. A last few breaths of home for whatever lay ahead.

But I was a liar.

I looked down the dirt road, snow falling in flurries and clinging to the trees. No one came.

And still I waited.

One minute turned into two, turned into three, into seven.

When ten minutes had passed, I knew it was now or never. I had stalled long enough.

I picked up my bag.

Stepped off the porch.

And went to my truck.

I climbed inside and closed the door behind me.

I stared up at the house.

I imagined Kelly was with me, sitting in the passenger seat.

He said, "Hold on to me."

He said, "As tightly as you can."

He said, "I know it hurts."

He said, "I know what it feels like."

My hands tightened on the steering wheel. "I know you do."

I sighed and reached over to my bag. I unzipped a small pocket on the side and pulled out a photograph. I touched the frozen, smiling faces of my brothers before putting it on the dashboard behind the steering wheel.

And then I left.

* * *

As soon as I'd gotten far enough away, I stopped.

I gathered the last of my strength.

I found the bonds within me, bright and alive and strong.

Could I do this?

I found out I could.

It was easier than I expected, slicing through them. At least at first. It wasn't until the end that I opened the door of the truck and vomited onto the ground, my face slick with sweat.

I gagged as the bonds faded.

My mouth was sour. I spit onto the ground.

"Kelly," I muttered. "Kelly, Kelly, Kelly."

It was enough.

The tether.

It was enough.

I pulled myself back up and looked into the rearview mirror. The stranger stared back. I flashed my eyes.

Orange.

Still orange.

I closed the door.

Took a breath.

I looked at the road ahead.

There wasn't another car for as far as I could see.

I pulled back onto the road.

A few minutes later I passed a sign telling me I was leaving Green Creek, Oregon, and to come back soon!

I would.

That was a promise.

ABOUT THE AUTHOR

TJ Klune is the *New York Times* and *USA Today* bestselling, Lambda Literary Award–winning author of *The House in the Cerulean Sea, Under the Whispering Door, In the Lives of Puppets,* the Green Creek Series for adults, the Extraordinaries series for teens, and more. Being queer himself, Klune believes it's important—now more than ever—to have accurate, positive queer representation in stories.

Visit Klune online:
tjklunebooks.com
Instagram: @tjklunebooks

THE GREEN CREEK SERIES

The Bennett family has a secret: They're not just a family, they're a pack.

The beloved fantasy romance sensation about love, loyalty, betrayal, and family.

Wolfsong is Ox Matheson's story.

Ravensong is Gordo Livingstone's story.

Heartsong is Robbie Fontaine's story.

Brothersong is Carter Bennett's story.

NOW AVAILABLE FROM TOR BOOKS!
The Green Creek series is for adult readers.

LOOK OUT FOR YOUR NEXT ADVENTURE BY *NEW YORK TIMES* BESTSELLING AUTHOR
TJ KLUNE

A magical island. A dangerous task. A burning secret.

Death is only their beginning.

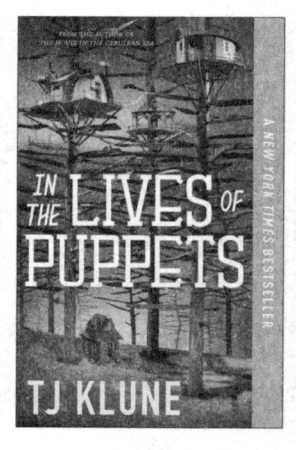

A real boy and his wooden heart. No strings attached.